## "That was a kiss, Annie. One helluva kiss, but it wasn't love."

Her muscles were liquid and aching and she couldn't seem to catch her breath. She waited for him to say something more since she didn't know what to say. What do you tell a man who has kissed you with that kind of hunger and then stares at you with hatred burning in his eyes?

"What was it then?" she asked finally. Somehow she made him look at her and she saw it again, that stirring of torment in his shadowed eyes. "What do I have to do? Teach me, Royce, I . . ."

His eyes squeezed shut as he tipped his head back. "Teach you to be a whore." Tremors seemed to race through his body. "I already allowed you to sell yourself for a roof over your head and now you want me to teach you to whore."

*No,* her heart cried. *Teach me what you want, teach me how to make you love me because I don't know how.*

*Other* **AVON ROMANCES**

# KATHLEEN ESCHENBURG

# SEEN BY MOONLIGHT

AVON BOOKS
*An Imprint of HarperCollinsPublishers*

This is a work of fiction. Names, characters, places, and incidents are products of the author's imagination or are used fictitiously and are not to be construed as real. Any resemblance to actual events, locales, organizations, or persons, living or dead, is entirely coincidental.

AVON BOOKS
*An Imprint of* HarperCollins*Publishers*
10 East 53rd Street
New York, New York 10022-5299

Copyright © 2004 by Kathleen Eschenburg
ISBN: 0-380-81568-0
www.avonromance.com

First Avon Books paperback printing: January 2004

Avon Trademark Reg. U.S. Pat. Off. and in Other Countries, Marca Registrada, Hecho en U.S.A.
HarperCollins® is a registered trademark of HarperCollins Publishers Inc.

Printed in the U.S.A.

10  9  8  7  6  5  4  3  2  1

So much time and emotion go into writing a book that the dedication is significant to the author. Those readers who follow Annabelle Hallston Kincaid through her journey will understand why this book must be dedicated to those men who have touched my life for too brief a time.

### *In Memory of*

Erroll R. Jenkins and Lee J. Stevens,
special men, exceptional fathers.
You walk through these pages.

Erroll Dana Jenkins,
brother of blood and spirit.
Your great capacity for love illuminated our lives.

Richard William Eschenburg
Words fail me,
but you could always see into my heart.
Always, my love.

# Acknowledgments

Writing a book is a solitary endeavor; bringing it to publication is a collaborative effort. My heartfelt thanks to my agent, Steven Axelrod, who believed in this book from the moment he turned the last page of the manuscript, and to my editor at Avon Books, Carrie Feron, for her patience and fortitude as we struggled to bring this story down to a publishable length and then struggled to find an appropriate title. I must also thank my friends and fellow writers at Compuserve's Writers Forum, who furnish both an understanding of the trials of bringing a story to life and a sense of humor on those days when the task seems impossible.

Two among that group deserve special mention: Carol Krenz, for her encouragement and unfailing writer's eye, and Diana Gabaldon, who read an early version of a critical scene and generously informed me that I was a writer. Thank you, Diana, for that nudge and a special thank-you for coming up with an evocative title.

Finally, in this collaborative effort, my children deserve special mention and special thanks for their patience with a parent who has a tendency to drift off into alternate realities as they are telling me their own important story. I consider myself blessed to have you as my children.

# Author's Note

The primary characters are figments of my imagination, although Royce Kincaid's war service is based upon the real-life service of General Turner Ashby and Major John S. Mosby. Some minor characters are real historical personages who appear in these pages as accurately as I could depict them. Riverbend and Merry Sherwood are fictitious estates. All the other locations are real, from Lee's Hill on Marye's Heights to Hope Mountain in the central Blue Ridge Mountains. If you go to Hope Mountain looking for the underground cavern, you will not find it there. Try Luray Caverns in Page County. As always, any mistakes in accuracy are my own.

# PART ONE

*Indeed, I tremble for my country when I reflect that God is just.*

—Thomas Jefferson, *Notes on the State of Virginia*

# Chapter 1

*Lexington, Virginia*
*March 1861*

Winter entered the little frame house, an angry gust of bitter wind ushering Carlyle through the door. Would spring never come this year? How she longed to see the red-plumed cardinals perched amidst the apple blossoms.

Annabelle stifled a sigh. Maybe tomorrow.

"Where's Bo?" asked Carlyle, as he removed his overcoat and tossed it on Papa's empty chair.

*Empty chair, empty house . . . empty Annabelle,* she thought.

"I sent him on some errands," she said. "I didn't want him here for this." It struck her for the first time. Carlyle had become a man. Handsome, in the same classical manner as Mama's people, but more so. Mama would be so proud of him now. Like Carlyle, Mama would have believed in this coming war, this coming madness.

Carlyle stared at her for the longest time, his blue eyes cloudy instead of bright. She held his gaze until, finally, he looked away, tugging at his gray uniform jacket.

"You don't have to do this," he said. "I'll figure out something."

"What?" she said, trying desperately to keep the sarcasm out of her voice.

"When Virginia secedes, we won't be militia any longer, we'll be army. I'll give you my pay. You and Bo can live on that."

"And when that grand day comes, Lieutenant Hallston, what do you live on? Your handsome Confederate looks?"

She turned her back on her brother, berating herself for her own stupidity. All those months, she'd believed Papa. *Don't worry, Annabelle*, he'd said. And like a silly goose, she'd believed him, had taken the five dollars, or the ten dollars, and paid Bo's tutor, bought food, coal, sent money to Carlyle.

*We women have to take care of our men.* Mama had known. Well, Annabelle knew now, too. She'd take care of her men, the two who were left to her. She just couldn't stand to look at Carlyle right this minute because something deep inside her wanted to scream at him: *Take care of me.*

He followed her into the kitchen. She scooped coffee beans out of the canister and dumped them into the hopper of the iron mill.

"Where's Gordon?" she asked as she proceeded to turn the handle.

"He's not coming."

She stopped and turned around.

"Don't worry," said Carlyle. "He'll go along with whatever you decide."

She could think of nothing to say. She turned back to making the coffee. Heavy hands landed on her shoulders.

"We'll sell the house. I don't need it, and you and Bo can live with Uncle Richard."

Didn't he know she'd racked her brain for days now trying to come up with a solution? Thought until her mind, and her heart, were both ready to explode while he dressed in a new gray uniform and marched with a new rifle. She couldn't stifle this sigh.

"The house is mortgaged for twelve hundred dollars. It isn't worth eight hundred, even with everything in it. There's Bo's education, the doctor bills, the funeral . . ." She turned around, shrugging out of Carlyle's grasp.

"Uncle Richard—" he said.

"Uncle Richard stopped by the other day on his way to Abingdon." *To train militia,* she thought. All of Virginia's sons gone mad with war fever.

"And?"

"And he's a little overextended, furnishing horses and guns

to the Confederacy. Could I please pay back the fifty dollars Papa borrowed. Not that there's any rush, mind you. Just when we get around to settling Papa's estate."

"Damn."

Two spots of color brightened his high cheekbones. She hoped, maybe, he felt a little bit guilty for all those months he'd been playing at war while Papa died from a tumor and borrowed money to keep the family fed. She suspected the color came from his impotent anger.

Annabelle brushed her hands down the front of her apron and turned back to making the coffee. She listened to the clicking of Carlyle's boots on the pine floor, each tap driving another nail into her heart. She'd filled the sugar bowl and poured cream in the little pitcher before he stopped pacing. She watched him jam his hands on his hipbones, and they stood like that, brother and sister, staring at one another while the coffee burped on the heat behind her and the harsh wind rattled the windowpanes.

"What was he thinking? I can't believe Father would do this to you."

She couldn't believe it either, but there was no point in dwelling on that riddle. She shrugged. The door chime sounded, and her heart ceased beating. She stared at the brass buttons on his uniform jacket and wondered if he knew how frightened, how humiliated she felt; wondered if he knew he was only making matters harder. And if he knew, did he care?

Lately, it seemed he didn't care about anything except *whupping* Yankees, not even Papa's lingering death. She could count on the fingers of one hand the number of times he'd visited their dying father.

Carlyle stepped forward and gripped her arms, squeezing painfully through the brown serge of her sleeves. "I won't let you do this, Annabelle."

She lifted her gaze. "You can't stop me." He let go of her arms, but his face remained hard. "Would you get the door, please?" she said quietly. "I'd like a minute alone."

He rubbed his face in his hands, a childish gesture of futility she hadn't seen him employ in years. She almost smiled; maybe he did care. He left her, his boots *tap-tap-tapping* down the hallway. She heard the front door open and the sound of male voices. She removed her apron, folded it carefully, and set it on top of the plank worktable.

*I can do this*, she thought, calming her racing heart. She lifted the tin coffeepot and transferred the contents into Mama's heirloom silver pot. *What am I doing*, she thought, as frantic laughter rose in her chest.

Annabelle bit her lip to hold back the craziness and pinched her cheeks to give them some color. She brushed her sweaty palms down the front of her dress and lifted Mama's silver coffee service into her hands. By the time she reached the parlor, her hands no longer trembled.

Royce heard the clicking of her bootheels down the passageway and looked toward the doorway. Her brother stepped forward, taking the coffee service from her hands and, for the space of a heartbeat, she looked as if she'd lost her anchor. With a slight brush of her fingers against her skirt and the tiniest lift of her shoulders, she regained control.

Peyton Kincaid and his lawyer, Mr. Jarvis, rose, each bowing. Royce intentionally remained seated, his legs stretched in front of him. He didn't want Peyton to think he'd come around to accepting this blackmail, and he sure didn't want to give her the wrong impression. Like maybe, Peyton's eldest son was really a gentleman. With slow, insolent deliberation, he checked her over like a filly in the auction tent. Not far off the mark, come to think of it.

She wore her pride like a suit of armor and it was a hell of a lot more becoming than that ugly brown dress. On the other hand, she should be clad in black bombazine, mourning her dear, departed father. If she had enough courage to flout that convention, maybe she had guts enough to face down the Kincaids.

He tried to remember the last time he'd seen her, before he went west. She'd have been about fourteen, usually barefoot, her skin a little too browned by the sun. As a child, she'd been an elfin little thing, a wood sprite hanging upside down from the branch of an oak tree or sprinting across the lawn with her skirts kilted up, skinny legs pumping through the air, always searching for Gordon and Carlyle. She'd grown up since then, not much taller, but definitely more womanly.

Ignoring his insolent perusal, she crossed over to greet Peyton. To Royce's surprise, his father leaned his royal, silver head down and brushed her forehead with a fatherly kiss.

"Annie, I remember another time, a night at Riverbend when a young lady danced her first waltz with an old man. Do you remember?"

His father smiled, waiting, he supposed, for an answering smile. If that's what Peyton waited for, she didn't cooperate. She closed her eyes and seemed to pull inside herself, as if the memory brought her pain. Royce felt the contempt swell up in his throat. He understood his father's Machiavellian scheming. He understood her own father's thoughts, tilting at windmills in his own bemused fashion. Royce doubted she had a clue to either. She recovered rapidly.

"I've never forgotten, Mr. Kincaid. I drank my first champagne that night, too," she said. Her voice sounded soft, lyrical. And immeasurably sad.

Mr. Jarvis cleared his throat, and she turned to face him. A smile tugged at Royce's lips. So far, she'd managed to ignore him completely.

"Will your lawyer be attending this, uh, meeting?" asked Jarvis, addressing his question to Carlyle.

Carlyle shifted from one foot to the other. "No," he said, avoiding his sister's warning glance by surveying the patterns in the worn Turkish carpet.

"I told Miss Hallston when she brought me these requests that she should have an attorney representing her interests. Didn't she tell you?"

"Carlyle represents my interests," said Annabelle.

Unexpected anger flooded Royce, watching her stiffen her spine while her worthless, hot spur brother shifted uncomfortably from one foot to another. They all knew she couldn't pay a lawyer.

"Shall we begin, gentlemen," she said, gesturing toward the table in the center of the room. "I'd like to have this over before Bo returns."

Unlike most parlor tables, hers lacked the heavy decorative cloth considered by most housewives as *de rigueur*. A single kerosene lamp sat in the center of the polished walnut top, the glass chimney free of soot. He guessed the table was a Duncan

Phyfe, an heirloom passed down from the glory days of her mother's family. Her pride was a palpable thing, evident in her surroundings as much as in her carriage. His indifference drained away, replaced with a crazy urge to protect her pride.

"Not yet, Miss Hallston," he said, rising. She shot him a startled look. He ignored both his father's patrician scowl and Carlyle's belligerence. He crossed the room in three strides, taking her elbow in his hand to prevent her from sitting. "Is there someplace we can have a word in private before we begin?"

She glanced at Carlyle, seemed to realize there was no help from that quarter, then nodded with visible reluctance.

"Papa's study," she said.

"I'm sure these gentlemen can find something to discuss while they wait," he said, guiding her toward the parlor door. Carlyle stepped in front of the passage. "The weather, the grand and glorious war we're about to embark on," he continued, holding his gaze on Carlyle's flushed face. Carlyle blinked and stepped aside. Royce dropped his hand from her elbow as they reached the hall.

"This way," she said in a quiet tone. Royce followed her down the hallway, thinking how strange it was that she made him want to smile simply by nudging her chin up defiantly while her ladylike voice said all the proper words.

Once inside her father's library, he deliberately closed the door and leaned against it. She met his gaze for the space of several heartbeats, then turned away, studying the shelves of leather-bound books as if she'd never seen them before.

He allowed the silence to grow, testing her mettle. Her iron-forged spine stiffened only a little. He controlled his urge to laugh.

"What did you want to say, Mr. Kincaid?" She turned around then, meeting his look. There was nothing coy or blushing about her. Instead, her demeanor was all business, one negotiator facing another.

"You don't have to go along with this coercion," he said.

"Really?" One delicate brow lifted. "Your father owns the mortgage to this house, plus several hundred dollars more he loaned my father based on that agreement. What happens to Bo if I refuse?"

"The old man might be bluffing."

She hadn't yet learned how to hide her emotions. Hope flashed in her eyes, followed by resignation. Her gaze dropped to her father's desk, and she began to trace her hand over the woodgrain top. "Where's Fort Laramie?" she asked.

"On the North Platte River," he said, startled by a question that was so far off the subject. She glanced at the large globe standing in the corner of the room as if considering whether or not to search for the North Platte River. "Nebraska Territory," he added.

She acknowledged the information with a slight nod. "How long have you been home?"

"I resigned my commission just after the election." Usually adept at keeping one step ahead of an opponent, he couldn't figure out where she was headed with this line of questioning.

"Because of this or because of the war?"

"Have I missed something? What war?" She gave him a withering look, and he wiped the taunting smile from his face. She hadn't asked for this any more than he had. "I didn't know anything about this arrangement either until after I'd been back a while. Actually, it was your father, not mine, who first mentioned it," he said, watching her closely for her reaction. She bridled immediately.

"That's not true. Papa was too sick to go to Riverbend, and you were never here."

Hurt darkened her eyes. He knew she didn't want to believe him. She'd evidently never figured out her beloved Papa had seen only his sons, while using his daughter as housewife and substitute mother. This was going to be hard enough on both of them. He could allow her to save some of her fantasy, but he wasn't about to make it more difficult by lying to her.

"Your father sent me a letter attempting to explain," said Royce.

For a moment, the rage overwhelmed him again, the same cold fury he'd felt when he confronted his own father. He shouldn't have been surprised. Peyton Kincaid had spent a lifetime manipulating others to his own purposes. Those few who wouldn't be manipulated he'd tried to bend, to break, usually successfully. Royce had spent his lifetime refusing to bend.

He was bending now and didn't like the sensation. But he'd go through with this farce if she was willing. Not for her sake. No, as far as he was concerned, the proud Miss Hallston could sink or swim on her own merits. He'd bend to his father's will for Gordon's sake and no other reason. Of course, Prince Machiavelli had known that and used it to his own advantage.

She turned away and walked toward the window. Drawing aside the dark velvet drapes, she stood perfectly still, gazing into the yard. Royce crossed his arms on his chest and waited.

"He's not bluffing," she said finally.

"What makes you so certain?" Royce knew the old man never bluffed; he wanted to know her reasoning.

"You're not here because you want to marry me, Mr. Kincaid." She turned back to face him. "He's got some sword hanging over your head, too."

He nodded, accepting her observation while refusing to comment on it. She waited expectantly, then her lips twitched, as if she wanted to smile.

"I won't ask, Mr. Kincaid. In fact, I'm rather certain I don't want to know what it is," she said, and he added perception to her growing list of admirable qualities. "I would like to know what my father said in his letter."

Her father had been one of the few men he respected, until the arrival of that letter. Then he suspected the unlikely friendship between Peyton Kincaid and Thomas Hallston wasn't so unlikely after all.

By forcing her into this arrangement, her father had provided for Carlyle and Bo while she paid the price for both. His father gained the satisfaction of bending his oldest son to his will and, once again, she was the one who would pay most dearly. He almost wanted to warn her away but didn't. He was just as evil as either of the two older men because he'd let her pay in order to save Gordon. She didn't recognize the ugly picture yet, and he suddenly hoped she never would.

"Your father saw a bloody war coming and a way to protect his children," said Royce, revealing only the kindest portion of Thomas Hallston's reasoning while couching it in terms that included her. A smile definitely played at the corner of her lips. An unfamiliar ache filled his chest.

*"He's mad past recovery, but yet has lucid intervals,"* she said softly.

Caught somewhere between sympathy and amusement, he gave her a wink. " *'Tis the only comfort of the miserable to have partners in their woes."*

"Papa was rather quixotic, wasn't he?"

The smile began in her eyes, a spark of gold in the twilight brown. And like a sunrise over the river, the light spread, creating a shadowed crease in her cheek and catching her lips in rosy splendor. It was a smile full of dawn's promise, and it transformed her into a rare and precious beauty. He dropped his arms to his side and straightened, for the first time wondering if maybe he shouldn't be the one to walk away before this went any further.

"If you can quote Cervantes, Miss Hallston, I'm sure we'll be able to find something to discuss at the dinner table," he said, taking her arm. "Now, I'm going to ask you a question."

She allowed his hand to remain at her elbow but looked away as he began to guide her from the room and for that, he was grateful. He chose his women based on the lushness of their bodies and the looseness of their morals. He didn't want to think about thin ladies with gold in their eyes.

"If you don't believe Peyton Kincaid is bluffing, why did you add conditions to his terms?"

She stopped and looked up, meeting his questioning gaze, while that smile once again threatened to explode. "Do you read Shakespeare, too, Mr. Kincaid?" she asked, and once again she'd outmaneuvered him with a question he didn't understand. He nodded. "Do you know what day this is?" she continued.

There was a method in her madness. He bit back a smile. "The Ides of March," he said. "You're testing, Miss Hallston— but do you remember what happened to old Julius?"

Gold sparked in her eyes. "Oh, certainly. It's just that I always wanted to live dangerously."

"Miss Hallston, I do believe you're going to get your wish."

Her smile exploded. He lost his breath.

\* \* \*

Carlyle met them as they reentered the parlor and he jerked his sister's elbow away from Kincaid's grasp. He wondered why she'd allowed it; surely her skin must be crawling. Carlyle made no effort to mask his hatred, confronting Kincaid's cold, gray eyes with his own hot anger. If the bastard felt any emotion, it was well hidden.

The other men, Jarvis and Peyton, were dressed appropriately in well-tailored black frock coats, gleaming white shirts with stiff, boiled collars, and silk cravats tied in the four-in-hand style. Carlyle had intentionally worn his dress uniform, the one Annabelle had made for him just two months before. Annabelle, probably hoping to make some kind of feminine impression on Kincaid, had dressed in her good brown serge instead of proper mourning attire. He doubted Royce Kincaid even noticed.

In contrast, Royce wore buckskin breeches that hugged his muscular thighs in an unseemly fashion. His collarless chamois shirt was cut loose and flowing, gaping open at the neck and displaying too much bronzed skin. He looked like some strange cross between a Plains Indian and a buccaneer, and handsome as sin.

Carlyle glanced at Annabelle. Her gaze followed Royce around the table. She didn't seem to realize she was outclassed, outgunned and outmaneuvered. She didn't stand a chance fighting on the same field as the disreputable Royce Kincaid, and there was nothing he could do to save her.

Except kill the bastard, which was an option he hadn't discounted yet.

Carlyle watched as Royce seated himself in the only remaining seat, between Mr. Jarvis at the head of the table and Peyton, who sat across from Annabelle. Royce angled the chair and propped his ankle on his knee. The posture was proof of the man's arrogance. The positioning was ideal, effectively removed from the proceedings while in a position to observe both Annabelle and Peyton without being obvious.

Jarvis waited for Royce to be seated, then cleared his throat. Already, Carlyle found that habit annoying.

"Four months ago, Mr. Peyton Kincaid and Mr. Thomas Hallston entered into a contractual agreement," said Jarvis.

"Both parties being of sound mind at the time, the contract was duly signed and witnessed and is therefore legal and binding upon the involved parties."

His annoyance escalating into anger, Carlyle interrupted. "We know that, Mr. Jarvis. What I'd like to know is why my sister asked for this meeting. She can say yes; she can say no. I see no reason for us to be sitting here today, and Annabelle has not chosen to confide in me."

He turned to Peyton Kincaid. "You've placed my sister in an untenable position, Mr. Kincaid, and there's no point in any of us pretending otherwise. Would you please instruct your lawyer to get to the crux of the issue because I, personally, find the odor in this room offensive."

Peyton fingered the carved ivory tip of his walking stick and smiled benignly. "Annabelle understands the terms of the agreement. She has requested that we consider a few changes—enter into further negotiations, so to speak—before she reaches a decision. Her situation is not as untenable as you fear, else we wouldn't be here today."

"Damn you." Carlyle bolted to his feet. "You're asking her to sell herself to the devil incarnate, and you tell me it's not untenable." He felt Annabelle's hand on his arm and looked down.

"Carlyle, please," said Annabelle. "Please sit down and listen."

"There's nothing to listen to." Her face drained of all its color, but Carlyle was too angry to care. "Father's supposed friend and his rogue son can sit here smirking as long as they want. I'll not be a party to this charade."

"If you're most concerned about your own pride," said Royce in a voice that carried the power of a hurricane in spite of its low tone, "please do leave. If you care anything about your sister, you'll sit down and listen."

The voice was compelling, but it was the warning in those barren, gray eyes that stopped him. Instead of vaulting across the table and smashing the arrogant bastard's face, which was what he wanted to do, Carlyle hesitated and instantly recognized the mistake. Without twitching a muscle, Royce Kincaid had won, and Carlyle didn't like the humiliating sense of defeat washing over him any more than he liked the acceptance in Annie's eyes.

"Please continue, Mr. Jarvis," instructed Royce, with a slight inclination of his head toward the lawyer, ignoring Carlyle as if he was a roach already squashed beneath a bootheel.

"Yes, well," said Jarvis, glancing nervously at Peyton Kincaid. "Shall I begin with the original agreement between the parties so we're certain everyone understands fully?"

"An excellent thought," said Peyton. He reached over and patted Annabelle's hand, as if in encouragement. Carlyle stifled his groan.

"Several years ago, Peyton Kincaid loaned Thomas Hallston the sum of twelve hundred dollars, said sum secured by a mortgage against a property in the city of Lexington which, I believe, is the house we're sitting in now."

The lawyer's eyebrow cocked, as if he didn't know exactly what property was under discussion. Peyton inclined his head once again. The acting was superb; the script stank. Carlyle swallowed his rage and watched Royce, who was studying Annie. Annie kept her gaze fixed on the lawyer's face.

"Over the course of time, Thomas Hallston borrowed additional monies, the sum of which amounted to five hundred dollars at the time of his death. In November of last year, Mr. Hallston and Mr. Peyton Kincaid entered into an agreement concerning the method of repayment of the entire amount of borrowed funds. The agreement is quite simple. In layman's terms, Mr. Peyton Kincaid has agreed to accept as payment in full whatever sum can be realized by the sale of the Lexington property plus all its furnishings, a sum estimated to be in the neighborhood of seven hundred and fifty dollars. A very generous concession by anyone's standards. He did stipulate, and Thomas Hallston agreed, that the sale would take place no later than March 31, 1861, a date only two weeks away."

"Please, in layman's terms," said Carlyle, his voice dripping with sarcasm, "refresh our memory on the second option, the pound of flesh this paragon is willing to take in exchange for not turning my sister and brother onto the street."

Royce's gaze shifted, first to Peyton, then to Carlyle. For an instant, laughter flashed in those cold, silver eyes, and Carlyle suddenly understood what was happening. Either Annie didn't realize she was some type of pawn between two strong men who hated one another, Kincaid *père* and *fils*, or she was too numb to care. In either case, Carlyle knew the sickening truth. The war was already lost, and to the victor went the spoils.

"The, er, second option is the crux of today's meeting." Jarvis avoided looking at any of them, directing his attention to the quill pen he held in his hand. "Mr. Peyton Kincaid is prepared to forgive the loan in its entirety, thereby passing said property to Carlyle Gault Hallston free and clear according to the terms of Thomas Hallston's Last Will and Testament. He will also provide a permanent home for Annabelle Hallston and Bohannon Hallston at Riverbend, a university education for Bohannon Hallston, and pass a farm property located in Augusta County to Bohannon Hallston in his own Last Will and Testament. For his own sons, Royce Magruder Kincaid will inherit the plantation known as Riverbend in its entirety, including chattel and contents. The younger son, Gordon Alistair Kincaid will inherit the contiguous property known as Old Riverbend. The only concession he asks is that Annabelle Hallston marries his son Royce Kincaid prior to March 31, 1861."

Jarvis finally lifted his gaze from his hands, although he seemed to be having difficulty meeting Annabelle's. "Do you understand, Miss Hallston?"

Annabelle's chin nudged up. "Perfectly, Mr. Jarvis."

"Mr. Kincaid?" asked Jarvis, turning to Royce. Royce nodded.

"Of course, neither of you is bound by the agreement between the senior Mr. Kincaid and Thomas Hallston. Either or both can decline the terms offered by Peyton Kincaid, and the original contract remains intact."

"My sister has a choice between losing her home or selling herself for seventeen hundred dollars while her proffered husband marries a woman he doesn't want to assure himself a valuable piece of property." Carlyle didn't care if his contempt showed, and he didn't care if he annihilated Annabelle's pride. The obscenity of the situation stuck in his throat, and he hated all of them, especially Royce Kincaid.

Royce's eyes narrowed, and his jaw tightened, but when he spoke, his voice remained low. "What changes has Miss Hallston requested us to consider?"

Carlyle realized that the man could control armies using nothing but that low, compelling voice and those icy eyes. He glanced at Annabelle. If she felt any of the panic that was rising in his own chest, she didn't show it. He wanted to hate her, too.

"Miss Hallston has made three simple requests. She asks that the ceremony be a civil ceremony held at Riverbend with only immediate family in attendance, that she be allowed to retain her maiden name, and that the marriage remains private knowledge among those in attendance until such time that she, herself, decides to announce the marriage. Of course, the last request complicates matters as it requires agreement between not only the principals to the agreement, but also Mr. Gordon Kincaid and her own brothers. She is willing to accept their signature on the contract as proof of intent."

"Mr. Jarvis, I actually made four requests," said Annabelle.

"Surely, you weren't serious, Miss Hallston," said Jarvis.

"Deadly serious," said Annabelle. She looked over at Royce, and Carlyle would swear he saw a smile hovering at her lips.

"Yes, well . . . in that case," said Jarvis. "She asks that the marriage ceremony take place on April 1 instead of—"

Royce's laughter drowned out the rest of the lawyer's sentence. Annabelle's lips twitched, but she managed to hold back her smile as she turned to Peyton Kincaid. Carlyle shifted his attention to the older man, and what he saw was so unexpected that he slumped in his seat, totally defeated. Peyton's eyes were a shade darker gray than his son's, usually as emotionless, but right now, they sparkled.

Peyton reached over the table and took Annabelle's hand in his own. "I always told Thomas he didn't know what a treasure he had in you." He released her hand and leaned back in his seat. "I would much prefer the world know Miss Hallston is my daughter-in-law, but I'm willing to wait for the recognition of that honor if that's what she wishes." His patrician face lost every vestige of kindness as he leveled his gaze on his son.

"Royce, I believe it's up to you now. Do you make me a happy man and accept her terms, or do you decline?"

Up to this point, between Carlyle's impotent anger, Jarvis's nervous twitches, and Miss Hallston's unexpected sense of humor, the proceedings had been more amusing than annoying. With his father's question, Royce knew the duel had commenced. Peyton got in the first thrust. Feint and parry.

"Your happiness doesn't concern me in the least, Father. However, I can accept Miss Hallston's stipulations if you can accept mine." The old man was good; he didn't even blink. Feint, parry. Thrust.

"Please continue, Mr. Jarvis," said Royce, taking the opportunity to glance at Annabelle. If her spine stiffened any more, she'd be in danger of permanent paralysis, but she didn't blink either. He wanted to give her an encouraging smile, but didn't. This was between the old man and himself.

"Mr. Royce Kincaid presented me with his own list just this morning. I have it in front of me, and I'll read from it now," said Jarvis. His hands shook as he pulled a pair of spectacles from his coat pocket. Everyone waited, watching his shaking hands maneuver the thin gold arms behind his ears. He picked up the single sheet of paper.

"Number one, if the marriage takes place and Royce Kincaid should be killed in the coming war, the plantation known as Riverbend shall pass in its entirety to his wife, Annabelle Hallston Kincaid. He does make the request that all slaves be freed if the war has not already accomplished that purpose."

Royce heard her small gasp of surprise, but his attention remained centered on Peyton. As yet, no reaction.

"Number two, if said marriage takes place and Royce Kincaid survives the coming war, his wife is free to seek a divorce after a period of five years or one year after the end of hostilities, whichever comes first. He stipulates that he will not counter her proceedings and further stipulates that he will settle Riverbend and the sum of twenty thousand dollars on her at the time the divorce becomes final. Whether or not she seeks the divorce, Mr. Royce Kincaid intends to return to the West. In either case, married or divorced, she must agree there will be no further contact between them from that time forward."

The lawyer emitted a small sigh and looked at Peyton, as if in apology. "Lastly, Mr. Peyton Kincaid must agree that Annabelle Hallston Kincaid will be the sole beneficiary of Riverbend and so stipulate in his own Last Will and Testament as well as in trust."

The lawyer set down the paper and swallowed audibly. A taut silence stretched across the room, becoming almost a sound in itself. As Royce expected, his father was the one finally to break the silence.

"Well done, Royce."

It was the same quiet tone that had once sent shivers down his spine. He wasn't a boy any longer and perfectly willing to meet Peyton Kincaid man to man. This time, the field was even level. Royce remained silent, waiting for Peyton's counterthrust. He didn't have to wait long.

"You didn't address the issue of children, however."

"There'll be no children," Royce said with finality. Something compelled him to look at Annabelle. She sat with her eyes closed, her hands clutched together in front of her while she bit her lower lip. Oddly, he felt a sudden surge of sympathy for her, but this couldn't be helped. He meant to draw blood on the old man, and the old man was equally determined not to bleed.

Peyton fingered the top of his walking stick, appropriately carved in the shape of a serpent. The ticking of the lyre clock on the mantel sounded strangely ominous in the quiet room. Finally, Peyton spoke. "I'll go along with those stipulations, son, if I'm assured those nonexistent children will have two parents."

By damn, the old man did bleed. Royce fought to hide his surprise at the ease of the capitulation. It certainly didn't take much effort to provide assurances for the welfare of children he never intended to produce.

"Mr. Jarvis," said Royce, "please add that in whatever language you feel is necessary." He directed his attention to Annabelle. "Miss Hallston?"

She tried for a haughty look, but the tears on her lashes spoiled the effort. Her brother offered her no assistance. He sat slumped in his chair, oblivious to her pain, looking as if he'd been punched in the gut.

"Your terms are more than generous," she said haltingly. "But it doesn't seem quite fair to Gordon."

Christ, he'd saddled himself with another innocent. If he had any sense, he'd knock the foolishness out of her right now. He just couldn't bring himself to do it, not with that vulnerable expression on her face.

"Annabelle, Gordon doesn't covet Riverbend any more than I do." He could see her pulse throbbing just above the cameo she wore at her throat. "What my father knows and your brother has failed to point out is that I've offered you nothing I'll ever miss. I have my land out West and the infamous English inheritance, which will remain safely in British sterling for the duration of this war. Twenty thousand dollars is a drop in the bucket."

"It's more than I want or need." She stared at him with those still, dark eyes.

"Take it or leave it, Miss Hallston," he said brusquely. He nudged his chin down, concealing his expression, and watched her as Jarvis scribbled the amendments to the agreement.

She turned to Carlyle, obviously seeking something: support, advice, a shoulder to cry on. Carlyle avoided looking at her. And then she did it again. Drawing a long breath, she pulled somewhere deep inside herself, somewhere safe and alone. Her gaze turned distant as she sat, perfectly still except for one thumb stroking the tabletop and it was as if that touch was the sole thing holding her here, in this world of madness. The quill pen scratched across the paper for several interminable minutes, making the only sound, as she sat, painfully alone in a room full of people.

He didn't know where it came from, and although he tried, he couldn't shove it away. It began with a tightening in his chest, passed through the vision of laughter and light in her eyes, and ended with the cessation of the scratching quill pen, while she continued to sit in the silence, alone and lifeless except for one thumb stroking a woodgrain table.

She made him feel, and she was going to make him hurt, and he hated her almost as much as he suddenly wanted to protect her from the madness. For the world was an indifferent place at best, heartless and cruel at its worst, and she was another innocent—this little woman with the golden brown hair and the golden brown eyes and the twenty-four-karat smile. Once again, the silence stretched taut and painful across the room while his own heart thumped and pumped and hurt with a pain he didn't want to remember.

"Are you finished, Jarvis?" said Peyton, breaking the silence.

The world spun crazily, and he jerked his gaze to his father, totally disoriented. The last time he'd heard that voice, that ache in his father's tone, was in another lifetime, the day Mother left.

Royce shook his head, seeking to reorient himself to the real world, the world of war and madness and hate. Jarvis shoved a piece of paper across the table. Peyton picked up the quill pen, dipped the point in the inkstand, and signed his name to the bottom. Wordlessly, he pushed the paper and ink toward Royce.

Royce might be a master at fooling others but never made the mistake of trying to fool himself. He knew if he thought, then he'd run—from Annabelle Hallston, from Peyton Kincaid, from himself. And if he did that, protected himself, then the younger brother he'd spent a lifetime protecting would be lost. Because Peyton Kincaid had no feelings, no blood . . . and only one son.

Royce signed his name, then set the quill on top of the paper and leaned back in his seat. Peyton slid the contract in front of Annabelle.

"Annie-girl," Peyton said, holding out the pen. It was the same gentle voice, and for another moment, Royce forgot to breathe.

She visibly trembled and brought herself back to the madness. It was her decision now. She absently took the quill from Peyton and once again turned to her brother. Carlyle lifted his gaze from his hands and stared at Royce.

*Help her*, thought Royce as he met the hatred in those blue eyes. Carlyle turned his attention back to his hands without meeting his sister's silent plea. Royce knew he could kill the man in a heartbeat and never regret it. Annabelle set the quill on the paper and looked uncertainly at the lawyer.

She couldn't do it. He was in the process of shifting his attention to Peyton, curious as to the old man's reaction, not wanting to think about his own, when he heard the back door slam.

"I'm back, Annie," called the young voice.

Everyone, even Carlyle, drew in a breath. Annabelle let hers out in a slow, deep-seated sigh. She picked up the quill and dipped it in the inkstand.

"Here's to living dangerously, Mr. Kincaid," she said. Without another moment's hesitation, she signed her name.

Royce inclined his head in a silent salute, garnering himself another stunning smile. She passed the contract to her brother.

Carlyle stared at the paper in front of him as the flush rose up his neck. About the same time the red flood reached his cheekbones, he stood up and glared at his sister.

"I'll keep the dirty little secret for your sake, Annabelle, but I'll not sign the agreement, and I'll not attend the ceremony." He stalked over to the door, then turned back to his white-faced sister. "I'll write, and I hope you'll answer, but I'll never set foot inside Riverbend, and I won't see you again until this farce of a marriage ends."

Royce jumped out of his chair, intent on breaking Carlyle's arrogant, chiseled nose. But Carlyle moved fast, and Royce stopped himself. He could always break that nose later, when Annabelle wasn't around to watch. Royce walked slowly back to the table. She lifted her gaze, and he saw the tears filling her eyes. But, somehow, she managed to keep them from spilling over.

"He'll come around, Annie-girl," said Peyton, reaching for her hand. "In the meantime, you're a Kincaid now."

*God help you*, thought Royce.

Bohannon Hallston appeared in the doorway, looking so much like a young version of his late father that Royce blinked. Until the boy smiled. When Bo smiled, his smile was as full of dreams and sunshine and promises as Annabelle's, and he was smiling now.

"I saw it, Annie," he said, bounding into the room and ignoring everyone but his sister. "It was snowing this morning, but I saw one anyway."

"What did you see, Bo?" asked Annabelle.

"A cardinal in the old apple tree."

She leaned back in her seat, head bowed, eyes closed, as if in prayer. When she looked up, meeting her brother's smile, tears shimmered like starlight on her dark lashes.

"I knew it," she whispered. "Spring always comes."

She was too young, still full of dreams and innocence, brimming with pride and grit, and Royce knew, if he didn't die in the coming war, he'd live to regret the coming marriage.

# Chapter 2

She felt so lost.

She wasn't actually lost. Just beyond the bend in the river, she could see the church spires of the town of Fredericksburg. Riverbend was only a mile distant, less if she abandoned the muddy roads and cut across the fields, the same fields she'd run with barefoot abandon as a child. She knew *where* she was, she just didn't seem to know *who* she was any longer.

The morning breeze brushed her face, lifted the escaped curls off her forehead, and moved on to ruffle the draping branches of the willows lining the riverbank. Sunlight glanced off the budding leaves, then sharpened, becoming painful, cutting prisms as sudden, unexpected tears filled her eyes.

"Mama," she whispered, and swallowed the knot in her throat. It had been years since she'd felt such an ache for Mama. She suspected the melancholy came from the drastic changes her life had undergone, changes Mama would never have expected or approved.

Annabelle swiped the tears away, then tilted her head back and raised her hand, splaying her fingers wide as she reached toward the blinding sun. Of course, like everything else, it remained just beyond her reach . . .

Annabelle had once believed if real life could be written like an epic poem, then in her story, she was fated to marry a hero.

23

Actually, back in the days when she still allowed herself to imagine, it was she who sallied forth from ancient castles to slay fire-breathing dragons. She could picture herself sailing into the Aegean sky, battling Trojans with drawn sword, following the ancient gods wherever they directed. She soon realized few people's lives bore any resemblance to the heroic actions in epic poems, in spite of Papa's ramblings on the subject.

She learned practicality early. Even in dreams, skinny little girls never grew up to be heroes. Little girls always grew up to be wives. A few years farther into the book of life, she realized, in her case, even that was doubtful.

The marriage of her parents had been a union of two unlikely lovers, but no one ever questioned their storybook love. Her mother, AnnaLee Gault, brought to her husband her great beauty, an aristocratic lineage, and an impoverished tobacco plantation near Suffolk. Thomas Hallston brought to his wife an equally aristocratic name, several libraries' worth of books, and a philosopher's brain. Annabelle's branch of the Hallston familial tree lived in genteel, aristocratic poverty.

By the time Annabelle was born, third child, only daughter, the tobacco plantation was gone, and the family lived in Lexington, where her father taught literature and philosophy at tiny Washington College. Six years and two miscarriages later, her mother gave birth to the last child, another son. They called him Bohannon, Bo for short. Mama was never the same after that. Bo became Annabelle's special charge, her special love.

In between several more miscarriages, the family traveled, as all Southern families traveled in those days. Sometimes, they took off without Papa, but he always joined them later, during college breaks.

Her favorite spot was always Merry Sherwood, such a fitting name for Aunt Hetty and Uncle Richard's plantation near sleepy Front Royal. Hetty had married more wisely than her sister, AnnaLee. Richard Sherwood owned land, chattel, and a large stable of blooded horses.

Never a girl had a more generous, indulgent uncle than Uncle Richard, who gave her ponies and pretty dresses and treated her with the same gallant chivalry he treated his own daughter, the beautiful Olivia. Annabelle loved Uncle Rich and Aunt Hetty almost as much as Mama and Papa.

They'd been at Merry Sherwood when Mama died, on another spring day deceptively full of promise. Annabelle had come in, laughing from the warmth of the sun on her face, the scent of dogwood and azaleas in the air. The laughter faded into a woman's cries and footsteps pounding up and down the stairs. She'd been sitting on Uncle Rich's lap when Aunt Hetty came for her.

"Come, dear," said Aunt Hetty. "I told her it was unseemly, but she insists. Your mama wants to see you." Aunt Hetty took her skinny hand into her own plump hand, and somehow, Annabelle's feet managed to climb those stairs, walk down that hall, and into her mother's room.

Neither of them cried. Mama was a blueblood, a lady. Annabelle was too scared.

"Why, Mama," she asked. Annabelle didn't know what she was asking. Why did this awful thing happen over and over again? Why was Mama dying?

"Hush, sweetling, and listen," said Mama, taking her hand. "One day, you'll love a man. You'll understand then. When that time comes, I pray you'll love wisely." She'd laughed then, Mama's special, molasses-sweet laugh. "But I needn't worry, my Annabelle has always been too wise for a little girl."

She didn't understand Mama. How could love make Mama die? She sighed. She'd never know the answer unless God made a miracle and let Mama live long enough for Annabelle to grow all the way up. Already, she knew grown-up ladies talked of things little girls weren't supposed to know.

"You must take care of your papa for me," said Mama. "Make sure his socks match, and there's food in the larder. Promise me that, Annabelle." Annabelle nodded, she couldn't find her voice to speak. "And Bo, you're already more his mother than I am. Love him well, Annie, he's too much like Papa for his own good."

"I will, Mama." Oh, she needed to cry; she was going to burst from the pressure of the tears inside. She didn't.

Mama squeezed her hand. "We women must always take care of our men."

"Yes, Mama." She wouldn't make Mama sadder, she couldn't. But she wanted to remind her she wasn't a woman yet. Without Mama, who would take care of her?

They sat for a few minutes gazing at each other, Annabelle trying desperately to memorize her mother's face so she could bring it out of her memories later and gaze on it again. She wanted to say things to Mama, but she didn't know what she wanted to say . . . all those things in her heart instead of words in her brain. So the love remained feelings, not words, but Annabelle always believed Mama could read her heart.

Aunt Hetty had taken her away then, dragging her from Mama's room. Annabelle had lain rigid in the bed that night, next to slumbering Olivia. She'd listened to the raindrops on the roof and the muffled screams and hurrying footsteps. Sometime, near dawn, when the sky lightened to the strange lavender of a spring-fresh mountain morning, the rain stopped and the screams stopped.

When the sun rose, lemon yellow in an azure sky, a cock crowed, and the blue jays answered. Inside, Merry Sherwood remained silent, not at all merry. Annabelle was ten years old, motherless, and the female head of Papa's household.

Eventually, they learned to laugh again, all except Papa. Most people considered Papa strange, and she guessed, if they never looked any deeper than his appearance, they'd be right. Papa looked rather too much like a scarecrow, all lanky, knobby bones and straw-colored hair with a tendency to stick straight up on his head. Annabelle didn't inherit his height or his coloring, but she did inherit the knobby bones and his love of books.

Papa loved her, she never doubted his love, but he knew nothing about raising a daughter and wasn't the kind of man to learn. She taught herself how to run a household, studied hard at her lessons to keep him content, and ran barefooted wild with the boys in her free time.

Her two older brothers allowed her to traipse after them. She learned everything they knew about hunting and fishing and riding. The ladies of Lexington might wrinkle their aristocratic noses in disapproval, but if that didn't bother Papa, she certainly wasn't going to let it bother her.

During practical moments, she realized Papa wouldn't recognize a wrinkled, aristocratic nose if it struck him between the eyes. Since her rationalization afforded her the happiest moments in her life, she didn't allow herself to be practical on the issue. She'd seen what happened to Olivia, raised as a proper Virginia aristocrat.

One winter, influenza struck hard in the little town of Lexington. It raced through the college, laying healthy young men low. Papa brought influenza home with him, and it raced through the Hallston household, too. They all recovered except Thomas, her oldest brother. He was buried next to Mama and the dead babies. What little light remained in Papa's eyes disappeared.

Papa never visited any of Mama's family after she died. Annabelle guessed it hurt him too much, remembering. He made certain the children continued the visits, putting them on the train and waving his black stovepipe hat in the air as it pulled away. He just never went with them.

He did go to Riverbend, every September before the start of the fall term. Riverbend, situated on the banks of the Rappahannock, belonged to his second cousin and only friend, Peyton Kincaid.

Annabelle couldn't make up her mind how she felt about the Kincaids, although she loved Riverbend itself. It was a grand old estate house set amongst the rolling hills, and Peyton Kincaid ran it in a grand style.

The mansion was a large affair, three stories in the center, two stories in each of the wings. She never knew exactly how many rooms it held, but once she'd counted twenty before something interrupted her impertinence. Long galleries swept across the front and back, pillared with those white columns that denoted Virginia's royal dwellings. Native oak, hickory, and magnolia graced the lawns near the house, while several old weeping willows draped their branches over the saw grass near the riverbank.

The house was always full of young men visiting the Kincaid sons, and in the later years, young ladies with dreamy looks on their aristocratic faces. There was always something going on too: formal dining, informal spend-the-days, frolicsome daytime rides, and at least once during their stay, an evening party held out on the sweeping lawn.

Papa would walk around on those nights with a befuddled

look on his face, his hands shoved in his pockets and his straw hair flying awry. But it was at Riverbend, during those evening parties, that she and her brother Carlyle learned to dance beneath the boughs of the old oak trees.

Carlyle was of the same age as the second Kincaid son, Gordon. They became great friends, as close as Papa and the royal Mr. Peyton Kincaid. Somewhere, a Mrs. Kincaid existed, but Annabelle never met her. She'd asked once, but Mr. Kincaid only patted her on the head and pretended not to hear the question. After that, she minded her manners.

There was another Kincaid son too, an older son, Royce, but he wasn't around much during those visits, and when he was, he ignored the Hallstons, all except Papa. It was odd, but Mr. Royce Kincaid seemed to understand Papa.

Once, the year she turned fourteen, she'd been standing on the side gallery, staring through the gnarled branches of the oaks, watching the sun rise. From there, she could see the two long rows of cabins facing each other across a wide expanse of Bermuda grass. A crooked trail led from each cabin door, ending at a broader path down the middle of the grass plot, beaten smooth and tan by the march of many black feet. On this morning, the servants, for no proper lady called them slaves, paused in their march and turned to watch the scene Annabelle longed to be a part of.

The hounds brayed in excitement. Thoroughbred horses stamped, fidgeting, then the horns blared. The squad of hunters raced off into the dawn mist, led by the dashing Mr. Royce Kincaid.

He looked splendid sitting astride a large blood bay in his hunting jacket, his black knee boots polished to such a shine the sun's rays actually blinded her as they glanced off. Of course, he didn't know she stood on the gallery watching. His gray eyes and deep laughter were directed exclusively to the aristocratic young woman riding next to him.

The lady wore a yellow riding habit with a large, floppy hat covering her blonde ringlets. Annabelle knew better than to ride to a hunt with a wide, floppy hat on her head, but right that minute, she'd have died for the opportunity to own a riding habit of daffodil yellow and a wide, floppy hat. Maybe, Mr. Royce Kincaid would notice her then.

Nobody noticed her, not even the servants coming up the path, which was probably the only reason she heard their conversation. After they disappeared in their different directions, she went looking for Papa, who never rode in hunts. As usual, she found him in the library.

"What's a scapegrace, Papa," she asked. "Is it the same as a blackguard?"

"Why do you ask, Annie?"

"I heard the servants talking about Mr. Kincaid." She didn't mind asking Papa questions. He never laughed at her and this time was no exception.

He set his book aside. "Mr. Peyton Kincaid?"

"Mr. Royce Kincaid."

"I see." He nodded. "Sit down, Annie."

Annabelle sat on the edge of the seat. She straightened her spine and folded her hands in her lap, for one always behaved like a lady inside Riverbend. Why, she even wore shoes, although Indian summer beckoned outside.

"*Scapegrace* and *blackguard* are unkind terms used to describe a man lacking both morals and prospects," said Papa in his stentorian lecturer's voice. "Do you remember your Plato, Annie?"

She nodded; she'd be a fool not to.

"Royce is a troubled young man, but he has the soul of a philosopher-king. Ignore what you hear and be kind to him." Papa picked up his book, and she knew she'd been effectively dismissed. Not that he meant to dismiss her that rudely; he'd simply forgotten she was there.

She waited until Papa went upstairs for his nap and slipped back into the library, where she borrowed all ten books of Plato's *Republic*. She fell asleep every night for the rest of that visit reading about just societies and philosopher-kings. She wanted to be nice to Royce Kincaid, but never got the opportunity. He didn't even know she was there.

By her sixteenth summer, she knew nature had played a nasty trick on her. She'd already recognized she would never be beautiful like Mama and Olivia. It was a disappointment, but as disappointments went, it could have been worse. She could have ended up looking like Papa.

She just wanted to grow. Something . . . anything . . . up or forward.

She lived in a college town. In the springtime, young men strolled the flower-scented paths, escorting young women who were all taller, softer, and rounder than Annabelle Hallston. Those same young men might ride to a turkey shoot with her and even be manly enough to compliment her if she bagged the largest number of turkeys. But they never invited her to stroll down a petal-strewn path.

A short walk away was Virginia Military Institute. Carlyle was now a cadet, and the family went often to watch the parades. Sometimes, Carlyle would brag about her to his friends. She could ride. She could shoot. By Jove, she could even cook. His friends weren't impressed. Like Carlyle, they strolled the pathways of VMI, making calf's eyes at young ladies with curves in the proper places.

Olivia tried to help.

"Are you sure you've been using that salve I gave you, Annie?" Olivia plopped a thick book on the top of Annie's head. "Walk," she commanded.

Annie figured it was the only use Olivia had ever discovered for a book. She walked, back and forth across Olivia's bedroom, balancing the book on her head while she talked.

"I use it. Religiously. Every night and every morning."

"Then I don't understand. It worked for me."

Annie stopped walking and stared at Olivia's corset-clad breasts. Melons. Olivia used the salve and grew lush, ripe melons. Annabelle used it and itched. *Not so inappropriate*, she thought. *God gave Olivia soft melons and me, itchy mosquito bites*.

"I don't even need a corset," she said, stopping in front of Livvy's full length mirror and studying herself. "There're no swells to push up or curves to pull in."

"Maybe you're just a late bloomer," said Olivia.

"Maybe I was meant to be a runty scarecrow," said Annabelle disgustedly. She took the book from her head and checked the title. Goldsmith. If anyone here at Merry Sherwood had read it, it could only be Uncle Richard. She tossed the book on the bed. She'd reread it tonight while Livvy snored. A wicked laugh bubbled up inside. "Did you know you snore, Livvy?" she asked.

"I do not! Ladies never snore."

"Then you're not a lady."

"Father says I'm the belle of three counties," said Livvy, her wide mouth grinning as proper ladies never grinned.

"Ding-dong. Ding-dong."

Olivia picked up a feather pillow and threw it across the room, catching Annabelle beside the head. Annabelle threw it back, and the battle was on.

Aunt Hetty finally heard them. "Girls!" said Hetty, standing just inside the doorway, her hands on her spreading hips. "Need I remind you you're ladies?"

"No, Mama," said Olivia. She caught a floating feather in her hand and used it to tickle Annabelle's nose.

"Of course not, Aunty," said Annabelle, grabbing the quill and pushing Olivia back into a pile of loose feathers. Aunt Hetty chuckled and closed the door.

Eventually, an ancient god took pity on her. She never grew taller, and she never grew anything resembling lush melons. But she did develop a waistline, and her breasts grew some. They no longer reminded her of mosquito bites, something more akin to poached eggs.

That year, Uncle Richard bought her a daffodil yellow riding habit and a ball gown the color of the wisteria that bloomed outside Livvy's bedroom window. Olivia helped her pack them both in layers and layers of tissue paper before she left for Riverbend.

That was the same year Mr. Hammond of South Carolina declared cotton as king. No one dared make war against King Cotton. Of course, in those days, she didn't spend much time thinking about wars. Heroes might battle in epic Greek poems. In Europe, ancient hatreds erupted into cavalry charges and flowing blood. But she lived in the United States of America. She was sixteen years old, a young woman trapped in a child's body, and full of soft, aching dreams.

The men discussed the debates between a Mr. Lincoln and the famous Mr. Douglas of Illinois. Annabelle listened to their talk and read the Richmond newspapers. Ladies never voiced their opinion, especially if the subject was politics. Annabelle wanted to be a lady, like Mama, but she couldn't always keep her mouth shut when she should. Not only did she speak when she shouldn't, she took the wrong side. She admired Mr. Lincoln's thoughts.

When she spoke out of turn, Papa's glazed, befuddled eyes would grow clear, and he'd look at her like he'd just remembered she was there. Once, she caught Mr. Peyton Kincaid's expression before he masked it. She guessed he rather appreciated a lady with a brain, although that summer, she'd have preferred to be a lady with a body.

She read *Uncle Tom's Cabin* during those weeks at Riverbend and thought it a little overwrought. At night, when no one would catch her, she read *Madame Bovary* by the light of a candle and wondered if she'd ever have a lover to die for.

The night of the soiree, she dressed in her new lavender gown and wandered down to the sweeping lawn. Chinese lanterns lit the soft autumn night. The river-scented air remained balmy, and she didn't even shiver in her off-the-shoulder gown. She'd stuffed her corset with a bit of cotton to give herself some cleavage. Carlyle stared at her chest. She wondered if he'd guessed. His gaze drifted up to her eyes, and he grinned. She knew he'd guessed.

Mr. Peyton Kincaid approached her, carrying two champagne glasses. He held one out to her. Annabelle didn't know what Papa would say, but she knew Livvy would be insanely jealous. Episcopalian ladies were allowed to sip champagne. Annabelle might be a Methodist lady, but she took the champagne anyway. She sipped some and managed not to shudder.

"You're growing up, Annie," said Mr. Peyton Kincaid.

"Do you really think so?" she asked hopefully. "I'd give anything to be another inch taller." Mr. Kincaid smiled at her. It wasn't the condescending adult smile she expected, more like an amused male smile.

"Thomas doesn't know what a treasure he has," he said. "Don't let anyone spoil you, Annie. You're like a breath of fresh mountain air."

She knew he was only being kind, but she returned his smile anyway. He blinked and seemed to lose his breath. She wondered if he felt ill and was going to suggest he sit for a spell when he asked her to dance.

She felt very grown-up, with her hair pinned up in a thick roll at the back of her neck, soft, satin slippers on her feet, dancing a mazurka with the patrician Mr. Kincaid. The night breeze brushed her bare shoulders and smelled of autumn, of pungent leaves and decaying bottomland, a scent she would forever associate with Riverbend and dancing beneath the stars.

After that, she danced a polka with Carlyle and a reel with Gordon, but none of the other young men asked her to dance, so she stood on the gallery and watched—as long as she could bear to watch.

She felt overcome by that wretched yearning to be something she wasn't meant to be. She wanted fiercely to know the trick of batting her eyelashes without looking owlish. She wanted to flirt with the ease of Olivia, have her beauty remembered in reverent tones, like Mama's.

More than that, she wanted to look up into some young man's face and see him gazing down at her with a special look, a look meaning she mattered. She wanted, wanted, wanted . . . somebody who knew she lived, somebody who noticed her, somebody who thought her the most special young lady in the world.

She bumped into Mr. Peyton Kincaid on her way back from the river. She didn't see him because of the tears in her eyes. He caught her elbow and kept her from falling.

"Why are you wandering alone down by the river, child, when there's moonlight and dancing on the lawn?" he asked.

"My slippers are too tight for dancing," she lied, but she feared he could hear the tears in her voice. To her great surprise, he leaned down and brushed a kiss on her forehead. To her great chagrin, a tear streaked down her cheek.

"Give them time, Annie-girl," he said softly. "They're too young to know what they're missing. In the meantime, would you share a waltz with a lonely old man down by the river?"

It was scandalous of course, dancing a waltz in the moonlight. But Annabelle didn't care. She decided she loved Mr. Peyton Kincaid almost as much as she loved Papa.

Her last day there, she dressed in her yellow riding habit and rode to the hunt with the young people of Fredericksburg. She learned that the aristocratic young lady she'd so envied two summers before had been sent to Philadelphia in disgrace. Royce Kincaid, the blackguard responsible for the young lady's disgrace, was in a place called Fort Laramie. Fighting Indians.

Perhaps Mr. Royce Kincaid would have his story told by an epic poet, in which case, she thought wryly, her childish imaginings would parallel real life since her fate was now linked with his. He was no longer out West, fighting Indians. He was in Richmond, fighting politicians—or so she supposed. She might be his wife, but she didn't know him well enough to be certain how he felt about the gathering war.

She heard a loud, frantic barking and looked toward the riverbank. Bo's new love, Major, bounded across the plain in pursuit of a rabbit. So like Bo, she thought, feeling the same mixture of amusement and tenderness she always felt with thoughts of her gangly young brother.

Told by Peyton he could choose from among the pedigreed fox hounds and retrievers raised here at Riverbend, Bo selected as his own a young dog of indeterminate lineage, whelped by a pure-blooded Chesapeake Bay retriever who had momentarily misplaced her aristocratic instincts. From the looks of Major, she guessed the father was some roving Newfoundland who had managed to gain his lady's love long enough to sire a litter of mongrels.

Although Peyton had laughed, she approved of Bo's choice. The dog possessed a temperament both spirited and loving; another gawky, young foundling who seemed to comprehend he'd been saved from a bleak future by a softhearted, thirteen-year-old orphan. As she watched, Major gave up on the rabbit and splashed into the river.

The wind puffed, catching her straw hat and flinging it into the breeze. She dismounted, allowing Bess's reins to dangle to the ground. She took two steps, reached for the straw, and the wind laughed, lifting the hat out of her reach and rolling it forward.

Cat and mouse, Annabelle played with the breeze, chasing the hat down the rise. Near the bottom of the hill, her bootheels hit a patch of slick mud, and her feet flew out from under her. She landed spread-eagled in the mud. Unhurt, she lay on her back and watched the clouds jostle and form in the deep blue sky. Suddenly, her heart skipped. If she stretched her imagination she saw it in the clouds—a cavalier's hat with a gray-white feather plume.

The air stirred as Major bounded up beside her, his brown, curly-haired body wagged by his tail. The dog's muscles quivered and suddenly erupted into an expansive, full-bodied shake. Annabelle ignored the shower of muddy river water and flung her arms around the dog's neck.

"We belong, Major," she murmured. "Papa and Mr. Kincaid did this for a reason, and I know the reason now." The dog licked her ear as she nuzzled her cheek against his grimy fur. "Just like Bo, they wanted to save the foundlings, to give them a home."

Gently, she pushed the marsh-stinking dog away, then pulled off her boots. She raised her muddy skirts, caught hold of her stocking tops, and rolled them down her legs. She shoved the stockings inside her boots and stood.

"Race you to the river, you silly mutt."

At the riverbank, she stopped and stared across at the opposite bank, into the sun. Major nudged her thigh, and she looked down. The dog carried a piece of driftwood in his mouth, his strong jaws wrapped gently around the wood as if it were a retrieved duck. He set the wood at her feet.

She leaned over and picked it up. Lifting her skirts with one hand, she waded into the river. The mud oozed between her toes, while her legs shivered from the cold water. She let her skirts drop and waded deeper. The rain-fed water eddied around her, sweeping the heavy material in the current. Beside her, the excited dog leaped and twisted, yelping with excitement.

Annabelle swung her arm back, then forward, letting go of the driftwood at the top of arc. The driftwood flew across the cloud-sprinkled sky and into the sun, where it hung suspended for the space of a heartbeat and came hurtling down to land with a splash and a gold-tinted shower in the flowing waters of the Rappahannock.

Major lunged into the current. Annabelle flung back her

head and laughed. While the dog paddled after the prize, she threw her arms wide and spun around in a circle while the laughter bubbled up from deep inside her. She spun around and around, the willows fading into river and back into willows, until the universe spun on its own without any help on her part.

She stopped, her arms dropping to her side as her whirling vision refocused on one gallant mutt, swimming toward her with the trophy between his jaws. With a new peace filling her chest, she lifted her water-clogged skirts and waded ashore.

She saw Royce then, at the top of the hill, sitting astride a black Arabian. His face was shadowed by the brim of his hat, but she could feel the lance of his gaze as they stared at one another. She swallowed and rubbed her palms down the front of her skirt. He pushed his hat back, revealing his face.

It was as if she was seeing him for the first time, this baffling man who was now her husband, with his sleek chestnut hair, the angular face of a centurion, and the lean, iron-muscled body of a warrior. He spurred his mount forward. She wanted to turn and run but held her ground, waiting.

He drew up beside Bess and dismounted. She watched him pat the Walker on her neck, then gather the reins in his hand. Once again, he started forward, one beautiful man with two beautiful horses trailing behind him.

Suddenly, she was painfully aware of her own condition: barefooted, her wet, mud-splattered skirts puddling in a droopy, black cloud around her legs. Her hair had come unbound, and the breeze blew it into her eyes. She pushed it back with her hands. She closed her eyes and lifted her face to the sun. Somewhere along the riverbank rested her ugly straw hat, useless in protecting her skin from turning brown.

She laughed aloud, a shaky laugh that caught and quivered at the end. Would she never learn? A true lady was always a lady. A lady kept her stocking feet where they belonged, inside patent leather boots beneath wide, crinolined skirts that somehow managed to stay starched and clean through both mud season and dust season. A lady would die before she'd wade barefoot in a muddy river, romping with a mongrel dog who was sadly lacking in pedigreed manners.

A colony of gulls took flight in a flapping of silver-gray

wings, cawing their disapproval, sounding so like the ladies of Lexington that she laughed again. Annabelle watched them flutter across the sky, a weaving, silver-white ribbon against the blue.

"What the bloody hell did you think you were doing?"

She jerked her gaze back to Royce. There was a rigid, arrogant set to his jaw and a tenseness in the way he stood, as if he expected her to answer his challenge with her own.

"Now there's a question, Mr. Kincaid," she said, fixing her gaze somewhere over his shoulder. "I would think it would be fairly obvious to a discerning gentleman such as yourself."

She slanted him a glance. He was not the type of man who shared her sense of the ridiculous. He didn't even smile.

"Well, it's not obvious, so why don't you tell me."

She had an unwelcome vision of an aristocratic young woman in a yellow riding habit and a wide floppy hat. A beautiful, clean, young lady riding to the hunt with the dashing Royce Kincaid at her side while a plain child stood on the gallery spinning dreams. Her chest tightened, and she fought an absurd urge to cry.

She shrugged and turned away, searching the riverbank for her missing hat. She didn't own enough clothing that she could afford to abandon the dilapidated thing. Her wet skirts clung to her legs as she traipsed through the cattails, gathering more mud along the hem until the weight seemed as heavy as her heart.

"Are you searching for something, Mrs. Kincaid, or do you simply enjoy trekking through the mud?"

Drat, the blasted mean man was laughing at her, not that she wasn't deserving of his laughter. She looked as respectable as a skinny piglet in a mud holler, and her nerves were as jumpy as popping corn in a hot fire. She couldn't very well hide the first condition, but she wasn't about to let him guess the second.

"Yes, Mr. Kincaid," she called over her shoulder, using her prim lady's voice.

"Yes, which?" The laughter sounded in his tone.

"Yes, both. I rather enjoy the feel of cold mud between my toes," she said, rising and beginning to turn. "And I seem to have misplaced my . . ."

He rotated the straw boater around and around in his hands while his lips turned up in that type of arrogant smile only a male could produce. A strange warmth budded inside her. He was teasing. Teasing was something friends did to one another, a sign of affection.

"Ugly old thing," he said, studying the hat as if it were a trophy of war.

"It is, isn't it?" She let her smile escape as she walked back toward him. "One of Aunt Hetty's hand-me-downs. Livvy had sense enough to make sure it went to me instead of her."

She took the hat from his hand. Major had obviously captured it at some point. It was as ruined as her dress. She held back a sigh.

"Who is Livvy?" He took a step closer, and she felt his heat wrapping around her. It took her a moment to find her voice.

"Aunt Hetty's daughter, Olivia. My cousin and friend."

"I see." He made two words sound as sultry as a hot summer night. She watched his long, brown fingers untie the crimson scarf at his throat. "Does this Livvy share your fondness for mud?"

"I, uh . . ." She swallowed, wanting to look away, unable to look away. "No, I don't think so. Livvy's a lady from the bones out; with me, it seems to go about skin deep."

"Ah, a lady. Fluttering eyelashes, no freckles . . . no mud," he said.

She stood motionless, mesmerized by the way the creases at the corner of his lips deepened when he spoke, paralyzed by the soft brush of the cloth against her skin as he wiped her face like she was some naughty child.

"I don't have freckles," she said stupidly.

"You don't have mud now either."

He stared at her mouth, and she fought a crazy urge to wet her lips. He stepped back, jamming the crimson cloth in his hip pocket as his almost smile faded. "Stay out of the river, Annabelle. The current is dangerous here at the best of times and killing during the spring floods."

Her spine stiffened of its own volition. It was more than the curt tone of his voice. She didn't understand the effect he had on her, these strange feelings like prickly heat on her skin and injured pride inside.

"I'm not some addlepated fool, Mr. Kincaid, and I don't have to take orders from you."

"You are Mrs. Kincaid, Mrs. *Royce* Kincaid," he shot back before she had a chance to catch a breath. "And you will take your orders from me."

Mrs. Royce Kincaid . . .

Annabelle fixed her unseeing gaze on the horizon. *Oh, Mama,* she thought. *I'm trying to take care of our men but everything is so different now. I'm married, but it's not a marriage— nothing like what you and Papa shared—and because of this marriage, Carlyle isn't speaking to me. But I didn't know how else to make a home for Bo.*

*Everything is changing, Mama, so fast, like when the creeks rise and rush down the mountain, sweeping away everything familiar . . .*

In September of 1859, the Hallstons didn't go to Riverbend. Papa was ill. In October, John Brown led a slave revolt in Harpers Ferry. He was captured the next day by Federal troops led by Bobby Lee of Virginia. Carlyle was among the VMI cadets who stood guard at John Brown's hanging in Charles Town.

Carlyle never spoke to her about the hanging although she knew he approved. The Hallstons didn't own chattel, but Carlyle was an aristocratic son of Virginia. He did speak often of Thomas Jackson, his military instructor. Carlyle thought Jackson to be a military genius and swore that when the war came, he'd fight in Jackson's regiment. Annabelle thought the grim Thomas Jackson was even stranger than Papa, and she knew there would never be a war.

The next summer, she put Bo on the train alone for the trip to Merry Sherwood. She didn't know what was wrong with Papa, but she knew he was ill. So she entrusted her little brother to Aunt Hetty and stayed home to make certain Papa ate well and slept regular hours. She and Papa didn't always sleep regular hours though. Sometimes, they sat up long into the night, talking.

Outside, a full harvest moon shed a soft light on the tiny rectangle of lawn enclosed in the white picket fence. She heard the night sounds of a drowsy little college town—the click of crickets, the soft moan of someone's cow, and, in the distance, the muted plod of a single rider on a dusty, red road. With such visions, such sounds, it was hard to imagine cannons and gunfire and mad, romantic cavalry charges. But that was all anyone talked about anymore.

"I think you must be the only Douglas Democrat in Lexington," she said to Papa.

"If that's the case, then I'm the only thinking Democrat in Lexington," he said.

"Why, Papa?" she asked, just like she'd asked Mama so many years ago.

Papa gave her his lecture on dividing the Union and state's rights and the ugly institution of slavery. He even threw in Henry Clay and John C. Calhoun for good measure. She listened and learned and, sometimes, she argued, but that wasn't what she meant by why. She was eighteen years old and still didn't understand.

What made men want to march away to die? What quirk in their nature told them war and romance were synonymous terms? Papa didn't know what she asked and wouldn't know the answer anyway. Papa might be a man, but he never thought like other men, like Carlyle. She didn't want Carlyle to die, alone and cold on some distant battlefield.

In November, Abraham Lincoln, the Republican, won the election. In December, South Carolina seceded. In January, Carlyle left to drill with the militia. He came home the next month, to pick up the new uniform she'd made him and to visit with Papa.

Carlyle stamped around their little house importantly, his chest bulging with pride while his mouth spouted nonsense. "We'll whip them in a matter of months, Annie."

"You're training with cornstalks and brooms and flintlock rifles, and you're going to lick them in months?" she asked incredulously.

"We believe in what we're fighting for. Any one boy in my company can lick three Federals with his arm tied behind his back."

"It'll be the bloodiest war the world has ever seen," said Papa. "And nothing will ever be the same afterward."

"There won't be any war," she said.

"There'll be a war, sparrow," said Carlyle, patting her on the head as if she remained a child.

She hated him when he called her by that nickname, and she hated him for the smile on his face when he spoke of war.

"Don't worry, it'll be over, and we'll all be home by next Christmas," said Carlyle.

She knew he was wrong.

By the end of February, six more states had followed South Carolina out of the Union and a new nation was born—the Confederate States of America. Virginia elected a secession convention. Lincoln set out for Washington while Jeff Davis struggled to build a government in Montgomery, Alabama.

All eyes, North, South, and border states, focused on the developing tension in Charleston Harbor, where Confederate gun batteries took the range of Federally held Fort Sumter.

March 4, 1861, dawned cold, gray, and windy. It suited Annabelle's frame of mind. She feared that her life, from this moment forward, would be forever cold and gray, full of blustering, raw March winds that would never again sweep away winter's death.

Annabelle stood between Bo and Carlyle, clutching a lace-edged handkerchief in her right hand while the winds whipped her black dress against her trembling legs.

Before her stood a man of the cloth, also dressed in black. Behind her stood innumerable men and boys, Papa's students, most of them dressed in gray. The minister read from a black book, but Annabelle didn't hear his words over the thrashing of the mad March wind. Oddly, her mind flashed to Lord Byron instead of the Twenty-third Psalm, but then, she was always more her papa's daughter than her mama's.

> *Let there be light, said God, and there was light.*
> *Let there be blood, says man, and there's a sea.*

Papa was happy at last. He rested beside Mama.

"Annabelle?"

Something in Royce's voice drew her attention. Annabelle shuddered before she managed to pull her distant gaze from the horizon and bring it back to him.

He glared at her, flat silver eyes showing nothing of his thoughts. She'd evidently frightened him by wading in the river, and her heart softened toward him for that. It meant there was a person behind those eyes, a man with feelings. For some reason, he'd learned to hide those feelings from the world. But she recognized the danger, too.

He was as dark and seductive as a fallen angel. Part of her wanted to flee from the darkness, and part of her wanted to grab hold of him and hold on for dear life while he carried them both through the coming fire.

She stepped back. From the corner of her eye, she saw his comeuppance in the form of a wet, smelly dog. Major bounded up beside him and uncoiled with a violent shaking. Stinking marsh water and great clumps of mud showered them both. Royce smothered an expletive.

She covered her mouth with her hand in an unsuccessful effort to hold back her laughter. He withdrew the scarf from his pocket and wiped the side of his face, then used it to pound his buckskin-coated arm. The fringes waved merrily with his effort.

"Goodness gracious, you are a sight," she said, stepping back another step and inspecting him from the top of his hat to the tips of his boots. "Who would believe a fine gentleman such as yourself would find pleasure in mud baths?"

To her surprise, a smile formed at his lips, the first true smile she'd seen from him. It mellowed the sharpness of his features and deepened the creases at the corner of his mouth into appealingly boyish dimples.

"I'm afraid whoever told you your husband is a gentleman was lying through his teeth."

"Oh, I figured that much out on my own, sir. Why, your language alone is so fancy, I do believe even the bullfrogs are blushing."

He looked her over again, starting with her muddy bare feet and working his insolent way up her stained and bedraggled dress. By the time he got to her hair, which hung about her face and over her shoulders so that even she could see the clumps of mud stuck in it, and doubtless giving her the appearance of last year's sparrow's nest, his laughter threatened to explode. She wanted to pull her arm back and slug him.

"Of course, you never sin," he said, stepping closer.

"Never."

The laughter deserted his features. The wind snatched her hair, plastering a wet clump across her face. He plucked it away, his fingers briefly making contact with her flaming cheeks.

"Church every Sunday," he said.

She nodded as he tucked the wisp of hair behind her ear, touching her again. She knew he was taunting her but she could hardly think with those silver eyes piercing through her and those callused, gentle fingers touching her.

"Morning prayers . . ."

"Every morning," she said.

"Evening prayers, too, I bet."

"On my knees."

His fingers slid across her cheek. He stroked her bottom lip, ever so gently. Her lips parted with the warmth of his touch.

"I highly recommend sin, Mrs. Kincaid. It's good for the soul."

He leaned his head closer, and she knew he was going to kiss her. She stared at the firm line of his unsmiling mouth, wanting his kiss, not wanting it. His breath caressed her face. Her insides tightened into a hard ball, and she closed her eyes, leaned ever so slightly forward, waiting . . . wanting . . . not wanting . . . waiting . . .

His low chuckle jerked her back to her senses. She opened her eyes to see him preparing to mount his horse.

"I'm not about to ruin what promises to be an interesting relationship by kissing you, dear heart."

"I didn't have any such notion in my head."

"Didn't you?"

He gave her a mocking bow and mounted his horse. She'd never felt so small or vulnerable as she did at that minute, with him looking down on her from his vast height, smiling a taunting challenge.

"You have my permission to sin, Mrs. Kincaid." He gathered the reins, turning his horse. "Just be discreet in your sinning."

A jumble of emotions tumbled around inside her: fury, humiliation, and that old, insane wanting. A cold nose nudged her hand, and she looked down. Major met her gaze, his brown eyes sympathetic while his great, bushy tail fanned the mud.

Absently, she scratched the dog behind the ear and looked toward the top of the hill. Her husband had stopped, in the same position she'd first noticed him, an eternity, a few minutes ago. She glanced down at the dog.

"Come on, Major," she said. Together, they bounded back into the river. The dog leaped and quivered and splashed next to her, delirious with the new game. When she was knee deep in the cold, she turned around so she could see the man she'd married. She lifted her straw boater and waved it over her head.

"Good day, Mr. Kincaid," she called out.

He swept his hat from his head with a flourish, swinging it in front of his chest as he half bowed in the saddle. A salute— good gracious, the horrible man was saluting her. She turned her back on him, but his deep, masculine laughter filtered back on the breeze.

It was the warm spring breeze that chased the chill from her body. It had nothing to do with a man's laughter or a cavalier's salute.

Royce pulled up in a clump of trees at the top of another rise. He sat in the shadows, hidden from her view, and watched her romp in the water with the dog.

She was so vulnerable, as evidenced by that unconscious withdrawal. He'd never met anyone who could pull so deep inside herself that she almost ceased to exist. He'd have to learn to temper his voice; he'd managed to send her into that private sanctuary with the anger in his tone.

She was full of life now, her laughter floating back to him on the wind. If she managed to keep from drowning, she'd probably catch her death from a chill. A man with any sense would yank her out of that dangerous water, by the hair if necessary, and turn her over his knee and smack some sense into her backside.

Oddly enough, he had no desire to do either. He found her defiance almost as erotic as her mouth. That wide, generous mouth with the lower lip a little too full, inviting a man to nibble and taste. He'd come too close to accepting the invitation and didn't like the near loss of control on his part.

Keeping his ears attuned to the sounds from the river in case she took a misstep and got caught in the current, he leaned forward in the saddle and gazed out over the land. Riverbend and Old Riverbend, together over three thousand acres of rolling hills on both sides of the river.

He hadn't been lying when he'd told her he didn't want it. He didn't, whether because of the old ghosts or because Peyton wanted him to want it, he didn't know and didn't care to contemplate. But, God only knew, he did love it, this beautiful land between the mountains and the sea. Loved it with a fierceness that made his chest ache and his eyes burn.

He'd sought to escape its hold by traveling west, only to discover another kind of beauty in the majestic Rockies, in the wide-open sky that made a man feel his proper, insignificant place in the universe. But even that beauty hadn't erased the old love.

Virginia held him in her subtle thrall, owned him, blood and guts. Maybe it was the history that haunted her like a lost lover—the whispers of the past that floated along her rivers, the old battle cries tangled in her forests. This land he loved was the staging ground for a nation, peopled with heroes and horse thieves, farseeing statesmen, hardy frontiersmen, and a few bloody idiots.

His mind wandered to the discussions he'd taken part in these last days in Richmond. Right now, Virginia's current crop of statesmen leaned toward remaining in the Union. He knew that mood could change in a flash, and the firebrands in Charleston would probably set the fuse. When that happened, this land of his blood would once again be the battleground for a nation, and he had no doubt she'd go down in ashes of glory.

Suddenly aware that the splashing and the yelping had both stopped, he jerked his gaze back to the river. Neither dog nor girl had drowned. One rolled in the mud while the other tied her boots around the saddle pommel. Annabelle took Bess's reins in her hand, and the trio started off along the riverbank. He couldn't help smiling.

He wished he could hear her, whatever one-sided conversation she was holding with her two four-footed friends. Every so many steps, she'd turn around, walking backward, while her head bobbed and her hands gestured. Damned if Bess didn't nod in response while the fool dog ran circles around both of them. Life held few such innocent pleasures, so he sat a while longer, watching the innocence.

She came to a sun-filled meadow and stopped. Like a bedraggled black butterfly, she waded into the patch of jonquils and early-blooming bluebells. She picked a handful of blossoms, then waded back out of the blooms to where the horse waited. She stuck several jonquils through the crown-piece on the horse's head. She leaned over and tucked some bluebells beneath the dog's collar, then stepped back as if surveying her handiwork. Evidently satisfied, she tucked the remaining blossom behind her own ear.

She turned so her profile was toward him, her chin nudged up slightly over the slender column of her neck. She stood like that for the longest time, gazing into the distance, and a strange peace settled over Royce. He'd made a wild leap of faith she'd feel it too, a faith based on her background, her bloodlines, and he suddenly knew he'd been right. She wasn't a lady of the manor house any more than he was a gentleman planter.

She was a child of the land, and she'd husband it through the coming fire and pass it on to the next generation, whoever they might be. But she'd teach those children of hers to love it and nurture it, and the line would continue through her, not him. He knew somewhere in the haunted, misty past, some common ancestor smiled in approval.

She settled onto the ground, sunlight bouncing off the cascade of her waist-length hair, sparking the damp brown curls with gold and platinum. The mutt settled beside her with his head in her lap. She stroked the smelly dog while her gaze lingered on the distance. Royce turned his horse and spurred him toward the estate house. He rode away from the wood nymph and her charges with a lightness of spirit he hadn't felt in years.

# Chapter 3

～⌒◯◯⌒～

Royce drew up in front of the smithy and dismounted, tethering his horse at the post just outside the door. He ran his hand along the broad rump as he skirted around and entered the small brick building. Heat and the sour stink of hot metal and sweat assaulted him.

Clarence acknowledged his presence with a nod and kept on working. A single bar of sunlight glanced off his flaring cheekbones, casting deeper shadows in the hollows beneath. Clarence flipped the tongs, turning the iron rod over the heat, and they both watched it change from dull red to hot yellow.

Royce moved forward and slung his hip on the workbench near the forge. He enjoyed watching a skilled man perform a task and knew Clarence reached for the same level of perfection he always set for himself.

"You get around to putting new shoes on Ajaque while I was gone?"

"Shoe that Thoroughbred so you can ride him off to war." Clarence squinted through the dusky smoke from the forge. "Seems to me that's a waste of good horse."

"That any way to be talking to your master?"

"Haven't you heard? Mr. Lincoln's gonna free all us worthless niggers."

"And send you back to Africa. Think you'll like Africa?"

Amazingly, Clarence shot him a grin, which Royce tried to match, but his face felt stiff with the effort. A clash of emotions filled his chest—anger and shame, exasperation, and something deeper—a kinship neither spoke of yet both silently acknowledged.

Air whooshed from the bellows, sending sparks floating lazily into the air. Clarence was whistling and somehow managing to smile at the same time. Even with the door open, it was unbearably hot inside the small building.

Royce removed his hat and laid it on the workbench beside his hip. "You smiling like an idiot because Mr. Lincoln's going to make you pay for your dinner in the future, or is there something else causing that look?"

Clarence looked up. Sweat dripped from his glistening hair and ran down his cheek in a rivulet. "Me and Miss Patsy's going to jump the broom come Sunday."

Royce thought for a minute. "We don't have a Patsy on Riverbend."

"No, we don't. Miss Patsy belongs to Johnson at the Willows."

Royce jerked to his feet. "Christ, Clarence. You couldn't pick a woman from someplace decent? It was Johnson's patrol that whipped your father to death."

Clarence took the white-hot iron from the heat and laid it on the anvil. "We're going to be married," he said with a stubborn firmness in his tone. "Slavelike this Sunday, Godlike and proper when things change."

Royce searched Clarence's face, but the mask had fallen over his features. All he saw was the sweat of hard work on the black man's brow and a proud rigidity in his jaw. The heat suddenly seemed even more oppressive.

"Johnson won't sell her, if that's what you're thinking."

Clarence rested the hammer on the anvil and looked up. "Johnson won't take money, but he sure covets that horse."

Royce pulled the handkerchief from his pocket and started to mop his own face, until he realized there was dried mud on the handkerchief. He swallowed a curse and shoved the cloth back in his hip pocket. "Which horse?"

"Jupiter."

"Jupiter's meaner than sin."

"He sure is."

Clarence was asking only for the comfort of having his

woman by his side, where he could protect her as best he was able. A basic right of a free man. The hammer rang against the anvil. Each hammerblow thrummed through his guts with an ache and a sadness as he watched Clarence shape the shoe.

Peyton owned the Riverbend slaves, but they were none of them free, not in this world of bondage and probably not even in the next. And they'd all, black and white, rich and poor, travel through hell before they solved that riddle.

"I'll try," he said.

Clarence straightened. Royce looked at that proud face glistening with sweat, into liquid brown eyes that were sad and wise and arrogant all at the same time. Clarence nodded. Royce picked up his hat.

Clarence said, "Young Bohannon, he won't ever be more'n a tolerable smithy, but we've been showing him like you asked. Clem says he's got the makings of a farmer."

"It'll be up to you to teach him, Clarence, you and the others."

The two men stared at one another across the distance that separated them; one self-educated black man with bulging, sweat-coated muscles gleaming in the shadowed light; one lean, hawk-faced, aristocratic rebel who had taught the black man to read and write.

"We take care of our own," said Clarence, turning back to the heat.

Royce was halfway through the door when Clarence called out to him. "That worthless horse of yours has got new shoes."

"Thank you," said Royce under his breath. Clarence didn't need to hear it. Royce was certain he already knew.

Royce turned the Arabian over to a groom, who led the horse toward one of the lesser stables. Royce headed for the main building, the one housing Riverbend's famed Thoroughbreds. Halfway down the length of the building, he stopped in front of one of the large stalls. A big blue, fully sixteen hands, stuck his head over the gate.

"Clarence was right," said Royce. "You are one worthless piece of horseflesh."

"You back already?" called out a voice from the shadows.

"I'm back." Royce patted the horse's muzzle, then wandered in the direction of the voice. He stopped several stalls farther along and leaned against the opened gate. Inside, Gordon and Bo curried Gordon's brown jumper.

Gordon looked up. "We didn't expect you for a couple more days," he said. "Any news?"

"Nothing yet," said Royce. "Seems Richmond and Washington are both waiting to see what happens at Sumter."

A shadow passed across Gordon's face. Royce would give his last breath to keep his brother out of the war. They never spoke of it however. Each would live up to his own code of honor; Gordon's to fight a war he didn't believe in, Royce's to allow him to fight.

Bo moved around the back of the horse, pulling hairs out of the currycomb. Royce found himself smiling for no reason, other than the boy looked like he belonged in a cornfield mounted on crossed poles.

"Didn't happen to see Annie on your way in?" asked Bo. "I told Uncle Peyton not to worry, she can take care of herself, but he's worrying anyway."

Royce lifted a brow. "*Uncle* Peyton?"

"Well, we're kinda like family now, and it makes him happy." The boy shrugged a nonchalant shoulder, but Royce guessed it made the boy kind of happy, too. He harbored a sigh. Naïveté must be a Hallston familial trait.

"I saw her," he said. "Down by the river with some mutt, both of them muddy from crown to tip."

"Shit," said Bo with an energetic shake of his head.

Royce held back a chuckle as his gaze met Gordon's. "What kind of language is that, son?" he asked.

"You said I should hang around the men and learn how to run an estate." Bo shrugged again. "So I'm learning."

"Learning to talk like a bloody damn roustabout wasn't what I had in mind."

A muffled voice came from the other side of the horse. "Stick around, Bo," said Gordon. "You can learn a whole new vocabulary from Royce Kincaid." Gordon's tawny head reappeared in front of the horse. Royce ignored the grin on his brother's face. "What's got you shitting anyway," Gordon continued. "The fact that your sister stole your dog?"

"I should be so lucky. I'm going to be reading all afternoon now." Bo backed away from the horse until he met the oak boards of the sidewall. He slid down, seating himself in the straw, his too-big hands atop his bent knees, with his head bowed between them. He looked the picture of total despondency.

"You're not making any sense," said Gordon.

"Because it doesn't make any sense. She gets mad at herself, and the next thing I know, I'm reading Shakespeare if she's only a little bit mad, Homer if she's medium mad, and, God help me, *Plato* if she's really furious."

Royce fought back a shout of laughter caused by both the sight of the gangly youngster and the intriguing piece of information he was inadvertently imparting. Not wanting to appear too interested, he waited for Gordon to probe further. Gordon didn't disappoint him.

"Keep talking, Bo, maybe I can help you unravel the mystery, but you're going to have to give me more clues."

"You know her." Bo tangled his fingers through his straw-colored hair and sighed. "She's got a devil on one shoulder and an angel on the other. She listens to the devil and acts dumb, then the angel pokes her and says something like, *What would your Mama say*. His head waggled from side to side as his voice hit a high falsetto. Royce nearly exploded with the laughter building in his chest.

"Next thing I know, I'm reading so's she can prove to the angel she's a proper lady and raising a proper gentleman." Bo rolled his eyes. "*She-it!*" he added for an emphatic finish.

"So what's mud on her dress? Shakespeare or Homer?" asked Gordon, his laughter having subsided to nothing more than shaking shoulders.

"Depends on what she's wearing." Bo sent a beseeching look in Royce's direction. "Tell me it wasn't one of those mourning dresses."

"Sorry, son. I guess it's going to be Homer," said Royce.

Bo closed his eyes and sent his supplication heavenward. "Tell me it's not ruined. She only had two."

Royce slouched against the gate and propped his bootheel on the wood. "Don't know enough about ladies' clothes to help on that one. But why in hell does she only have two dresses?"

He saw a look pass between Bo and Gordon and knew there was some secret hidden there they didn't want him to know. It would be easier to pull it out of the youngster, so Royce ignored Gordon and leveled his gaze on Bo. Bo squirmed and swallowed and squirmed some more. Royce didn't back off.

"Well . . . see, she didn't really believe Papa was going to die until right at the end and she didn't have anything black when it happened and then she found out we didn't have any money and she had to borrow—aw, shit, she's going to kill me for telling you that."

"Look at me, Bo." Royce waited until Bo lifted his gaze. "I'll save your sorry ass for you if you tell me who loaned her the money."

"My sorry ass will already be dead if I tell you that."

"Bo." Royce narrowed his eyes, giving the youngster his hardest look.

Gordon came from around the horse and leaned over, taking the currycomb from the boy's hand. "Run over to the smithy and get Clarence for me. I want him to check Aster's shoes."

Bo leaped up as if saved from the devil. Gordon gathered the currying tools while Royce watched in silence. Horses shifted inside their stalls, the soft-sounding movement emitting the sweet scent of fresh bedding. He loved the sounds and the smells of a stable. He loved his brother, who had suddenly learned to keep secrets.

"You loaned her the money," said Royce, as Gordon passed by.

"She's already paid me back."

Royce swung the gate closed and latched it. For an instant, their gazes locked, and Royce stared into Celeste's eyes, almond shaped, slightly lifted at the outside corners and the deep blue of a vesper sky.

He seldom remembered her eyes or her beauty because he didn't want to remember, but at times like this, when he actually looked at her son, really saw him, he always felt the jolt of memory. Celeste Fortier Kincaid, the New Orleans belle who had whelped God only knew how many sons. Not for the first time, he wondered what Peyton thought when he looked into Gordon's eyes.

He waited until Gordon had stowed the brushes, then fell into stride beside him as he came back up the length of the barn.

"I'm going to make one lousy husband," Royce said quietly.

"You seem to have started out that way."

Royce detected something in his brother's tone of voice. His guts twitched with a foreboding he'd made a horrible mistake. Most men didn't talk about their hearts, about loving. Gordon wasn't most men, and Royce had to know, although how the devil he'd straighten it out at this late date he couldn't fathom.

"Are you in love with her, Gordon? If that's the case . . ."

"Once, a long time ago." Gordon pushed his hat back and expelled a breath. "She never saw me as anything more than another brother, and I got over it."

They came to a stop just inside the wide doors, both men staring out. He wanted to look at his brother but didn't. He knew what he'd see. Another small loss, self-deprecatory amusement, the bittersweet shadow of first love. Gordon wore his feelings on his face, and sometimes Royce hated him for that. He didn't want to know everything about his brother. Knowing made the charge and the responsibility too great.

"That last summer they came to visit—you'd already gone west—Peyton threw one of his lawn parties like always. Only that time, she was old enough actually to take part in it. Somebody had done her hair up, and she had these little ringlets around her face and a bunch of lilacs caught up at the side. I looked at her and suddenly, she wasn't annoying little Annie with the scraped knees, she was the young Miss Hallston and pretty as a bay filly in a flower bed."

Gordon brushed the toe of his boot through the hay scraps littering the floor. Over by the cookhouse, slaves moved in a flurry of clanging activity as they loaded the wagons to carry dinner to the field hands. A turbaned mammy herded a group of black children toward the nursery building, their high-pitched voices mingling with the sounds of the stable hands and the livestock.

Royce took in the normal activity of the estate, while his mind pictured the other scene his brother painted.

The soft light of the Chinese lanterns on the front lawn reflecting off the shiny leaves of the big magnolias, their white blooms giving off the sweet smell of a summer night. The parade of beautifully gowned women escorted by men in frilled shirts and silk scarves, alighting from tall carriages and sleek barouches, each driven by a distinctly uniformed black servant and pulled by a matched team of horses. And a young girl dressed for her first foray into that shimmering world, a world already receding into misty memory.

A sick restlessness filled his guts. It was all coming to an end, as it should, yet everything he'd heard in Richmond pointed to that end coming by violent means. No one could guess what havoc war would wreak, either for the little black children disappearing into the nursery or for the pampered young ladies and their attendant beaus.

"She was wearing this off-the-shoulder gown," said Gordon. "The same color as the lilacs in her hair. I asked her to dance a reel. She smiled at me, and I knew I was in love."

Royce pulled himself back from the dark abyss and focused his attention on Gordon's story. He could actually appreciate that last comment. Annabelle's smile and her lips were a potent combination.

He started aimlessly forward with no particular destination in mind. Gordon followed, and they ended up at the worm fence, elbows set on the top rail. In the distance, he could see the not-quite-a-lady on her return trek. Behind them, Clarence and Bo passed on their way to the stables.

"So you danced a reel and gave the lady her first kiss under the magnolia," said Royce. He'd kissed many a woman beneath the boughs of that giant magnolia, and done other, more unmentionable, things in other places about the grounds. He couldn't remember the innocence of his first kiss, probably because he'd lost his innocence long before the event.

Gordon laughed softly. "To borrow Bo's turn of phrase, I should be so lucky." He shook his head and turned around, leaning his back against the fence. "No. Carlyle, the bastard, came up afterward, laughing like the idiot he is, and told me she'd stuffed cotton in her corset. All I could think of was getting her under the oaks and finding out whether he was telling the truth. I was so damned irritated with myself I had to drink a couple of Peyton's rum punches before I could ask her to dance again. By the time I reached that state of drunken courage, she'd disappeared."

Royce tilted a smile in his brother's direction. "Never did find out, huh?"

"Didn't matter. You won't understand this, but I dreamed about those breasts for months. Rather uncomfortable dreams, I'll admit. Like I said before, she never shared the attraction, and I got over it."

Gordon thought his big brother was so damn tough. What would Gordon think if he told him the truth? Told him about the scores of times a much younger Royce Kincaid had walked through the streets of Fredericksburg, peering through the curtained windows and dreaming he lived inside one of those less grand dwellings. Inside those houses, real families lived, with a mother and a father and well-loved sons.

The dreaming had come to an end long ago, but the terrible yearning had never left him. The yearning to have a home—grand mansion or sod shanty didn't matter—so long as it was filled with the warmth of a real family.

"I still love her though," said Gordon. Royce looked at Gordon to seek the meaning beneath his words, and Gordon flashed him his wide, boyish smile. "She's been like a little sister since forever. She needed some money—couldn't ask her uncle Richard, wouldn't ask Peyton—so I gave it to her. She's the one who insisted on paying me back."

He watched Bo and Clarence walk across the stable yard toward them. Clarence's irritation showed on his face.

"Where'd she get the money to pay you back?" asked Royce, before Bo reached hearing distance.

"Sold her mother's silver gravy ladle."

Royce thought of the little house in Lexington with its shiny floors and well-polished furniture. He pictured the gleaming heirloom coffee service in her hands and guessed how much the loss of that small piece of her past must have affected her. Royce half listened to Gordon and Clarence as they argued over the condition of Aster's shoes. Then he shifted his attention to Annabelle, who had come into the yard.

The dog chased after a stray chicken. A groom dodged the dog, then the chicken, then the dog again and finally made it to Annabelle. As she handed over the Tennessee Walker, she said something to him that caused him to laugh. As the small black man led the horse away, she walked over to the well, released the bucket, and reached for the crank.

She used all of her slight body to turn the crank. He doubted she'd have the strength to raise a full bucket and was preparing to go help her when the situation suddenly became too interesting to interrupt. He nudged Gordon with his elbow. The other men stopped talking and turned to watch.

Jules, Peyton's personal servant, strutted across the back lawn with his normal august formality. He was dressed in a black frock coat and starched shirt, the snowy linen matching the color of his hair. A white towel draped over his forearm and ruffled like a flag in the breeze.

The crazed mutt ran circles around him, which he tried to ignore as he headed purposefully toward Annabelle. She straightened, pushed her tangled hair off her face, and flashed Jules one of those smiles.

"Aw shit," said Bo, apparently seeing her condition for the first time.

"Homer?" asked Royce.

"Plato," said Bo with disgust.

Jules set the towel on the side of the stone well and proceeded to work the crank. She stepped back as the bucket reappeared. Jules dumped the cold well water on the dog, and the mutt leaped stiff-legged into the air. On landing, Major took off yelping with his bushy tail tucked between his legs.

All activity in the neighborhood ceased as whites and blacks alike broke into laughter. Jules never cracked a smile. He brushed his gloved hands together in front of his waistcoat, then went back to refilling the bucket.

"If that's really your dog, Bo, don't you think you should be cleaning him?" asked Royce without taking his eyes from the entertainment.

"Yes, sir," said Bo.

Bo took off in a lope, chasing the still-yelping dog. After a few circles and countercircles, he managed to herd the mutt back by his sister. Annabelle grabbed the dog's collar and Jules showered the mutt again. The old slave's condition was beginning to resemble Annabelle's.

Jules ignored the return shower from the shaking dog and handed Bo the linen. Annabelle looped her arm in Jules's, and the two of them strolled toward the house, Jules still dignified, Annabelle in animated conversation.

"I'll be," muttered Clarence. "Old Jules got his hands dirty."

"Annabelle Hallston is one special woman." Gordon strode after the servant and the girl without a backward glance.

"What did I say that got him all riled?" asked Clarence.

Royce chuckled. "He's riled at me."

Jules and Annabelle had stopped, waiting for Gordon to catch up with them. Her bedraggled condition hadn't improved during her homeward journey.

"That Patsy of yours wouldn't happen to be a lady's maid by any chance?" asked Royce.

"Seamstress."

"Could she learn?"

"If the lady can teach her."

"Not bloody likely." He was looking at Clarence when he heard the frothy trill of Annabelle's laughter. The sound brought the old, forgotten yearnings pummeling through Royce with such unexpected force that he actually shuddered.

He closed his eyes against the bright sun and willed the terrible ache away. He felt Clarence's hand on his arm, and only then realized his own hands were clenched into fists at his side.

"Why'd you do it, Royce?"

The marriage Annabelle wished to keep secret had already spread among Riverbend's slave population, not that he was surprised. Speculation, maybe, or a remark overheard by a house servant. He knew old Jules, the only servant actually informed of the marriage, hadn't spread the knowledge. Jules was . . . Jules was special.

"Does everybody know?" asked Royce.

Clarence nodded. "The grown ones anyway."

"Peyton's handiwork," said Royce. "She wasn't any more interested in me than I was in her, and that's all I'm going to say on the subject except that she's got sense enough to want it kept secret for a while. Can you squelch the drums?"

"Nobody's talking off the estate."

Clarence was silent but Royce knew he wasn't finished and for some reason he didn't understand, he waited.

"Royce, I'm way out of line here, and you can tell me to go to hell . . . but you could do a lot worse than that little woman."

Anger flashed, burning hot in his chest. Anger at Clarence,

Peyton and Celeste, Annabelle and himself—mostly himself. He walked away without answering, unwilling to let Clarence see the anger and unable to hide it this time.

*The line ends with me*, he thought bitterly. *The ignoble end of the Kincaids of Riverbend*.

Annabelle gladly excused herself from the dining table, leaving the men to their port and cigars and knowing as soon as she disappeared, the conversation would turn to secession and war. She'd had enough of that topic to last her a lifetime. Bo made no move to follow, so she leveled her stern mother's look on him. He squirmed but remained seated. She was preparing to call him to task when Royce spoke, seeming to read her mind.

"Bo will stay with us," he said in his low baritone.

She'd never heard Royce's voice raised in anger, or any other emotion for that matter. It was always smooth and soft-spoken and she suspected the greater his emotion, the more dangerously soft-spoken his voice would become.

Right now, his tone brooked no argument, and she capitulated with a slight inclination of her head. As she left the dining room, she saw a movement from the corner of her eye and almost turned back, then thought better of it. She'd fight that battle when Bo wasn't around.

Annabelle walked down to the immense front hallway, past the hall stand and hat rack and stopped at a small mahogany table. She pulled the calling cards from the card receiver, thumbed through them, then proceeded to file them in the enameled box sitting next to the card stand. As she closed the lid to the card filer, she noticed another small box and lifted the cover. Her new calling cards had been delivered, black bordered cards denoting her mourning status, printed with her maiden name.

She ran her finger along the black border and sighed. Now that the new cards were here, she no longer had any excuse to avoid the obligation of returning the social calls, and she dreaded them because of the deceit. She was stuck in a trap of her own making and didn't know how to extricate herself gracefully. She'd presented Peyton with those conditions without any belief he'd actually go along with her, and now she was caught between Scylla and Charybdis.

She could live the lie and hope when the marriage became known, people would assume it was an ill-fated love match fueled by the fever of wartime and proximity. Or she could toss these calling cards away, print up proper cards with her married name, and try to live down the humiliation of being in a loveless marriage of convenience.

She didn't like either option and didn't like herself because she knew she was going to take the coward's way and live the lie. She replaced the lid on the stationery box, avoiding her reflection in the mirror above the table as she turned away.

A deep loneliness invaded her soul tonight: Papa dead, Carlyle lost to her, even Bo showed signs of growing up, which meant growing away. Unwilling to dwell on the losses, she headed for the second parlor, where she'd left her knitting box. She could finish the socks she'd started for Carlyle and send them with tomorrow's post. She hoped his anger had cooled enough he wouldn't toss them in some mudhole in disgust. He'd need good, thick socks if war came.

Jules had carried in a tea tray and placed it on a tiny gilt table in front of the fire screen. Annabelle seated herself nearby and pulled out her knitting. The needles clicked in her hands, the fire crackled behind the screen while the low murmur of the men's voices drifted from the dining room. She tried to concentrate on the task she'd set, but found herself listening for Royce's voice.

She thought of the morning down by the river when she'd believed they might become friends. She tried not to think about her foolish behavior, waiting for a kiss from the most handsome man she'd ever met, a man who had both intrigued and frightened her since the days of her childhood.

She let the knitting drop in her lap and leaned her head against the tufted upholstery. Jules had left the pocket doors open between the first and second parlors, and her gaze settled on the portrait hanging above the mantel in the formal first parlor. She dropped the unfinished sock in the knitting box and gave in to the sudden urge to study that portrait.

A much younger Peyton Kincaid stood beside an elegantly

gowned Mrs. Kincaid. Royce had inherited much of his father's appearance—the gray eyes and lean build, thick,
straight hair the deep reddish brown of a fresh-plowed field,
even the same proud, almost arrogant, set to his broad shoulders.

Strangely, Gordon didn't resemble either. Gordon was
taller, broader across the chest, with golden waves of hair and
deep blue eyes. She turned her attention to the woman in the
portrait and suddenly saw Gordon in the blue eyes looking
back at her. But only in the eyes and the wide mouth. Mrs.
Kincaid's hair was black, and the body clothed in the Empire
folds of a turquoise gown was both petite and voluptuous.

"*Pater patriae* and Lady Bountiful, a lovely pair if I must
say so myself."

Annabelle started, then caught herself. She'd been so involved in her thoughts, she hadn't heard Royce come up behind her. She ignored the sarcasm in his tone and kept her gaze
fixed on the portrait.

"Your mother is almost as beautiful as mine was," she said.

He chuckled. "A lady would have lied and claimed equal
beauty for the two women under discussion so as to avoid in-
juring my tender feelings."

There seemed to be a current beneath his words, but the current ran too deep for her to fathom. She slanted him a glance,
seeking whatever it was he wasn't saying, but his expression
didn't give him away.

"You're wrong," she said. "A lady would have couched that
statement in so many superfluous words it would take you
weeks to figure out she'd insulted your mother. And a gentleman would never have sneaked up on me like you just did,
half-frightening me out of my wits."

"Ah, but you haven't been listening. The ugly truth is, I'm
rotten all the way to my black heart, Mrs. Kincaid, and when
your five-year sentence is up, I predict you'll be more than
happy to obtain your divorce."

His bantering tone belied the sting of his words, and she
wished for the hundredth time that she'd learned, somewhere
in her youth, the secrets of flirting. He looked so masculinely
beautiful in a knee-length blue coat with a black velvet collar,

worn open to display the yellow-and-gray-plaid silk waistcoat beneath.

She thought of Carlyle's nickname for her. She'd never felt so sparrow-like in her life, dressed in her plain black silk over a hopelessly old-fashioned narrow hoop. But it was her sole mourning dress since she'd irreparably ruined the bombazine the other day and she didn't have the courage to flout the convention although she secretly considered the strict mourning customs to be wasteful.

"I'm afraid I'm no more a lady than you are a gentleman," she said, trying to meet his bantering tone and knowing that statement was impossibly dim-witted.

"Ermined and minked, bedecked and bediamonded, silked in their words as well as their gowns, such is a lady."

Fancy language rolled off his tongue with astonishing ease. She tried desperately to think of something witty to say, but he stood there studying her, not bothering to hide the fact he was judging her as a man judged a woman, and she knew she'd come up sadly lacking.

She waited, in spite of herself, for his mocking derision. Instead, he reached out and took her wrist, pulling her forward. Cupping her chin, he tilted her head back and stroked her cheekbone with his thumb. She closed her eyes and swallowed, feeling his touch all the way to her curled toes.

"No mud tonight," he said.

"No freckles either," she managed to whisper.

Somewhere, in another world, she heard Bo and Gordon laughing; in another world the house servants shuffled about on their never-ending duties. Her world had shrunk to the unbelievable sensation of a man's thumb stroking ever so gently, back and forth, Royce Kincaid's thumb caressing her face.

"Forget ladyhood. Ladyhood is incredibly boring," he said, and she knew she was in danger of losing her heart to this man who would only break it.

He dropped his hand and stepped away, turning slightly so that she saw his profile as he gazed at the portrait. His jaw tightened, and she sensed an increase in the tension that seemed always to roil just beneath his surface.

"I remember your mother well," he said finally. "AnnaLee

was a beautiful woman, while her kindness saved her from being perfectly boring."

"And your mother?"

All these years she'd wondered about the missing Mrs. Kincaid of whom no one ever spoke, and yet whose portrait hung in a place of honor in the first parlor. Maybe if he revealed that secret, she would discover a clue to the dark spirits that drove Royce Kincaid.

He made a low, scornful sound. "That portrait doesn't do her justice. She had an air the artist didn't capture, probably because he was so smitten by her he couldn't see her."

Annabelle moved and stood beside him, pulled by something she couldn't define, something like sadness that seemed to be so bone-deep in him he couldn't let it go. She wanted to reach for his arm, but before she found the courage, he spoke.

"Celeste Kincaid wasn't a lady, she wasn't kind, and she wasn't my mother." He spun on his heel and strode out the door.

Annabelle pulled the paisley shawl over her shoulders and walked out onto the side gallery. He hadn't gone far, only as far as the hitching rack on the other side of the porte cochére. He was leaning against the rail, his long legs crossed at the ankles. A lit cigar dangled from the fingers of one hand. It was a relaxed pose, yet tension radiated from every hardened line of his body.

Although the sun had dropped, it wasn't yet night. The twilight gloaming cast flickering shadows on the box hedges and meandering garden paths. The magnolia leaves shivered in the breeze, and, somewhere, a meadowlark sang. The scene was perfect, except for the unspoken suffering in the man.

She stood looking at his profile: the sharp angles of bone under the dark, tight skin, the hard line of his lips. She no longer believed that those taut, cruel lines came from cruelty. He turned his head, and his unemotional eyes stared back at her. The wind blew chill between them, and she drew her shawl tighter over her shoulders.

"Mr. Kincaid . . ." She began haltingly.

"We live in the same house, we're married for God's sake,"

he said. "Don't you think we can dispense with propriety. My name is Royce."

She looked away, toward the river. "I didn't mean to pry, and I hope you'll accept my apology."

She heard a sound, a boot scuffing through dirt, and turned her head to look at him. He shifted his position and took a slow draw on the cigar. She waited, not knowing what more to say.

"My mother was Rebecca Bullard," he said quietly. "Does that name ring any bells?"

She thought for a minute. Bullard? Then she almost smiled. She'd heard Aunt Hetty's whispers over that ancient scandal, but that wasn't Rebecca.

"A Bullard eloped with some poor English earl, and her father disinherited her," she said.

"Marianne, my mother's only sister. And it turned out the earl wasn't poor. He inherited a fortune from some relative, duke somebody or other, then managed to get himself killed in India, leaving Aunt Marianne a very rich widow. She didn't live long enough to spend much of it and died childless. Some relative of his inherited the title and estate, the rest came to me."

"The infamous English inheritance you once mentioned."

He slanted her a twisted smile. "Peyton and Rebecca married about a year before that scandal. Rebecca had a big dowry, Peyton had a big plantation, and as far as I know, that was the sole basis for their marriage."

Her heart ached for him, the son of a loveless marriage, now stuck in his own loveless marriage, and she couldn't even claim a dowry to present him. She couldn't imagine what coercion Peyton had used to induce his son into the trap.

"I was born September 10, 1832, exactly ten months after the wedding. Rebecca died the next day." He stopped and lifted the cigar, taking another long pull. She wasn't about to pry any deeper and made a motion to leave him alone with his ghosts. His voice stopped her.

"Celeste was Gordon's mother and the only mother I ever knew. She lasted five years, and her name is never mentioned in this house. You don't want to know the story, Annabelle. It's as ugly as all the Kincaids: Peyton's father, Peyton, me. The only exception is Gordon. For some unknown reason, he seems to have escaped the curse."

She wanted to tell him he was wrong. Peyton wasn't ugly or evil, maybe overbearing at times, but she remembered a waltz with an unhappy young girl and the words he'd used to describe himself. *A lonely old man.* She knew in her heart he'd manipulated his son into this marriage for both their sakes, to provide for her and Bo, maybe with the deluded hope of taming his own son. Royce didn't want to hear that, wasn't ready to hear it.

She flipped through her memories of Royce. The scandals were there, of course: the rake, the black sheep. But she saw other things, the frequent small kindnesses he'd shown to her father over the years, the interest he took in Bo now, but mostly, the easy, laughing camaraderie he shared with his brother.

She might not know her husband very well, but she knew Gordon inside out. Gordon wouldn't stomach an evil man as his boon companion. Royce wouldn't accept that observation from her either. She walked over and placed her hand on his forearm. His muscles hardened beneath the cloth.

"Would it be easier for you if Bo and I left—went back to Lexington?"

A muscle jerked along his jaw. She ached for him. She wanted to pull his head to her breast, stroke her fingers through his hair and tell him it didn't matter, the past was the past, and he had to let it die.

"Aren't you afraid of Peyton?"

"No," she said.

His mouth tightened. "Stay put, Annabelle. There's a war gathering, and although there won't be any safe place in the entire state, you'll be better off here with Peyton offering some protection."

"Was that an answer? I asked you what *you* wanted."

The shadows lifted in his eyes, and she saw a bewildered anguish before he blinked, and the look disappeared. He tossed the cigar butt into the dirt and ground it beneath his boot.

He took her wrist and lifted her arm. He studied her arm for the longest time, and it was all she could do to keep from trembling. She was beginning to wonder what abominable stain he saw in the paisley print that must be invisible to her own eyes when his face changed, a beautiful, gentle look that deepened the creases of his mouth without really moving his lips.

"I knew I'd find it there." He pretended to pluck something from her sleeve and made a production of dropping the imaginary object into her palm. "Your heart, Annie-girl. Put it away . . . somewhere safe," he said softly, curling her fingers over her empty palm. "I don't want it, and I don't want to be responsible for breaking it."

She felt his suffering as if it were a deep, empty hole within her own soul. He didn't know there was no longer any safe place for her to put her heart. He'd conquered it in that single moment. She longed to say something kind and soothing, something that would ease the shadowed pain he hid so well. Instead, she slipped her hand inside her pocket.

"Consider it done," she said. "Now, do you think we could be friends?"

"What a novel concept, Mrs. Kincaid." He drew the edges of her shawl together at the base of her throat. Her pulse beat madly just beneath his lingering fingers. "Husband and wife and friends to boot." He lifted her hand and, with a courtly bow, kissed her palm. "If you weren't so much your mother's daughter, and I wasn't such a blackhearted scoundrel, I do believe I might be inclined to marry you by choice."

He was teasing, of course. Only his self-mocking teasing. But teasing meant he cared, at least a little, and she couldn't help herself. He released her hand and she closed her fingers over the kiss, keeping it safe, while her heart rose like a Phoenix, soaring from ashes to dreams.

# Chapter 4

Royce had once tried to convince Clarence they were brothers of the blood. He couldn't have been more than seven, which would have put Clarence only a year older at eight, but infinitely wiser to the ways of their Southern world.

In his memories of the day, Peyton had been in Richmond with his new wife, politicking and socializing; Clarence had finished his apprentice hours with his father in the smithy, and the two boys were lolling on the riverbank. The sun was brutal, the glare of it from the water like a slap across the eyes. It beat down so hard, Royce could feel it through his big straw hat.

Clarence reached in the jar between them and grabbed a fat bloodworm. Royce swallowed as he watched the worm curl around Clarence's long black fingers even as he was spearing it with the hook. Royce grabbed his own bloodworm and swallowed harder. He quickly cast his baited hook and wiped his hand on the side of his rolled-up pants. Clarence's summer pants were rolled to just below his knees, too, although they were already too short, and it would be three months or better before he got his new winter pants of heavy kersey.

"If we were brothers, that would mean you'd be at least half-white," he pointed out, so smug inside his superior skin.

"I don't want to be white no more'n—"

"Any more."

"Any more'n I want your daddy lying with my ma. Don't you know nothin'?"

"Anything." Royce ignored the puckered brow of concentration on Clarence's sweat-streaked face—it was his normal expression whenever Royce corrected his grammar—and watched the cork bob on the current, contemplating the mystery Clarence evidently knew and he didn't, wondering whether he should reveal his ignorance by asking, or let it slide. Curiosity won out.

"Know what?"

"How a man plants a baby inside a woman."

"Criminy, you make it sound like he's harrowing a furrow."

Clarence snorted. "Ain't—isn't—far wrong. The man sticks his willy inside the woman's privates, then he humps up and down, grunts a lot, then his seed spurts out. That stuff stays inside her, and if the moon's right, then it makes a baby."

Royce had seen a bull mount a cow in the pasture, so he believed what Clarence was telling him. Only something about Clarence's version wasn't quite right. Royce reached down between his legs and rolled his balls in his hand. It shamed him sometimes, the way that felt good in a hot, prickly-tickly kind of way. A gentleman wasn't supposed to play with his privates, but sometimes he just couldn't help himself.

"How's he get his willy to go in her?" he asked.

"It gets hard all by itself. Ma says that's a man, thinking with the part between his legs."

Royce didn't need to contemplate that one. He wasn't exactly thinking *with* his willy just then, but touching himself there was causing it to firm up, and he sure wasn't finding it hard to think *about* the interesting sensations going on down there.

Royce tried to picture his patrician father with his beautiful new wife, sticking his willy between her white thighs, but the picture he conjured up seemed dirty somehow, so he wiped his imagination clean.

"If I were a woman, I don't think I'd like it much."

Clarence rolled the piece of straw from one side of his mouth to the other. "Nah, in the quarters, you hear things at night. They like it just fine when it's one of their own people."

Royce felt the shock slam into his gut. "My father never went to the quarters to stick his thing inside a slave woman."

"Not your pa. Your gran'pappy, though. Sometimes, he'd

bring his company down with him. Slave woman don't have to like it. She owned, so she can't say no."

Maybe it was then that he'd started to understand something of the absolute power certain white men wielded over their plantation fiefdoms. The power was seductive, but the closest thing Royce had to a family was Clarence sharing his.

If he, Royce, were to play his role right—prince of the fiefdom—then he'd be giving up all that: the smell of Sophie when she hugged him to her large bosom—which he wasn't supposed to like any more since he was growing to a big boy instead of a little boy now—the deep, rumbly voice Holder used to say grace at the meager supper table, the quiet satisfaction he got from breaking the law and teaching Clarence's family everything he learned in his own schoolroom.

"When I grow up, I'll set you free," he said, and Sophie and Holder, too, he silently vowed. And their other children, if they ever had any more. Clarence had had three older brothers once, but they'd all died from some sickness before Royce was born.

Maybe Sophie was too old to drop any more babies. Maybe that was why she allowed the white boy to be under her feet all the time. It didn't seem right to be thankful for someone else's sorrow, but if he didn't have Sophie taking care of him—well, Royce didn't know how he'd get by without that. Probably shrivel up into a ball and die from loneliness. Not that he was *that* lonely.

"Law says a freed colored man's got to leave the state." Clarence kept his gaze fixed on the river, but his jaw clenched. "This is my home, too, my people here. I don't want to leave. I just want to be *able* to leave."

"I'm sorry, Clarey. If I were you, I wouldn't want to be my blood brother either."

"Ain't your fault, Royce. You were born white. Just plumb lucky, that's all."

And there the matter had rested for almost three years, until the time Clarence pushed open the door to the old brick gatehouse and found Royce huddled in a ball on the bare wooden floor, naked from the waist down, reeking of shame and a carnal scent no boy should ever bear on his skin.

Clarence had said nothing, simply draped a blanket over his

shivering young master and slipped away, pulling the door closed as he left. In the silence left behind, Royce started to cry—great gut-wrenching sobs that rolled up from his belly, through his tight throat, and burst out of his mouth and nose and eyes so hard it made his head ache. It was, Royce thought, the last time he'd ever cried.

By the time Clarence returned, the tears were little more than dry hiccups. He'd been afraid Clarence would bring Sophie back with him, and he didn't want Sophie to see his shame, but Clarence came by himself, carrying a bucket of warm water, a bar of lye soap, and a clean pair of his own stiff canvas pants thrown over one shoulder.

Clarence hummed a slave song as he washed Royce's body, his work-roughened hands as gentle as if he were bathing an infant. Afterward, he handed Royce the canvas pants and turned his back while Royce stepped into them and tied the knot at the waist with fingers that still trembled. When Royce finally gained the courage to look up, Clarence was holding a fishing knife clasped in one fist. Blood welled from a fresh cut on the heel of his palm.

Wordlessly, Royce extended his own hand. Clarence grasped it and sliced a matching line in the fleshy pad below Royce's thumb, then turned his larger, darker hand so their palms touched.

"Blood brothers," he said, and Royce knew then a wave of love so pure it frightened him. Then Clarence raised his face so their eyes locked and held, and Royce knew from what he saw in those deep brown depths that Clarence felt it, too.

Clarence wasn't his brother any more than Gordon was his brother. Men didn't have to share blood to feel brotherhood.

The sun beamed from a cloudless sky the rich blue of a robin's egg, chasing the morning chill from the air and into the shadows beneath the trees. Royce's bootheels sank into the soft dirt as he turned up the lane leading to the Johnson estate house. Willow trees lined the carriage road, their draping branches soft with new leaves and swaying in the warm breeze.

He wasn't sure why he'd chosen to walk here this morning, other than that restless sensation he couldn't quite shake no matter how many hours he spent riding the fields during the day and poring over estate ledgers at night.

He stayed away from the Big House as much as possible, and that was easy, as his own living accommodations were in the office dependency. Still, with Peyton returned to Richmond with the recall of the Secession Convention, he'd felt a responsibility toward Annabelle to at least take his meals with her.

While Jules shuffled around the table with serving dishes, and Bo and Gordon talked, Royce didn't study his wife with quick little furtive glances the way she would do with him; he studied her openly. She was soft-spoken and gracious to Jules, easy with both of the brothers, and yet she disturbed Royce in some manner he couldn't even begin to formulate, let alone put into words.

They'd been alone together only twice. Once down by the river, and that night when he'd searched her out.

He'd lain awake the previous night turning that last conversation over again and again in his mind, examining it from every angle like it was a piece of fine porcelain and he was searching for the flaw. There was a flaw there somewhere; there had to be. No one was as good-hearted as she appeared to be. Damned if he'd found it yet, though.

*Now do you think we could be friends,* she'd asked him, her face looking up so that even in the shadowy dusk he couldn't miss those warm brown eyes shining with hope.

*No, Mrs. Kincaid,* he thought. *I don't think we can be friends at all.*

The whole world seemed edgy anyway; waiting, he supposed, for some fool to set the match to a cannon fuse and get the shooting war under way. In some strange way, it would be a relief to end the shouting war and get down to the serious business.

"You bloody son of a bitch," he muttered, dodging Jupiter's teeth as the stallion reached for his shoulder to take a nip. It was a valuable bay Thoroughbred, one of the two colts they'd bought from a stud in Ireland. Ajaque was a prince compared to this mean bastard. He hoped the horse took a sharp bite out of Moulton Johnson, almost wished he could stick around to watch it happen.

He reached the top of the lane, the bay sidestepping and pulling at the end of the lead, and saw Johnson's trainer just outside the paddock near the stud barn. Royce angled his steps in that direction, and it was only as he came around the side of the brick estate house that he became aware of the crowd of sullen black faces gathered near the summer kitchen.

Royce kept going toward the trainer, who caught sight of him and waited. He knew him from rubbing elbows at various shed rows throughout the racing circuit. Franklin, that was it. A slave, but a damn good trainer, too.

Franklin lifted a cap from his head and ran a knuckle along his grizzled brow. "That's one of your Irish studs," he said, eyeing the bay who, out of sheer perversity no doubt, had turned suddenly docile.

Royce nodded.

"That's the one—Jupiter, right? He beat my Tall Chief by two lengths in that two-year-old meet in Richmond."

"The same," said Royce, as Franklin approached the bay.

Instead of biting, the damn-fool horse lowered his head and nickered. Franklin crooned some nonsense while he rubbed the animal behind the ears, and the horse looked like he'd roll his eyes in delirious happiness any second now.

"Think Mr. Johnson would be interested in obtaining this horse for his stud?" asked Royce, pretending nonchalance while keeping a sharp eye on Franklin's profiled body, which enabled him to catch the small lift of a brow before the slave mastered his expression.

"Oh, he'd want the horse, sure enough. Depends on how much you're asking though. This time of year, he ain't usually . . ." Franklin seemed to realize he was saying too much, too openly, to a white man. His sharp brown eyes turned dazed and mulish, then he lowered his head to gaze at his feet.

It was a safe expression to assume in front of a white slave owner. Royce didn't have to like it when it came directed his way, but he could understand and accept it.

"Clarence took a wife last Sunday, one of your people. A woman called Patsy. I thought I'd see if Johnson would take a trade."

Franklin lifted his head then, but instead of looking at Royce, he gazed at the throng around the summer kitchen. A cow lowed in a pasture somewhere. The fresh breeze, scented with apple blossoms, brushed his face.

"Patsy?" he asked, feeling a heavy weight settling on his shoulders.

"The missus claims she stole a pickle."

"Did she?"

"Wouldn't matter. Missus said she did, so she'll get whipped."

The hell with Richmond. If—when—war came, he'd go to Washington, offer his services to the US Army if they'd take him back. Colonel Lee had been called back from Texas; he might still be in Washington City. If Lee went with the Union, then Royce could, in good conscience, go with the Union as well.

But he'd already had that conversation with Lee in a dusty army camp in Texas. Lincoln would probably offer Lee command of the Union armies—he'd be a fool not to—and Lincoln was no fool. Lee would go across the Potomac to Arlington and search his conscience through one more sleepless night, then, unless Royce missed his guess, Lee would offer his own resignation to the army he'd sworn to serve.

Virginia, the pitiless whore—she owned the both of them.

He handed over the leather lead to Franklin. "Tether Jupiter somewhere," he said. "I'll see what I can do."

It didn't take long. Moulton Johnson had the winning game—and knew it from the opening gambit—there was no reason for Royce voluntarily to offer up a valuable stud for trade unless he wanted that trade desperately. Consequently, Royce didn't manage to capture the additional pawn he'd decided to try for, but he'd gotten the pawn he came for. He'd have to be satisfied with that.

On his way out to collect Patsy, he met up with Johnson's youngest sister on the back porch. Aurora was dressed in a wide hoop skirt with at least a dozen rows of pink dimity flounces. She tossed her blonde hair over her shoulder and gave him a coquettish smile. He kept going, down the steps. He had one innocent female at his own father's house to deal with, and that was one too many.

"Is Gordon going to the flag raising this afternoon?" Aurora asked.

Royce stopped with one foot on the bottom step, one foot on the ground and so close to escape he could almost taste it. He fingered his hat while he looked back up at Moulton Johnson's sister. A pretty little thing, he decided, with a natural pink blush to her cheeks, pale blue eyes with more wisdom in them than her years should allow, her body just beginning to come into womanly curves. He pitied her, having to live under her brother's iron-fisted control.

"How old are you, Aurora?" he asked, smiling because she was a child playing at being a woman.

"I'll be fifteen next month."

"I hate to be the bearer of bad tidings then, but I think Miss Raleigh's going to capture the prize before you're even old enough to get in the race." Royce laughed, watching her round face fall into a practiced pout. He lifted his hat to his head and tugged on the brim, shielding his own expression. "I've just bought one of your slaves, a woman named Patsy. Can you point her out to me."

Aurora raised one languid hand to her brow and peered across the yard. "That one, wearing the red turban."

Royce ignored her dramatic posing and turned to look. The Willows was a smaller estate than Riverbend. A white-painted fence enclosed a small back lawn of clipped grass, separating the family from the area where the slaves lived and worked. He heard the clang of metal against metal as somewhere out of sight a smithy worked iron. The aroma of frying chickens drifted from the summer kitchen.

Two laundresses stirred household linens in a large tin washtub, aided by several young children who ferried buckets of water from the well and tended the fire. Two men and one woman too old for field labor were engaged in weeding the extensive vegetable garden with wooden hoes. Small half-naked black children played in the dirt in front of one of the three plank wooden cabins where the Johnson slaves lived in communal misery. Even from this distance, he could see into the cabins from the chinks in the wood.

Royce suddenly realized it was the relative silence that was bothering him. At Riverbend, no one made the inane observation that at least their slaves were happy, but at least their slaves weren't silent. There was a constant hum of voices in Riverbend's yards and outbuildings. Not here. The silence made his skin crawl.

He found the red turban on a woman who was sitting on an overturned barrel just outside the cookhouse door. None of the other slaves going about their business in the yard would even look at her, as if fearing a whipping might come their way if they so much as spoke to the alleged thief.

Royce studied her as he crossed the lawn. Patsy was probably tall, he'd know for certain when she stood. Slender, yet full-breasted, she was dressed in a faded blue cotton rag of a dress that fell above her ankles. Barefooted, of course.

He wanted to see her face, but from a distance he couldn't tell if she was handsome and didn't want to stare too hard when he got closer. Patsy didn't look up when he stopped in front of her. Shadows slanted across her downturned face, so he still couldn't see well even the small amount she was allowing him to see. Her hands were nice though, skin the color of toffee, with long, slender fingers and clean nails.

"You're coming with me," he said, and waited for some spark of life to appear.

She simply nodded, eyes still downcast, and slowly stood. The woman was scared down to the bone. Clarence wanted her, so presumably she had some spirit left in her. Let Clarence bring it back to life.

He led the way back to the stables with Patsy walking three paces behind him all the way. He stopped; she stopped three paces behind. Franklin had tethered Jupiter to the paddock fence and was leaning over with the horse's right foreleg folded back while he cleaned the hoof of embedded mud with a small pick.

"Take good care of him," Royce said. "He kicks at the least little movement behind him."

Franklin looked over his shoulder at Royce, then beyond Royce to where Patsy stood in misery, not knowing what was happening to her and too frightened for it to be of any use for Royce to try and explain. Then Franklin straightened to his full height and looked Royce in the eye.

"You done a good thing," he said.

Royce lifted his hat and ran his fingers through his hair. "I tried to buy you too, Franklin. I never bought a person before in my life, and this morning here I am trying to buy two. If that ain't a hell of a fix."

"Johnson wouldn't sell me," said Franklin.

"No, he wasn't having any of that." Royce studied the hat he still held in his hand. It was the first hat he'd grabbed on his way out the door this morning—an old straw planters' hat. It wasn't in much better condition than the straw boater Annabelle had misplaced down by the riverbank. He felt himself wanting to smile at the memory of the defiant wood sprite and her animal friends.

And there she was, sneaking into his mind. Since he didn't want her there, he forcibly shoved her right back out, turning his attention back where it belonged.

"Someday, well, if it ever turns out you need a place," he said to Franklin, "there's a job waiting for you at Riverbend. If you want it."

"I'll remember that, Marse Royce." Franklin shifted his deep brown gaze from Royce to Patsy, then seemed to sigh. He reached in his pocket and pulled out a horehound drop. "Take this, girl, if'n you're hungry," he said. "You go on with Marse Kincaid now. He's taking you to your Clarence."

So that's what Royce did: He took the slave woman called Patsy to Riverbend, walking down the middle of a dirt road, carrying on a monologue the whole way while he wondered what Annabelle would have to say when she was presented with a lady's maid he instinctively knew she didn't want.

They reached the boundaries of his own land, and Royce took the shortcut across the cow pasture. As soon as they left the road he sensed an increase in the tension that had held Patsy in silent thrall throughout the length of their trek, but since he didn't know what was causing her to tighten up like a coiled spring, he couldn't know how to relieve it.

They topped a small knoll, and Riverbend finally came into view. He figured it was a toss-up as to which of them felt the greater sense of relief. He hustled Patsy through the work yard, ignoring the grins on the faces of Riverbend's two cooks who were watching him hustle her, to the single cabin where she would live with Clarence.

The sight of the wilting tulips Clarence had picked and placed in a jelly jar to welcome his woman was worth every second of the morning's aggravations.

The look on Clarence's face when Royce handed over the papers—a bill of sale and a writ of manumission for one slave woman named Patsy—well, that look was worth ten times the price of an imported Thoroughbred stud.

As long as the white massa stood inside talking to Clarence, Patsy remained standing. She kept her eyes downcast and concentrated on breathing through her nose. In, out. In, out. Lordy, it felt like a whole hive of honeybees was swarming inside her belly.

Massa Kincaid handed Clarence some papers and took his leave, closing the cabin door as he left. Patsy sank down on a three-legged stool near the brick fireplace. She thought she should say something to Clarence but didn't have the sense in her head to make words just yet, so she watched the man she'd joined in a slave marriage last Sunday.

She'd already taken his weight on top of her, so she knew he was a big man, but he seemed even larger as he moved around inside this cabin. He walked through a slice of sunlight as he passed in front of the single window. His skin was so many shades darker than her own that she thought he must be all black. If he carried any white blood inside his veins, then that blood came far back in his line.

He hadn't said anything to her either, and she gradually became aware that he was carefully wrapping those papers the massa had handed him inside a folded piece of oilcloth. He tied the oilcloth with a piece of string, then placed the bundle inside a pottery jar. He placed the jar on the top shelf of a wooden corner cupboard, then turned and stared at her.

No one, she thought, could ever whip the pride out of Clarence. He stood with his shoulders back, massive chest bursting against the ties of a clean white shirt, nappy head held high. His eyes were big and round beneath straight, thick tufted brows. When he laughed he used his whole body to produce the sound, throwing his head back with the rumbles coming from deep inside that massive chest. He wasn't laughing now though; his dark-eyed expression was serious.

"Your mama?" she asked, when he continued to look at her, causing those bees inside her belly to swarm again.

"She moved in with Reba, a room behind the kitchen. It's warmer there in the winter."

She didn't want to believe what he seemed to be saying. "All this? Just for us?"

"I'm a good smithy—the best in these parts. That makes me valuable." He inclined his head to the far side of the room where an opening in the wall was covered by a quilt pieced from rags. "That's where we'll sleep," he said. "It's a small room—the bed takes up most of the space, but there's fresh ticking to lie on. You won't find no crawly critters in my house."

She smiled then, and he smiled back. Slowly, she looked around. The room they were in was large, about eight feet square. Narrow bunk beds, covered with two faded quilts, were built against one wall with wooden pegs on the wall nearby to hang clothing, although nothing was hanging there.

Iron cook pots were lined up on a shelf over a fireplace that was large enough to cook in. Someone had swept it clean of ashes; she could see the charred bricks that made up the floor. Over it all was the strong scent of pine soap that warred with the freshness of the breeze fluttering the thin yellow curtain at the window, and underneath those scents was the darker male scent of Clarence.

A corner cupboard held pottery dishes and several pottery jars, with tin eating utensils standing upright inside a real glass jelly jar. The floor was wood, not dirt, and the pine slats had been scrubbed so many times with harsh soap that the color had leached to pale gray.

Patsy stood, her legs suddenly strong with the sense of delighted disbelief flooding through her. She went first to another wooden shelf in the place of honor on the far side of the hearth. She took down the first book and ran her fingers over the black leather grain.

"That's a Bible," said Clarence in a deep, quiet voice from behind her. She nodded and spent a minute turning the pages, looking at the ink markings inside. Those were the Lord's own words, right there in her own colored hands if she could only read them. She closed the Bible and placed it back on the shelf. She touched the next book, a thin one.

"Shakespeare's sonnets."

That meant nothing to her so she continued to the next in the line.

*"The Life and Times of Frederick Douglass,"* said Clarence's voice, and she removed her hand as if it had been scorched. "Go ahead, touch it; open it if you want," he said. "Royce gave me all those books—that one he brought with him when he came back from Texas."

She took the book down and stared at the picture inside the stiff cover for a long time. Frederick Douglass, born a slave just like herself. She felt the stirrings of pride and bitterness and happiness and sorrow, all tangled together inside her head. She couldn't make sense of anything in this strange day that just might change her life for the better, after all, so she put the book back.

"You called him Royce, not Massa Royce," she said, asking Clarence to tell her what was the safe way to behave here, at Riverbend.

"Always have," said Clarence. "I call the others proper, Marse Peyton and Marse Gordon."

*Marse, not massa*, she thought, tucking that difference in a safe place to be remembered at the right time. She'd been born on a rice plantation in South Carolina. There the colored folks spoke Gullah among themselves and a different black English to the whites in their big houses. She missed the safety of that private slave language the white folks didn't understand, but then she'd been virtually silent for the last months anyway; ever since she'd been locked in a coffle and herded north to a slave block in Richmond.

The trees had been dropping their leaves the day her son was sold in Charleston. The world outside had turned green again, but she thought there would always be a touch of winter inside her soul. Her boy, nine summers old, with skin as pale as the massa who sired him and soft black hair that fell in strong waves over his brow.

She pulled herself back from that well of despair. Her child was lost to her, and there was nothing she could do to change that. She had Clarence now, and he claimed to love her, so maybe there was a reason to keep on living after all.

She walked to the pine table in the center of the room and

set her hands on the top rung of a slat-back chair—*rush seats*, she thought idly, and there was one chair at each side of the long table scarred with years of use. Only then did she see the tulips, the same color as the turban she wore wrapped around her hair, sitting in another real glass jar in the center of the table. Tears welled in her eyes.

Strong arms came around her waist and pulled her backward against a hard chest. She leaned her head back and breathed through her nostrils, taking in all the powerful scents of this man who had claimed her. She felt the weight of his head pressing against her turbaned hair.

"Royce said you were hungry," he said.

Was it only an hour ago she'd been at the Willows, facing the inevitability of a beating that would probably kill her; wondering in some distant part of her mind what Clarence would do when he discovered she'd died for the taste of a pickle?

She hadn't listened to anything Massa—Marse—Royce had said, either on that long walk here or inside this cabin. But Marse Royce had evidently kept his silence about the circumstances he'd found her in, and Patsy didn't want Clarence to know either. Clarence's anger was slow to rise, but when it came it was a frightening thing. He'd only go over there—too angry to be thinking sense—and end up with Marse Johnson killing him. So she kept silent about the pickle and the two days of starvation punishment that had led to the theft.

"Ma's cooked up some black-eyed peas and ham hocks," he said, enticing her empty belly with the promise of food while his big hands were wandering up to cup her breasts, enticing her body toward the fulfillment of a different hunger.

"Fresh pone, too." His thumbs rubbed her nipples, and she jerked, then leaned farther into him. His hands were so warm through the thin cotton covering her breasts, kneading them now, oh Lord, this man could make her pant with wanting him.

"We've got the whole day though," he murmured near her ear, sending a shiver down her spine. "No work until Monday morning."

She held back a whimper as he moved one hand down her belly to cup her between the legs, his other hand still holding her breast, thumb moving back and forth across her hard nipple.

"There's a slave party tonight," he said, his breath warm and moist inside her ear. "Lots of folks for you to meet then . . ."

His tongue inside her ear now, his hand drawing her skirt up her thigh, then slipping beneath the cloth to touch her—open her—for his finger to penetrate. She made an animal sound of need, of heat and desire, as his finger thrust deeper and yet not nearly deep enough.

"I don't want to wait, woman," he said, and she turned in his arms, throwing her own arms over his shoulders, digging her fingers into the muscles on his back.

She lifted her face, and he took it between his callused palms, holding her in place while he kissed her hard and long and deep. Then without speaking they were moving together into the other room, hands grasping at cloth to pull it away until both of them were naked, lying skin to skin with limbs entwined on top of the soft new ticking.

She wrapped her legs around his hips, lifting to meet him as he thrust into her, and nothing mattered at all, except the thrust and draw of his sex inside her, the smell of him on her skin, the sounds from deep in his chest, and her answering cries.

Later, maybe later it would all be important again, but for this moment, she was hers alone to give, and she gave herself over to loving him.

# Chapter 5

"**P**ut it away, Annie."

Annabelle looked up from the sewing machine as Gordon strolled across the room. His face was wreathed in a broad grin. She hid her own smile as she turned the woolen cloth and positioned it to run another seam.

"I want to finish this." Her foot worked the treadle, and the needle plunged up and down with amazing rapidity. Access to a sewing machine was the greatest luxury she'd discovered at Riverbend.

Gordon fingered the gray cloth, turning it over to see the red lining. "For Carlyle?" he asked. She shook her head and his grin widened. "For me!"

"Silly man. Yours is next."

An expression passed across his face, as if he wanted to say something and had decided against it. She guessed his unspoken warning and ignored it. Thoughts of her husband still caused her heart to trip like the sewing needle, whether safely or not, she didn't really care. Gordon placed his hand beneath her elbow and raised her from the chair.

"You've declined all the social calls since you've been here and gone nowhere but church on Sunday." He guided her toward the door. "I've got the phaeton hitched up and waiting. We're going to a flag raising."

She stopped and pulled her elbow away. "Secesh?"

"Is there any other kind?"

Sometimes he had a way of smiling that wasn't at all a smile, something more akin to a superior being watching the foibles of humankind from atop a lofty mountain and shaking his head in sorrow. The look passed, and he was once again just a handsome young man determined to enjoy a day in the spring sunshine.

"You're coming," he repeated, lifting a black Tudor hat from the hall rack and handing it to her.

"I've never won an argument with you." She stood in front of the hall mirror and proceeded to pin the cockaded hat at a jaunty angle. "I'd think you'd let me win at least once."

"Not this time when the young ladies of Mrs. Pettigrew's sewing circle have labored so long and lovingly for our glorious Cause." He helped her into the shiny blue phaeton and went around to the other side. He climbed in beside her.

Annabelle tugged on her black lace gloves as he spanked the reins. The vehicle pulled away smooth as country butter. "What's her name?"

He reached over and patted her knee, one of the things she loved most about him. He always treated her with an easy, brotherlike informality.

"Now, now, Annie," he said, turning his head to look at her. She saw laughter in his eyes. "Just because I'm dressed in my finest suit of armor, freshly scrubbed and clean-shaven with my boots polished to a mirror shine does not mean I'm out to win some fair lady's heart."

"Then what does it mean?"

"That I'm out to win some fair lady's heart."

"Oh, you." She punched him lightly on the shoulder. "If you won't tell me her name, at least tell me all the gossip before we get there, so I'm not hopelessly lost."

She settled back against the leather seat and half listened to Gordon. Mostly, she reveled in the balmy spring day. Gordon was right. She'd been hiding at Riverbend. The time had come to face up to her own actions and live with them.

They came to a small church near the junction of two country lanes. Heavy forests, brightened by the white bracts of blooming dogwoods, surrounded the small plot. Gordon maneuvered the phaeton to a shaded spot beyond the other carriages, amongst the tethered horses and mules. He jumped down with his usual long-legged grace and came around to assist her.

She suddenly didn't want to be here, raising a secesh flag, passing herself off as Miss Hallston come for a long visit at Riverbend, and wished she'd fought Gordon with more determination. Her feet touched the ground, and she guessed Gordon must have sensed her feelings as he gave her hand a firm squeeze before letting go. For a moment, she disloyally wished she could trade him for Carlyle.

She put her social look on her face and followed Gordon as he worked his way among the milling groups. He seemed to have a destination in mind, and she tried to keep from staring at the group under the chestnut tree although curiosity consumed her. Before they made it that far, Mrs. Pettigrew stopped them.

"How good to see you here, Gordon," she said. "Has your father left for Richmond yet?"

A former governor of Virginia, Peyton had been elected as one of the county representatives to the Secession Convention. Annabelle wondered if Mrs. Pettigrew recalled he'd been elected as a Union man. Kincaids had too much at stake to upset the status quo unnecessarily.

"He went back last week," answered Gordon, his gaze wandering toward the chestnut tree. Mrs. Pettigrew switched her attention to Annabelle.

"I was so sorry to hear about your father. It was so thoughtful of Peyton to bring you and your brother to stay with him. They were such good friends, you know."

"Yes, ma'am," she said, interrupting with the hope she could forestall the direction of this conversation. "We haven't missed all the excitement by our late arrival, have we?"

"Oh no, dear. Such a wonderful flag we've made." Mrs. Pettigrew turned to Gordon. Her face was flushed, either from the warmth of the sun or the heat of war fever permeating the air. "You're enrolled, of course?"

Gordon nodded. They all knew what she meant. Home Guards and militias were forming all over the south.

"And your brother?" Mrs. Pettigrew's eyes narrowed.

"Royce came home."

"We must all do our part to resist aggression. It's our duty and our honor." Her intended insult to the elder Kincaid son appeared to hit home with the younger son, but Gordon had been well trained and sat a notch higher on the social level.

He lifted one brow. "Aggression, Mrs. Pettigrew? Have you some news the rest of us don't know?"

"Have your sons enrolled?" asked Annabelle in an effort to distract Mrs. Pettigrew from the anger on Gordon's face.

"Of course, dear. And you must tell Mr. Royce Kincaid the same thing I told my own sons. It's our duty as women to see that our men preserve our independence. You must tell him *exactly* what I told my own dear boys. Death is preferable to dishonor."

Annabelle could think of nothing to say that wouldn't be considered both rude and dishonorable, so she merely nodded. Someone called out to Gordon, and they were able to make a polite escape.

They'd taken but three steps when Mrs. Pettigrew called after her, "You must join us next week, Miss Hallston. We're making haversacks for our boys next week."

Annabelle turned, taking two backward steps, and waved. "Thank you, Mrs. Pettigrew," she answered noncommittally, and swung back around. She took Gordon's arm and murmured in a low breath, "If I loan you my squirrel gun, will you promise to keep the old biddy away from Charleston Harbor?"

He threw back his head and laughed. "Annie, you're incorrigible." She lifted him a smile. "Come on," he said. "I predict you'll like this lady's company."

She did. As children, they'd met at Peyton's informal daytime frolics, but Augusta Raleigh had grown up, too. She didn't have Livvy's stunning beauty, but then, few did. Gussie was demurely pretty in the way that made mamas feel proud and young men feel manly.

Annabelle surreptitiously studied Gordon. Yes, he definitely felt manly. Or maybe it was roosterish. If his broad chest puffed out any more, he just might explode. Afraid she might giggle aloud with those thoughts and have to explain, she forced her attention back to the less amusing conversation.

"I saw you with Mrs. Pettigrew," said Augusta. "Did she give you her death and dishonor speech?" Annie nodded, and Augusta shook her head. "Whenever I hear that, I always wonder how honorable she's going to feel if it's one of her sons who comes home in a coffin."

Annabelle took Augusta's hand and squeezed. She knew she'd found a friend, another person who saw something besides romance in all this excitement and preparation. She decided she'd allow Gordon to fall madly in love with Miss Augusta Raleigh; she was perfectly suited for him. From the soft-eyed looks Miss Raleigh was bestowing on Gordon, she guessed the suitable young lady was already in love with him.

Annabelle listened to their lightly flirtatious conversation, beginning to feel like a fifth wheel on a farm wagon, when the arrival of some more young men on horseback diverted her attention. She tried to catch Gordon's eye, but his interest was focused squarely on the lovely brunette standing between them. She reached out and touched his arm. He seemed to recall her presence.

"Bo?"

Gordon glanced at the new arrivals. "He asked Royce if he could come."

"He should have asked me. He's thirteen years old, and I don't want him here," she said.

Seeing Bo in this group of war-crazy young men sent a sickening weight settling around her heart. Suddenly, a gun's report cracked the air and for the briefest moment, she thought the war had begun, right here in the yard of this tiny wilderness church. Then she heard the laughter and jesting from a group on the shady side of the building.

She didn't know whether to go after Bo and send him home, embarrassed or not, or to follow after Gordon and Miss Raleigh, who were heading in the direction of the laughter. While she stood alone trying to decide, Gordon made the decision for her.

"Do I have to drag you everywhere today?" he said, pulling her elbow. He glanced in the direction of her gaze. "Let him be, Annie," he said softly. "Bo has to make his own way."

She looked at him in surprise. He sounded like his brother,

speaking on two levels, words on top and something different underneath. She pondered the new puzzle and allowed him to drag her with them. They rounded the building, and she came to a sudden stop.

About a dozen young ladies stood in a wavering line, attended by assorted young men of the county. She gathered from the overheard bits of conversation and the paper targets tacked to the tree trunks that they were taking potshots at the *Yankee* hickory tree. Off to the side, Royce attended to one very beautiful young woman Annabelle didn't recognize.

The lady was seated on a log in the shade of an old oak. Her bright muslin flounces billowed in the breeze, displaying a little more of her green morocco-clad feet and silk-stockinged ankles than was seemly. Royce lounged on the ground nearby, his attention directed to the part of the flowered dress that had no neck.

Annabelle recovered quickly, until Gordon cupped his hand around her elbow and gave it a gentle squeeze; then she wanted to cry. Royce glanced in their direction, and she knew exactly when he caught sight of her. He shot her an impudent grin that put her in mind of an ill-mannered tomcat.

Augusta leaned forward. "Isn't she scandalous?" she whispered.

"Who?" asked Annabelle, pretending she hadn't noticed.

Augusta nodded toward Royce and his lady. "That's Ellen Cady, up from Charleston with her father. They say she was quite compromised last spring when she went carriage riding with a man and stayed out after dark. Of course, her parents expected him to marry her, and the gentleman agreed. But *she* refused. Can you believe that?" finished Augusta breathlessly.

Annabelle stood silently, watching her husband and Miss Cady. "I believe she's got something stuck in her eye," she said finally.

Gordon gave her an approving wink. It didn't help. Her heart wasn't in someplace safe. It belonged to the man in the blue coat and mustard-color britches lounging on the ground with his long, booted legs crossed negligently at the ankle while he laughed and talked with a Charleston belle.

She'd spent most of her life on the side, watching. She knew how to smile through hurt. She couldn't even justify anger at him because he'd tried to warn her. It was her foolish heart that refused to listen. She turned her back to the sight.

Bo rounded the corner and waved. Her heart clutched when she looked at him, so young and yet on his way to dangerous manhood. He left his friends and walked across the lawn toward her in his usual long-legged lope. She wanted to grab him up in her arms like she used to do when he was small, to run with him, somewhere, anywhere, so long as it was a safe place without promise of war.

The sun dazzled her eyes, and she blinked back the tears. A gentle breeze rustled her skirts. Bo and Gordon, Augusta and Annabelle, laughing and gay amidst the sharp reports of pistols aimed at tree trunk Yankees. Her head swam. Dogwoods and apple blossoms. Shots and laughter. Breathe in the sweet air, smile through the gun smoke. Bo and war. Royce and a Charleston belle.

Smiling, smiling. Smiling.

"Annie, come on. You haven't taken a shot."

Young men and young ladies she remembered as children, calling her to war. Annabelle shook her head to clear the dizziness and shook her head to decline the honor. She heard her husband's deep laughter. She wouldn't look at Royce. He laughed again. She looked.

With feline grace, he unwound his heavily muscled legs and stood up. The blue cloth coat stretched tautly across his broad shoulders as he reached out to assist Miss Cady. The black-hearted scoundrel continued to hold the lady's hand as they walked across the grass to join the group at the line.

"Miss Cady tells me she'd like to try," he said.

Gordon frowned. Royce's face darkened, went taut, then his mocking smile reappeared. With a small sigh, Gordon handed his brother the pistol and stepped aside. Gordon looked toward her, and she recognized the sympathy in his eyes. She forced a smile. She mustn't let it show, this hurt.

"I've never shot a gun before," purred Miss Charleston Belle, batting her lashes.

"Point it at the tree," said Royce as he nudged her hand in a safer direction.

"Which tree? There're so many." Flutter, flutter.

"Would you like some assistance?"

Oh, they were good, Miss Feline and Mr. Tom. Of course, they'd probably both been practicing since they left nappies behind.

Royce stepped as close to the lady as he could get without knocking her down. Miss Cady giggled as he reached around her and supported her arms. Annabelle couldn't see her face, but from the wide angle of the bullet, she guessed Miss Cady had been fluttering her lashes when she pulled the trigger. Royce deftly removed the pistol from the lady's hand before he let her go.

Miss Cady bestowed her fluttering lash look on all the gentleman present. "Did I hit anything?"

"I think you managed to miss every tree in the forest, my dear," said Royce.

"Come on, Annie." Augusta gestured her over. "You're the only one who hasn't shot."

"She's the best shot in Rockbridge County," said Bo loudly to the assembled group.

She knew he was trying to be helpful, but he was making it worse. Royce Kincaid wasn't impressed by a lady who could ride, shoot, and cook any more than those long-ago cadets at VMI had been impressed. Men wanted something more from their women, something she didn't possess and didn't know where to find, whatever *it* was.

Royce looked over to where she stood with Bo. His silver eyes sparked a challenge. She glanced at Gordon and found no advice in his expression.

Annabelle expelled a breath. "All right," she said, stepping forward. Royce handed her the gun, an elegant little Colt revolver. She ignored his air of sardonic amusement and took her position on the line.

"Pretend it's a Yankee," shouted someone in encouragement. She lifted the gun, pretending no such thing.

"Pretend it's wearing a blue coat," murmured Royce near her ear.

Annabelle laughed, and fired a bull's-eye.

Royce half listened to the chatter coming from the coquette at his side. Miss Cady was an empty-headed piece of fluff, but she served his purpose today, and her lack of intelligence made it ridiculously easy to play the part of the ardent rake without damaging her pride or already questionable reputation.

He normally avoided these types of gatherings. Speeches extolling the virtues of the South and her brave young lads were meaningless to him, and he wondered how his neighbors could be so willingly blind. Honor and valor might win some battles, but the war would be won by armaments, factories, and manpower, all things the North possessed in abundance and were sadly lacking in the South. He'd pointed out that little truth enough times this afternoon to find himself conveniently shunted to the sidelines and ignored, which also suited his purpose.

He'd come today because Gordon told him he was bringing Annabelle. Annabelle had become like a burr beneath his skin, a source of constant irritation he couldn't scratch away and could no longer deny.

Gordon's group accepted her as one of their own, and she appeared to be comfortable within that group of landed gentlemen and gently reared ladies. Yet even there, an indefinable something set her apart.

From the time of her mother's decline, she hadn't been gently reared; she'd been virtually ignored, and maybe that was the difference. She didn't know she was supposed to hide her intelligence behind feminine wiles. He'd like to think her intelligence was the irritating burr beneath his skin, but he couldn't blame it on that either since he'd always appreciated anyone, male or female, who had the good sense to use that God-given gift.

The speeches came to an end with the pastor pronouncing himself, "ready not only to preach the cause of liberty from the pulpit, but to go myself and join the ranks, to take up arms in the battle."

Six blushing young ladies marched forward, proudly bearing the fruits of their labor, and presented the secesh flag to the ardent Rebel pastor. With the aid of several young men, the flag was thrown to the breeze from the branch of a tall, straight tree. Repeated rifle volleys followed in salute of this achievement while the crowd applauded and whistled.

His gaze sought Annabelle. She stood with her head bowed and her eyes closed. When the volleys stopped, she turned, searching for someone. Oddly, his heart seemed to halt with the thought she searched the crowd for him, but her gaze passed over him and settled on Bo.

Love and fear waged war in her dark eyes, and it was all he could do to keep from going to her. He understood too well; he felt the same whenever he looked at Gordon. The war hadn't yet come, but when it came the inevitable result would be the loss of precious lives, young men sent recklessly into the presence of their Maker to answer for the sins of their fathers. All they could do was pray the end came before Bo's generation grew up.

As if in mockery of that wish, a red-faced West Point cadet proceeded to round up a group of Bo's compatriots. He soon had them marching to drill. Annabelle's attention was diverted from the display by Gordon. His own attention was diverted by the precipitous arrival of Miss Cady's father.

Mr. Randolph Cady swung off his lathered horse, made a bow in the direction of his daughter, then strode through the milling crowd in search of someone. Royce straightened. When Cady made contact with the Reverend Quincy, Royce knew. His heart collided against his chest. Off to the side, rifle shots once again pierced the pastoral stillness. The West Point cadet had his young charges shooting at trees.

Royce reached out and grabbed the arm of a passing young man. "Leighton, have you had the honor of being introduced to Miss Cady?" he asked. He ignored her startled look and directed his attention to Leighton. He saw an amusing combination of surprise mingled with hope on Leighton's bulldog face.

"Miss Cady's father just arrived, and in order to save her from his justifiable ire for being seen in the company of a reprobate like me, I'm entrusting her to your care." Royce bowed to the lady and, with an ease born of much practice, made his escape.

He didn't know if he searched for Gordon or Annabelle or Bo, not that it mattered. They were all three of them innocents, and he felt only that old driving compulsion to save the innocents from the world's lunacy. He wanted them gone, all three of them, before Mr. Cady's certain, peace-destroying announcement. He found Gordon and Annabelle together, watching the youngsters shoot.

"Ladies and gentlemen, may I have your attention." The

voice was the Reverend Quincy's, and his excitement was palpable. The crowd came to instant stillness. "Mr. Cady, our
friend and visitor from our sister state, South Carolina, has just
arrived with important news."

Royce exchanged glances with Gordon and knew as certainly as the sun would rise on the morrow that Gordon had
also guessed. The crowd seemed to take a collective breath as
Mr. Cady stepped forward.

"Friends, and I hope soon to be fellow countrymen, it is my
great pleasure to be the bearer of this information. Before
dawn yesterday, our brave Confederate forces opened fire on
Fort Sumter in Charleston Harbor." He paused for an oratori-
cal breath. "Sumter surrendered. The war has begun with a
great victory for our glorious Confederacy."

Annabelle turned to Gordon with a look of pain in her eyes.
Gordon drew her into a hug. "It's not war for us yet, Annie-
girl," he murmured. "Virginia hasn't taken a stand either way."

Royce suddenly hated his brother. He hated him for his
dreams and his optimism, his lies and his truths. But most of
all, he hated Gordon because his wife turned to him for comfort. And that feeling made no more sense than the war fever
surrounding them. He didn't want a wife, and, God only knew,
he'd seen enough of life to know marriage was nothing more
than a bitter joke.

He felt a hand on his forearm and looked over. Bo stood beside him, also watching Annabelle and Gordon. The boy held a
double-barreled shotgun in his other hand. Royce resisted the
impulse to grab the weapon and hurl it into the woods. There
was no choice to be made; Bo had to grow to manhood. And
because Bo needed to become a man, sooner now rather than
later, Royce treated him as a man.

"You're a good shot," he said, nodding toward the weapon.
"You'll be putting birds on the table at Riverbend with that
thing."

Annabelle stepped away from Gordon. She used the back of
her hand to wipe her cheek. Royce resisted another insane urge
to pull out his handkerchief and wipe the tears away for her.

"I just wish I'd meet three Yankees on the way home," said
Bo. "Two anyway," he added as he contemplated the double
gun barrels.

Annabelle bristled. "And how will you recognize these Yankees?" she asked, reaching out for the shotgun. Bo gave it up without resistance. "Perhaps they'll be feathered like your cousin Brett in Kentucky, or maybe like Mama's Ohio relatives. Will you shoot them then, because their feathers are blue not gray? Need I remind you blood is red. Your blood and Yankee blood, doesn't matter, my brave, stupid little brother. *Red*, that's the only color that's going to matter."

Royce stepped between her and Bo. "Go on with your friends, Bo," he said quietly while taking the shotgun from her and handing it over to Gordon.

"The only place he's going is home with me. *Now*." She glared up at Royce. "He should never have come in the first place."

"Not quite right," said Royce, taking her elbow in his hand. "*You* are coming home with *me*."

"Stay out of this. You've already barged in where you don't belong once today, so barge out now." She jerked her elbow away. "Go back to the company of your lovely lady and leave my brother to me."

"I'll leave your brother to my brother and drag you out of here one way or another," he said in his low voice. She took a breath in preparation for another angry tirade, and he cut her off. "You want a scene, I'll make a scene."

"You've already made a scene, Mr. Kincaid. You've been on everyone's tongue all afternoon—you and Miss Cady."

"That's nothing, *wife*," he said. "Just wait until I toss you over my shoulder, arse to the sunshine, and carry you through this crowd."

"You wouldn't."

"I would." He smiled and knew from the sudden fear in her eyes that the menacing smile was more effective than the threat. "And with every step, I'll be singing, *have you met my wife, the former Annabelle Hallston*." Gordon made a motion to intervene. Royce shot his brother a cold glare, warning him back. "To the tune of 'Dixie's Land,' " he added.

"Dear merciful heaven."

A ragged gasp of laughter caught in her throat. But her eyes, the color of the river at twilight, gazed steadily back at him, and he saw in the dark depths an emotion he didn't want to understand. He knew a sudden fear of his own. She'd already touched his soul in places he didn't want touched and made him feel things he didn't want to feel. He cast those unwelcome thoughts aside.

"I'll drive her," he said to Gordon. "You ride Ajaque back and make sure Bo gets home." He already had her elbow and began steering her toward the parked vehicles.

"I don't want to go with you, Mr. Kincaid," she muttered, while managing a small smile for the astonished faces they passed.

"It doesn't matter what you want, Mrs. Kincaid," he said while doing his own part to still the wagging tongues with a polite nod. "We'll settle that issue right now. I wear the pants in this family."

"Blast you." She inclined her head and smiled for Mrs. Pettigrew, and the pride he felt in his little secret wife swelled in his chest.

When they reached the phaeton she turned to him. The sunshine through the leaves dappled her face, highlighting the classic lines of her high cheekbones. She stared at him for a moment, a still, stark gaze. His breath caught. Even without the sunrise smile, his wife was a beautiful woman. A natural beauty so different from the gushing belles he was accustomed to that he'd never noticed until now.

"What have I done?" she said under her breath

"You made a pact with the devil." He squeezed her elbow until she flinched. "And now you're living with him."

She bit hard at her lower lip as he assisted her into the phaeton. He didn't expect her silence to last long, maybe about as long as it took to leave the clearing behind. He could tolerate her anger, suspected he might even enjoy it, but he knew it was far better for her to be angry with him than to let her humiliate Bo in front of his new friends.

He spanked the reins against the matched pair. The carriage pulled away at such a clip that she jostled against him as her hand instinctively reached for her hat. Her body was warm and surprisingly soft. She stiffened and scooted as far away from him as she could get without actually falling out of the vehicle.

He glanced at her, her face in profile to him with her chin nudged up. A tight pain filled his chest, a pain he didn't understand and because he couldn't understand the effect she had on him, he allowed his own resentment to churn.

"You should have let the hat blow," he said. "It's every bit as ugly as the last one."

"You, sir, are a degenerate louse."

"Throw in a few hells and damns, and I might get to thinking you actually mean it." He reached over and patted her knee in an effort to annoy her further. "Now, out West, the proper phrasing would be something along the lines of—"

"Spare me."

He heard buried laughter in her voice. She wasn't a woman to stay angry. He said nothing as she unpinned the black hat and settled it in her lap. He had a sudden vision of her the other morning with bluebells tucked in her tousled hair, bedraggled and charming. He cast her a glance. Pensive now, turning the boxy little hat around and around in her fingers. They rode like that for several long miles, and he wondered if her quiet was caused by his mocking insult over the hat or over the scene with Bo. He heard a small sigh.

"I don't want him to grow up," she said.

"He's going to grow up whether you want it or not."

"You don't have to push him." She made a little sound, something between a snort and a sob. "Sitting at the table with the men, smoking cigars . . . Whatever possessed you to offer him a cigar?"

"You saw that?" Royce shrugged. "Actually, it was a cheroot. And I gave it to him because he's going to try anyway. Better for him to choke and turn red in front of me than in front of the local bully."

Royce turned off Telegraph Road onto a country lane. All around them, nature loomed large and tranquil. Beneath the stands of oak and loblolly, abundant wildflowers shot rainbow colors against green shadows. Over it all hung the rich scent of river mud. He tried to picture the land covered with the camp tents and fires of an army on the march and failed. But he had no doubt that army would arrive in the near future. She must have been reading his thoughts.

"It's coming," she said softly. "I can't allow Bo to be a part of it. No matter what you say, he's still a child."

"On his way to manhood. And if you try to keep him tied to your apron strings, you'll destroy him."

She snorted. "I never thought you'd sound like Mrs. Pettigrew."

"Mrs. Pettigrew is a peahen, but she's right about that one thing." He pulled the horses to a halt on a rise just beyond Marye's Heights. "People like us, you and your brothers, me and Gordon—we have a heritage to uphold, Annabelle. Our forefathers fought at Valley Forge and Yorktown, sat in the Philadelphia Conventions. They were leaders. They made mistakes, God only knows, we're going to pay for the biggest one now; but they were there, and they didn't flinch." She was looking at him, her eyes wide and dark. "For people like us, death *is* preferable to dishonor," he said quietly.

Did she believe that? He couldn't tell. The sun had begun its descent, painting the sky in front of them with broad strokes of brilliant orange and red. A chorus of bullfrogs and peepers lifted a discordant symphony.

She gazed steadily ahead, but he saw her throat convulse and the rapid blinking of her eyes as she fought to hold back tears.

"You don't really believe in this war either," she said, and he was amazed at her perceptive abilities.

"No. But I'll fight."

She shook her head slowly. "I'll never understand."

"You understand, you just don't like it."

"I hate it."

She leaned against the blue leather and closed her eyes. Her pert little nose pointed up, her nostrils flaring as she took a deep breath. She was so young, hardly more than a child herself, yet she'd carried a mother's load since forever.

He slapped the reins. Not trusting the unfamiliar ache in his chest, he avoided looking at her and concentrated on the clink and rattle of the harness traces, the steady gait of hooves on the soft red road. They drove past fresh-plowed fields redolent with the musty odor of damp earth, through a grove of whispering hardwoods, and came to a hillside covered with bluebells and blooming wild ginger.

Impulsively, he drew to a halt and jumped down. He traveled halfway up the hill before stopping. He heard the creak of the carriage springs and turned. She walked toward him in her ugly black dress, carrying her ugly black hat. Walking toward an ugly, blackhearted man who'd married her for all the wrong reasons and suddenly regretted the marriage for all the right reasons.

Her silk skirts rustled as she walked, mingling with the sough of the breeze and it sounded to him like soft music. She stopped a few feet in front of him.

She had summertime looks; sun-kissed hair and sultry night eyes, a warm wash of roses across her fragile bones. He didn't realize he was staring until she gave a little fluttery sigh. As if she couldn't bear the strength of his gaze, she leaned over and picked a single blossom.

"Why did you stop?"

Her voice sounded as thick as a humid July night. She straightened, clutching the blossom in one gloved hand, bright blue petals against black lace. She buried her nose in the petals and inhaled deeply. He stepped forward and took both the hat and the blossom from her hands.

"Let your hair down." Her eyes clouded with uncertainty. "Let it down," he repeated.

He could feel each beat of his heart as he watched her trembling hands pull the pins. She gave a shake of her head, and the golden brown waves cascaded down her back. He held out the hat, and she placed the hairpins in the crown.

He dropped the little black hat to the ground and purposely crushed it beneath his boot. She drew in a tiny gasp. He silenced her by placing his finger against her lips. He felt the fire for a moment so brief, he wondered if he imagined it, a jolt of lightning from his fingertip to his soul. Careful to maintain a casual air, he pulled his hand back. Just in case it was real.

"No more black, little wife," he said. "Your father doesn't deserve it, and you look awful in it anyway."

She turned away, standing with her head proud and her narrow shoulders vulnerable. War fever must have crazed his brain, one minute wanting to hold her, to protect her, the next minute feeling pleased for having insulted her. She murmured something. He stepped forward and turned her by her arm.

"Sparrow?" he asked, wondering if he'd heard correctly. Her voice was so low, he had to lean forward to hear her.

"Carlyle's nickname for me."

He remembered that now. Gordon, too, for that matter. *Little brown sparrow.* Whenever they'd been annoyed with her trailing after them, they'd break into a singsong of torment until the tiny girl went running in the opposite direction, usually in tears. God, he hadn't simply insulted her, he'd touched a hurt so old and deep she probably couldn't see the truth in a looking glass. Damn Carlyle, damn Gordon. Double-damn Royce Kincaid, the great protector.

"You're not poor anymore, which is about the only good thing I can say will come from having married me."

He tucked the bluebell behind her ear. His finger snagged on a wisp of hair, and he crimped the gossamer strands around the petals. She kept her gaze somewhere over his shoulder, but he heard her breath catch as his hand brushed her ear.

"Go into town tomorrow, pick up Miss Raleigh and her mother, and go shopping. Do it now, Annie, before it's too late." She looked at him then, rebellion evident in the square set to her jaw.

"No black," he repeated. "If you can't stand the heat of the Mrs. Pettigrews, make up some white dresses for propriety. But I want to see you in something expensive and pretty." Their gazes locked and held. "You'll do that for me because we're friends."

"Are we really friends?"

He gave her his nastiest smile. "As long as you do things my way."

Her laughter started with a little gurgling sound deep in her throat that erupted into a full-bodied melody. His head reeled with a strange dizziness, as if he had swung around too fast and too long. He shook his head, trying to regain his equilibrium.

"I don't know why I'm laughing, when the truth is, you frighten me to death," she said.

"Well hell, Mrs. Kincaid, you should be scared."

She leaned over and plucked another blossom. Her advance

took only two steps, but he felt as exposed as a lone picket in front of an advancing legion. She took his coat lapel in her hand and inserted the flower in a buttonhole. Maybe he breathed, and maybe he didn't. A gaggle of geese passed overhead with loud, raucous squawks. The racket jerked him back to a larger world, so it was no longer just one tiny, lavender-scented woman patting the chest of one cold-sweating man.

"There," she said, smiling up at him.

She turned and started down the hill. After several steps, she swung round, her arms tucked behind her as she continued walking backward. Her posture stretched the black cloth tight against her uplifted breasts. He jerked his gaze back to her face.

"I'll do it your way on the clothes." Her sunshine smile glowed brighter than nature's sunset. "And my way with Bo."

"Defiant little wench."

He started after her. She whipped around and raced for the carriage, her laughter lilting and mingling with the frog symphony. He let her win, stood to the side, and watched her climb into the low-slung phaeton unassisted. He took the driver's seat and lifted the reins.

"Do I frighten you too, Mr. Kincaid?"

"Just another pretty little firefly on a hot summer night, my dear."

She folded her hands in her lap and stared over the horse's ears. They traveled the last mile to Riverbend in silence.

As he pulled beneath the porte cochére, he caught sight of Gordon and Bo leading the horses into the stable. Laughter and singing drifted from the slave quarters.

"I'm afraid you're going to have a cold supper tonight," he said. Little Rufus appeared like a specter on silent feet. Royce climbed down and circled behind the phaeton as the servant held the trace of the lead horse. Annabelle stood.

"It's getting dark. You'll fall." His hands spanned her waist. She was so small, she'd have to turn twice to make a shadow. Through the layers of cloth, he felt a warm, natural, woman's body. She didn't need whalebone and overtight stays. He told himself to let go, but she looked up at him with a soft light in her eyes, and his hands lingered against the warmth.

The big door opened with a gentle swish, and he looked over to see Jules come out under the portico. Jules bowed, and she rewarded him with her smile.

Jules fought back a grin as she came abreast of him. He fought harder when he looked at Royce. Royce quelled the threatening smile with a look and pulled the offending flower from his buttonhole. He crushed the petals in his palm and flung it into the stones. Jules's forehead creased in a frown.

"A package came for you this afternoon, Miz Annabelle," said the elderly servant, pushing the door open for her to pass through. "I put it on the table in the big hall."

"From Carlyle?" she asked.

"Didn't say who it was from, little missy."

Royce regretted not breaking Carlyle's nose when he'd had the chance. She hadn't received one letter from her brother. Each day, she met the mail packet with a hopeful expression and turned away crestfallen.

Her steps quickened. Royce pulled off his driving gloves and handed them to the servant. "Was the package from Richmond?"

"Yes sir, it sure 'nuff was."

Royce followed the clicking sound of her bootheels down the corridor to the big hall. She stood with her back to him as she tore open the wrapping. He leaned against the newel post and watched her from beneath the concealing brim of his hat.

An odd little sobbing sound escaped her throat. She started to turn, but stopped halfway around, as if she couldn't bear to face him. She rubbed her fingers over the ornate silver handle, stroking the cold metal as if she needed the touch to see.

"Does it match?" he said.

"This is from you?" She turned all the way, and he saw confusion on her face.

"It's not every day a woman gets married, and I never gave you a wedding present."

"Who told you?"

"Not Bo, and I tried like the devil to get it out of him."

"Gordon," she murmured. Her face lit with a soft smile, and he wished the smile was for him instead of his brother.

"Mr. Kincaid . . . Royce . . ." Her brown eyes glistened.

"No one ever gave me . . ." She stopped as her slender throat convulsed. "Thank you," she said with a whispery sigh. Their gazes met, held, and then she smiled for him. A soft, tremulous smile on sultry lips.

He stared at her, stunned, unable to breathe or move or think. Wherever it had begun, maybe in her parlor in Lexington, maybe the firing line at the wilderness church, maybe on a petal carpeted hillside—it no longer mattered. It ended here in the big hall at Riverbend with a punishing twist of his gut.

He could define that irritating burr; he wanted more than her smiles. He wanted to take her beneath him with hot, hard-breathing lust. He wanted to thrust himself deep inside her, to master her, own her, and he wanted to hear her moans and cries as he did. She turned away but not before he saw it in her eyes. His sweet little wife thought she was in love with him.

He might have stood there staring at her stiff back and trembling shoulders for the space of a heartbeat or an endless eternity; he would never know. He was conscious only of her immense physical pull and the need to resist it.

Christ, he was no better than every Kincaid before him. *God help her*, he thought as he turned and lurched for the door.

# Chapter 6

❦

Annabelle sat on the step of the back gallery, listening to the sounds of revelry coming from inside the nursery building. Someone played a lively fiddle, and she could hear the foot-stomping and hand-clapping of the dancers.

She looked up as Gordon came out on the gallery. He leaned against the nearest column with his hands in his pockets. Unlike her, he seemed to ignore the party sounds, directing his gaze toward the fields.

"Is this a special Riverbend holiday?" she asked after several minutes of companionable silence. She knew only that the slaves had been given an extra day off. Only the most necessary labor would be undertaken between now and Monday and she couldn't recall any instance at Merry Sherwood, except Christmas and Whitsun, when the servants were given extra time off.

Gordon seemed taken aback by her question. "Didn't Royce tell you?"

She shrugged. She hadn't seen Royce since he'd left her standing in the big hall with her tears threatening to fall. He hadn't even appeared for supper.

"Clarence took a wife last Sunday," said Gordon.

"Then why wasn't the party on Sunday?"

"Johnson doesn't allow his slaves to party."

She wondered exactly when her life had turned into a riddle. Nothing seemed to make sense anymore, not even Gordon.

She lifted a questioning look, hoping he'd explain himself, but his attention was once again focused on the fields. He straightened, and she followed the direction of his gaze.

She heard the galloping hoofbeats first, then saw them silhouetted in the moonlight: Royce on Ajaque, taking the hedgerows with the ease of a winged Pegasus.

"Bloody fool," muttered Gordon.

Gordon was right. Only a fool would ride a valuable Thoroughbred at a racing pace through dark fields where a single rabbit burrow could cause instant death for horse and rider. But she guessed Royce knew what he was doing. A man who rode with that much grace valued his mount and wouldn't risk its destruction.

"I don't think I've ever seen anything so beautiful," she murmured.

Gordon huffed. "Royce never does anything halfway."

He was talking on two levels again, and she'd grown tired of the riddles. She moved beside him, placing her hand on his forearm. "What's bothering you tonight, Gordon? Sumter or your brother?"

"You."

"Me?"

"Royce didn't tell you about Clarence's wife?" he asked. She shook her head, confused. He stared at her, then said, "You've worked your fingers to blisters making him a uniform he won't bother to thank you for. He was rude and insolent to you this afternoon, and you went along with it when you'd have slugged anyone else who treated you like that. You're damn right, it worries me, because I'd swear you're falling in love with him, and you're only going to get hurt."

She folded her arms across her chest and looked away. "Do you think he's noticed?" she asked in a small voice, tacitly admitting the truth of his words.

"Who knows with Royce? He doesn't let anyone close enough to know what he's thinking," he said. "Maybe not. Royce doesn't know you as well as I do."

She thought of the night when Royce had stolen her heart, the night she sensed his loneliness, saw the glimpse of a wounded, tender man. Gordon's words only substantiated her conviction. "Doesn't anybody know him?" she asked.

"The parts he allows people to know, or wants us to believe. We're supposed to think he hates Peyton, hates Riverbend and everything it stands for. He'll tell you before you ask that he's a blackhearted scoundrel, then turn around and do something so basically kind and decent it takes your breath away. Of course, you're not supposed to notice that." He paused, his gaze hard on her face, then shrugged. "Maybe Clarence knows him, maybe not. Every time I think I've got a handle on him, he slips through like an eel."

"But you love him."

His mouth lifted in an ironic twist. They stood, each immersed in private thoughts. She finally worked up the courage to ask Gordon another question. She could only hope he'd answer because she knew she'd never learn the things she needed to know about her husband from her husband.

"Why would a servant know more about him than his own brother?"

"Because they're so much alike they should have been brothers. Clarence's mother was Royce's wet nurse. Maybe that explains it."

His lips were pressed tight together, as if the whole subject was distasteful to him. She wondered if the bitter taste came from jealousy over a black man, a piece of property and, therefore, less than human. She gave silent thanks that the Hallstons had never owned slaves. She didn't want that burden on her shoulders.

"You want me to help you, Annie, and I can't. Royce is eight years older than I, and he's devoted his life to hiding the truth from my tender sensibilities. Whatever happened before I was born, no one talks about. No one talks about why Celeste left. I was four years old, and all I know is that my mammy had dressed me in my fancy tucked dress and I thought this time, Mother was going to take me with her, wherever it was she went in her shiny black carriage."

He huffed a derisive laugh. "I was on the gallery waiting, and she swept past me without so much as a glance. By the time I figured out she was going without me, the carriage was halfway down the front lane. I went tearing after her, tripping all over that pretty white skirt, falling more than running . . ."

His collar moved as he swallowed. "Anyway, the next thing

I knew, Royce had me, carrying me back up the lane . . ."

He trailed off. She thought it a sad story, this family that had so much more than they needed in material things and so little in the way of important things.

"Peyton met us at the foot of the steps," he said, finally. "He made Royce put me down, then stood me in on the top step and wiped my face with his handkerchief. 'We will never speak of this day, boys,' he said. And nobody ever has. But that picture hangs in the parlor still. Maybe you can figure it out, I can't. All I know is from that day on, Peyton has lived his lie, and Royce lived another."

"Gordon, maybe it's because they love you."

"And maybe it's all because of me."

"What do you mean?"

He jammed his hands in his pockets and leaned against the column. "According to slave gossip, which I'm not supposed to have heard, Celeste is my mother, but Peyton isn't my father."

"Gordon, perhaps—"

"My guess is my brother, who doesn't have any feelings, married you for the same reason you married him."

"To save a brother," she said softly.

"Exactly."

She looked up at his shadowed face. She saw something: guilt maybe, maybe fear.

"I owe them, Annie, both of them. Peyton for giving a bastard a name, Royce for treating me like a blood brother. I can't let them down."

She touched his arm. "Of course you won't. You've never let anyone down."

"You. I should have told you this before you signed that contract."

She suddenly understood why Gordon hadn't come to that meeting although she had begged him to come. "You didn't let me down," she said. "I still would have agreed because Bo needed a home, and I couldn't provide it for him." She shrugged. "Maybe Royce and I are more alike than you think."

"Don't make that mistake, Annie-girl."

"Don't make what mistake?" The new voice was low and deep.

She swung around. Royce stood at the end of the gallery, lighting a cheroot. He took a slow draw, and the tip flamed like a single orange eye in the night. She wondered how much he'd overheard, but as usual, his expression didn't give any clues.

"Of thinking you're a gentleman," said Gordon.

"Well hell, brother, I already told her that myself."

Gordon, in his formal dinner clothes with every golden hair in place, looked exactly what he was, a gentleman planter. Royce, with his dark hair tumbled by the mad ride, with his shirt collar open and moonlight glinting off the strong column of his neck, appeared both dangerous and fascinating.

As long as she could remember, she had loved the younger one; a safe, comfortable, unthinking love. There was nothing safe about the older brother. With Royce, she felt the gathering of a summer storm, the tingle and the slow heat, the shivering anticipation of both the fury and the beauty. And the fear.

He moved on cat's feet, supple, stealthy, until she found herself standing between the brothers. She drew in a deep breath and smelled Royce, night and sweat and man.

Gordon's mouth twisted. "It's not enough that you trade away a good stud, you've got to try and kill another horse?"

"Weevils in the wheat." Royce lifted the cheroot and studied the thin stream of smoke curling from the tip.

More riddles she didn't understand, but Gordon visibly softened. "Johnson send the patrollers?" he asked. Royce only nodded.

*Patrollers.* The word sent shivers up her spine. Devils in white skin who beat the bushes for runaways, patrolled the roads and the fields for slaves traveling without passes; men who took perverse pleasure in whippings and chains. She'd never seen a patroller on Riverbend.

"What did you tell them?" Gordon's voice remained quiet, but she sensed an undercurrent of alarm.

Royce took his time answering, puffing first on the cheroot, then watching the smoke twist and rise. "I told them the next time they showed up here, they wouldn't be patrolling my fields, they'd be fertilizing them."

"Tarnation, Royce." Gordon rubbed his thumb across his upper lip. "Poor white trash would just as soon kill you as kill a slave."

"I'll take more than my share down first."

"Has one of your servants done something wrong?" she asked, wondering if her quaking knees came from fear for the slave or fear for her husband.

Royce gifted her with a cocky smile. "Just stupid, little wife. Seems marriage is a catching disease; but in Clarey's case, he claims to love his woman."

Gordon stared at his brother, love, disgust, and anger all present on his face. "It's not enough that you gad around all afternoon with that Cady woman, now you're going to rub it in real good. Damn you, Royce, you might not have any feelings, but other people do."

"You want her, brother?" drawled Royce. "How about we make a trade, kind of like the deal with Johnson. My wife for your horse."

"You've been drinking."

"Not enough. I aim to remedy that oversight real soon though."

Tension arced between the two men like heat lightning over the mountains. Gordon raked his fingers through his hair. Annabelle stepped forward and put her hand on his arm.

"Stay out of this, Annie. He's been spoiling for a fight, and he's going to get one."

Royce flicked the cheroot. The tip traced an orange flare in the darkness, trailing sparks. She saw his hand clench and unclench at his side.

"I'm not fighting you." Royce took a step onto the lawn.

Gordon reached out and grabbed his brother's arm, swinging him around. "You'll apologize, or you'll fight."

Royce stiffened, holding his brother's gaze until his brother dropped his hand. His lips curled as his gaze sought her, raking her from tip to toe.

"Please accept my apologies, little wife. I can't imagine what possessed me to trade a fine Thoroughbred stud for a worthless lady's maid to give a wife I don't want." He leaned into a mocking bow. Gordon's fist connected with his jaw on the way down.

The force of the blow brought Royce upright and wheeling halfway around. He staggered himself straight, shaking his head. His laugh sounded over the noise of the party. "Didn't like my apology, huh?"

Royce moved so quickly, Annabelle didn't see it coming. Evidently Gordon missed it, too, as he doubled over from a hard punch to his belly.

Gordon groaned in a breath and groaned it back out. "I thought—I thought you—didn't want to fight."

"Changed my mind." Royce held himself ready, managing to look cocky and impudent in spite of the tense set to his shoulders. Suddenly, Gordon lunged. His raging-bull bellow brought slaves rushing out of the party and into the yard.

The brothers huffed and snorted, landing punches that sounded like hoofbeats on hard ground, reeling and grinning at each other like listing lunatics. A circle formed around them, the male slaves loudly making bets on the outcome, reminding her of the one and only cockfight she'd ever witnessed.

Annabelle stepped up to the nearest slave, a big black man standing with his arm around a woman's waist. His grin was as broad as that of the cockeyed lunatics. He looked down at her.

"Make them stop," she pleaded.

"Nothing's going to stop those two until one of them's flat on the ground."

Annabelle looked around for something to throw or use to get their attention. Nothing. No rocks, no boards, no sturdy tree limbs. The brothers staggered backward from each other, and she saw her opportunity. She rushed into the melee, dimly aware of the black man's hand reaching out to stop her.

Royce was the closest to her. He half turned on unsteady legs, shaking his head as if he couldn't believe his fluttering vision. She put every ounce of power she possessed into the effort, feeling mighty pleased with the solid thwacking sound as her bony knee connected with his groin. He dropped to a tight ball, clutching himself between the legs.

"Christ, woman," he bleated, before rolling to the ground.

Annabelle stood over him, watching him writhe. Satisfied he wasn't going anywhere, she turned to glare at Gordon. Gordon swayed like a cattail in a stiff breeze. He wiped his bloody mouth with the back of his hand, then grinned.

"Where'd you learn that trick, Annie-girl," he wheezed.

"From you."

"Thanks, brother." Behind her, Royce gave a pained snort. "Warn me next time before you bring in reserves."

She turned her back to both of them, feeling an uplifting sense of power as she heard the retching sound behind her. Her gaze locked with that of the laughing black man. She brushed her hands together in front of her waist.

"One of them's flat on the ground," she said.

"He's about as flat as he can get," agreed the slave. He looked around the circle of dark faces. "Party's over, folks. Don't think any of you want to be around when Marse Royce gets back on his feet."

The circle broke up, most of the laughing voices heading back for the nursery building and not the individual quarters. The one who'd sent them on their way stepped toward her, pulling the young woman with him.

"I'm Clarence, Miz Annabelle, and this is my wife Patsy." He pushed the woman forward. "Royce said you could teach her to be a lady's maid. I'd be much obliged if you kept it at that."

The black woman gave her a shy smile. Annabelle looked at Clarence. "Patsy might have other ideas."

She grinned at Patsy, and Patsy's shy smile broadened into a matching grin. It was two women, a sharing of secrets, a sharing of power. It wasn't often that the little woman brought the master to his knees.

Annabelle moved past the slave couple, heading for the Big House. She grinned again when she heard Gordon speaking behind her.

"Don't be such a ninny, Royce," he said. "All she hurt was your pride."

"To borrow Bo's turn of phrase—*shee-it*."

She stopped grinning. Tomorrow, that boy would be reading Plato all afternoon.

# Chapter 7

Annabelle leaned back on her heels, pulled off the heavy gardening glove, and ran her finger inside the choke collar of her dress. She turned her head at the sound of riders coming up the front lane. Peyton and Gordon had returned from Richmond.

Annabelle grabbed a sucker branch of one of the cabbage roses. "Ouch," she muttered, lifting her thumb.

She pulled a large thorn from the fleshy pad. Absently, she lifted her hand to her mouth, drawing in the metallic taste of blood and the grit of Riverbend's soil while she watched Gordon and Peyton ride toward the stables.

She lifted the heavy coil of hair from the back of her neck in a vain attempt to feel a cooling breeze, then returned to her task of pruning the cabbage roses. She concentrated on the peaceful sounds of late afternoon in the country in an effort to soothe her growing disquiet. She suspected peace was soon to be only a memory. A dark shadow loomed across her vision, and she looked up.

"The gardener can do this, Annie-girl."

Peyton's voice was calm, but she sensed the note of strain beneath and couldn't miss the furrows in his brow. They looked at one another. Time seemed to stop, the very air growing heavy with the weight of future tears.

Peyton held out his hand. She took hold and he raised her up. She didn't trust her voice, so she said nothing as Peyton enveloped her in a hug. When he released her, she saw Gordon standing beside them.

"Did you see Carlyle?" she asked, wiping her sweaty brow with her sleeve.

"Why does it seem I'm always mopping dirt off your face?" Gordon pulled a handkerchief from his pocket and brushed the cotton cloth across her brow. "No, I didn't see him," he said. "The outlying militia companies are just beginning to come into Richmond. It'll be a while before the Valley companies arrive."

She nodded and blinked against the annoying pressure at the back of her eyes. "How long before you leave?"

"Two, maybe three days."

She drew in a deep breath and regretted it. The mingled scents of flowers and earth seemed suddenly cloying and she felt slightly sick.

"I'd like to see you in my study before dinner," said Peyton. "We've some important matters to discuss, but I think Gordon and I are both in need of a scrubbing first."

She studied his handsome, impassive features, so like his firstborn son. She swallowed back the rising nausea. "How did you vote?" she asked.

"I'm a Virginian, Annie-girl. I voted the only way I could."

They were all Virginians, and she understood the words no one had spoken. Virginia had seceded from the Union.

All her life, she'd accepted her place. Women belonged in the home, minding the hearth and the children while men, in their wisdom, ran the world. Somewhere, someone had made a big mistake. Men had no wisdom.

She could end this war by tomorrow night. Jefferson Davis, in his wisdom, called for the firing on Sumter. Abraham Lincoln, in his wisdom, responded by calling up troops. Annabelle Hallston Kincaid, in her superior wisdom, would place the honorable Mr. Davis and the honorable Mr. Lincoln on a field of honor with a set of dueling pistols. May the best man win, and every other mother's son go home unharmed.

Nobody asked her opinion.

Annabelle picked up the woven basket and made her way inside. A bead of sweat trickled between her breasts, and she discreetly pulled at her bodice. Ruefully, she eyed the hem of her sleeve, grimy with the afternoon's efforts in the garden, and wondered again the secret of keeping starched and clean.

She trudged up the stairs to her room, her mind shifting to Carlyle. His war had come. She'd give her right hand to see him, hold him close one more time before he marched into the guns. Not knowing where he was, she couldn't even write. All that was left to her were prayers for his safety. She didn't find that thought consoling. God was male, after all.

She shoved open the door to her room, seeing Patsy with an empty bucket in her hands.

"Your bath's ready, Miz Annabelle," said Patsy. "And I got your dinner dress all laid out."

Annabelle nodded as she set the gardening basket on the floor by her bureau. Since coming to Riverbend, she'd come to understand the seductive pull of the life led by the planter class, the ease and the leisure that came as a direct result of the labor of black-skinned men, women, and children. She still felt uncomfortable having her every need addressed before she even realized she had the need.

She found her relationship with the silent and proud Patsy even more disquieting. The sentiment remained unspoken between them, but each was intimately aware of it. Annabelle didn't want to own another woman. Patsy refused to be owned.

"If you be needing anything more, just ring the bell."

Annabelle turned to face the black woman. Patsy was half a foot taller, her skin the rich color of burnt coffee. She wore a length of bright calico wrapped around her head, hiding the glossy black hair that made Annabelle suspect Indian blood in her background.

"Mr. Peyton is back," said Annabelle.

"Yes'm."

Patsy retained her bland expression, the mask she hid behind, the weapon she used to keep herself to herself. Annabelle understood it was the only protection she possessed and normally tried to respect Patsy's need. Today, she wanted to reach out and take Patsy's hand and ask a hundred questions. She wanted to talk and share her woman's fears. She picked up the gardening basket and held it out instead.

"I saw you planting flowers in front of your quarters the

other night," she said. "I thought maybe you'd like some cuttings from the roses. They should take real good in the corner."

Patsy's mask slipped, and surprise registered on her handsome face. It was gone just as quickly as it appeared. "Thank you, ma'am."

"Patsy," said Annabelle softly, reaching out the only way she knew how. "It's here. War, changes . . ."

"Miz Annabelle, you're wanting somebody to talk to, and it can't be me." She stared into the basket as though seeing in it the ghosts of her past. Annabelle suspected right this minute, Patsy preferred those known ghosts to the frightening overture of friendship.

"I'm a slave."

"You're a woman."

"And that's my heavy load. Before I came here, Clarence told me Riverbend's white folks aren't like some others. Might be he's right, can't say I've seen anything tells me otherwise. But that don't take away what already happened."

"Would you tell me what happened if I asked?"

Patsy wiped away a trickle of sweat that ran down her temple. "Are you asking?"

Annabelle nodded slowly, sensing some warming in the older woman's demeanor and loath to give up.

A small, bitter smile touched the corner of Patsy's lips. "I don't fear dying being as I've seen Hell already, and I don't fear this war. Can't nothing happen to Patsy any worse than what's already happened. That be all I'm wanting to say."

"Can I ask you one more question?"

Patsy seemed to think for a moment, and then she nodded.

"Do you love your husband?"

"Any day, white folks can decide to sell one of us." Patsy's throat convulsed as she swallowed. "What happens to this broken heart when that day comes?"

Hot as it was, Annabelle felt a shiver like ice trickling down her spine. "Husband or children?" she whispered.

"My boy was the massa's," said Patsy in an eerie voice devoid of feeling. "His missus wasn't one to take kindly to that. Don't know where my baby is and won't never find him, war or no war, freedom or no freedom. Johnson at the Willows bought me, my boy was sold South."

Annabelle knew she was supposed to hear nothing, feel nothing. Patsy was, after all, only a slave. Annabelle was heir to a way of life that defined people by their color. She'd never fit the common mold as a child and evidently, she never would. She couldn't deny her own humanity or that of the terrorized woman standing before her.

"Patsy, I'm sorry," she said. "It's wrong, as wrong as this war."

"Yes'm, it is, and sorry don't help none."

Their gazes met, brown eyes staring into brown eyes, each coming from a different direction and arriving at some understanding. A woman's knowledge of loving and losing, a woman's subjugation to men's power.

"You can go on and fix your husband's dinner," said Annabelle softly. "I won't be needing anything more tonight."

She watched Patsy leave, her long back stiff with pride, the only thing her white masters couldn't steal from her. Golden rays slanted across the oak floor as the sun dropped into the west behind the distant mountains. Through the open window, she heard the field hands returning from their day's labor.

Annabelle walked over and drew back the voile curtains. The first stirring of the evening breeze ruffled her hair. She leaned her shoulder against the window frame and listened: to the breeze, to God's creatures, big and small, hearing the symphony and a heartrending cry.

*Go down, Moses, way down in Egypt's land.*

An army trudged over the fields, a barefoot army of men, women, and children dressed in kersey and calico, armed with hoes and shovels.

*Go down, Moses, let my people go.*

Annabelle stopped just outside Peyton's study. She smoothed the front of her bodice, took a deep breath and knocked on the partially open door. Peyton's voice welcomed her, but Jules's face greeted her as he pulled the door open.

Gordon rose from the settee. "You look even more charming than usual tonight," he said with his normal gallantry. "New dress?"

It was a new dress, and she could remember a time in the not-so-distant past when a new dinner gown with eight flounces and a wide hoop would have caused her to clap like a child with joy. Tonight, clothing, whether old or new, struck her as extremely inconsequential.

She curtsied anyway and returned Gordon's gallantry with a tilt of her head and a smile. She took the lady's chair, the only seat that would accommodate her wide hoop, and gave silent thanks for Jules's foresight in carrying the chair from the parlor into the male domain of Peyton's library.

"Sherry?"

She glanced at Peyton and considered her options. According to Carlyle, bourbon and branch possessed a quality guaranteed to soothe any Southern soul. Her Southern soul needed soothing tonight.

"Sherry will be fine," she said.

Peyton resumed pacing while Jules poured her drink. She took the crystal glass from his white-gloved hand and sipped at the sweet liqueur while she studied Peyton.

As usual, his attire was impeccable, but the scrubbing had done nothing to erase the lines of fatigue that etched his strong features. She suddenly realized he was no longer a young man, and the events of the past three weeks had brought the years out in his face. She added Peyton to her growing list of men to be cared for, prayed for—men to be loved while time permitted.

Jules refilled Peyton's brandy and left the room, pulling the door closed. Annabelle glanced at Gordon. He'd resumed his seat, his long legs stretched in front of him. His attention seemed to be focused on the amber liquid in the glass he held cupped between his hands, studying it as if the secrets of the future could be divined in its murky depths.

Peyton leaned his hip on the edge of his desk and cleared his throat. "Annie, this subject might seem indelicate to you, and I don't bring it up to cause you any distress."

She looked up sharply. His gray eyes, normally as impenetrable as Royce's, seemed clouded with some grave concern. She told herself it was secession causing that look, but his words caused a prickle of fear. Without anything more to go on than his words and her confusion, she only nodded in response.

"Unlike most girls of your age," he said, "you've been

schooled as well as your brothers. You've got an understanding of both history and politics and a healthy disregard for the virtues of Southern womanhood. Although I used to tell your father he was making a grave mistake in the manner he raised you . . ." At this point, a slight smile escaped. "Or didn't raise you . . ." She smiled in return. "I have to admit I'm appreciative of these qualities now. You'll have an advantage over the wilting flowers as the heat thickens."

She supposed he meant that as a compliment and accepted it as such although Mama was definitely twisting somewhere.

"Now, the indelicate part." He took a deep drink of his brandy and then set the glass on the desk. "You and Royce signed a marital contract that puts Riverbend in your name upon my death. Since I don't intend to die anytime soon, I foresee certain problems and have taken action to forestall a calamity."

She turned to Gordon, feeling somewhat less skittish when he met her gaze with a slight wink. At least he knew what was happening and didn't seem upset.

"As you know, when I went to Richmond, I went as a Union man. Davis acted like a fool when he allowed the firing on Sumter. By firing the first shot, he forced Lincoln's hand, and no one should be surprised by Lincoln's response. But that's neither here nor there. The fact is, it happened, and now we deal with it. For those of us who preferred to stay with the Union, everything changed when Lincoln called on Virginia to supply troops for his invasion. It's not a rebellion, it's secession, an implicit right of each and every state. We didn't initially choose to join them, but we won't furnish men and arms to invade our sister states when they are *right*. Do you understand so far?"

She nodded again and took another sip of sherry, trying to ease her dry throat.

"That's the broad issue and will be settled on the battlefields. The narrow issue is what happens to Riverbend, now, and later when the war decides whose vision of the country will prevail."

She saw his direction and felt the same cold chill she'd felt when talking with Patsy. So many issues, so many conflicting sides. She wondered if anyone really knew what this war was

going to be fought over. She wondered if it even mattered anymore. But she understood Peyton's fears.

"Honor if we win," she said softly. "Treason if we lose."

"I will not see Riverbend confiscated by an invading army
simply because I voted my conscience."

"How can you avoid it?" she asked.

He stood up, walked behind his desk, and pulled open the
drawer. She watched him withdraw a sheet of paper.

"By filing this deed drawn up by Judge Pleasonton the same
day you married my son. Dated April 1, 1861. Long before
Sumter, long before I voted for secession. If you'll give me
your permission, knowing your married name will be available to anyone searching courthouse records, I'll have this
deed filed and Riverbend will be safe for your future children."
He paused, his eyes piercing her with the same fierce gaze of
his eldest son. "Will you give me that permission, Annie-girl?"

She felt caught in a river at floodtide, swept along by events,
in danger of drowning from the breathtakingly rapid changes.
"Royce," she managed to say. "Have you mentioned this to
Royce?"

Peyton gave her a look half-rueful, half-amused. "We spoke
in Richmond. He found the situation highly gratifying."

"He laughed like an idiot," said Gordon from the side.

"Did he mention the slaves? Didn't he want them freed?"
she asked, recalling both her conversation with Patsy and the
initial discussion of the marital contract.

Peyton's face hardened. "I retain ownership of the slaves
and will not free them on the eve of this war."

She reminded herself who she was, how much this man had
already given her and Bo. She was turning into an absolute
coward anyway, grateful he kept that burden on his own shoulders, saving her from a moral decision that could only end in
either public or private censure.

Peyton set the deed on his desk and walked over to the window, peering out into the gathering dusk. He stood quiet for so
long, she wondered what he saw; the moon rising over the
magnolias and oaks, or the shadows of the past. Maybe even
the future.

"What happens to the very old and the very young if you
free them tonight? What happens to the field hands, without

skills or farmland or any education?" His voice sounded melancholy. "The North doesn't want them in their cities any more than they want the Irish fresh off the boats. The strong always survive, but not everyone is strong."

She thought she knew Peyton Kincaid, but she didn't. Tears lurked at the back of her eyes. "Uncle Peyton—"

He turned. "Let me finish," he said with a wave of his hand. "I predict that no matter who wins this war, life as we understand it has already ended. If you want freedom for those people out there, you've got a responsibility, Annie. You risk your own reputation and you risk their lives by educating them. And you promise me no Riverbend servant will ever be turned away from his home. You feed the old and the sick, even if it means you go hungry. You protect them from the white trash patrollers. It's a burden you've escaped up to now, but it rests on every Southern shoulder. Mine, my sons, all of us. I will free them, but not until they are prepared for freedom."

"I never knew you felt that way," she said.

"Don't give me credit where none is due. I could have taken those steps any time in the past thirty years, and I didn't," said Peyton with a glance at Gordon. She looked to Gordon but his normally expressive face remained blank.

Peyton shook his head, one side of his mouth turning up a bit. "Kincaids have done their fair share of sinning. Every mulatto you see out there in the quarters is a Kincaid. Unlike some, we don't sell our own blood, but that's never stopped us from propagating our own quarters."

Heat flooded her neck. Merciful heaven, this conversation couldn't be happening. Why, in mixed company, even a piano rested on limbs, legs being too indelicate a term for female ears.

"Do I shock you, Annie?" Peyton's voice sounded hard.

"Yes," she murmured, unable to lift her gaze from her gloved hands.

"If you wonder, to my knowledge, Royce has managed to avoid that one particular sin."

She closed her eyes. Even her gloved hands, hiding the calluses from gardening, suddenly seemed obscene. So many hidden faults beneath the illusion of perfection. She felt a presence behind her, then the weight of a hand on her shoulder.

"I'm sorry, child," said Peyton in a softened voice. "It's been a long time since we had a lady gracing our family. But you must understand the truth if you're going to be one of the strong. The most horrible thing I ever did was to sell a River-bend slave, and I'm certain that neither God nor Royce will ever forgive me." He patted her gently. "These are the things you have to know, however painful they may be."

She placed her hand on Peyton's and looked over to Gordon. Gordon's face had gone white.

"Whom did you sell, Father?"

Peyton's muscles tightened beneath her hand. "It doesn't matter now."

"It matters."

"Gordon—"

"It matters, Father. You sold Clem's father because Mother made you sell him." He jerked to his feet. "Or is that just another ugly slave rumor—that the poor man happened to walk into the wrong place at the wrong time? Was that the instance when I was conceived, Father, or don't you know?"

Annabelle let out her breath in the silence that gave Gordon his answer. She squeezed Peyton's hand and heard his sigh.

"I loved your mother," said Peyton, and she thought he sounded as if his heart had been torn from his chest.

"You're a bloody fool, Father." Gordon slammed down his glass. "A bloody damn fool."

Annabelle made a motion to go to him, but before she could move, he wheeled and was gone. She thought of the portrait in the front parlor. Gordon had the answer to his riddle now. It hung there because the silver-haired man had never stopped loving his wife, no matter what sins Celeste had committed. For the first time, she realized love could be a double-edged sword, as capable of destruction as it was capable of comfort.

Absently, Peyton patted her shoulder once more, then returned to the window, where he stood gazing out, his hands clasped behind his back. She sat for another minute, wondering if Peyton even remembered she was here. Finally, she managed to push herself up and cross the room to stand beside him.

"There's something I don't understand," she said softly. Peyton looked down at her and lifted one silver brow. She said,

"You love Riverbend so much. Why did you agree to give it to me, especially with . . . well, Royce's terms were nothing more than a bribe to get me to divorce him, yet you agreed to it all, knowing your family would lose Riverbend if I took your son's bribe."

One corner of his mouth lifted in a strange little smile. "Annie-girl, people of our station never get divorced. It just isn't done."

She thought of the wife he had somewhere unknown and felt another wave of love and pity for him. "I *am* a Kincaid now, as you said once before. I'm afraid I'm not a very brave Kincaid." His stiff shoulders seemed to slump, and she hastened on. "Protect Riverbend by filing your paper whenever you want."

He gave a brief nod. "But you're asking me to say nothing publicly?"

"I'm asking you to give Royce and me a chance to find something besides duty in this marriage."

"We meant you no harm, your father and I. I hope you understand that, Annie."

"I understand. Your son doesn't." She looked out the window, but she couldn't see the shadows that haunted him, and for that she was grateful. She considered leaning up and kissing his cheek. She didn't. Beneath the armor of pride, he appeared too fragile tonight for that display of affection.

"Would you like me to send your supper in here?" she asked.

He nodded. She'd reached the door before he spoke.

"Thank you, Annie-girl," he said without turning.

"You're welcome . . . Father."

She waited until she saw his shoulders straighten, then quietly pulled the door closed.

Peyton listened to the soft footsteps of his daughter-in-law until the sounds faded into nothing. Country quiet filtered through the open window, frogs and insects, the muffled beat of the swollen river, the sigh of the breeze.

It had been a night such as this the first time Peyton looked into the eyes of the woman who would become his second wife. He'd been hosting a barbecue on Riverbend's lawn and she had come on the arm of another man, a Democratic congressman from Louisiana. As soon as their eyes met over the carcass of a roasting pig, Peyton had known he had to have her as his own.

Later, he decided it was the whimsy of the moment that seduced him, but it had really been her beauty—that flawless ivory skin and shiny black hair, the rose-petal softness of her generous mouth, and her eyes . . .

Gordon had those same eyes of midnight blue.

Not that Peyton would ever forget her anyway. He wouldn't allow that cowardice on his part. She had given him Gordon—sired by one of her many lovers—but fathered by Peyton himself because he loved the boy, had loved him from the first moment he'd laid eyes on the bundle wrapped in a soft blue swaddling blanket. It was that love that had caused him to lie to Gordon tonight, and he'd been shocked that Gordon had already known.

He might have threatened Royce with exposing Gordon's bastardy as a lever to force Royce into a marriage he would never think of on his own, but Peyton would never have exposed Gordon to that kind of social humiliation. He'd spent the past twenty years of his life protecting his youngest son from just that thing.

Not that Royce would believe that. Royce saw himself as Gordon's protector, and perhaps he was.

Royce . . .

Peyton sighed. In so many ways he'd failed his firstborn son. It was his greatest wish—his father's wish—that Annabelle might touch Royce's heart. God only knew, Peyton himself had not managed to reach through that hard veneer of pride and distance the boy had carried with him into manhood. He didn't deserve Royce's forgiveness and would not ask for that grace, but he would gladly give up everything he owned to save Royce from his own life of bitter loneliness.

Annabelle. A chance at happiness . . . if the war didn't kill Royce first.

Peyton said nothing when Jules entered, listening to the familiar shuffle of Jules's feet, the tiny clink of glass against the silver tray as Jules collected the drink glasses.

Jules, his mulatto half brother, given by their mutual father to the white son as a piece of property on his fifteenth birthday.

Peyton had once drawn up manumission papers for Jules, the only Riverbend slave he'd ever offered his freedom. Jules had turned him down, well not down, exactly.

It had been the first anniversary of Rebecca's death. Peyton knew he was feeling sorry for himself, had spent the entire year hiding from his unhappiness, his baby son, his responsibilities at Riverbend. Politics was an excellent excuse. He didn't want to be governor; he simply needed something to fight back the aching, echoing emptiness inside him. It had come as something of a shock to learn how lonely a man could feel in a crowd of people.

He'd wanted to feel good about himself instead—or maybe he was looking for something more—a connection with unacknowledged kin that might kindle a faint touch of warmth in all those cold places inside. He'd called Jules into this very room.

He remembered, Royce had been just learning to walk, and the child was toddling on fat little legs and splayed toes, his arms lifted forward as he staggered across the carpet toward Jules.

Jules looked at the manumission papers, then at the child—and Royce had been a beautiful child.

Jules said, "You weren't here yesterday for this boy's first birthday."

Peyton slowly lowered the papers to the desk. "I know." He swallowed that perpetual knot in his throat. When had he started to love Rebecca? Too late, that was all he knew. "I couldn't get away in time."

Jules snorted, which was about what that patent falsehood was worth. The black gentleman's valet—who hadn't served as a gentleman's valet in many months—leaned over and picked up the child at his feet, disregarding the body soil filling the nappie and sending a potent odor into the room.

Jules carried the boy toward the closed door. He reached for the knob, then turned slightly. "You bring home a wife who'll be a decent mother to this boy, and I'll take those papers. Until then, I'm staying."

But Peyton had brought Celeste.

The way things worked out, Jules had stayed on at River-bend; it was Celeste who left.

When had he recognized the depth of humanity in his dark-skinned half brother? The combination of honor and love that had held Jules here when freedom was only a paper away?

Like his love for Rebecca, and his hatred of Celeste, the knowledge had come too late to be of much value. He couldn't quite bring himself to cross the great divide and tell Jules just how much it meant to him—that Jules had seen what his own eyes, smote blind with accumulated losses, had missed.

Even big sins begin with little deeds, so Peyton had learned to his sorrow. It wasn't any one thing a man did, but all the moments and deeds and choices that, put together, created the mosaic of a life. Or the mosaic of a nation.

# PART TWO

*A house divided against itself cannot stand . . . I do not
expect the Union to be dissolved—I do not expect the
house to fall—but I do expect it will cease to be divided.*

—Abraham Lincoln, Republican State Convention,
July 7, 1858

# Chapter 8

He gripped the rifle tighter and peered into the inky blackness across the Potomac. High on the menacing black recesses of the Bull Run Mountains, blue lights winked ominous signals, flashing terror into his heart.

Behind him, the rest of his company filled the narrow river valley, their campfires fanned by a stiff breeze. He tried to draw comfort from the support of so many friendly guns at his back but his mind kept shifting to the reports of the scouting party sent across the river earlier that afternoon.

A band of horsemen, dressed in rebel gray, had been spotted galloping down a country road. Jackson was known to be near Harpers Ferry; Ashby was reported farther north along the B. & O. Railroad. No one in the Maryland Guard posted on the bank of the river had been able to identify this body of Rebels. The war was only weeks old, yet already the borders were in turmoil, owing primarily to the bands of gray-clad partisans wreaking havoc against the ill-prepared Northern troops.

He thought of Ma back on the farm. He couldn't miss the war because Ma needed help getting the corn planted. He'd be home in time to get the harvest in; everyone knew this war wouldn't last long.

A mysterious splashing sounded. Should he fire a warning? No. It was only the little sounds heard along any river at night, the gurgles and glucks of night creatures. He'd be the laughingstock of the company if he fired to warn the men sleeping in tents along the ridge that a catfish was jumping in the inky river.

He glanced over his shoulder. The campfires created moving shadows against the black trees and billowing white tents. A raucous laugh sounded as some officer cursed his luck in the tent where the nightly card game went on.

The blue lights flashed in a cluster. Another noise sounded, upriver from him. He lifted the rifle, pushing back the unwelcome thought that he covered the last picket post in the line strung along the riverbank.

Minutes passed in silence and he eased his tension on the trigger. Only a rabbit, after all.

Suddenly, a shot rang out on the near side of camp. One, two, three, in quick succession, then a barrage of explosive noise and activity. His scalp tingled as the blood rushed around in his body with the same wild uproar and general confusion as the scrambling men in the camp.

In the eerie glow of the campfires, it seemed the white tents had taken on a life of their own as men struggled to find their rifles in the dark and squeeze themselves out of the narrow openings. Finally, answering bursts of flame opened up from behind the trees, more firing from along the ridge.

His heart hammered with every successive wave of sound, quick spurts of flaring death as each weapon hurled its load of lead. Men dodged like shadows in the flickering light. Shouting, explosions, bristling fire . . .

A new sound rose above the tumult, an inhuman sound that screeched down his spine. His rifle dropped to the ground, a quiet thud at his feet that was lost in the cacophony surrounding him.

His legs moved of their own volition and he was running from the screeching cry of the Rebel banshees. His blood hammered in his ears as he ran through tangled underbrush and whipping pine branches.

He smashed into something with such force, he was hurled backward, landing flat on his back. His lungs strained to pull in air. Someone chuckled and he opened his eyes. A huge man stood over him, holding a revolver.

"Move slow, Yank," said the gray-clad giant. His yellow

mustache seemed to quiver with suppressed mirth. "Got a name?"

"Abner."

"Well, Abner, if you'd run the other direction, I expect we'd both be a lot happier. As it is, I haven't got any choice but to take you with me."

Abner rose slowly, still gasping in quick little breaths. Before his frightened mind could grasp the situation, he found himself mounted on a horse, the Rebel giant pressed to his back, the giant's gun muzzle pressed to his ribs.

The horse picked its way down a dark path and into a clearing. Another half dozen men on horseback waited. The band of Rebels responded to some silent command, turning their horses as one and heading into the dark woods.

He kept expecting them to turn for the river, take him as a prisoner into the land of secession, but they continued along the narrow valley between the ridge and the Potomac. As dawn crept from the east, another band joined them, this one led by a dark man wearing a felt hat with the brim pinned up at the side. The dark man rode up to the giant.

"Orders were no prisoners, John."

"Not much I could do about it after he ran into me."

The undercurrent of amusement in the giant's voice rankled. Abner stiffened, then froze as the gun muzzle jammed hard against his rib cage.

The man in the hat must be the leader even though he wore none of the chicken-gut braid favored by secesh officers. Someone's mount blew a snort, which was quickly cut off. Abner suddenly realized these unknown Rebels had captured dozens of horses from the Union corral. From the leader's quiet commands, Abner guessed they'd captured an artillery piece as well, although he didn't see it anywhere in the clearing.

"Get down, son." It was the Rebel officer, his voice strangely compelling in its quiet authority.

Abner didn't need any encouragement. He slid off and prayed his knees wouldn't quake when his feet hit the ground.

"How old are you, son?"

"Seventeen, sir."

The leader tugged his hat forward, shading his expression. "Where's home?"

Abner swallowed. He wouldn't give them any information. They were the enemy.

The Rebel officer pulled out a revolver and studied it intently. With slow deliberation, he half cocked the pistol and turned the cylinder, each tiny click sounding like gunfire in the deathly quiet. "Where's home?" he repeated.

"Farm near Sharpsburg, sir." Abner's voice squeaked, but there was nothing he could do about that besides blush. He hoped he didn't wet his pants.

"William." From the lips of the gray-eyed officer, the name sounded like an order, as it must have been. The circle parted and allowed entrance to another rider. "You know this boy?" asked the leader.

The soldier studied him, then lifted his hand and scratched his red chin whiskers. "That's the widow Ransom's youngest boy."

"How old is he?"

"Not more'n fifteen. The Ransoms are all big for their age."

"Take him home. John will meet you at the Crossroads tomorrow."

Abner found his courage, even if it was a bit late. "That's desertion. You can shoot me, or you can let me go, but I'm not deserting my army." He pulled himself up as tall as he could manage. "Yup, you'll just have to shoot me."

Another audible click sounded as the leader let down the hammer. "Strip out of that uniform," he ordered in his low voice, casually pointing the gun barrel in the direction of Abner's thundering heart.

Courage fled. With little hopping motions, Abner stripped down to his dingy white nether garments wishing he'd washed laundry at least once since leaving home. William dismounted, gathered up the pieces of blue uniform, and handed the wadded ball to the giant. Abner saw the giant's yellow-brown mustache twitch again. He thought if the man laughed, he'd burst into tears and thoroughly humiliate himself. The giant didn't laugh. Instead, he exchanged glances with the leader, and a spark of warmth seemed to kindle in those cold gray eyes.

"Tomorrow at the Crossroads."

"Yes, sir," said William. "He'll be home one way or another."

The leader nodded and spurred his horse. All except William fell in behind him, and the band faded like specters into the still-dark forest.

"You goin' home on horseback or in a pine box?" asked William once the last rider had disappeared from view.

"Do I have a choice? Really?"

"You heard him, same as I did."

"Guess Ma could use some help with the planting."

William swung onto his mount. He held out his hand, and Abner grabbed hold as the older man pulled him up to the saddle. They rode for several miles with their backs to the rising sun. William reached for his canteen, opened it, and took a noisy swallow. He handed the open flask behind him. Abner took it gratefully and swilled the water into his parched throat. He handed it back.

"You know I won't be fifteen until next month," he said.

"Didn't want to embarrass you any more than you already were," said William. "Where'd you get the dang-fool notion to sign up anyway?"

Abner shrugged away the question. "Guess Ma'll want to know the name of the man who said to let me go."

"The last of the cavaliers," said the widow Ransom's brother, Abner's uncle, otherwise known as William Savage.

*General Lee,*

*It is my pleasure to report the results of the raid we discussed a week past. Enemy casualties estimated at six killed, fifteen wounded. Employing a force of twenty men, we captured fifteen cavalry mounts and eight draft horses as well as one rifled artillery gun and eight new Sharp's carbines. Our losses were none.*

*It is with some dismay that I also report the capture of one Federal picket, a mere boy of fourteen who fled the field of fire and managed to literally run into Captain DeShields. I made the command decision to release the child, sending him home in the company of one of my* men who, by happenstance, turned out to be the boy's uncle. Sgt. William Savage has already returned to duty, reporting the boy's mother will do her best to hold the child until he attains fighting age.

R. M. Kincaid, Major
Virginia Volunteer Army, Detached Service

Major Kincaid,

Received your report of May 29. We congratulate you on the success of the raid and commend you for sending the young picket home. We do not wish to fight those people's children.

Please leave your command to Captain DeShields and return to Richmond for further discussion.

R. E. Lee, General

# Chapter 9

~~~◇~~~

Royce mulled over the conversation he'd just had inside Army Headquarters, idly watching a regimental band pass by on the street in front of him, while he waited for the orderly to bring his horse from the depot. He was so deep in reflection he started when a hand touched his elbow, and a low voice said, "Sir?"

It wasn't a headquarters orderly but his own sergeant. "Couldn't get through the crowd," said William Savage. "Your horse is over on Ninth Street."

Royce began to pull on his riding gauntlets as he fell into step beside Savage. "What are they celebrating today?"

"I believe this one's a welcoming parade for Mrs. Davis."

Royce supposed it was inevitable that once Virginia joined the Confederacy the politicians would move the capital to Richmond. Jeff Davis had arrived a week or so earlier; his wife and children had come in just yesterday. Politically, the move made sense. He thought it was a strategic mistake for the armies and a disaster in the making for Virginia. Already the Northern battle cry was "On to Richmond!"

A blast of drums and brasses sounded as the regimental band burst into the "Marseillaise." They turned the next corner, and he realized Savage was saying something to him. Royce tilted his head in the direction of the fading music, signaling he'd been deafened by the noise.

Savage shrugged. "I never heard so many bands in my life

as I've heard since you ordered us back to this city. A man can't hardly think through the din."

"Stirring marches slue past the brain and go directly to the gut. Plato banned martial music in his ideal society for just that reason." Royce looked ahead, seeing the bright midday sun shining on the burnished waves of his brother's hair.

Gordon was far down the block, near the R. F. and P. railway depot, but Royce could pick him out of the crowd by his hair and the way he sat his horse. Gordon was holding the reins of Ajaque and Savage's favorite gelding.

"What's he doing here?" Royce tried to decide if he was relieved that now he wouldn't have to waste hours searching the teeming city for his brother, or alarmed that his brother had come searching for him.

Gordon kept in close touch with the family at Riverbend. Peyton's health would be fine; if not, the gossips would have gleefully informed his eldest son in somber tones while struggling to hide their curiosity as they waited for a reaction. But the boy . . . Bohannon wasn't a sickly boy, but he wasn't the strongest one going either. And Annabelle, even as a child she'd been too thin and too ready to take the world's responsibilities on her own narrow shoulders.

Annie . . .

Forget her. Forget her.

He had asked for Gordon's assistance. Gordon was here to report. Nothing more than that.

"He was looking for you at the depot," said Savage.

Royce stopped Savage with a touch on the arm. The information he had to impart would leak out eventually, but for now it was vital the circle be kept small.

"We're striking tents," said Royce. "I want the men formed up and ready to move out by first dawn."

"You convinced him," said Savage, grinning between his red whiskers.

"The raid convinced him," Royce corrected. "We'll be carried on the charts as a battalion, order of line through Jackson but detached to Lee's sole command. We can recruit from any company. I want to take that part slow though, handpick the right kind of men."

"Everything—dad-blamed, if that ain't everything you wanted."

*Nearly,* thought Royce, and that felt sweet. He wondered how much the ties of kinship and old blood had influenced Lee's decision. Not much, he decided. Lee was a general, not a politician.

"Where's DeShields?" he said.

"Spotswood Hotel."

"Who is she this time?" said Royce in a tone that was half amusement, half exasperation.

"Aw, heck, Major. Long as he fights when he's supposed to." Savage shrugged. "He brought us young Geary from one of those soirees he attended. It ain't all play."

"Got you fooled, does he? You head for the Spotswood and remind him that uniform he's wearing has a higher purpose than slaying impressionable young ladies. We'll meet at the Fairgrounds, my tent, in two hours."

A big elm cast deep shadows onto the sidewalk, and a stiff breeze blew in off the James River.

"I'm going to need more captains," said Royce in a low, careful voice.

Most companies elected their officers. Royce wasn't running a democracy. His officers were appointed by him, and if the troops didn't like it, they could serve under another commander.

Savage slanted him a glance. "You off to buy new insignia?"

"No."

"Then neither am I. The way I figure it, someone's got to look out for you. I'm that man."

"You're a lousy cook," said Royce, deflecting the emotion that was clouding his thoughts while tacitly acknowledging Savage's desire to stay put. Protecting, thought Royce, the back of the commanding officer who had made a decision that might have been humane but certainly wasn't momentous—unless you were the child involved or the child's kin.

They had reached the corner where Gordon was waiting. At the depot, a wood-burning locomotive hissed and snorted, belching clouds of resinous smoke and a shower of sparks. The clank and clatter of link-and-pin couplings ran down the line of cars. Ajaque shied, and Royce took the reins from his brother's hands.

He calmed the gray with a soothing stroke along his neck. "Two hours," he said to Savage.

"I'll have him there." Savage swung into his saddle. He tipped his hat to Gordon, who was dressed in full uniform with captain's insignia at his shoulders and braid at his cuffs. Savage saluted generals and colonels, if glared at long enough. Lesser rank got a tip of the hat at best.

Royce bit back a smile as he gathered his own reins and mounted Ajaque. He turned the horse and rode up beside his brother. Neither man spoke as they picked their way through the traffic. It was only when they had passed beyond the congestion that Gordon turned his head and gave Royce a slow look, from the tip of his dusty cavalry boots to the top of his comfortable, well-broken-in slouch hat.

"Is it Colonel Kincaid or General Kincaid?" Gordon wasn't smiling.

"Major Kincaid," said Royce, ignoring both the hard expression on Gordon's face and the irritation it engendered.

"I've known you all my life," said Gordon. "But I'll be damned if I'll ever figure you out. Why did you turn down another command?"

Royce allowed a small sigh. "Listen, Gordon, and learn. Colonels get noted by the other side. Generals *have* to be noted. Order of battle is the first information their spies are after, and you better believe this city is teeming with Northern spies. No one on either side is going to take much notice of a mere major leading a handful of companies. That's the best weapon I've got right now, and you can be bloody damn sure I'm going to use it to my advantage as long as I can."

Royce tugged his hat forward and carefully gazed at a spot between Ajaque's ears. "I could use you," he said.

He waited, not exactly hoping, but something close to that emotion. For a long time, the only sound was the dull thud of the horse's hooves then Gordon said, "Maybe. Augusta's here though."

Royce looked up. "Richmond?"

"No, she's still in Fredericksburg, but that's closer than she'd be if I was riding with you."

Damn. Who was talking?

"How much do you know, Gordon?"

"Nothing really. I just know you, so I can put the pieces together. You were the unnamed commanding officer in the papers last week—that story about the child picket with the Maryland Guard."

"That could have been any one of a hundred soldiers."

Gordon snorted. "Right." He guided Aster around a pile of steaming horse droppings in the road. "Your secret's safe with me, as long as it lasts," he said. "They'll figure it out eventually though."

Royce couldn't deny the truth of that observation, so he didn't try. They had ridden into another Richmond now, the disreputable perimeter of Camp Lee, where the bars, speculators, and prostitutes flourished. A Louisiana Zouave swaggered out of a so-called boardinghouse, his arms thrown over the shoulders of two of Scuffle Town's finest.

The prostitutes paled in comparison to the Zouave's sartorial splendor: billowing red trousers, embroidered blue jacket, and gold-tasseled fez. It was the uniform of the hodgepodge of Mississippi boatmen and recent convicts who roamed the city making off with chickens and garden vegetables as defiantly as they walked into saloons, drank what they wanted, and walked out telling the proprietor to charge it all to the government.

The sun glinted off the hilt of a bowie knife the Zouave had tucked in his boot. For some reason he didn't want to examine too closely, the sight reminded Royce of the onerous duty he'd set for himself to complete before he left Richmond. Presumably this was the reason Gordon was riding at his side.

"Did you find Carlyle?" He'd made his own cursory search in the little time he'd had available. It was easy to discover that Lieutenant Carlyle Hallston had been assigned to Jackson's staff. The problem had been finding Annabelle's brother anywhere near Jackson's staff headquarters.

"I've always known where he was," said Gordon "You didn't ask until now. Tom-Fool has him overseeing training details."

That last nugget of information bore contemplation. Training itself wasn't much—cadets from VMI were mostly responsible for whatever real training took place. But Jackson had placed Carlyle in an administrative position of some importance. Royce had spent too many years in the US Army to respect administrative soldiers. Paper-pushing popinjays, the lot of them. His reading of Carlyle was as a fighting soldier.

"Mark my words, no one will be calling Jackson *Tom-Fool* once the real fighting starts," he said mildly. Gordon managed to convey utter disdain with the lifting of one eyebrow. Royce laughed. "Lead the way, brother."

"Tell me why I feel like I'm making a big mistake," said Gordon, and Royce laughed again.

It was early yet, but already the avalanche of carriages from town was under way, jockeying for a good viewing position for the daily afternoon parades. As he and Gordon rode by the parade ground, a woman beckoned to them from inside a black barouche. Normally, Royce ignored the socializing that went on after drill—he was fighting a war, not attending a damn barbecue—but those were the Stannards' carriage horses, and Mrs. Stannard knew she'd been seen.

He wasn't looking forward to his interview with Carlyle anyway. Royce shared a look of mild exasperation with Gordon, then they both nudged their horses toward the open barouche, where three modishly dressed women were seated on the green leather seats.

He tipped his hat to Mrs. Stannard, a lady of Peyton's age and the same charmed circle of Virginia's peerage, and again to Mrs. Chesnut, a recent arrival to Richmond's glittering social scene whose husband was a Confederate congressman from South Carolina. Royce used his polite smile as Mrs. Chesnut made the introduction to the attractive young lady sitting next to her.

Constance Cary, he'd heard that name from John DeShields's lips just last night. Royce flashed his most audacious grin and for the next several minutes flirted unconscionably with Miss Cary, simply for the pleasure of seeing John's riled expression when John, inevitably, heard the tale.

A corporal barked orders, and they all turned their heads to watch a blue-clad Alabama battalion attempt a close-order drill on the parade grounds.

"Every man of them looks a hero," said Miss Cary. "Don't you agree, Major?"

"Well," drawled Royce, allowing the devil to take hold of his tongue, "I'm more reminded of the music at Mrs. Pettigrew's parties, where every guest sings the chorus to the tune he knows best."

Mrs. Chesnut laughed. "Come now, Major Kincaid," she said. "It's an army to be proud of."

In time, yes, an army would emerge out of this motley collection of lords and knaves and innocent, willing country boys. But not yet. "One day, Mrs. Chesnut." He touched the brim of his hat. "Enjoy the parade, ladies."

Gordon, who had remained uncharacteristically silent throughout the entire exchange, made his polite leave-taking and turned his horse so they rode off together. Royce didn't realize the tactical mistake he'd made until he slung his brother a sideways glance and saw the expression on Gordon's face.

"What?" he asked, although he was certain he already knew.

"You were flirting with Miss Cary."

"So?"

Temper flared on Gordon's face. "So you're a married man."

"It's a marriage in name only, and *Annabelle* doesn't want anyone to know. I'm protecting her secret every time I engage in a little innocent flirting in public."

"You're not protecting her. That's the last thing you were thinking about just now."

*The hell I'm not*, thought Royce.

When Annie had looked at him with her soul in her eyes, and he'd suddenly realized exactly what he wanted to do to her, he'd left Riverbend so fast the wind whistled behind him. He hadn't been back, and he hadn't written.

The days were easy; he was kept too busy for all but fleeting thoughts of Annabelle Kincaid. It was the nights that were torture. Too many times he'd awakened with his cock at full staff and his mind cloudy with lingering dreams of cool sheets and moist skin: Annabelle arching up beneath him, tongues and limbs twisting together, and hips mating. He hadn't had a wet dream since he was a fifteen-year-old boy. She'd reduced him to that.

Like hell, he wasn't protecting her.

Royce blew out a breath. "Whatever you're thinking, it's wrong. You don't know me like you think you do."

"I can only hope; otherwise, I'm leading the wolf to the hen-house."

Something edgy and mean was beginning to churn in his belly, so Royce bit back his instinctive response and listened to the soothing rhythm of Ajaque's hooves clip-clopping on cob-blestones, thudding on hard-packed dirt, then a hollow knock-ing as they rode across a small wooden bridge.

In mutual testy silence they left their horses in the care of a corporal from Gordon's company and proceeded on foot. The air was heavy with the scents of gun oil, bacon, and boiled cof-fee. Soldiers swapped insults in loud, carrying voices as they moved between the orderly rows of tents. The sun hung high, bleaching color from a heat-hazed sky.

Royce allowed Gordon to pull ahead of him so it was Gor-don's taller body Carlyle would see first. They came into a small square of hard-packed dirt ringed with tents, and the scent of boiled coffee grew stronger. A half dozen soldiers lounged on folding stools around a camp stove, holding tin mugs in their hands. A black boy was taking down the wash that was hanging from a line strung between tent poles.

Royce stepped from behind his brother's back, and Car-lyle's welcoming smile twisted into a harder, meaner look.

Carlyle said, "Why'd you bring him here, Gordon?"

"You got a problem with him, then tell him to his face."

*Thank you, brother*, thought Royce.

"Your tent?" Royce asked, with an accompanying nod of his head. He could tell by the way Carlyle's eyes slid away from him, then back, that he'd guessed correctly. It was a large can-vas tent, still gleaming white. Naturally—only the best for Carlyle Hallston. Royce wondered where he'd obtained the cash to outfit himself, while his sister was selling her heir-looms to buy mourning dresses.

"Consider that an order, Lieutenant," he said, narrowing his gaze.

Carlyle's mouth parted as if he might speak, but then he closed it and led the way to the tent. Gordon would have fol-lowed them inside, but Royce stopped him with a jerk of his head, and Gordon nodded, then turned back to join the curious watchers around the camp stove.

The air inside was hot and still. Royce let the tent flap fall behind him anyway. Carlyle looked over his shoulder, shrugged, then proceeded to light a lantern. He turned the wick low and hung the lantern by a hook from the ceiling.

Royce removed his slouch hat and looked around. The tent was furnished with two narrow cots, a square wooden table, and a metal trunk. The interior walls were streaked with mildew.

Carlyle lowered his arm and turned. "Well?"

Royce walked over and set his hat on the table beside a small wooden writing desk. He lifted the hinged lid. Inside was one bottle of India ink, writing paper, several quills, and a small knife for cutting the nibs.

"I was going to offer to buy you some writing supplies," he said, fighting back the edge of anger inside him.

Red patches of color suffused Carlyle's pale cheeks. "I wouldn't accept anything from you."

"The offer's been rescinded." Royce let go of the lid so it closed with a satisfying smack. Carlyle closed his eyes, but Royce thought that deep inside him something had flinched.

"Why haven't you written her?"

Carlyle turned halfway away, waving his hand. "I haven't had time."

Royce smiled. "Try a different tack."

A muscle flexed behind Carlyle's jaw, but the gaze he turned back to Royce was filled with an odd kind of bewilderment. "Always the goddamn savior, Royce. Why can't you just let it alone?"

Royce stared back at this man who once, long ago, had been a child running the green lawns at Riverbend, whom he'd once pulled from the river when he got caught in the channel current and saved him from drowning. "Because you matter to your sister," he said. "She's lost her father, her home . . . All she has left in this world are you and Bohannon."

"Bo." Carlyle's eyes closed for a moment, and when they opened again Royce saw genuine anguish in the depths. "I lost my father, my sister, and my little brother. What good is that little house in Lexington if it's empty?" He waited a beat, then carried on. "You bought my sister, the same way you'd buy a black wench for your quarters."

The ground rolled precariously beneath Royce's feet. "You selfish son of a bitch, don't you understand anything?"

"Oh, I understand." Carlyle actually laughed although tension arched his back like a bow. He looked down and saw that his fists were clenched, and he relaxed them, splaying his long fingers out wide. "How many men have you killed, Major Kincaid? Would you believe I've never killed anybody? I've never owned anybody either."

The edge was rushing Royce now, like the roar of a cataract. Part of him was aware that Carlyle was stepping toward him at last. He could hear Carlyle's breathing, smell Carlyle's sweat.

Carlyle stopped in front of him and spread his hands out from his sides. Sweat glistened on his upper lip and held a lock of sandy hair against his forehead like sticking plaster.

The red flood receded. "I didn't come here to fight with you," Royce said, pitching his voice soft and low. He touched the scarred top of the writing desk with one finger. "Just write her so she knows you're all right. That's all."

"What am I supposed to say? Dearest sister of mine, I had to choose between you and the army and because I chose honor over duty, you've become Royce Kincaid's whore?"

Royce smiled and shook his head, and let fly with a left jab to Carlyle's mouth that sent blood and spittle spraying into the air.

The punch didn't knock Carlyle to the ground, but it sent him staggering. His leg clipped the corner of the metal trunk, and that spun him around and he fell to his knees, letting go with a grunt and great whoosh of breath as his upper torso splayed across the cot. He pushed himself up with both hands, but by the time he'd turned to rush Royce, Gordon was between them, arms extended.

"Royce, dammit!" said Gordon, and when Royce only shook his head, Gordon turned, placing both palms flat on Carlyle's heaving chest, and shoved. Carlyle resisted, his chest pitching forward even while Gordon was forcing reluctant backward steps.

"Stop it," Gordon said. "Stop. Do you want every soldier outside this tent to know what's going on in here?"

Carlyle made a sound like a rag tearing, then the backs of his legs hit the cot and he sat hard. Blood ran from the gash across his mouth, dripped from his jaw, and stained the front of his gray tunic jacket.

Royce had a sudden vision of Annabelle hunched over the

sewing machine at Riverbend, making the gray dress uniform stored in his own army trunk. She'd made her brother's tunic jacket; Royce knew it, and the first band of guilt tightened his chest.

He could still feel the blood pulsing in his neck, but his hands felt useless and heavy at his sides. He closed them into fists, then opened them, closed and opened, closed and opened, and breathed slowly through his nostrils.

Carlyle slumped forward and covered his bruised and bloody face with his hands. "Oh, God, Annie," he choked. "I'm sorry. I'm so sorry."

Gordon pulled a handkerchief out of his pocket. "Wait outside, Royce."

Royce made himself smile like the mean-assed bastard he was supposed to be. "He asked for that one."

"Tell it to your wife next time you see her."

Royce picked up his hat. He looked back once, from the tent flap. Gordon was on his haunches in front of Carlyle, gently wiping the blood from his jaw.

Royce drew in a deep breath, smelling the mud in the drainage ditch and the hot wood at his back. He was outside, leaning against a quartermaster's depot, although he didn't know how long he'd been standing there.

Gordon stood in front of him. Warm color flushed his face.

"Is he all right?" asked Royce. It was a rhetorical question. The Carlyles of the world always cried foul, and someone came along to put the game right for them again. Gordon shrugged.

Royce's gaze cut away. In a vacant part of the bivouac across the drainage ditch some soldiers were playing baseball. The smack of the bat against the ball echoed in the humid air. His hand hurt. He made a fist and looked down at the raw place where the skin had split across his knuckles.

"That wasn't like you," said Gordon. He was leaning against the building now, too, with his arms crossed over his chest, his lids half-lowered against the brassy glare of the sun. "What did he say that caused you to lose control?"

Royce cradled his bruised hand and shut his eyes. A wrenching guilt ran through him. "It doesn't matter," he said, his voice feeling thick in his throat. "He hit close to home, that's all."

Royce wanted to tell his brother he was wrong about him, that Royce Kincaid wasn't hard or tough or unfeeling. But he could find no words inside to show he was only another man fighting to find his way through this life with the least amount of pain to himself, or to those he treasured.

No words inside him, and no hope. *Maybe,* he thought, *if you lived the lie long enough, you would come to believe it yourself, and then it became your truth.*

"Whatever he said that set you off," Gordon said, "it was his shame doing the talking. That's why he hasn't written her and probably won't write her anytime soon after what happened today. I feel ashamed myself whenever I remember I wasn't there with her in Lexington. She'd asked me to come, did you know that?"

"No," said Royce. A Negro woman wearing a yellow turban was going through the camp on the other side of the ditch, selling fresh strawberries from a wheelbarrow. He watched her for a while, then said, "Annabelle did fine that day, all on her own. You'd have been proud of her."

He squinted, checking the angle of the sun. "I have to be getting back." Royce pushed away from the wall. Gordon moved with him, and Royce slanted him a glance. "Are you going to Riverbend anytime soon?"

"I've got a four-day leave starting Thursday," Gordon said. "I won't say anything about this to Annabelle."

Gordon moved away and went to the ditch, crossing it with one long-legged bound. He went a few rows back in the tents, where the Negro woman was selling her strawberries. Royce kept going around the outer perimeter of the encampment, toward the far western side, where his troop was bivouacked.

A supply wagon lumbered by, chain traces rattling, gritty dust boiling around the wheels. The mule skinner leaned over the side and hawked a glob of spit. Royce wiped the perspiration from his brow with the back of his sleeve and watched Gordon come back carrying several plump strawberries.

Gordon picked the green caps off with his thumbnail, tossed them to the ground, and popped one whole strawberry into his mouth. He chewed, and his mouth puckered at the tart sweetness of it, the way a child would do.

It was part of a Virginia childhood, thought Royce, eating ripe strawberries fresh from the field. He had done it, and Gordon had done it, but it was one of the many things they had never done together. They were eight years distant in age, and when you are a child, eight years is an unbridgeable chasm.

Gordon reached for his handkerchief, muttering a mild curse when he couldn't find it. Royce handed him his own.

"I'd like you to stand up with me at my wedding," Gordon said as he wiped the sticky juice off his mouth.

Images tugged at the edges of Royce's thoughts: Annabelle, her face white and pinched as she stood beside him in Riverbend's formal parlor, taking their civil vows. Annabelle turning to him for a bridal kiss, and him giving her only a sardonic smile. Royce and Gordon standing together on one side of the room, watching her serious face watch them back, as she stood all alone. It shamed him to remember it was Gordon who had gone to her.

Gordon blew a hollow laugh through his nose. "You are coming?"

"God willing," said Royce. Gnats and mosquitoes boiled up from the drainage ditch, hovering in a swarm over the thin strip of saw grass. Royce leaped the ditch, and Gordon followed. "If something keeps me away, ask Bo."

Gordon laughed. "He'd like that, wouldn't he."

They passed through a pool of shadow made by an oak tree. His boots crushed the dried acorns that lay scattered on ground that would be a morass of ankle-deep mud at the next heavy rain.

Somewhere in the distance a long-winded bugler struggled with the notes to reveille. On an empty patch of field nearby a cadet officer was drilling a cavalry company, horse's hooves clip-clopping on hard dirt, spurs and bits jangling, crying out in a high-pitched voice, "Stand to horse! Mount! No! Ragged! Ragged!"

"Do you ever wonder why you're doing this?" said Gordon at his shoulder. "Sophie and Holder raised you; I had Jules for all those times no one else was around to care. Yet here we are, both of us wearing gray uniforms."

The high white sun had turned the day into a scorcher, and the cook fires in front of the mess tents sent more heat waves floating into the sky. Royce breathed in the stench of a shallow latrine trench and listened to the constant drone of thousands of men going about their business. Riverbend seemed so distant from this madness it might have been nothing more than imagination.

He would be pulling his own men out of this breeding ground for disease and back to the healthier air of the mountains, within hours. Royce stopped and gazed out over the sea of billowing white tents.

"No more than a quarter of these soldiers own slaves," he said.

"So maybe they're asking themselves the same thing. What brought us to this?"

Royce shrugged. "Slavery for certain, and the way that issue is all caught up in state sovereignty. Unfair tariffs, Northern control of credit, the way the North raised a fanatical abolitionist to the status of martyr—and there you're touching on slavery again. The constitutional right of secession. Ask any man out there, and you'd hear all those reasons and more."

Royce watched a South Carolina palmetto flag flutter in the hot breeze. He thought he could hear a banjo playing, but it seemed a long way off.

Gordon said, "If you'd gone with the North, I'd have gone with you."

Oh God, the pain of it. Royce closed his eyes and took a moment to concentrate on breathing. He was not his brother's keeper, but always—*always*—he'd felt he had to be.

When he had himself under control he said quietly, "How did you know I was even thinking that?"

"Brothers," said Gordon, and Royce heard a smile in his voice. "I watched you that week we spent together in Richmond last April. Even when we seceded I could tell you were still fighting a battle with your own principles. You're not fighting it anymore."

"No," said Royce. "I'm not."

"What changed?"

"They invaded Alexandria, and it wasn't theoretical anymore. I knew then that not even for Clarence's sake—God forgive me—there was no way I could raise my sword against my native state."

He looked at his brother's face: the arresting dark blue eyes, the film of hot dampness on the strong arch of cheekbones, the wide mobile mouth that had always smiled and laughed so easily. Royce suddenly felt a wrenching fear that God, the Prankster, would ensure that he'd never see Gordon looking so vitally alive, so damn beautiful, again in this world.

Because he *was* his brother's keeper after all, and because of him, Gordon had stayed with the South.

Royce reached for a casual tone of voice. "Come to my tent tonight," he said. "I've got a half bottle of good sour mash left."

Gordon took his hat in his hands, studying it as he turned it around and around. Then he looked up, and their gazes locked.

*You're riding out again,* said the look in those deep blue eyes.

Royce blinked once: *yes.*

It happened on a cool misty morning near the iron spans of the Cheat River viaduct. The fighting was desperate—with pistol, saber, bayonet, and fist. There was such a tornado of noise and smoke that it took Royce a moment to realize that the hammer on his Navy Colt was falling on an empty chamber.

He shoved the empty gun in a saddle holster, shifted the reins, and drew his last loaded revolver from his hip holster with his freed hand. Royce raised up in his stirrups, waving his arm in a circle and shouting. Ajaque pivoted beneath him, and the fighting withdrawal was under way.

Royce was through and beyond the Federal line, carbine and revolvers all spent, with Savage riding hard beside him. He threw a glance over his shoulder just as John's horse stumbled into a cattle guard, unseating its rider.

John rolled and was up, grabbing for his horse, but he was set upon by two, then three men who pummeled him to the ground. Royce pulled back hard on the reins, so that Ajaque reared and swung around.

*Surrender, John,* flashed through his mind at the same moment he realized the Federals were not giving John a chance to surrender. Blue-sleeved arms raised a bayonet in a two-fisted grip, and brought it down. John screamed.

Royce spurred Ajaque. He galloped back through his own retreating column, swamped by a red tide of fury, only marginally aware that his own men were stopping, swinging around, beginning to raise weapons. Lead bullets danced around him like hail.

He heard Savage yell, "Shit!" then the staccato burst of carbines, giving him cover. He didn't remember what came after.

Now, Royce was on foot and someone was calling his name, he thought it might be Savage, but Royce didn't answer for he was scrabbling over the bloody, littered ground, dragging his right leg because it was throbbing and didn't want to work properly. He knelt beside John DeShields and covered the hole in the man's groin with his hands. Dark crimson blood ran hot through his fingers.

John's eyes fluttered open and focused on his. "I forgive you," he said, the words faint and huffy, "for flirting with Miss Cary."

"Miss Cary was flirting with me. She knows a better man when she sees one." Sweat poured down his temples and into his eyes and Royce tried to jerk it away with a toss of his head, but the motion made him dizzy. "I don't fall off my horse."

"Damn fools, the both of you," muttered Savage, kneeling on the ground beside them. He gently nudged Royce's hands away and pressed a thick wad of bandages on John's wound. "You'll make it, DeShields," he said. "Can't have all those pretty ladies in mourning."

Royce realized the men were already beginning the business of searching the dead and tending to the wounded. Somehow a retreat had been turned into a victory, and his mind held none of the images. Sometimes it was better that way, although he'd have to pick Savage's brain later when they were alone.

"Parker," called Savage. "Get over here and wrap the major's leg. Geary, bring up the ambulance for Captain DeShields."

"Sergeant Savage," said Royce, "both of those men outrank you."

Savage wasn't amused. He was almost foaming through his chin whiskers. "Just what do you think I am, a four-handed monkey?"

Royce dropped his chin and looked, in some bemusement, at the angry saber slash on his outer thigh, then flopped over on his back. The ground was still cool, and moisture seeped through his tunic and shirt to his skin.

"God *is* a prankster," he said, allowing his eyes to shut.

# Chapter 10

"Tired, Annie-girl?"

"No," she lied, gratefully leaning against Peyton's strong body as he slipped his arm around her waist and gave her a gentle squeeze.

"Well, I have to admit I am. In my day, weddings weren't these rushed affairs we've been racing to over the past weeks."

Annabelle watched couples form for the opening reel, Gordon and Augusta in the place of honor at the head of the line, their faces lit with a soft glow that had nothing to do with the hundreds of beeswax candles illuminating Riverbend's parlors.

Peyton was right. Since early June, they'd attended three weddings in the county, propriety and courtship rituals having been pushed aside in the rush of war preparations. Together, she and Peyton had spent the past several weeks in a flurry of activity, readying Riverbend to host the wedding of Gordon Kincaid to Augusta Raleigh, a wedding the *Fredericksburg News* dubbed the social event of the year.

The house brimmed with guests, including most of the county's soldiers, home on furlough. Colonel Stuart had sent his regrets but, magnanimously, given Gordon five days leave while the Southern army continued to form its ranks.

Now, as a cloud-tossed moon rose over the river, with the formal ceremony behind them, the ladies rested and the gentlemen fed, the musicians took their place at the top of the parlor. Tonight, the laughing, gray-clad men formed ranks with young ladies dressed in their finest organdies and silks. Long, strong legs, as adept at dancing as they were at riding, quick-marched through the dance figures, flashing stripes of artillery red and cavalry yellow.

Peyton nudged her, and Annabelle pulled her gaze from the kaleidoscope of reeling color and looked at him. His face was lit with a soft smile as he nodded toward the corner.

"You'll have to teach him to bow," she murmured, watching Bo's ungainly efforts at courting a very young lady.

"He seems to be doing fine without my help," said Peyton, as the young lady blushingly dipped into a curtsy.

A gentle rain throughout the afternoon had forced the party inside, but watching Bo, she was reminded of those other Riverbend dances, those soft, summer nights when she and Carlyle had practiced dance steps beneath the cover of the old oak trees. How she missed him. Even the wedding of his best friend hadn't weakened his resolve. She shoved that lingering ache aside.

"Aren't you supposed to dance with the bride next?" she asked.

"The bride, then the bride's mother," said Peyton with a small sigh. "And how many cousins does she have here to-night?"

"At least a dozen." Annabelle tried hard not to laugh at the grimace that passed across Peyton's face. "Don't forget me, you must save one for me," she added teasingly.

"That one I'll enjoy, so don't fill up your dance card."

*Not very likely*, she thought, as he stepped into the milling crowd. Since she was intent on being the perfect hostess for this, her first effort, she sidled backward into the hallway. So many small details to attend to. She backed into an immovable object, the impact sending the front of her hoop skirt sailing upward. She managed to get her hands forward to stop the motion somewhere short of total humiliation.

"Whoa, little wife." Royce grabbed her waist and turned her.

She squinted her eyes closed, afraid to look at him, even with the humor in his voice. "I didn't hurt you, did I?"

"If a Yankee bullet couldn't unseat me, I'm sure you haven't a chance."

Her stomach knotted with a newfound fear. Until he'd arrived home two days earlier, no one had known of his wounding. Even now, he kept silent on how and when he'd received the wound although the gossip and rumors she'd heard today placed him everywhere from the Ohio River to the outskirts of Washington, before the first battle had even been fought.

"Where's your cane?"

"A blackhearted scoundrel can't dance with a cane," he said, guiding her back into the makeshift ballroom.

He looked dashing in his full-dress uniform, a fitted, gray coat with buff collar and cuffs. A wide gold sash circled his trim waistline, the effect emphasizing the breadth of his shoulders. His pants were the regulation dark blue she'd made for him months ago, but somewhere, he'd had a tailor add the narrow, gold braid down the outer seams. The total effect was stunning, and she thought he lacked only an ostrich-plumed slouch hat to be the cavalier of her dreams.

His arm settled around her waist and the knot in her belly tightened. She spoke to the double row of brass buttons on his coat. "Is it my imagination, or is everyone staring at us?"

"Gordon has eyes only for his new wife. Otherwise, you're about right. I really must speak to your chaperone about whom you're allowed to dance with tonight."

"I don't have a chaperone."

"Then I'm impelled by my better nature to perform the duty. My conscience has a thousand tongues and I try to listen to one or two occasionally."

"And every tale condemns you for a villain," she teased.

"The Bard knew of what he spoke, dear heart." His palm pressed against her back as he led her in a sweeping circle. "With my extensive knowledge of villainous behavior, you couldn't ask for a better chaperone. In spite of the temptation, you'll shutter that little defiant soul of yours tonight and follow my instructions. No more than three dances with any one scoundrel, no champagne, no scandalous waltzes."

"Isn't this a scandalous waltz?"

"True, but I'm the chaperone. It's a comedown for me, and I

hope you appreciate that my own reputation will be in shreds before the night's over."

She looked up, ready to laugh. His lips turned at the corners so his dimple appeared. Their gazes locked and held. His smile thinned and she looked away as a shivery sensation raced through her. She seemed to have forgotten everything she ever knew about dancing and tripped over his boot, causing them to miss a step.

"Drat," she muttered.

"I really must teach you to curse properly. Drat has way too much starch."

"Not starch—soap," she said, with a slight giggle that came from budding craziness. "I ate more than one bar of soap for saying *drat* where Mama could hear me."

"What makes me suspect you saw that as an invitation to blow bubbles?"

The laughter came. She tried to hold it back with her lips, but it burst out in the form of an unladylike snort. She looked over his shoulder, unwilling to meet his gaze, certain he would be laughing at her.

Candlelight and shimmering jewels reflected back from the pier mirrors. The room spun crazily around her, and she blinked. His thigh pressed against her leg, and she felt the hardness of his body before he took another step and they parted.

She looked up and lost her breath. He held his gaze on her face, her mouth, and it was as if he caressed her with a look. She fought back a shudder as that shivery feeling raced through her once more.

*It's only a dream*, she told herself. She tried to think of something to say, but her mind wouldn't work, so she closed her eyes and basked in his warmth while her feet floated on the strains of the music.

*We loved each other then, Lorena, more than we ever dared to tell.*

He faltered as he took his weight on his injured leg and although he tried to hide it, she knew it pained him. "Royce."

His hand burned into her back as he gathered her closer. "Dance, little wife," he murmured, sweeping her into a glide as if to prove his manliness against his pain. Her chest grew so tight she could hardly breathe.

*Our heads will soon lie low, Lorena, Life's tide is ebbing out so fast . . .*

She tried to shut out the words and the music as an ache of tears swelled up inside her. Dip and glide; Royce's arm around her waist. This wasn't part of the dream, but then, she was no longer a child. A woman now, in a war-torn land, she knew the fear that went hand in hand with the dream.

"It's only a song, Annabelle."

"Yes, it's only a song," she whispered, finding the courage to meet his gaze and wondering how he'd read her mind.

The gray fog lifted in his eyes, and she thought she saw clear to his tortured soul. "Is it so awful to love?" she asked in a small voice.

"Yes, little wife. So don't make the mistake."

"You're wrong."

"Don't do this to yourself, Annabelle."

"But I'm your wife. I *want* to be your wife in every sense." Pain flashed across his face, and this time, she knew it didn't come from his wounded leg. "And you want me."

She didn't care that her voice broke with those words. She'd seen love in his eyes. And denial. He took her hand and pulled her after him, down the hallway to where it jogged toward the porte cochére. Mercifully, they were alone there, if only for a minute.

"I'm only going to say this once," he said in that quiet, menacing tone. "Our marriage is a charade that ends in five years. I do *not* want you for a wife. I never did and never will. You're not my type of woman, Annabelle. Leave it at that."

"You're lying."

"You're determined to make me hurt you, aren't you?"

"I'm determined to make you face the truth." She placed her hands on his chest and felt him flinch, then harden, at her touch. "Kiss me," she said.

"No."

She leaned up on her toes, bringing her face as close to his as she could get. His breath was moist and hot against her mouth. "You, Major Kincaid, are a coward."

A muscle jumped along his jaw, but his eyes remained veiled in that gray mist he used so well. He pushed her away. "I like my women lush and loose. You don't qualify in either sense." A mean smile hovered at the corner of his lips. "Loose, you're improving on."

"I'll just have to practice some more."

She swung around, determined to hide her own hurt and equally determined to spend the rest of this suddenly horrid night learning how to be a loose woman. Lush, she'd given up on years ago. He reached out and grabbed her wrist, swinging her back around, squeezing so hard she wanted to wince.

"You'll behave like your mother's daughter," he said.

"I'll play by the same rules you do."

"There *are* no rules in this game, Annabelle. You're playing with a fire you don't understand. Don't blame me when you get burned."

She was already nothing but ashes inside, but she'd die before she let him see that. "Just because you don't want me, Major Kincaid, doesn't mean nobody else will."

She gave a toss of her head, just for practice. His gaze settled on her mouth. She felt helpless with fright and an odd kind of excitement. He acknowledged no rules, no rules in love or war, and she was playing his game.

A burst of laughter sounded nearby, followed immediately by the appearance of the Pettigrew twins. She saw the mask slip over Royce's features and hoped she did as well in hiding her own tumultuous emotion.

"I say, old boy," said Chauncey Pettigrew. "You had to go and beat the rest of us to the war." His fist pummeled into Royce's shoulder. "If you won't tell us where the fighting is, the least you can do is show us where the good bourbon's hidden."

"Try the dining room." Royce's gaze flicked from Chauncey's face back to her, as if warning her to behave or accept the consequences.

"Major Kincaid's leg is bothering him," she said, smiling at Chauncey. "I'll show you."

The twins exchanged a startled look. She wondered if she ought to smile more often. But then, maybe that startled look came only because they never expected to see plain Annie with the scourge of the county's young flowers.

"Show both of us," said Willis. He crooked his arm. "The major's been guarding you all evening. Time for us lesser mortals to have a shot, don't you agree?"

"No." Royce stepped between the twins, taking each by the elbow. "I don't agree. However, I'll join you in a drink." He ushered them down the hallway with the practiced ease of a stout mammy before she could gather her wits enough to make a stab at wanton behavior.

She leaned her back against the wall, easing the burden on her rubbery legs. Chauncey slung her a lewd wink over his shoulder, and she covered her hand with her mouth in a vain attempt to hold back a giggle. Almost immediately, the crazy giggle transformed into a sob. She rubbed her face with her hands, and when she took them away, she saw a movement in the shadows down the narrow hall.

"Miz Annabelle, I didn't mean to listen," said Patsy, coming forward into the light. She held a silver drink tray in her hands while her face heated with a strange blush. Annabelle sensed the servant's fear. "I just didn't have nowhere to go without Marse Royce seeing me."

"It's all right," she said, reaching for her cover of pride. "Just, please, don't say anything to anybody."

"Loving don't never come easy, Miz Annabelle, and I think you ought to know your marriage isn't a secret here. All the colored folks know about it, but they're keeping quiet because they like you."

"Dear merciful heaven," she whispered, as humiliation washed over her in waves. She slung her head back and swallowed. Patsy's hand landed on her forearm.

"Some dreams are worth the heartache," said Patsy in a quiet, husky voice.

Annabelle placed her hand over Patsy's. Every woman learned the danger in dreaming. Sometimes, the dreams came true.

The moon rose higher as time sped by in a whirl of color and sound and motion. Annabelle had no intention of watching Royce, and it didn't matter. He lived up to his threat and watched her. She was becoming exceedingly tired of her self-appointed chaperone. How could a lady act loose when Major Kincaid swept down like an avenging angel on every effort?

She saw Chauncey's face go flat and knew the trumpeter of the Last Judgment was swooping in behind her. She smiled at

Chauncey, who gave her another lewd wink. He was actually quite good at that winking business. She'd flutter her lashes for him if she only knew how.

Royce took the fluted glass out of her hand and held it up to his nose. She gave him an innocent look. "Lemonade," she said sweetly.

"Humph." He handed the glass to Chauncey and grasped her elbow. "Sorry, Lieutenant, you've already danced three times with Miss Hallston."

"You're quite good at snorting, Major." She lifted her hand and waggled her fingers over her shoulder for Chauncey's benefit. Royce pulled her hand back down.

"I have never made such a ludicrous sound as a snort in my entire life," he said.

"Humph." She thought she heard him chuckle. "Who are you giving me to this time?"

"Leighton."

"Goodness gracious, but you've given me to him five times already." She huffed a breath so he'd recognize her disgust. "I won't be able to walk tomorrow if he steps on my feet one more time."

"You won't be able to walk tomorrow if I catch you with Chauncey one more time."

She tilted her head with what she hoped was a flirtatious air. "Jealous, Major?"

"No. And tomorrow you'll thank me for protecting you from yourself."

"Not bloody likely."

He squeezed her elbow so hard she flinched. She fluttered her fan in front of her face as Royce handed her over to Leighton with orders to bring her back at the end of the polka. She'd sidestepped that admonishment four times already and wondered when her husband was finally going to recognize that small triumph on her part.

Her cheeks were sore from so many smiles, but she forced another one. Leighton's baggy lids blinked several times. She entertained herself by picturing Corporal Leighton Sumner forty years hence. By then, his heavy jowls would probably be resting somewhere in the vicinity of his collarbone. She'd giggle at the thought if the tears weren't closer to the surface. She and Leighton were actually well suited to one another; both of them something less than beautiful and totally inept in ballroom skills.

Good gracious, he was asking her a question, and she hadn't been listening. She winced as his foot landed on her toes and managed a small smile. "I'm sorry, Leighton," she apologized, "but I didn't hear you over the music."

"I said, do you think I should speak to Major Kincaid or to Mr. Peyton?"

She shook her head, trying to clear the fuzziness. "About what?"

"Permission to come courting." Leighton's cheeks jostled with his earnestness. "That is, if you don't mind, Miss Hallston."

Her first and only proposal, from a man she didn't love, and she was already married to a man who wouldn't love her. She wondered which ancient god was playing this ludicrous trick. Her heart actually went out to dear, earnest Leighton. He was too nice to suffer hurt, especially from someone as mean-spirited as her.

If only Livvy were here. She could dash off to the corner, grab some advice, and dash back. Livvy wasn't here. She was on her own.

"Would you escort me to the supper room?" He looked so relieved, she almost laughed. By the time they'd worked their way through the crowd, she'd concocted her story, and the tale had so much truth involved, she didn't even feel guilty.

". . . and so you see, Leighton," she finished with a theatrical sigh, "it has nothing to do with you. You're much too worthy for me. It's my own broken heart that must heal before I can love another."

"Miss Hallston, war is a terrible thing." He handed her a flute of champagne and lifted his own in a toast. "To true love and hearts that mend."

She'd drink to that. She did. Dimly, she became aware the polka had ended. Time to avoid her dark guardian angel. "Will you excuse me, Leighton," she said with an earnestness that matched his own. "I really must check the kitchen; the trays in here need to be refilled."

He bowed. She escaped. Willis Pettigrew captured her on her way back into the ballroom.

"Isn't my name on your dance card for the next mazurka?"

She didn't remember stopping for anyone's name on her dance card. She'd been too busy trying to avoid Major Kincaid, anger Major Kincaid, and keep the food and drinks coming in all the while. Not that it mattered; Willis swept her onto the dance floor anyway. He danced like a dancing instructor and she gave herself over to the whirling fun. Something stopped her midwhirl. She huffed another breath and turned around, planting her hands on her hips.

"*Really*, Major."

"Four dances with Willis." Royce shook his head. "Not allowed."

Willis rubbed his handlebar mustache with his thumb, but she saw the smile peeking out beneath. "He's more than a little insufferable tonight, don't you think, Annie?"

"Humph." Royce took her elbow and steered her away. She lifted her hand and waggled her fingers over her shoulder.

"Would you stop that," muttered Royce.

"When you stop snorting."

"I don't snort."

She saw no point in arguing with him. "Who this time?"

"Peyton."

"At least my toes are safe."

"Humph."

She slanted a glance at Royce's face. He didn't look the least bit amused. The smile she gave Peyton was real and didn't even hurt her overworked muscles.

"Who's left she can dance with when we're done?" asked Peyton.

"You, Gordon, and Leighton," said Royce.

"Not Leighton. I think he's already proposed to every female in the county at least once. Sweet thing he is, he didn't want to leave me out." Royce lifted a brow. She tweaked him a grin. "I told him my heart belonged to another."

"Humph."

"If he does that one more time, you're going to have to build him a bull pen." Annabelle watched Peyton fight the tremors at the corners of his lips. She didn't want to look at the snorting bull.

"Dance with me, Annie-girl." Peyton swept her into a waltz. "I don't know what you're doing, but don't stop now."

"Oh, Father, I don't know." She wanted to bury her head in his chest and weep. He seemed to sense her ache, drawing her in a little closer.

"Laugh, child. It hurts less," he said softly.

She looked up at his face and saw understanding in his eyes. She settled against him, and they finished the waltz in comfortable silence.

"A glass of champagne is what I recommend." Peyton placed his hand on the small of her back and steered her forward, somehow managing to avoid Royce. He reached out and lifted two glasses from a passing servant's tray. They settled against the wall, partially hidden between two large ficus plants.

She took a sip of the champagne and regretted it. The bubbles refused to stay in her stomach and kept rising back into her throat. She took another sip to hold them down.

Her gaze settled on Royce. He leaned insolently against a pillar while he talked with a tall, golden-haired girl. She said something that caused him to throw back his head and laugh. Suzannah Pruitt; she was tall and lush and had a hundred beaux. Annabelle swallowed against the bubbles floating in the emptiness inside her. Peyton followed the direction of her look.

"He's not interested in the Pruitt girl," he said.

"He's not interested in me, either."

"Not so, Annie-girl, not so." Peyton took the glass from her hand and set it on a small table. "Another dance with an old man?"

She shook her head. "I need some fresh air. But would you mind checking the supper trays for me?"

"Consider it done."

They split up, Peyton toward the dining room, Annabelle toward the gallery. Someone had lit the Chinese lanterns along the paths. Soft light glinted off wet grass, so each raindrop seemed a sparkling star fallen from the heavens. The night air drifted lazily through the magnolia leaves. She stopped at the edge of the porch, taking in the perfection. The devil inside her wanted to blow milkweed seeds over the manicured grounds. The child inside her wanted to cry while the woman she was only ached.

She strolled down to the end of the gallery, away from the light spilling through the windows. The night breeze brushed her bare shoulders, and she shivered. Leaning against the last column, she closed her eyes and listened to the music. Time stood still.

"If I'd known you were cold, I'd have brought you a shawl instead of champagne."

She started herself back to reality, suddenly aware she'd been rubbing her arms. She couldn't find a smile for Chauncey; she was too tired and too achy.

"Not cold, just overheated." Manners forced her to accept the glass he held out, but she shook her head. "I don't know . . . I think I've had too much champagne already."

"No such thing." With that comment, she smiled, and Chauncey smiled back. He nodded toward one of the dark oaks. "Remember the time you got stuck up in that tree?"

"I wasn't stuck. I just hadn't figured a way down yet."

He gave a quiet laugh. "You were always different from the rest of the girls. None of us knew what to make of you then."

"Not much has changed." She watched the bubbles rise to the top of the glass and die a sudden death. Her own was lingering. "Chauncey, even if I knew how to flirt with you, which I don't, I'm too tired to make the effort."

"The world is full of flirts, most of whom are boring as heck. Don't try to fit yourself in that mold."

She looked at him, startled beyond measure.

"I'm not flirting with you, Annie. I'm asking if we can still be friends, like in the old days."

She wondered if he could see the tears filling her eyes. For a moment, she couldn't speak over the lump in her throat. His hand lifted and brushed a loose wisp of hair off her cheek.

"If I were your beau, I couldn't do that. But since I'm your friend, I can," he said in a soft voice. "And I can listen and try to help."

The knot in her throat grew larger while the tears threatened to spill over. She took a sip of champagne and managed to dislodge the lump in her throat.

"Where's Carlyle?" he asked. "It's not like him to miss Gordon's wedding, and all the rest of us got furloughs when we asked for them."

"It's me. He doesn't want me here."

"He never did like Royce."

"Chauncey, I didn't say anything about Royce."

"You didn't have to, sweetheart. It's as plain as that pretty little nose on your pretty little face."

She could laugh, or she could cry. Peyton said laughing hurt less, so she laughed. Not much, but enough.

"Do you want to talk about it?" he asked.

"No."

He shifted his position and gazed over her shoulder. "Then I'll tell you about Major Kincaid. Rumor has it he turned down the commission that went to Stuart, which is more than rumor, it's true." She gave him another startled look. "My father's in the War Department, remember?" She nodded.

"Royce fought like the devil to get a detachment, all regular cavalry instead of Partisans, but the idea's the same. Small, guerrilla bands striking the rear and stinging the Union Army to death. As usual, he's good—too good for his own health. His raids are already filling the Union papers as well as our own. I know you've read them; the one about the child picket he captured and sent home was all over the papers."

"The Last Cavalier," she murmured, suddenly realizing that somewhere deep in her heart, she'd known the softhearted warrior was Royce Kincaid.

Chauncey hesitated, then lifted a shrug. "They haven't discovered who it is yet; but they will eventually, and if we lose this war, he'll be in about as deep a mess as Jeff Davis."

"Why are you telling me this?"

"Because you need to know what might happen, and the Kincaids won't tell you. They'll die protecting you from life's harsh realities without stopping to think the deception can hurt you more."

She heard something in his voice. "You admire him, don't you?"

"I'd give my grandfather's Revolutionary War saber for the chance to ride with him."

A movement caught her eye. "Then I'd suggest you skedaddle because the cavalier is on his way—intent on protecting my virtue."

Chauncey's mustache twitched. "Don't you dare drop that glass of champagne," he said, as his arms swept her into an embrace.

"Chauncey—"

"Doggone it, Annie, stop laughing and act serious."

"Stop grinning, and maybe I can."

"Right." He replaced his grin with a lewd snicker that would do any villain proud. She dropped her forehead on his chest. He swung around so his broad back hid her quaking shoulders from Royce's view.

"Stop laughing," he murmured on a low breath.

"You're tickling me," she muttered, then laughed harder as he prodded the small of her back with his thumb.

"*Lieutenant.*"

*There went Chauncey's prospects of riding with Major Kincaid,* she thought. Chauncey didn't seem disturbed and didn't skedaddle either, although he did let her go. She decided he was both brave enough and dumb enough to be a stinging guerrilla. She tried to avoid looking at her husband. Royce reached for her glass. She cradled it against her chest.

"Champagne," she said in her prim lady's voice.

"Methodist ladies don't drink champagne."

Merciful heaven, he was not amused. She slanted a glance at Chauncey. He was very amused.

"I'm an Episcopalian lady now." She lifted the glass and took a deep swallow. She blinked back the sudden moisture in her eyes. "Tell him you saw me at church last Sunday, Chauncey."

"Sure did," drawled Chauncey. "And pretty as an angel on her first communion."

She gave Chauncey a look of disgust. He shrugged as if to say that was the best he could do on short notice. Sudden, crazy laughter rose in her chest. Royce made a motion to reach for her glass. She quaffed down the remains and held the empty crystal out for him. Royce handed the empty glass to Chauncey.

"Skedaddle, Lieutenant."

"Ohhh, I don't know . . ."

*Very dumb, Chauncey,* she thought. Royce shot him one of those looks that would freeze a flowing river in August. Chauncey backed up, maintaining his air of insolence. He even winked.

"Save me a waltz, Annie."

She waggled her fingers. Royce grabbed her wrist.

"How much bloody damn champagne have you had tonight?"

"A good bar of lye soap would cure that gutter language."

She felt proud of her swift retort until she remembered he'd never known a mother's love, let alone one who loved him enough to wash his mouth with soap. Another piece of her heart cracked loose and fell away into that bottomless pit inside her. She closed her eyes and willed him to let go of her wrist. If he didn't let go, she thought she'd break into a million pieces and float away like the champagne bubbles, float up and up . . . until she popped and died.

She swayed, and he didn't let go. His arm came around her waist.

"No. Don't," she pleaded.

"You're going to fall down otherwise."

"Wrong." She nudged her chin up and pulled away. She leaned against the column and gazed out on the lawn, avoiding the silver glare in his eyes.

"How much champagne have you had?"

She didn't know how he could make a question sound like an accusation, but whatever his secret, he was really quite effective.

She fisted her hand, holding it in the air between them. "Leighton," she said, raising her forefinger. "Peyton." Second finger. "And Chauncey." She wiggled her fingers. "Three."

"You are an abject failure as a loose woman."

He might as well have said, *You're a failure as a woman.* He'd be right either way. Her hand dropped heavy at her side. She closed her eyes and leaned her head back, drawing in the scents of hot summer night and angry man. Inside was light and laughter and love. Out here was night and silence and pain.

The silence grew, and grew. She sucked in a deep breath that caught on the jagged edges of her heart and hurt. He stood so close, she couldn't move without brushing him, and her skin was too fragile to bear touching him. But she couldn't stand here, breathing the same air and sharing nothing. She straightened her spine and tried to sidle around the pillar. He reached out and snagged her arm.

"Chauncey Pettigrew is engaged to a girl in Richmond."

"She's a lucky girl."

"Annie, what the bloody hell is going on?"

He let her arm drop, and she forced herself to look at him. The clouds parted, and moonlight washed the harsh planes of his face with a silvery glow. He was all those heroes of her dreams, a cavalier sculpted in moonbeams, masculine and beautiful, and she was . . .

She was plain Annie.

"I guess I can't hide things like you can. Chauncey thought he could help by making you jealous. If he'd given me a chance, I'd have disabused him of the notion." Muggy river air brushed her face, too thick to breathe. "I can't even hate you for making me look like the pea-brain I am."

His chest expanded in a deep sigh. "You're right, you can't."

"Even a blackhearted scoundrel could have argued a little."

"Our marriage had nothing to do with love, dammit!"

The bubbles inside her burst in a tremendous explosion of pain. She whirled and took two stumbling steps onto the lawn.

"Oh, bloody damn!"

He grabbed her arm and swung her around. She landed against his chest, causing those few parts of her that remained to shatter and fall at her feet. She recoiled as if he had physically struck her. He pulled her back with a roughness that should have frightened her but made her heart thunder instead. She was playing his way, without rules, knowing he would only hurt her.

"Kiss you, Annie? You want a kiss?" His fingers grasped the coil of hair at her nape. He yanked her head back. "Bloody damn, I'll kiss you." She caught the flare of fire in his eyes before his mouth slammed against hers.

His lips were hard, no . . . soft. Demanding and hot. His mouth molded against hers, pulling, sucking, filling her with his moist breath and the sweet-sour taste of bourbon. She grabbed his arms and her fingers dug into his muscles to hold on to something. Her lips parted, and his tongue slid in.

Dear merciful heaven, his tongue was in her mouth, tasting her as she tasted him, and the intimacy, the pure, stabbing intimacy fed the flames inside her until she was like a wildfire in dry tinder, burning out of control. She moaned and arched into him, pressing against him, trying to appease the fierce heat deep in her belly. His tongue slid against hers, wet and hungry. His hands pulled her tighter to him, and the burning place inside her grew larger and hotter.

Slowly, he raised his head. She sucked in a breath before his mouth was back, drawing on her bottom lip. He started to pull away, then brushed her mouth with gentle lips. And again.

He set her back. She wanted to reach up, touch him where the pulse beat wildly in his neck, but his taut, fierce face scared her. His breathing was rough and his nostrils flared wide, the way a stallion's does when it has been run too hard. Or frightened by something it can't understand.

Her muscles were liquid and aching, and she couldn't seem to catch her breath. She waited for him to say something since she didn't know what to say. What do you tell a man who has kissed you with that kind of hunger, then stares at you with hatred burning in his eyes?

"That was a kiss, Annie, one helluva kiss. But it wasn't love."

"What was it then?"

Somehow, she made him look at her and she saw it again, that stirring of torment in his shadowed eyes.

"What do I have to do? Teach me, Royce, I . . ." She faltered, knowing what she needed from him, not knowing how to put it in words. She doubted she'd ever be able to explain it even to herself.

His eyes squeezed shut as he tipped his head back. "Teach you to be a whore." Tremors seemed to race through his body. "I already allowed you to sell yourself for a roof over your head, and now you want me to teach you to whore."

*No*, her heart cried. *Teach me what you want, teach me how to make you love me because I don't know how.* She turned away, unwilling for him to see her choking back tears.

"All my life, I've listened to the other girls, the pretty ones. Listened and smiled and pretended it didn't matter. But I never stopped dreaming that somewhere, there was a someone for me." She tried to force a laugh, but it came out as a small, despairing sound. "I didn't know I was dreaming of you."

"Come here," he said softly as he pulled her back into his arms. "Sniveling little virgins cannot be beautiful. It's an antithesis of terms."

Tears clogged her throat, building and building until she thought she would burst from the pressure, but she couldn't let him see her cry. Her eyes burned as if she had already cried too much.

"I didn't mean . . . I don't want . . ."

"I know what you want. If I were a different man . . . but I'm not." His hands stroked her back, across her bare shoulders. Finally, she gave one funny little hiccupping sound and stilled against him.

"Are you done blubbering all over my uniform?"

"I wasn't blubbering."

Her cheek rubbed the choice woolen cloth covering his chest. Her throat hurt. She couldn't make herself look at him. Shame. The pain was gone, and all that was left inside her was sickening shame. She stepped away from him, careful to keep her face averted. She sniffled and rubbed her nose with the back of her hand.

"For God sakes, Annie, what would your mother say?" He handed her a handkerchief of fine Sea Island cotton. "I'll make you read Plato all afternoon if I ever see you do that again."

A strangled sound escaped around the balled-up cloth she held at her mouth. Suddenly, he was there, wrapping her back in his embrace. Oh, dear heaven, it was better than any dream, to be held so gently in his warrior's arms, surrounded by his strength and heat. She nestled against him, drawing in the bouquet of bay soap and tobacco and another male scent she'd never recognized before. She wanted to fuse herself into him, absorb his scents and his textures through every pore of her skin.

He held her with one hand pressed against the small of her back, the other stroking her nape. She brushed her lips against the pulse at his neck, tasting salty skin, feeling his heart throb against her mouth.

He tilted her head back. He looked feverish, the color high in his cheeks. His gaze fastened on her mouth and her lips parted in invitation. He dipped his head, his breath caressing her face—

"Annie-girl?"

They separated languidly, as if neither had the strength to move. Peyton walked slowly down the length of the gallery. He stopped when he saw them.

"Mrs. Raleigh was looking for you," said Peyton, and she knew he spoke to her although his hard gaze was fixed on his son. "Something about needing a lady's maid for one of the cousins."

Her gaze met her husband's, but his thoughts, his feelings, were shuttered behind the gray mist in his eyes. Soon, he'd be gone again; gone to war, maybe death, and she would never know what he wanted. Or how to make him love her.

"Go on inside," Royce said. "Just remember, little wife, everything you see in there is an illusion. A trick of masks and mummery and deceit."

She nudged her chin up. "I feel sorry for you, Major Kincaid. Nothing but pity."

His lips turned up at the corner in a look that might have been regret. Or cynicism. She turned and walked away.

Royce watched his father watch him, both of them waiting for the other to make the first mistake. Finally, Peyton's shoulders heaved in a sigh.

"Don't hurt her, son," he said.

"You should have thought about that earlier."

"She's in love with you."

"No, she's in lust with me. It won't take her long to recognize my totally degenerate character and move on to some respectable gentleman." For a moment, a taut silence stretched between them. Then Royce said, his voice rough with a pain he couldn't hide, "Christ, Father, you bought me a mother once. Didn't you learn anything from that? If I'd wanted a wife, I could have bought one of my own choosing."

"I've seen the women you choose. You'll damn your soul to perdition."

"You can't damn the already damned." Royce stared at his father's handsome, patrician face. "But then, you know all about that, don't you, Father?"

He thought he saw pain, raw and deep, flash in the gray pools of his father's eyes, but they turned flat and empty as his own. Peyton turned on his heel and walked off with proud, stately strides.

He watched until his father disappeared into the house, into the laughter and music, into the illusion. He groped behind him, felt the cool plaster of the column and leaned against the support. He rubbed his hands hard against the bones of his face until the violent sound of his breathing subsided.

But he didn't move for the longest time, waiting for his legs to stop shaking.

# Chapter 11

L eighton Sumner lifted the faceted glass to his lips and shuddered as Glenfiddich slid down his throat. He let out a deep sigh. "I say, old boy, Riverbend must keep the best cellar in the South."

"After tonight, I'm certain the cellar will be a barren wasteland." Royce's voice was full of aristocratic ennui. His posture emulated his tone in spite of the fierce stabs of pain that shot down his thigh with every motion.

He wondered why Gordon's friends insisted on addressing him as the *old boy*. He wasn't more than seven or eight years older than any of them. Maybe the truth was obvious; he'd been old ever since his ninth summer, an innocent, carefree child too young to be exposed to life's bitter secrets.

"It's all my fault," said Leighton, waving his glass.

For an instant, Royce thought Leighton was reading his own thoughts, then he followed the direction of Leighton's gaze. Annabelle. He watched her because he couldn't help himself.

She wore a simple white gown of watered silk, trimmed with narrow black ruche at the modest bodice. The skirt draped over a wide hoop that swayed with every step she took. A black organza sash circled her tiny waist and tied in a stiff bow at her back. He couldn't even compare her to the over-flounced, bejeweled women undulating across the dance floor with their bosoms threatening sudden exposure. She was like a

167

graceful swan thrown into a gaggle of fat, raucous geese. Just watching her caused his body to harden.

He couldn't understand what it was about his skinny, sweet wife that caused this physical reaction in him, couldn't understand what it was about her that made him act so contrary to his usual reprehensible behavior when his body spoke this way. She was his legal wife, and he'd be within his rights to take her into his bed and relieve this pain between his thighs. He didn't want these feelings, the itch in his groin or the ache in his chest, and couldn't push either away.

Sweet, innocent Annabelle. Not so innocent she didn't know what she offered; much too innocent to understand the price she'd pay. But when he was with her, when she gazed at him with those gold-flecked eyes that saw everything and revealed her soul, God, he wanted to believe again . . . believe in a kind of love that lasted beyond the next sunrise, believe in her. Hell, she almost made him believe he could change himself into the man she wanted him to be.

"All my fault," repeated Leighton although the words slurred together with this effort. "She was fine until I asked if I could come calling. Shoulda warned me, old boy, shoulda warned me." He waved his glass then held it in front of his nose. His eyes crossed as he stared at the liquid. "How was I supposed to know about her young man, died from the camp trots he did before he ever got the chance to kill a Yankee. Sad, sad . . ."

"Not for the Yankee who's still breathing."

Leighton responded with a solemn shake of his head. "I see your point, Major, really I do. But it wasn't the Yankee I was speaking of."

Royce thumped Leighton on the back. "You'll get over it."

"Sure I will. I've asked them all, you know, and all of them turn me down. But none of them ever smiled like Miss Hallston when they're doing it. A smile like that makes a man's blood run hot. Yes, sir, Major, *hot*."

Royce picked up the bottle of Glenfiddich and tipped it over Leighton's glass, filling it to the brim. "Forget hot, Corporal. Think cool and smooth."

Leighton shrugged his beefy shoulders. "Thing is, sir, she's not smiling anymore, and it's my fault for making her remember. Never forgive myself, I won't." He shuddered dramatically and tipped the glass to his lips. He smacked his thick lips. "Cool and smooth. Yessir, cool and smooth helps a man forget."

"Good, and I'll forget we had this conversation." He handed Leighton the half-filled bottle. "Run along, Corporal. And forget hot."

Leighton's fist gripped the bottle neck while a huge grin spread across his face. "Thank you, sir. I'll just find me a corner somewhere and forget hot." He lurched forward a step, then stopped and turned back, listing slightly to one side. "Glad to know she's got you looking out for her. You might not be famous for protecting a woman's virtue, but I can tell you're not thinking about her that way. Girl like her, she needs a man protecting her from young blades like me. Specially now, with her condition and all."

"You be sure and warn all those young blades they'll have to answer to me if they play with the lady's affections."

Maybe Leighton was too drunk to catch the irony, but he saw the bitter, derisive truth. It wasn't the young blades she needed protection from; it was Royce, himself.

Royce shifted his full weight to his good leg and leaned against the mantel, watching Annabelle. She stood within a group that included the Pettigrew brothers. Chauncey seemed to have taken her under his wing. He'd walk over and punch Chauncey Pettigrew if he hadn't seen him with his own woman in Richmond and recognized the fevered glint in his eyes. Annie was safe with Chauncey, at least until his fever for the Richmond girl died out.

Royce looked away, listening for her laughter, that wonderful sound that caused his blood to rush. It didn't come. He turned his head and fixed her with a glare, willing her to smile, to laugh. As if she felt the weight of his gaze, she looked across the room, meeting him with her dark eyes.

*Smile, damn you.*

The sunrise didn't come. He pushed himself away from the mantel and left the parlor, unable to keep his bad leg from dragging. He didn't feel the pain in his thigh; the force of her gaze following him was like a knife in his black heart.

* * *

Gordon stood beneath the oak tree and watched Royce massage his leg. Royce's face was hidden, and he wondered if his brother allowed his pain to show when he thought he was alone. He doubted it; Royce was too much a master at hiding himself to let his guard down even then.

"Did she kick you again?"

Royce slowly straightened. "Not this time. Can't blame this on anything but my own damn stupidity."

It was a lazy, self-mocking drawl, nothing in it of the commander who had gone galloping back into a field of fire, his own pistols empty, armed only with a spent carbine and a bowie knife—to rescue a wounded man inadvertently left behind. The wonder of it was that either of them survived, although only one told the story.

"I saw DeShields in Richmond," said Gordon.

Royce tipped his head back. "Ah," he said and it was almost a sigh. "Well, I'm certain whatever John told you was heavily exaggerated. Building the myth for the benefit of the public is a tactic. Puts fear in those weak Yankee hearts so they'll run when the battle finally comes."

"Royce, are you trying to get yourself killed?"

"Far from it." Royce huffed a bitter laugh. "This might be a depraved, worthless hide, but it's the only one I've got, brother, and if you were thinking with your head instead of the equipment between your legs, you'd take the transfer I got for you and join us."

"Why? So you can risk your worthless hide saving me next time? Dammit, Royce, you might mean well, but it's growing a little thin from where I stand." He searched Royce's face for a flicker of emotion and saw nothing but an enigmatic mask. Gordon fought back a sigh. "You knew Stuart at West Point, and you know he's good."

"He's good. He's also out for fame and glory; Beauty can't help himself. Cavalry captains get killed that way."

"He's fighting my kind of war, out in the open."

"He keeps a bloody banjo picker at headquarters!"

Royce started to turn aside and Gordon seized his arm. "For once, I'm going to be a man. I know why you married Annabelle, and I let it happen. Dammit, I let her ruin her life because of your misbegotten notion you had to protect the bastard son."

Royce peeled Gordon's fingers off his sleeve. "Stop worrying about Annabelle. She's got more guts than every soldier dancing inside that pretentious house put together. She knew what she was doing, and she did the right thing. Wars are ugly things, Gordon. She and Bo not only have a decent home now, they've got Peyton's protection."

"She didn't plan on falling in love with you."

"I seem to have had this conversation once before tonight. I'll tell you the same thing I told Peyton. She's not in love; she's in lust."

"And you can't pass up a woman in lust."

"Stick it up your arse, *brother*."

"That's the issue, isn't it?" Gordon barked a harsh laugh. "*Brother*."

"That is not the goddamn issue." Royce leaned forward. Moonlight slanted across his face, accenting the bitter set of his mouth. "You think Miss Raleigh would be Mrs. Gordon Kincaid if I'd let Peyton make his announcement? You think those hypocrites in there would be dancing at your wedding? Grow up, Gordon. You'd be a social pariah through no fault of your own. Blame Peyton, blame the bitch that bore you, but don't blame me."

Gordon stared at that handsome, worldly face and wondered where he, himself, would be if this man hadn't sacrificed his own youth for the younger sibling. The pity was, Royce had lost more than his youth. He'd lost all hope. Royce's faith was in the utter depravity of mankind, Gordon's in the ultimate goodness of human nature. This war would probably prove one of them wrong and he hoped to hell Royce's conviction was the invalid one.

"I don't blame you. Just don't hurt her. Please."

A taut silence filled the night. Royce's head drifted back, his lids squeezed tightly closed. He drew in a deep breath and let it out in a sigh. "If I have to hurt her, I'll make it as quick and clean as I can," Royce said, his voice rough with some emotion Gordon didn't understand.

Gordon wanted to smash his fist into that arrogant face; he wanted to hear words of love from his brother, love for Annabelle, love for himself. His fists clenched and unclenched at his side in frustration.

He envied Royce his courage, his strength of will, and pitied him for those same virtues that kept him from admitting his own torment. But most of all, he loved Royce, and nothing the man would ever do could change that.

Gordon turned on his heel and walked toward the house, back to his waiting wife. Augusta knew the truth. But he knew in his heart Royce was right. She would never have been allowed to marry the bastard if society knew his shameful roots, and, for that, he owed Royce another debt. And he hated his brother for laying one more obligation on his shoulders.

"Gordon."

He stopped, holding his breath, waiting to hear Royce speak the words that would make everything right between them again.

"Come fight with me."

He turned slowly. Royce stood, deceptively loose, staring back at him with those unemotional gray eyes. He felt a pang at the sight of that harsh and elegant face, shadowed by both night and intent. The beloved and hated face of the man he called brother.

"I can't do that and call myself a man."

Gordon left him alone in the night, unable to stay, unable to watch Royce fight his personal battle. He thought he should feel triumph, but he didn't. What he felt was love. And a terrible, aching sorrow.

Royce Kincaid leaned against the tree, his face blank except for a twitching at the corner of his lip, and watched his brother go. He stayed that way, propped up by an ancient oak, until the river breeze cooled the sweat on his brow and the party began to break up.

He walked across the grounds to the plantation office, cursing silently against the weakness in his leg that caused him to limp. Pride or stupidity, he couldn't make up his mind which, but he shouldn't have disdained the use of the cane tonight. He'd damn near fallen on his ass when he tried to dance with Annabelle, and the pain had been a torment ever since.

He let himself into the dependency that had been his home since he'd returned East and groped in the dark for a candle. He struck a match, and the room jumped into focus.

He normally used the second floor for his living arrangements, but his wound precluded the use of the stairs. In the midst of all the wedding preparations, Annabelle had seen to his needs here, having the bed and trunks brought down and arranged in the corner, setting up a bathing area behind a screen. She'd even brought out throw rugs and arranged vases of flowers to lighten the atmosphere. It wasn't the lap of luxury, but it was a damned sight better than the way he'd lived out West or the way he was living now, dodging Yankee patrols.

Once, this room had been his sanctuary, the nerve center of the estate, the place where he could bury himself in the details of husbanding the land and breeding the livestock. Only here had he ever been able to forget that Riverbend was the ultimate illusion, for when he worked, when he sweated and toiled for Riverbend, the illusion became real even to him.

It belonged to Annabelle now, God help her. He huffed a bitter laugh. A country torn asunder, both sides claiming God for their own cause. If such a Being existed, He was too preoccupied to worry about the likes of Annabelle Hallston Kincaid or her debauched, degenerate excuse for a husband.

He lowered himself onto the rope bed that hissed in protest against his weight. He kneaded his aching eyes with the heel of his palms. Damn, the look on Gordon's face—self-hate, despair. On his wedding day. Royce thought of those things Celeste had stolen from him, himself; childhood and innocence, the belief that somewhere in this world of enslavement and corruption there remained a tiny, bright shred of decency and honor. Maybe even love.

All this time, he'd thought to save Gordon from those losses and evidently failed. How long had Gordon known and said nothing? And now, because of Gordon's silence, he had Annabelle as his wife.

Damn her, she'd been all but begging for it tonight, and he sure as bloody hell had wanted to give her what she asked for. He should have swept her up in his arms, up to her room, and taken what she offered.

And he would have destroyed everything that made her good.

He had to leave here, go back to the war, away from her.

He'd start riding tomorrow, strengthen his leg so he could fight again. McDowell was getting ready to move out of Washington anyway. He had a duty to fulfill, a duty to lead his command into the coming battle.

He reached over his head and gripped the slatted headboard, tensing his muscles and willing away the burn in his thigh. He stared up at the wooden beams stretching across the ceiling. The candle glow flickered, and he watched pine knots transform into . . .

Her eyes, so dark as to be almost black, deep, turbulent pools that made a man want to drown himself in their depths. He saw her hair, gilt-tipped waves of ash brown strewn across his pillow like liquid sunshine, saw himself burying his face in those waves, filling himself with her scents, the cool scent of lavender overcome by the hot scent of sweating woman.

She'd be small everywhere, small, golden breasts, perfectly proportioned, an exact fit for his hand. He saw himself tasting her nipples, watching her writhe as he tasted more of her appealing, too-bony body. He'd spread her skinny legs and bury himself inside her while he kissed that too-wide, laughing mouth senseless. *Teach me, Royce.* God, the things he could teach her to do with that luscious mouth, that skinny body.

He jerked himself up, causing fire to shoot down his leg. The fire did nothing to ease his bulging sex, which strained hard and painfully against his pants. He limped across the room and yanked the door open. He stood in the doorway and gulped great quantities of hot, sultry air.

The clouds were gone, and the moon had risen full in the sky, bathing the lawn with a soft luster. The Big House stood in silhouette, the windows dark. His gaze drifted to the second floor, to her room, and because he thought of her, he knew she'd be there.

She stood outside on the portico, dressed only in a white night rail. The breeze caught the flimsy material, molding it against her body. She turned her head and looked toward him. He wondered if she could see him standing in the shadowed doorway and knew it made no difference. There was something between them, something that drew one to the other. Whether she saw him or not, she knew he was there, watching her.

He backed up, all the way over to the bed. He stared at the flagon of bourbon sitting in invitation on the desk. Between the pain from his wound and the pain between his legs, the only respite lay in drinking himself senseless. He wasn't that weak yet. He sat on the edge of the bed and held his hands over his knees. He stared at his hands until the trembling ceased, then set them atop his thighs.

Love. A shining scrap of decency somewhere. A sunrise that didn't destroy hope. All of them, nothing more than illusion. As if in proof, the candle sputtered out in the breeze, shoving the room into darkness. A great shudder racked his body. His head dropped back, and his eyes drifted closed.

"Annabelle," he whispered into the hot and empty silence.

# Chapter 12

"**Y**ou shouldn't be in the smithy, Miz Annabelle."

For a moment, her lighthearted sense of relief disappeared inside a big, black cloud of disgust. *Obey the rules, Annie*, she admonished herself. *For Clarence's sake if not your own*. Annabelle said nothing, but returned to the doorway, standing where anyone could plainly see her.

"Patsy told me she's . . . I mean, that you . . ." She drew in a deep breath as Clarence looked at her with amusement playing around his eyes. "She told me she's expecting to find something in the pumpkin patch in a few months," she said, smiling softly. "I'm happy for you both."

Clarence nodded and turned his back to her, walking over to the workbench. She couldn't possibly know his thoughts; he was male and he was black and she had no experience being either. But she understood why his smile faded.

Because of Patsy, she knew of his freedom jars buried behind his quarters, filled with the coins he earned as a blacksmith off Riverbend. Peyton allowed him to keep those earnings for his own, and Patsy had told her of his dream to buy freedom for himself and his family.

"The last guest left this morning," she said, changing to the real purpose of her visit. "We can go back to the lessons tonight if you want to spread the word."

"I'll do that." Clarence picked up a hole press. "They're tired, don't expect too many."

"Tired or scared, Clarence?"

"Paddyrollers have been right busy since this war started. War hasn't improved their dispositions any."

They were frightened; she wondered if any of them suspected she was terrified. But she was equally determined to teach those who wanted to learn at least the rudiments of letters and sums. They played a dangerous game, and she wasn't so naive as to be unaware of the repercussions if they were caught.

"I'll do my best to protect them. I can't promise anything more."

"I expect you will, Miz Annabelle. Can't anyone ask for more'n that." He picked up a handful of clench nails and went back to work.

She stood for another minute watching him. His shirtsleeve was cloaked in sweat, and she could see the dark muscles quivering beneath the cloth. Gordon was right. Clarence and Royce shared many qualities, both of them proud, arrogant perfectionists with a tender heart they'd die before they revealed. She gave a silent prayer of thanks God had saved her from the affliction of being born male. She turned to leave him to his work.

"You stay away from the river today, Miz Annabelle. There's a storm coming."

She tilted her head and saw blue sky, clear and cloudless to the horizon. Laughter started deep in her belly and rumbled up like a river in floodtide. She laughed because the wedding guests were finally gone and because summer spread its lazy magic over the land. She laughed because for three days she'd been dying from the shame of throwing herself at Royce, dying from his rejection, and if she didn't find some reason to laugh, she'd die crying.

Annabelle followed the path that wended its way through a green corridor of sugar maples and twisting morning glory to her own special place on the river. Here the water swirled around big rocks, forming deep pools where black bass lived. A land spit rose not far offshore, populated by river otters and shorebirds and sundry crawling creatures. Major didn't deign to wait for her. The dog scuttled down the bluff and bounded into the water. Bluebottle flies rose from the surface, swarming around the dog in iridescent clouds.

She sat on a rotting log and peeled off her boots and stockings. She picked up the hickory pole and tackle, slung her book under her arm, and clambered down the bluff to the narrow beach. It was a summer day in the Piedmont, the air languid and soggy, the rough sand beneath her bare feet blistering hot. She waded into the river and curled her toes in the cool, mucky bottom. She hitched the book farther under her arm and ran, laughing and splashing, to the little island.

She dropped to the ground beneath the shade of a scrappy willow. As Major gamboled around her, showering her with refreshing sprays of river water, she baited her hook and cast it into the deep pools beyond the rocks.

For several long minutes, she watched the cork bob in the current. Somewhere behind her a warbler trilled. Major came and settled beside her, placing his big head in her lap.

She stroked the dog behind his ears and closed her eyes against the glare of sun on water. The water purling over the rocks sounded a gentle lullaby. Swept by a sudden wave of drowsiness, she forgot about the fishing pole held between her knees and stretched out in the willow's shade. She rolled to her side, threw her arm over the dog, and fell asleep.

When she stirred, the sun was gone behind ominous clouds, the dog was gone somewhere unknown, and Royce was there, staring at her with an empty look in his eyes. She thought she was dreaming.

He moved, and she realized he was real. She wondered how long he'd been standing there, watching her sleep. The thought made her feel naked and defenseless. She scuttled backward like a sand crab, her wet skirts dragging through the dirt.

He stiffened. "Be still, Annie." His voice was low and insistent, his eyes as dark as the gathering clouds. "Goddamn it, don't move!"

Dear heaven, where did the revolver come from? A cold chill racked her body. She clenched herself into a ball and shoved her hands against her ears. A gunshot exploded, the sound smashing into her belly. The air stank of sulfur.

The world went utterly still, as if the river had stopped flowing and every creature waited to breathe.

"Annabelle?"

Slowly, she raised her head and looked at him. His body was stretched so taut she thought he'd twang if anything touched him.

"If you'll harness that weapon, I'll promise never to throw myself at you again."

"Christ, woman." His head drifted back and his eyes closed. He seemed almost to sigh. In three long strides, he was beside her. He hunkered down next to her, reaching out with his hand. She flinched, and his hand dropped to his side.

Something moved in his tarnished eyes, something wispy and shapeless, like drifting fog. His gaze was so intense, she actually felt it against her skin, the way she'd feel a summer breeze caress her face. Her chest tightened, squeezing around her heart until she thought she must scream if he didn't look away. His gaze dropped, and she let her breath out in a slow sigh.

"Are you all right?" he asked.

"I've got burrs stuck in my behind-her, but that's no reason to put me out of my misery."

"You were about to be lunch for a cottonmouth, little wife."

She jerked to her feet so fast the world tilted sideways. "Oh my," she said. Not two feet from where she stood lay the remains of a snake, at least five feet long. The bullet had blown off its head. "You sure it wasn't just a brown snake?"

"His mouth was open, ready to strike." He grabbed her and gave her a rough shake. "Clarence told you to stay away from the river. Do you ever do anything you're told?"

She pulled herself free and took two steps. Ignoring his ridiculous question, she nudged the snake with her foot. "Big old bugger, wasn't he?"

He let his breath out, like a hiss of steam. "About as big as you are."

He moved and stood beside her and she was suddenly buffeted by a whirlwind; feeling safe because he stood beside her, a man with his man's size and strength; feeling lighthearted and carefree because his voice sounded light in her ear. And at the same time, feeling a hollowness deep inside herself—because she needed him desperately, and he needed her not at all.

Thunder rumbled nearby. Heavy clouds rolled across the

sky, as black as the bottom of a witch's cauldron. "Major!" she said, suddenly worried for the dog. She cupped her hands around her mouth and called, "*Maa—jor.*"

"No need to sound the trumpet, dear heart. I already saved your unrepentant life once today."

"Not you, silly man. Major was here, helping me fish, and now he's gone."

"Silly me, I should have known that as soon as I spotted the mutt on the riverbank chewing on a hickory pole." His eyes opened wide, as if he was struck by a sudden inspiration. "He didn't catch any fish, so he consumed the pole for dinner."

"And you killed the snake before he consumed me for dinner, and they all lived happily ever after."

"They did not live happily ever after. The snake has a violent headache from which he will never recover; the dog got a splinter caught in his mouth, and you, why you, Mrs. Kincaid, are about to be taught a lesson you'll never forget."

He advanced on her, evil intent writ large on his face. She backed up, into the water. "Don't, Royce," she said, holding up her hands to fend him off.

"Which would you prefer, a couple of sound whacks on your pretty little behind-her or a good dunking like an ugly old witch of old?" A light crept into his eyes. "Both, I think. It's exceedingly difficult to get your attention, and a smart man will take advantage of the opportunity when it presents itself."

"No," she shrieked, spinning around. Her legs flailed against the heavy weight of her skirts as she tried to run through the water. She heard him splashing, then he lunged, seizing her around the waist. The impact toppled them both into the water.

She came up spluttering and laughing. He grabbed her and dunked her under again. When she came up, she puckered her lips and shot a stream of water, catching him in the face. He swore, then began to laugh so that their laughter joined, hers light and airy, his husky and deep. The sound floated on the soggy air—his laughter and her laughter, entwined together like lovers.

His died first. He was staring at her mouth, and a tautness had come over his face, as if his skin was stretched too tight over the bones. She wondered what he saw when he looked at her. Not a lady; somehow, he always managed to catch her at her worst when even her best wasn't good enough. Self-consciously, she pushed her wet hair off her face. Thunder rolled like a thousand drums beating at once and she jumped as lightning split the sky.

"Out of the water." His voice sounded harsh.

She started toward the island and he seized her arm.

"Wrong way, little wife."

"My book, the tackle . . ."

One brow lifted. "Plato's *Gorgias*, I presume."

"*Wuthering Heights*."

"Filling that empty little head with more romantic nonsense." She smiled at him, and his face softened before he turned her around. "Out," he said, punctuating the command with a sound whack on her behind-her.

Annabelle waded out of the water. She stopped at the foot of the bluff to wring out her skirts, and when she looked up, he was beside her, staring at her bare legs. She thought at first the heated look in his eyes was her imagination, but she began to realize she held some kind of power over him, too. He might claim he didn't want to kiss her, to touch her, but he lied. If she knew how, she could make him love her in spite of himself.

He held out his hand, and she grasped it. He had left Ajaque hobbled at the top of the bluff. He nodded for her to mount. She had her foot in the stirrup, ready to haul herself into the saddle, when she spied a feather at the edge of the bluff. She jumped down. Smiling to herself, she snatched up the gull feather and shoved it in her pocket. Turning, she saw him staring at her again.

"What's the matter?" she asked.

"Get on the bloody horse before the storm hits."

"We're both already soaking wet, Major."

He lifted her into the saddle and stood grinning up at her. "Delightfully so, Mrs. Kincaid. That ugly old dress clinging to all your nonexistent curves is most enchanting. And certainly God will strike me dead with a bolt of lightning to my black heart for speaking such sacrilege, which is why I intend to run for cover."

He swung up behind her, his arms coming around her to take the reins. The heat of him seeped through her clothes. He urged the horse into a trot, the motion causing her breast to press against his arm. She drew in a deep breath and let it out slowly.

"Do you have thoughts of ravishing this skinny body?" she asked.

"Didn't anyone ever tell you that ladies are to be meek of spirit and terrified of rapacious blackguards such as I?"

"You are such a fraud, Major Kincaid."

His breath was hot and moist against her neck. His arm jostled against her breast, and her nipples tightened, rubbing almost painfully against her cotton shift. She'd never experienced this sensation before, this tightness everywhere and at the same time, loose and floating as if she were going to come apart in a million pieces.

He might have answered her, but she didn't hear him as the storm cut loose, the rain slashing in wind-shoved drifts, flattening the grass and hitting the hardwoods with a snapping noise. Lightning flashed, silhouetting the trees and the distant mountains against a sky the molten color of his eyes. He hunched over her, protecting her from the lashing rain, and urged the horse onto a side trail.

"Where are we going?" She had to shout over the tumult of the storm. She felt his answer, but the wind grabbed his words before she heard them.

After several minutes, they came into a clearing, and she saw a small brick building ahead. Royce nudged the horse into a gallop, then drew up in front of the structure. He dismounted and helped her down.

"Old Riverbend's gatehouse," he shouted over the beating rain. "Get inside while I tether the horse."

The hinges squealed as she pushed open the door. The room was dark and dank. As her eyes adjusted to the murkiness, she made out a table with two slat-back chairs, a brick hearth, and, against the back wall, a wooden bed covered with an old brown blanket. She heard him behind her, and, suddenly, she felt shy and nervous and very, very cold. She hugged herself and shivered.

"Christ, I've got to get you warm." He came up and wrapped his arms around her from behind. The shivers became shakes, and he dropped his arms as if she'd lashed out at him.

"Strip down to your shift and wrap up in that blanket." His voice was hoarse, like it hurt him to speak.

"I don't think that's a good idea."

"To what do we owe this sudden ladylike behavior?" He laughed and gave her a gentle shove forward. "Do as you're told for once while I build us a fire. I promise I won't turn around until you tell me you're covered."

She did as he said, stripping down to her lace-tucked shift and cotton drawers, careful to keep her back to him in case he peeked. Her skin felt odd and prickly and too tight for her body. She pulled the pins from her hair and shook the coil loose. Wet hair fell across her shoulders and down her back. She pulled the blanket off the bed and wrapped it around her. She turned but said nothing, watching him this time.

He crouched on one knee while he set another faggot on the fire. His pants stretched tautly across his powerful thighs. Water dripped from his thick hair and ran in rivulets down his back.

He pushed himself upright, and she could tell his wound still pained him. Yet he had gamboled with her in the water like a carefree boy and used those same thighs to control a powerful horse during a violent storm. His self-will was awesome. She had another sudden insight; that same self-will would be both her protection and defeat, and the thought filled her with a profound sadness.

She walked across the room and stood beside him, both of them staring into the flames. "There's a sheet on the bed," she said softly. "Don't you think you should get dry, too?"

He turned sideways, placing his hands on her shoulders and turning her so they faced one another. He lifted one hand and stroked her cheek with the backs of his fingers. "Are you happy here?"

His question surprised her as much as his touch. "I miss Carlyle," she said, then she recognized another truth. "But I think I've always been happy at Riverbend."

He said nothing, studying her for the longest time, then his expression changed—a subtle gentling of his mouth and softening of his features, as if her admission had touched him deeply somehow. She could have stood there forever, watching him in wonderment, but something must have shown on her face, because he dropped his hands and turned away to pull the chairs nearer the fire.

She watched him retrieve her dress and stretch it over one of the chairs to dry. He gave her another funny look, this one half amused, half apologetic, then pulled his shirt over his head. He placed the shirt, wrong side out, over the back of the second chair.

An awkwardness washed over her. Dark hairs curled across the breadth of his muscles, the hair tapering down toward another part of him she couldn't even imagine. She wanted to stare at those powerful muscles, the beautiful bronzed skin, but she looked away, whether from shame or propriety she was uncertain.

She sat on the floor in front of the grate. She leaned forward, toward the heat, and wrapped her arms around her knees. The wind whistled down the chimney so that the fire leaped, hissing and crackling like an angry cat. She heard him behind her, his bootheels tapping as he walked. She turned her head, resting her cheek on her upraised knee, and he came into her sight.

He stopped in front of the single window, staring out at the lashing rain. He stood with his hands loose at his side, doing nothing.

There was something to his pose, something in the tilt of his head, that made him seem very alone and very vulnerable. It would not please him to know she thought such things, to see her traitorous face as she thought such things, so she turned back to watching the fire.

The silence stretched out, filled by the drone of the wind and the beating of the rain, and still she kept quiet. He was the one who could speak in circles and somersaults while saying nothing. For her, the right words were important, and they'd never come easily. So it wasn't strange that when the quiet was broken, it was by him. Nor did she find it strange that when he spoke, he spoke utter nonsense.

"You look like an Indian princess," he said.

"Silly man." She twisted her head on her knee so that she saw him coming toward her. Firelight sputtered red in his wet hair and cast flickering shadows across his face, so she couldn't tell if he smiled or not. But she smiled because she felt very much alive. She was with him, somewhere safe, and she was happy.

"I bet you knew a thousand Indian princesses out West, and every one of them was in love with you."

"At least a thousand." She laughed, and he flashed her a devilish grin. "A hundred anyway," he drawled.

He leaned his shoulder against the brick face of the hearth. "You know there were Indians here, too. Did you ever hear the story of Hurit, the Lost Maiden?"

"Only Pocahontas."

"Hurit was long before Pocahontas. She wasn't a princess, her father was a shaman, but there was something very special about her that made everyone love her, especially the brave who was to be the next chief. The brave was the one who gave her her name; you see, Hurit means beautiful, and to him, she was the most beautiful maiden who ever lived.

"War came between the tribes, and the brave crossed the river to fight. During a battle, he was captured by the evil spirit that lived near the sea. We'd call the evil spirit a witch, and she was an ugly old witch, so ugly she had to wear a mask over her face, otherwise even the crabs turned away in disgust—why are you laughing? This is a very serious story."

"This is a ridiculous story, and you're making it up as you go along."

"I assure you, I am not making it up, and if you insist on giggling your way through it, I'll stop now and you'll never know the ending."

She bit at her bottom lip, holding back a smile.

He stared at her mouth. His face grew taut and strained. She suddenly realized he was very serious, that this man who usually used language to hide himself was now trying to tell her something important about himself, about them. She no longer had any urge to laugh. She feared she would soon be weeping.

"Where was I?" he said finally. "Ah yes . . . The ugly witch cast a spell, so the only time the brave could cross the river was when the water flowed upstream. Since everyone knows water never flows upstream, she thought she was making it impossible for him to return to his maiden. And the spell worked for the longest time. When he didn't return, Hurit pined for her warrior until everyone in the tribe feared she would die from the heartache. But remember, Hurit's father was the shaman. He called up a mighty storm that grew in the ocean and blew west, pushing the river water back to the mountains . . ." His voice faded.

"And the warrior crossed over to his maiden," said Annabelle because she wanted it to be so.

"No. The shaman's magic wasn't strong enough."

She stood and moved to stand in front of him. She wanted to tell him to stop, but she couldn't. He was telling her something, and she needed to understand the story to understand him.

His throat moved as he swallowed. "The warrior had just reached the bank when he saw her running across the dry riverbed. He stopped because she was so beautiful with her hair flying behind her, and he just wanted to look at her." Royce took the edges of the blanket wrapping her and pulled them tight together at the base of her throat. "So the brave was standing on the riverbank, helpless to save her, when the water rushed back and carried his love out to sea."

"That is a horrible story," she said in a choked voice. "Didn't anybody tell you when you make up fairy tales you must always give them a happy ending?"

He cupped her face between his hands. "Ah, but Annie-girl, don't you see," he said, dipping his head. "There are no happy endings."

His mouth touched hers, gently first, then growing hot and demanding. She opened her mouth, giving him her tongue, and he took it, giving her his. Her body exploded with the same violence as the storm hammering outside.

The blanket slipped from her shoulders and landed at her feet. She seized his waist, and her arms slipped around him, her nails digging into his back. His hand moved to her breast and she gasped as his fingers tugged and pulled at her nipple through the rain-wet cotton shift. She clung to him as he devoured her lips and mauled her body, and she couldn't get close enough. They were two mouths, two bodies, crushing together in a desperate effort to become one.

"Annabelle," he breathed into her mouth. His hand thrust through her hair, fisting and pulling her head back. His lips slid across her jaw and down her neck. She moaned softly, twisting her head as he came to rest at the pulse throbbing in her throat. "Annie . . . dear God, Annie, I have to—"

He shuddered and straightened, pushing her away with such violence she stumbled. She lifted her gaze up the length of his body, coming to rest on his face.

They stared at one another. His bronzed, muscled chest heaved with his breathing. He could deny he wanted her, but the evidence of his desire bulged prominently against his breeches.

Her throat burned as if she'd gulped great swallows of smoke. Slowly, feeling his eyes watching her, she retrieved the blanket from the floor and carried it over to the bed. She drew on her wet petticoat, reaching behind to tie it in the back. Still, neither of them spoke. She flipped the blanket in the air and let it settle cloudlike on the bed. She smoothed the wrinkles, then pulled the foot up, folding it back so the wet spot would dry underneath. When she turned, his tortured eyes searched her face as if he both longed to see something there and feared he might find it.

"You don't understand," he said.

"No, Royce, I don't." She walked over to the chair and gathered her dress in her arms. She slipped it over her head, and, suddenly, he was behind her.

"Lift your hair," he said in an eerily gentle voice.

She gathered her hair in her hands. His long fingers fumbled with the tiny buttons at the back of her dress, almost as if his hands trembled. By the time he was finished, her knees were jelly. She wondered where the laughter had gone, the wonderful sense of being alive. She felt as if she'd died a thousand deaths and feared there were another thousand ahead of her. All of them to be faced alone.

"You asked to keep our marriage a secret, and yet you're wearing my ring tied to your shift. Why, Annie?" His hands on her shoulders felt like the weight of the world.

Instinctively, she reached up, cupping her hand over the gold band she'd forgotten was there. And now he'd seen it, and that was another humiliation to be borne. She turned around.

"I am your wife," she said, nudging her chin up. He narrowed his eyes, tilting his head slightly. She was helpless to resist. "I was ashamed," she admitted in a small voice. "Ashamed and embarrassed because my father spent his last days making some horrible arrangement to get his plain daughter a husband to take care of her. And I guess I was too proud to want to admit that to anybody."

He clutched her hands, holding them between their bodies. "You are not plain. You're every bit as beautiful as the Indian maiden."

She shook her head because she knew he lied. He studied her face as his thumbs rubbed her wrists in slow, gentle circles. He laughed, a laugh so unlike him, soft and almost wistful.

"Oh yes, little wife. You are beautiful—inside and out." He lifted her hands and pressed them against his chest, then flung them off. "Here," he said in a bitter voice. "Of all the places in the world, I bring you here and almost force you like she did to me."

She looked around the barren, musty-smelling room and saw nothing except a dying fire and dust. She thought of his defenseless, vulnerable pose in front of the window. For him, this place held some awful meaning. She stepped forward and placed her hands on his chest. Beneath her palms, his skin was hot. She felt his heart tripping like a frightened animal.

"Who, Royce? What did she do to you?"

He lifted her hair, his fingers barely brushing her neck, then let it drop to her shoulders. "I was eight years old the day I sought shelter here . . . a thunderstorm just like today. What I found was Celeste coupling with a riverboat captain." He swallowed so hard his throat moved. "She was mother to me then. I thought the man was trying to kill her, and I wanted to kill him, tried to kill him."

His chest hitched, then the words went on in a rush. "There was nothing I could do or say because she threatened to have Clarence sold if I did. You cannot believe, cannot imagine, the years that followed." He ran his fingers down her cheek, so gently. "You see, little wife, I don't want you to understand my world."

She watched him as tears welled up in her eyes, studied his face with its sharp bones and shadowed eyes. Her heart cracked and bled for him, for herself, for all the things he could not say and she could not imagine.

"The ugliness, Annie, so much ugliness. The great Senator Julian Kincaid hotfooting in and out of the slave quarters while his wife suffered in silence and everyone pretended not to notice the yellow babies. Peyton never fell prey to that abomination, but he never realized what an abomination he'd brought into our home. She even asked for a divorce so she could go off with some Frenchman, and he refused to divorce her. To this day, they are married."

"But if you never told him, how would he know?"

"He should have known. A decent father would have realized what was happening and gotten rid of her faster than wildfire in the wind."

"But don't you see, he loved her," she said softly. "If anything, he deserves your pity. He loves you and Gordon. Forgive him, Royce. Forgive him and go on with your life."

"You are too young, Annabelle." His mouth twisted in a bitter slant. "It's not love or forgiveness we're talking about—neither exists in the real world. It's hate and retribution. I'm a Kincaid. Dishonorable, disreputable bastards, all. And like every Kincaid before me, I'll destroy everything I touch."

He was warning her, and she thought that alone was proof he was wrong. She couldn't change what he believed in his heart any more than she could remove the horrors from his past.

Low thunder rolled in the distance. She smelled the clean scent of rain-scrubbed air as the returning sun lightened the darkness inside the building. She looked at him through a wash of tears and saw nary a trace of light in his eyes.

"And the man who lives to protect his brother, the man who sent the child picket home from the war. Who is that man?"

"He's a bloody fool."

*You are wrong*, she thought. *He's what became of the brave little boy robbed of his innocence, robbed by an evil witch who wore a beautiful mask on her face.*

But she didn't say the words. He could not bear to hear them.

# Chapter 13

Color and shapes rushed past her eyes; green-brown grass and sentinel trees, a white ribbon of fence against sun-speckled sky. She felt the mare's muscles gathering beneath her, and they soared, up, up . . . hanging suspended in blue air for the space of a heartbeat, then the earth rushed to meet pounding hooves. It was like straddling lightning and riding it across the sky.

They took the last jump in the series, and Annabelle slowed the bay mare to a calming pace. She laughed from sheer pleasure—the wind on her face and the sun on her back, a powerful, sleek horse beneath her. Some days, she understood how good it was just to be alive, even in this new world of war-madness and impossible love.

She rode up to the paddock fence. Bo sat on the top rail, his large mouth spread in a toothy grin. Beside him, Peyton leaned against the fence. A white planter's hat shaded his eyes, but she saw the creases at the corners of his mouth.

"Glory, Annie. When I learn to ride like that will you let me follow the hounds?"

Annabelle reached out and gave the brim of Bo's hat a play-ful tug. "You can ride to the hunt as soon as you grow to fit your name, Bohannon Ewell Chandler Hallston."

"What do you think of her?" asked Peyton.

"She's wonderful." Annabelle stroked the mare's neck. "I think her legs have wings."

"She's yours, Annie-girl."

A bundle of heat stole up her throat. She loved Peyton Kincaid while her heart ached for his heartaches, and, at times, she thought he cared more for her than even Papa had cared. He'd given her too much already.

"No. I'll love riding her, but I can't accept—"

"She's yours," he said. "Let me know what you decide to name her so I can enter it in the book." He straightened and gave her a gray Kincaid glare. "Come on, Bo, we're riding out to check the tobacco fields this morning."

"Father—"

He'd already turned, walking away from her with his shoulders set stiff and proud. She guessed at least six hundred years of arrogance had been bred into the Kincaid line.

"Never look a gift horse in the mouth, sis."

She transferred her gaze to Bo, who grinned back at her. "Skedaddle, squirt."

He swung his long, skinny legs around and jumped down from the fence. "Guess I can take a hint. Unlike some people I know who shall remain nameless, I wasn't born stupid." He turned to follow Peyton, tossing his hat in the air and catching it as he walked. "No sirree, someone got the smarts in the family, and it wasn't Annie or Carlyle."

She laughed as he broke into a whistling, squeaky rendition of "Dixie." She saw Royce come out of the smithy, and her laughter died. He said something to Bo as the boy passed by, then jerked his hat on his head, tugging it down with a gesture that bespoke fury. He came toward her, his hitching stride leaving a swath in the dew-damp grass.

She'd been about to dismount and lead the mare to the stables, but she hastily reconsidered. For once, he could look up at her. He stopped when he reached the fence.

"Get down," he said, his voice fraught with leashed anger.

"Why, Major Kincaid, from your behavior, a lady would think you have burrs stuck on your behind-him," she said in the most dulcet voice she could summon.

"A lady would be wrong. I have a feather in my cap, a pain in my arse, and a powerful urge to beat some sense into you, which I am doing my damnedest to control since the effort would be wasted."

"You're angry."

"How perceptive of you, little wife. Now get off the bloody horse before I jump the fence and pull you down."

She nudged the horse forward. She reached out and lifted his slouch hat from his head. The morning sun glinted on his hair, lighting it the russet shade of a banked fire. She settled the hat in front of her.

"It was just a joke," she said, twisting the feather until she was able to pull it free from the thread she'd used to sew it on last night. She held out the hat, featherless now.

He took it from her hand, slapping it against his leg as he studied her. "I liked the feather, woman. It's the kind of joke that reaches my irreverent soul. Are you going to get down?"

"No."

"Why doesn't that surprise me?"

She was trying to read both his mind and his face when he dropped the hat to the ground and slung himself over the fence. She had no idea how he could move with such grace and speed while still suffering from the wound in his thigh. The horse shied, doing a nervous little sidestep. She gathered the reins to calm the mount and took a deep breath to calm herself.

"What are you doing?" she asked warily as he approached.

"Your seat's bad; you'll break your skinny neck riding that way."

By spouting fury one second and concern the next, he had her as confused as a headless chicken. She looked down at his bent head as he shortened the stirrups. She wondered what it would be like to press her lips where his hair curled at the nape. She touched him there instead. His hair was surprisingly soft, like a child's, and already damp from the summer heat. He went utterly still beneath her fingers.

She withdrew her hand and gripped the reins, clutching the leather tight in her fist. She had the oddest feeling that by touching his man's body, she'd touched his man's soul—and he didn't want her touching him either place.

He finished adjusting the stirrups and stepped back. He stood with his hands on his hips and glared at her. "School is over, Mrs. Kincaid. There will be no more classes until this war is ended. When that blessed day comes, you can teach the slaves to your heart's content."

She looked at him but didn't see him. She saw instead black faces, Patsy's and Reba's, Rufus's and Clem's. She saw brows creased in concentration as they struggled to grasp the printed word and saw those same faces breaking into a wide grin when they discovered the key. She thought of the courage inside their hearts and the weakness inside her own.

"You haven't answered me," he said, and his voice jerked her back to this moment. The sun was a hazy yellow ball behind him. The breeze plastered his shirt to his chest. His skin showed dark and muscular beneath the white cloth. She wondered if he knew she hadn't been listening to a word he'd spoken.

"Do you understand what I'm telling you?" His mouth was set in a hard, angry line. This was the same man who'd taught Clarence to read and write. She knew from that his fear now was for her safety, not the normal white fear of an educated black.

"Do you love me, Major Kincaid?"

His brows lifted. "No."

"And our marriage ends in five years?"

"Yes, Mrs. Kincaid, five very long years." A crease appeared at the corner of his lips, as if a smile wanted to break free.

"Then I'll do as I bloody damn well please."

Royce stepped back as she turned the mare. "You're getting the words down right," he called after her, "but the tune's still a little squeaky."

He heard her laughter, then watched, his heart in his throat, as woman and mare took the fence and thundered across the field. She was laughter and sunshine, defiance and courage, and he'd never known a woman like her. She drank of life, gulped it down in great swallows, and held out her hands for more.

She was his for the taking.

Her hair blew behind her like streamers in the wind, the color of sunburnt river sand. Something swelled in his chest so that he could hardly breathe . . . a terrible, fierce hunger for a thing that never was.

He could ride after her, take her down in a bed of pine needles, possess her for a moment in time. But only a moment.

Because time never stood still, and love didn't exist, couldn't exist, in this world of war and hate and madness. She thought she loved him, but soon life would teach her the ugly truth as it had taught him when he was a child. Love, like dreams, ended with the next sunrise.

He hoped he wasn't around when she learned the bitter lesson. He would be the Indian brave standing on the riverbank, and he couldn't bear watching the joy-light die in her eyes, knowing nothing could save her.

He stood motionless until long after she'd disappeared. A jay squawked somewhere behind him, bringing him back to the morning. He took one step and stopped. Leaning over, he picked up a feather, a scraggly, gray-white, seagull's feather. Absently running his fingers along the vane, he looked to the horizon where she had vanished, then slipped the feather in his pocket.

The Kincaid curse had been cast while they sat in her little parlor and signed a marital contract. He'd known it then and regretted it with every fiber of his being now.

He leaned against the stable door, watching her ride back into the yard. She was dressed in a lemon yellow riding habit that had seen its better days. She was hatless, but somewhere along the way she'd stopped and picked daisies, sticking one in her hair and several through the mare's crown piece. An intriguing combination of seductive woman and ingenuous child, just looking at her filled him with a boundless joy and an unbearable sadness.

She slowed, and he walked forward to meet her, hating himself for what he'd already done and hating himself for what he had to do now. He laid his palm against the mare's neck and looked up at Annabelle. Light blinded his eyes. She was wrapped in sunshine, dressed in sunshine, and she flashed him that sunshine smile.

"Don't look at me like that," she said. "I'll have you know I've had a perfectly respectable afternoon in Mrs. Pettigrew's parlor. Sewing haversacks and gossiping." She laughed that joyous champagne laughter, the sound that made his blood surge and his chest ache. "You put the feather back in your hat!"

He tried to match her smile, but his lips felt stiff. "I told you

I liked that feather," he said, reaching up to help her dismount.

His hands spanned her waist and he felt as if he was crushing the life out of her. He set her on the ground. She looked up, meeting his gaze, and it was all he could do not to look away. Her smile dimmed.

"What's wrong?" she asked.

"A telegram came this afternoon from Gordon." He swallowed hard, trying to find the right words. "Annie . . . oh, damn, Annie . . . it's Carlyle."

Her eyes grew wide and dark. She moved away until she stood by the horse's head. She drew the mare's forelock over the brow band, parted it and smoothed it, then patted the bay's forehead in an absentminded way.

"How?" she asked, and he knew she'd guessed what he hadn't yet found the guts to say.

"Measles."

She nodded, her hands still smoothing the mare. "Funny isn't it, he couldn't wait for this war to start . . . gonna *whup* himself some Yankees . . ."

"Annie."

"He didn't even make the first battle." Her voice sounded as soft as a spring breeze. He wanted to touch her, hold her. He couldn't touch her. She'd break into a million pieces.

"I have to tell Bo. Dear, merciful heaven." Her voice caught. "What do I tell him?"

"Bo knows. He's with Peyton." He wished she'd cry or scream, blame him and Peyton for this misery. She only nodded again, still patting, smoothing. "Gordon's waiting for your instructions. Do you want Carlyle buried here?"

She pressed her forehead to the horse's muzzle. "Nooo," she breathed. "I can't do that, not after what he . . . how he . . ."

She raised her head and looked him square in the eye. He saw the teardrops shimmering on her lashes and the pride that kept them from falling. He heard Carlyle's angry voice, *I'll never set foot inside Riverbend, and I won't see you again until this farce of a marriage ends.*

"Lexington. I'll go pack now." She took a step, and he stopped her.

"No, Annie," he said, pulling her into his arms, knowing he

had to strike another blow. "Gordon will have to take care of it. I can't let you get on that train, not now, with two armies converging toward Manassas Junction."

She seemed to collapse inside herself, small and smaller still, until soon there would be nothing left in his grasp but air. His arms tightened around her.

"I'm sorry," he murmured. He dipped his head, rubbing his chin in her hair. "I'm so goddamned sorry."

She seemed as fragile as a sparrow's wing. He drew in her scents, lavender sachet and horse, the musky scent of a woman's sweat. His vile, depraved body hardened, and he set her back. She raised her head and fastened her wide, sad gaze on his face.

"It's not your fault." She tried to smile, and he thought his heart was going to crack with her effort. "I could have gone to him and made it right between us."

Christ, she was comforting *him*. "Annie . . ."

He couldn't find the right words, could never find the right words when they were important. He reached out and stroked her dry cheekbone. Her skin felt hot and fevered when it should be moist with tears. She placed her hand over his.

"Don't," she whispered, her eyes drifting closed. "Please, don't."

He was a full-grown man, infinitely more experienced than this speck of a girl with the giant-sized heart she wore on her sleeve. He knew better. But already the light was dying in her eyes, and he couldn't bear it.

His arms came around her, crushing her to him. His mouth covered hers in a long, deep kiss. He needed to taste her, drink in her sorrow and swallow her pain. Give her his breath and make her whole again. Her hands curled, fisting around his shirt, and she leaned into him, giving herself while he took and, oh God, he'd never tasted anything so bittersweet. For that moment out of time, she was his, and she filled his universe.

Until she pulled away. She rested her cheek on his chest, and he stroked her back, trying to ease her shivers. His head dropped forward against her hair, and he closed his eyes, stung with remorse and regret and a thousand other feelings he couldn't name.

"Your brother was right, Annie-girl. I am a first-class bastard."

She stepped back and shook her head slowly. The daisy drooped forward against her cheek. Wisps of hair, damp with heat, curled about her face. He sucked in a breath. She lifted her hand and dragged the wilting flower from her hair. For a long moment, she stared at the flower as if wondering where it had come from. A small, haunting smile formed at her lips.

Her gaze lifted, and he took the impact like a blow to his gut. She was gone, pulled deep inside that place where no one could touch her, and he had driven her there.

"Annie," he said softly, reaching out with his hand.

She stepped back again, out of his reach. "I must go to Bo."

The daisy dropped to the ground, crushed beneath her boot as she walked away from him. He stared at the crushed flower. He couldn't endure the sight of the beaten woman.

He telegraphed Gordon to ship the casket to Lexington, where he would personally see to a proper burial. It was the least he could do for her, even if she never knew. He didn't want her to know. He'd leave here as soon as possible; in the meantime, he kept to the office dependency when he wasn't riding.

He saw her once the next afternoon as he was coming in from the fields. He drew up beneath the spreading boughs of an oak and watched her cross from the cookhouse.

Some of the things that so intrigued him were there; the way she preferred to leave her hair unbound, allowing it to fall free down her back, the simple way she dressed, in petticoats instead of those ridiculous hoops, the unconscious grace and willful pride in the way she carried her body. Already gone were those other things, her sunshine smile and gamine laughter.

He wished he could make it different for her, for him. Maybe she could be what she thought she could be for him. And maybe he could become the man she thought he was for her. They would never know now, not with the war on their doorstep.

The nature of war was blood and destruction, and it had only just begun. He was a soldier for the duration, duty-bound to follow the drum whether it led to death or honor, and death was far more likely than honor. She was a woman, to be left behind. He

wouldn't, couldn't, leave her pining for a love he was incapable
of giving. Let her learn to hate him and let her start now.

She stopped at the well with her profile toward him. He
watched her reach for the gourd and dip it in the water bucket.
For the longest time, she seemed to forget what she meant to
do, staring ahead, her body motionless. And then she turned
her head and looked directly at him. Whatever it was, a sense,
a power, or maybe only a hunger; whatever it was, it spoke to
her, too.

He backed up his horse, turned and rode away.

Annabelle pushed open the French doors and stepped out on
the portico. She leaned forward against the railing and drew in
a deep breath, filling her lungs with dew-dampened air. She
looked toward the river, flowing rose-gray, the ripples gilded
by the sun's first light. Something had wakened her from a fit-
ful sleep. She shifted her gaze toward the stables, knowing
what she would find.

The man in the Confederate uniform was already mounted
on the powerful gray charger. He turned the horse, and, suddenly, the sun crested the horizon, capturing him in a misty,
golden haze.

He was her love, the cavalier of her dreams. And he was
leaving without even saying good-bye.

Her head told her a man could want a woman he didn't love,
and he'd tried to tell her so. Her traitorous heart loved him anyway. She loved his gentle hands and irreverent humor, the way
his cheek crinkled when he smiled. She loved his quiet, deep-
toned voice, his warrior's face and knight's honor. She loved
all those things and more. She loved the way he . . . was.

He didn't love her.

She felt as if she'd swallowed the sun, and it was choking
her breath. She watched through misty, unshed tears as he rode
across the field, away from peaceful Riverbend, toward war
and flowing blood. She watched, waiting and hoping.

It hurt, but it didn't surprise her. He wasn't a man to look back.

# PART THREE

*It is good that war is so terrible, or we should become too fond of it.*

—General Robert E. Lee, CSA, Battle of Fredericksburg

# Chapter 14

❦

*December 11, 1862*

A nnabelle leaned against the newel post and expelled a forceful breath, causing wisps of hair to flutter against her forehead. She rubbed her temples with the heel of her palms, seeking to ease the headache that had been pounding since dawn. She looked up to see Patsy bearing down on her. Annabelle straightened and tried to buttress herself for whatever grim news Patsy was bringing.

"Miz Annabelle, another carriage just drove up. I don't know where we going to put any more of these folks."

"How many this time?"

"Six. It's them Sutters from over by Hanover Street."

"They have young children." Annabelle went back to rubbing her temples while she thought. "We're out of mattresses, blankets, and pillows, but we'll find something—maybe bed them down in the dining room after everyone's fed." Patsy stared at her, the desire to argue apparent on her face.

Annabelle felt a small smile growing. "I know, I've already heard it," she said. "Them white folks haven't got the sense the good Lord gave a turkey, and that ain't worth sticking in a pot for boiling."

"Didn't hear that from me." Patsy turned and stalked off, muttering under her breath, just loud enough to be heard, "No ma'am, if'n Marse Robert had told this turkey to fly, this turkey woulda been flapping her way to Richmond long before now."

In spite of her exhaustion, Annabelle laughed and found, to her surprise, the headache eased with the laughter. She told herself to stick that lesson in her pocket and pull it out when the next crisis struck. She couldn't imagine a worse crisis than the evacuation of Fredericksburg, but she was learning that war went beyond her ability to imagine anyway.

She wandered out to the front gallery. The wind gusted in a frigid blast, catching her skirts and whipping them against her legs. She crossed her arms on her chest as some protection against the cold and leaned against the pillar.

Striated ribbons of purple and rose streaked the sky. In the distance, a large column of smoke rolled gently upward, ascending to a vast height where it drifted northward, shaped like a feather plume. It seemed all of Fredericksburg was burning.

She looked over Riverbend, what she could see from the gallery. The front lawn and gardens survived intact, but many of the fields were near ruin. Miles of fence railings were gone, burned in the campfires of Confederate troops who had encamped here for almost a week. They had pulled out yesterday, into position around Marye's Heights. All she had left to contend with now were the refugees from Fredericksburg, and, somehow, she'd find a way to feed and house them until this battle ended, and they could make their way home—if home still existed.

Stabbing flames pierced the dusk as the artillery guns fired another barrage. The shells screamed and whined as they flew across the river from Stafford Heights into the burning town, where they exploded with a violence that shook the ground. The smoke clouds turned crimson against the darkening sky.

She thought of the long-ago battle at Manassas Junction that had seemed so terrible at the time. So many battles since then, fought at places no one had ever heard of: Shiloh and Donelson, Balls Bluff, Gaines Mill, and Antietam Creek. The Shenandoah Valley belonged to General Jackson, but Vicksburg was under siege, and New Orleans had fallen. Neither side had won the Cannae victory, and neither side was ready to quit. Now, war had come to Riverbend.

"You're going to catch your death out here, Annie-girl."

Peyton's voice startled her out of her musings. He draped a

woolen pelisse across her shoulders. She drew it tight across her chest. They stood silently for several long minutes, both of them watching the impossible beauty of war.

"Gordon is out there somewhere," she said quietly.

"Yes."

He slipped his arm around her waist and drew her close. She guessed his thoughts followed her own, but she didn't speak her thoughts, and he respected her silence. Royce belonged to the past, that long-ago summer of laughter and hope. An innocent time when dreams were real and wars were only dreams.

"It's not fitting," declared Jules. "Ladies do not go gallivanting off to battlegrounds."

"I'm not gallivanting anywhere," said Annabelle. "I'm bouncing in a farm wagon, listening to a silly old fussbox spout nonsense."

The battered farm wagon jounced and rattled down the new road hastily constructed behind the lines by Rebel engineers. The back was loaded with as much in the way of provisions as Riverbend could spare on this cold, foggy morning, the second morning since Fredericksburg had been taken by Union forces.

"Just watch who you be calling old, little missy. If'n anyone's old, it's that fool sitting on the horse there," said Jules, nodding toward Peyton, who rode beside the wagon. "He's so old, he's gone senile. Letting you come out here—"

The wagon hit a deep hole, giving a sudden, violent lurch and cutting off the rest of his tirade. Annabelle grabbed the seat with one hand and her hat with the other.

"You're going to kill me long before the Yankees get the opportunity to try," she said, trying not to laugh. "And if you keep hitting every rut in this road, I'm going to take the ribbons and drive myself."

"Isn't fitting. Ladies don't ride in farm wagons, let alone drive them."

Annabelle exchanged an amused glance with Peyton.

"May as well give up, Jules," said Peyton. "The lady in question didn't listen to me any more than she's listening to you."

A grunt followed this final pronouncement, whether because of disgust or because the wagon hit another frozen rut, she was uncertain. Drawing on her bottom lip to hide a smile while holding on to the wagon bench for dear life, she looked at the passing countryside. Her urge to smile faded. No longer was this a beautiful land of rolling hills, heavily timbered between pastures and tilled fields. Two armies had come, bringing desolation with them.

A slow wind pushed cold, damp fog through leafless tree branches. Peyton rode ahead, then disappeared into the heavy mist. Jules continued to mutter beside her. She absently patted his knee to soothe him and ignored whatever he was saying. Within several minutes, Peyton reappeared like a ghost rider out of the smoke. This time, he was accompanied by a young soldier. The soldier tipped his hat when he saw her perched precariously on the jolting wagon seat.

"If y'all just follow me, I'll take you to headquarters."

"Isn't fitting," muttered Jules as he spanked the reins, causing the wagon to lurch forward again. She tightened her grip on the bench seat.

They climbed a hillock, and the white tents of staff headquarters came into view. By the time Jules pulled the wagon to a halt, Peyton was already dismounted and deep in conversation with an officer.

"You stay right here in this wagon, little missy," ordered Jules, as Peyton and the officer walked off, headed toward the front of the hill, where several officers stood conversing.

She jumped down, resisting the urge to rub her aching bottom as she pretended not to hear him. The gray fog had thinned, revealing the two church steeples and the courthouse spire, rising like battle spears out of the blanketing fog.

The hilltop was a beehive of activity, with staff officers and enlisted men swarming about on whatever duties such men performed in preparation for war. The scene was both exciting and frightening, and goose flesh rose on her skin, a cold, nervous tingle that had nothing to do with the winter wind blowing her cloak against her legs.

Peyton and the officer returned, the officer tipping his hat when he saw her. "Major Sorrel, ma'am," he said. "General Longstreet's aide."

"You must come and pay us a visit at Riverbend, Major. We

haven't yet had the opportunity to entertain our Carolina friends."

"Riverbend's hospitality is already famed in our army. I suspect we'll be camped near here most of the winter, and I would be honored to take you up on the invitation."

"The honor is ours," she replied, thinking how ludicrous was the display of drawing room manners on this winter-draped hilltop bristling with soldiers and arms.

Within minutes, the major had a crew of soldiers unloading the provisions from the back of the wagon. She stepped out of the way, moving to stand in front of a campfire that gave off small, fluttering bits of warmth against the damp cold. Peyton and the major soon joined her.

"General Lee said to give you his regards," said Peyton, nodding toward the group of officers. "I didn't know you knew him."

"His wife and Mama were dear friends," she said. "But, still, I'm surprised he remembered me. He wasn't at Arlington much in those days."

Peyton chuckled. "If it was the same little girl visiting Arlington that visited Riverbend . . . well, you're hard to forget, Annie-girl.

She sucked in her cheek, hiding a smile, as she studied the Confederacy's most revered soldier. Tall and comely, he was neatly dressed in a thigh-length gray sack coat with only the three unwreathed stars on his collar to designate his rank. He wore his beard close-clipped, its iron gray color giving away the passage of time since she'd last seen him. Still, his figure was lithe, and he moved with a deftness that disguised the fact he was somewhere in his midfifties.

Beside Lee stood another general, a large, burly man with shaggy brown hair. She assumed he must be General Longstreet. Another officer stood with them but he had his back to her and she gave up trying to guess his identity.

Peyton and the major were deep in a discussion of the probabilities for battle today. She was half-listening to the conversation when the third officer turned and started toward them.

She couldn't believe her vision and if it hadn't been for the scraggly dark brown beard and those piercing blue eyes, she wasn't certain she'd even have recognized him as the man she'd known in Lexington. In those days, he'd paid even less attention to his appearance than had Papa. Even now, he was famous for wearing a homespun uniform and a mangy old cadet cap into battle.

"You look splendid," she said. "Mrs. Anna would be very proud."

"Some doing of my friend Stuart," General Jackson muttered, giving a disdainful brush to the gold braid on his sleeve.

Major Sorrel laughed. "He's dressed so fine, we're all wondering if he's going to get down to work today."

General Jackson leveled the major with a glare, and she suddenly understood how he had come to be known as "Old Blue Light" to his troops. He turned his attention back to her.

"Miss Hallston, your brother gave his life for the Cause just as certainly as if he'd died in battle. He was a commendable addition to staff and a fine soldier. I know you miss him, but he died well, for something he believed in."

A sudden lump rose in her throat. "Thank you, General," she said. "I'll try to remember that."

Peyton's hand enclosed her own, and she returned his gentle squeeze. General Jackson cleared his throat. He turned his hat around and around in his hand, and she guessed he had more to say.

"The Stonewall Brigade is positioned over there." Jackson nodded to the right, toward Hamilton Crossing. "All Valley men—boys you know." He paused again, as if wondering what he was trying to say, then went on in a rush. "Our field hospital is set up at Belvoir, and if your uncle would give his permission, perhaps you would return there tonight or tomorrow to minister to the wounded."

Her heart gave a sudden leap. "Perhaps I will go there now, General."

"Annie," said Peyton in a warning tone.

"Is Stuart's cavalry over there, too?" she asked. Jackson nodded, and she turned to Peyton. "What if one of them is Gordon?"

Peyton's expression remained grave as he studied her. "Will she be safe there?" he finally asked the general.

"My men may have failed to take a position, sir, but they've never once failed to hold one. She'll be as safe there as at Riverbend," said Jackson.

"Annie-girl, your father would kill me if he knew I'd allowed you to do this."

"Thomas Hallston never knew where his daughter was until long after she'd arrived home and decided to admit her folly," said Jackson. She was holding back unexpected laughter when the general's grim visage cracked. A wonderful smile broke through the pieces. "If you'll give your permission, sir, I'll send a detail to escort her safely to Belvoir."

Peyton stared into the fire. She waited, consumed with the desire to do something more worthwhile than attend to the needs of dozens of complaining civilian refugees. He seemed to reach a decision and took her hand, pulling her aside.

"What if Royce is here? What if he's one of the wounded brought in?"

"He doesn't fight these kinds of battles," she said. "As we speak, he's probably in Fairfax capturing some poor Union general in his bed."

"What if you're wrong?"

"Then he's just another soldier," she said in a quiet voice. "It doesn't matter anymore, Father."

Annabelle stood by the wagon, a grinning Major Sorrel at her side, as Peyton climbed into the seat beside a still-grumbling Jules.

"Isn't fitting," muttered Jules. "Just cause they're soldiers doesn't make 'em gennulmen. A lady—"

"If you don't hush up, old man, I'll send you across the river and let you entertain Burnside. The war would be over in a matter of hours," said Peyton.

Jules huffed and slapped the reins. The mules lurched forward, and Peyton lurched backward, almost rolling into the wagon bed.

"Don't expect that damnyankee Burnside got much more sense than you do." The remainder of Jules's commentary was lost in the squeaking of the wagon wheels as they jounced and swayed down the lane.

A mounted courier rode up the hill, pulling his horse to a

sharp halt. He swung out of the saddle, flicked her a surprised glance that he quickly hid, and lifted a salute to the major.

Major Sorrel returned the soldier's salute and held out a gloved hand into which the courier placed an envelope. She stood quietly while Major Sorrel read the dispatch. He favored her with a slight bow. "Duty calls, Miss Hallston. If you'll excuse me, I'll turn you over to Lieutenant Green until your escort arrives."

"You've been most gracious, Major."

The young lieutenant stood looking at her with an expression bespeaking his total loss as to what to do with her. She smiled, and he suddenly pulled his hat from his head, almost dropping it in his haste.

"Would you care to wait in the general's tent?" he asked. "You'll be much warmer there."

"Why don't you show me where there's a nice fire and get me some water. May as well make myself useful, and I've yet to meet a man who didn't appreciate a cup of hot coffee on a cold winter morning."

Almost three hours later, she was still there, bent over a campfire located on an eminence forever after known as Lee's Hill, surrounded by a collection of staff soldiers when the fog suddenly lifted like a curtain in a theater. Hearing an odd sound like the buzzing of a million bees, she straightened.

Brilliant sunshine bathed the plain in front of the hill, revealing the city and all its attendant destruction. She drew in a sharp breath, feeling a sickening sense of nausea and, at the same time, a strange excitement.

Dark lines of infantry troops spread across the plain, bright with colored regimental flags and polished muskets glinting in the sunlight. Countless numbers more crossed the swaying pontoon bridges in a tramping step that sounded like distant thunder. Another long line, actually miles away although they looked like wooden soldiers she could reach out and touch, snaked down the Richmond Stage Road to the south. Deadly-looking caissons were drawn up at intervals between the brigades.

For a breathless moment, she understood the siren call for audacious young men with dreams of adventure. Suddenly, a great turbulence of crashing sound and fuming smoke boiled up into the sky.

Her hands shook as she handed a steaming cup of coffee to the young lieutenant. His face was flushed, his eyes, bright sunbursts, like he suffered a raging fever.

"Isn't it splendid, Miss Hallston?" he shouted.

She'd begun with fear and gone hurtling past every emotion in the spectrum, ending at sheer terror. She swallowed hard. "Splendid," she said dryly.

His face became grave. "I forget myself, ma'am. If you're frightened, I'll be glad to escort you to the general's tent."

"There are a hundred places I'd rather be right now, but inside a tent waiting for an unseen artillery shell to land on my head is not one of them."

She heard laughter behind her and swung around. The man was thin with a pipelike neck and a thick mustache. He wore a tall gray hat and a red coat with very wide shoulders, almost like wings.

"Spoken like a true soldier," he said in the clipped tones of a British accent. He bowed. "General Arthur Freemantle, late of Her Majesty's Coldstream Guards, at your service, ma'am."

"Miss Annabelle Hallston," she said, managing a wobbly smile. "The petticoat sergeant, late of His Majesty Peyton Kincaid's grand estate, Riverbend."

He threw back his head and laughed. "With ladies such as yourself on her side, the Confederacy must surely win this war."

Another thundering barrage sounded, answered by the deeper voice of the big guns across the river, then the clamoring thunder and spitting fire became constant. She shuddered as the booms shook the ground beneath her feet.

A fleeting image crossed her mind, of the cresting sun striking a gray-clad warrior, making a perfect illusion—and a perfect target. She pushed the thought aside. Royce hadn't looked back that long-ago morning, and she wouldn't look back now. He was somewhere else, fighting a different sort of war. She was here, in a place she didn't belong, and the best thing she could do was keep herself busy and out of the way while she waited for Jackson's men.

She returned to her self-appointed task of preparing coffee. Her heart ceased clamoring with every blast of fire as she realized they were almost out of range of the cannonballs. Only once did one land nearby, and that one failed to explode. She lost track of time. Without warning, a huge cry lifted. She raised a questioning gaze to the soldier next to her. He pointed to the right.

"They're driving them back," he shouted. "Jackson's boys have done it again."

Annabelle followed the direction of his pointing finger and understood what he meant. Over the snow-pocked flats, tiny blue soldiers fled a withering fire, hotly pursued by Rebel infantry storming out of the timber, across the railroad, and down into the plain. As the Federals fell back toward the river, answering fire opened on the Rebels. Each side seemed to withdraw, disappearing into trenches and timberland and leaving a plain strewn with broken bodies.

She looked to the front of the hill where the generals stood. General Lee lowered his binoculars and turned to General Longstreet, making some comment. They were too far away for her to hear. Both men seemed almost serene. In the basin in front of them, another wave of blue soldiers fell to the sword-swoop of Rebel fire, adding to the carnage in the sunken road.

Annabelle clasped her arms about her waist as the terrible significance of what she was seeing dawned on her.

All morning, column after column had moved up, only to be broken against the Confederate fire. Another immediately formed behind, moving forward without hesitation, polished rifles gleaming in the December sunlight—the Union Army, uncountable in number, moving forward endlessly in burnished rows of steel and undeniable courage. An army led by stupid generals, but an army which, somehow, kept coming on, and would keep coming on until victory was theirs.

She stood shivering by the fire, listening to the winds of war whistle through naked tree branches, mingling with the shrieks of wounded men. Her chest ached from breathing the raw smoke of battle. She rocked on her heels and hugged herself tightly, thinking of Carlyle and all those other young men—sons and brothers, husbands and fathers—sacrificed to a futile cause.

A pain grew inside her, in her bones and her flesh and her blood. *Why*, her mind railed. Only the booming guns answered.

The guns were still blasting on the hills outside Fredericksburg when Annabelle arrived at Belvoir. An unceasing procession of ambulances was arriving from all directions to augment the number of wounded already spread about the grounds in various degrees of suffering. Most of the operating tables were placed in the open where the light was best, protected by tarpaulins or blankets stretched upon poles.

They rode past one such tent-fly, and her gaze fell on one of the surgeons, a large man dressed in a linen duster that reached nearly to the ground. His sleeves were rolled up to his elbows in spite of the cold. Crimson blood coated his hairy forearms as well as the linen apron, which she guessed had once been white. More blood lay in shiny, icing pools on the ground and already, a pile of amputated arms and legs rose at the foot of the table like a grisly collection of broken doll parts.

Two assistants lifted a shrieking man onto the table. The surgeon held his knife between his teeth as he fingered the leg wound, then yanked the leg into position. He grabbed the knife from between his teeth and wiped it against his blood-smeared apron. Annabelle looked away as a wave of nausea engulfed her.

Somehow, she managed to get her stomach under control within the few minutes it took to ride beyond the house. They dismounted and hobbled the horses near the cookhouse, which was a swarm of activity. She smelled soup and coffee, the aroma of baking biscuits. Her stomach lurched again and she instinctively pressed her palm against her abdomen.

"We'll find Dr. Stringer," said the lieutenant who had escorted her from Lee's Hill. "He'll be awfully glad to see you."

She gave him a wan smile, wondering if she could hide her distress and keep the doctor from sending her home. They had taken but two steps when someone called her name. She turned to see Mrs. Neal, a friend of Mrs. Pettigrew's.

"You're one of the first to arrive, Miss Hallston," said Mrs. Neal. "Have you ever done this before?"

"Not quite like this," she said. "I nursed my father when he was dying and helped out at the hospitals when our boys were in Fredericksburg last spring, but they were sick, not wounded."

Mrs. Neal gave her an appraising glance and handed a steaming bucket to the lieutenant. "Take this coffee into the house," she said. "You'll see somebody in there who'll direct you to Mrs. Franklin, she'll tell you where to put it."

Mrs. Neal took Annabelle's arm, guiding her forward. "You'll find these men different from the sick you dealt with before. They want water, a gentle hand, and kind words, in that order. There's little you can do to relieve their suffering other than keeping the bandages moist and listening to what they need to say. Can you stand that?"

"I hope so, Mrs. Neal. I really want to try."

Mrs. Neal nodded as if that sentiment was enough. "If you feel like you're going to faint, try to get to some fresh air. Failing that, sit down and put your head between your knees. Whatever you do, watch where you walk. You don't want to step on some poor soldier's recently amputated stump."

Annabelle swallowed hard and tried not to look at the ghastly sight of mangled men deposited in rows on the ground in front of the tent-fly, waiting their turn to undergo the surgeon's knife. A man, dressed as a medical officer, separated himself from a group of bloodied walking wounded and approached them. Mrs. Neal introduced him as Dr. Stringer. Annabelle twisted her hands in her cloak as he leveled her with another appraisal.

"We need you," he said, his voice gruff. "Can you do it?"

She stiffened her spine and nudged her chin up. "I can."

He studied her for another minute, during which she stiffened her spine a bit more, then gave a shake of his head.

"The barn, then; I think you can probably handle what you'll find there. Mrs. Neal will show you what to do." He turned his back without another glance and returned to his own pressing duties.

Several lanterns relieved the gloom inside the barn. Straw had been spread on the floor, and the men lay in the straw, most of them without blankets beneath them or to cover them. Those who had knapsacks used them as pillows. Many were without shoes or jackets in this bitter cold.

The barn smelled of horses and straw and less pleasant

odors she didn't want to define. Mrs. Neal wasted no time in putting her to work, and she soon found herself swept into the needs of these men and away from her own thoughts.

Left on her own, she knelt beside a young man whose right arm was gone. A bloody bandage covered the stump just below his elbow. "Hello, soldier," she said softly, aching to reach out and brush the shock of brown hair from his forehead. His eyes widened as he focused on her.

"Miss Hallston?"

"Yes," she replied. "But how did you know?"

"I went to school with your brother Carlyle."

She decided that allowed her to touch him. She brushed his hair back and tried to smile. "Can I get you anything? Some water . . . tea or coffee?"

His skin stretched taut and white across his broad cheekbones, giving him a wild appearance, but his words were gentle and kind. "I'm doing fine, ma'am, but my friend . . ." He gestured with his good arm. "That boy over there. His name's Charlie, and he's not doing so good."

She tilted her head to the side. "I'll see to Charlie in just a moment, but I think while I'm here you ought to take advantage of it. Thirsty?"

His eyes clouded with tears as he nodded. She managed to raise him so he could sip water from the tin cup and then she eased him back so his head rested on his knapsack. "What's your name?" she asked.

"Ellis. Winston Ellis."

"I'll be back, Winston. If you need anything before then, call me. I'll be listening."

She was stopped three times by outstretched hands as she worked her way to Charlie. When she reached him, an ache filled her chest. He could be Bo, he looked so young. He even had the same straw-thatch hair sticking up on his head. A bandage wrapped around his middle, black with oozing blood. He lay clutching his hands across his midsection and whimpering like a baby. She knew without asking that his wound was mortal. She sat down and drew his head into her lap.

"Ma?" he muttered.

"Nooo."

"Need to go home—see Ma."

"Soon, Charlie. You'll be going home soon." A pressure built behind her eyes and she blinked against the ache. She stroked his hair and saw his eyes open, cornflower blue and filled with his soul.

"An angel. I'm seeing the prettiest angel I ever did see."

"How many angels have you seen, soldier?"

A grimace of a grin stretched his lips. "Not many. But you're still the prettiest."

She sat with him for several long minutes, wiping his fevered brow with cool water, stroking his hair. As long as she remained with him, he seemed calm. She knew she couldn't stay forever and made a motion. His eyes opened again.

"You'll be back, won't you, angel?"

"I'll be back, Charlie." As soon as she moved away, she heard his crying begin.

The hours passed in an immeasurable drift. She discovered she had helpers, soldiers whose wounds were not serious who moved among their comrades dispensing fluids and wry humor, carrying buckets for her.

Charlie lingered in his suffering, and she found herself drawn to him again and again, although he seldom recognized her now. She was stroking his brow and humming a lullaby when his eyes opened, showing recognition. He even managed a wan smile.

"I'm going to die, angel," he said.

The lump of tears choking her throat prevented her from answering. She nodded.

"In my knapsack . . . Ma's Bible. Would you send it to her?"

"I will." She stroked his cheek. His skin was baby soft, prickled with a downy new beard. She hummed another lullaby, and he slept, maybe his last sleep.

"Was it worth it, Charlie?" she whispered around the knot in her throat. To her surprise, he smiled. And nodded *yes*.

Somehow, Winston had managed to move so he lay next to Charlie. She caught his dark eyes studying her and gave him a weak smile. "Do you remember Bo—Carlyle's youngest brother?"

"Little squirty thing with yellow hair?"

"Not so little anymore. Your friend reminds me of Bo."

"Charlie, there, he's the youngest in his family, too. His brother was my roommate at VMI. Died last summer at Sharpsburg. I promised him then I'd look out for Charlie." He tried to shrug and grimaced with the effort. "Didn't do such a good job, did I?"

"I expect you did as well as anyone could have done." She held back a sigh as she dipped the cloth in the water bucket. She squeezed out the rag and proceeded to wipe Charlie's face. "Bo's been accepted at VMI, and even though Carlyle would be proud, I wish he'd go anywhere else next fall. I don't want him to be a soldier."

"A boy's got to grow to be a man. Can't be any other way."

"Someone else once told me the same thing."

"He was right, Miss Hallston."

"Maybe."

Annabelle tossed the rag in the bucket where it landed with a small *plop*. Her hands were chapped raw from the combination of water and cold. She was rubbing them between the folds of her apron when she looked up, and saw him.

# Chapter 15

He stood just inside the barn doors, half-turned toward her as he conversed with Dr. Stringer. Lanternlight flared on his warrior's face, casting shadows beneath the sharp bones. The doctor gestured toward the opposite side of the barn and Royce nodded, then walked in that direction. He still moved with that lazy, lean-hipped grace, like a cat on a hot summer day.

He crouched beside a suffering private, then reached out and gently patted the man's shoulder; a commander visiting his wounded after the battle was over. She heard Gordon's voice: *He'll tell you he's a blackhearted scoundrel, then turn around and do something so basically kind and decent it takes your breath away.*

Dear merciful heaven, how she had loved him. How young and foolish she must have seemed to him, laying her heart at his feet, believing that was enough.

"The orderlies just brought in some hot broth," Annabelle said, shifting her attention where it belonged, to the wounded, in this case, Lieutenant Winston Ellis. "Do you think you could keep it down?"

"Maybe. Sounds good, something hot."

She nodded and stood, careful not to look toward the side of the barn as she did. By the time she returned with the broth, Royce would be gone, and he'd never know she'd seen him, or that her stomach was clenched in a tight knot.

216

The heat seeped through the tin cup, scorching her raw hands, as she worked her way back down the rows of wounded men. She watched where she placed her feet and concentrated on not spilling any of the precious broth on a wounded soldier. She'd almost reached the spot where Winston waited when a man stepped directly into her path.

She drew a deep breath and looked up. His dark hair hung loose and shaggy against the collar of his greatcoat. With a slow, deliberate motion, he thumbed his hat back, revealing those compelling, silvered eyes. She could say nothing. It hurt to look at him, and it was wonderful to look at him—that handsome, strong-boned face; the face that still haunted her dreams.

"What the bloody hell are you doing here?"

"For once, your observation is well-spoken, Major," she said, her voice as icily soft-spoken as his. "I'm here trying to make hell a little less bloody. Now if you would kindly move out of my way—"

He reached out, as if to grab her arm, and she stepped back with such haste the broth sloshed over the cup rim, burning the sensitive flap around her thumb. He dropped his hand. She sidled around him, settling herself beside Winston.

"Annabelle."

She ignored Royce and tried to produce a smile for Winston. He floundered, pushing himself up onto his good elbow.

"Is that man bothering you, Miss Hallston?" he asked. "We'll just send him on his way. Enough of us in here, we can manage to get two good arms and legs together to throw him out with."

"Not to worry, he always leaves on his own," she said, supporting Winston's shoulders as she maneuvered the knapsack beneath him. "Do you want me to hold the cup, or do you want to try?"

Winston's gaze flicked from her to Royce. "If you'll just keep your arm around my shoulder, I think I can handle the cup."

She kept her arm around Winston's shoulders and handed him the cup. He held it front of him like a weapon he intended to hurl in her defense.

Royce glared at her for a long minute, during which she

managed to match his glare, then turned on his heel and strode away. Her gaze followed his proud, arrogant back until he disappeared through the barn doors. With a sigh, she shifted her attention back to her wounded friend. Winston was studying her.

"Who was that?" he asked.

"Major Kincaid."

"*The* Major Kincaid?"

"The same."

"Good Lord Almighty, if I live, I'm going to be court-martialed," he said, slumping against her.

She brushed his hair back from his face and took the cup from him. "I know you're going to live," she said, easing him back down. "You're too brave to die."

The wind picked up, wailing through slits and chinks, deepening the chill and adding a dolorous note to the cries of broken men. Dr. Stringer caught up with her as she was tucking a rag carpet over the shoulders of a violently shaking man. "I told you hours ago to get something to eat," said Dr. Stringer.

By the hard set of his jaw he wasn't going to listen to any argument. Annabelle nodded and started for the door. She stopped as she reached Charlie and knelt beside him. She pulled her cloak over Charlie's shoulders. "I won't be long," she said to Winston, who tried to smile for her.

It seemed to take a tremendous effort to open the barn door. She suddenly realized how tired she was, recognized the dull ache between her shoulder blades and the heavy weight in her legs. Annabelle shoved the door closed and took several faltering steps to the side of the barn.

She crossed her arms on her chest and tilted her head back. Her eyes drifted closed. Her mind floated in an eerie nothingness, and she had no idea how long she'd been standing there when her own shivering pulled her to her senses.

She opened her eyes to the witch scene in *Macbeth*. Men in motley, ragged uniforms were gathered in groups around dozens of faggot fires. Iron stanchions loomed like skeletons over the flickering orange light, black cauldrons suspended over the heat, their contents steaming up to drift into the wispy fog.

The ground was frozen solid, the cold seeping through the worn soles of her boots, yet she saw soldiers huddled beneath blankets and rag carpets, sleeping as soundly as if they were enclosed in the warmth of a feather bed. Other soldiers milled around, chatting quietly while smoking tobacco and sipping from tin mugs. It seemed they all wore bloodied bandages—arms in slings, shoulder pits hunched over rough crutches.

They were Jackson's foot cavalry, and her heart gave a leap for these boys from home, from the rough mountain dirt farms and the gentle valley croplands.

Light beamed from every window of the brick manor house, and she could see moving shadows as other ladies went about nursing the officer wounded. Someone had told her General Gregg was in one of those rooms, dying.

Inside were food and warmth. Out here were the boys from home. The decision was easy. Some of the tiredness eased from her bones as she crossed the yard to the nearest fire.

A deep voice drawled, "Make way, boys, it's our petticoat sergeant."

A loud whoop went up, and she stopped in confusion. A tall soldier, dressed in the rough blue kersey usually reserved for slaves, took her arm and pulled her nearer the fire. All around her, she heard it, *petticoat sergeant*, and she had no idea what they meant. Someone shoved a tin cup in her hand. It was hot and gave off the aroma of overboiled coffee. She cradled the cup in her palms for the warmth and looked up into the face of the nearest soldier.

"Annabelle Hallston," he said, "late of Riverbend, but born and raised in Lexington." He lifted his good arm and tipped a mangy cap. "Sergeant Lance, born and raised in nearby Salem, ma'am. And you're the talk of two army corps tonight—standing up there on the hill with the generals, directing battle. Why, I heard tell even Old Blue Light, himself, was heard to speak highly of you, '*commendable, commendable,*' he said."

This last was such a perfect imitation of Jackson's somber tone that she laughed. "It wasn't quite that way," she said. "And I was only there because he forgot to send the escort he promised until after the shooting began. But how did you hear, anyway?"

"The Anglo-Rebel that follows Longstreet, what's his name?"

He scratched his jaw. "Doesn't matter," he said. "But I hear he's the one . . ."

She remembered then. "Freemantle, late of Her Majesty's Coldstream Guards, and if he comes by Riverbend for hospitality, I'll be certain to doctor his coffee."

That brought a laugh from those who heard it. A barefoot soldier rolled a log close to the fire and gestured. She longed to offer him her own boots, as worn as they were, yet knew it was hopeless. Her feet were maybe half the size of his. As she stepped over the log to sit, she made a mental note to come back tomorrow with as many blankets as she could scrounge. If nothing else, they could wrap their poor, bloody feet in wool.

She sipped on hot coffee and swapped stories of home with the hardened soldiers around her. A corporal from Stuart's cavalry told her he'd actually seen Gordon, and her mind rested easy for that.

A soldier settled on the ground next to her, elbows resting on drawn-up knees. A bloody bandage peeked out beneath a forager's cap. His face and body were those of a mountain man, a hardscrabble farmer toughened by a difficult life even before the coming of war. He tipped the cap with his thumb and stared into the fire, saying nothing.

The fire's heat did little to surmount the cold. Annabelle hunched forward over her knees, shivering. She felt a weight on her shoulders and reached up. Someone had given her his rag carpet. She was getting ready to give it back, it was time to return to the barn anyway, when she heard a voice and shivered more.

"That's all right, soldier," said the low voice. "Keep your blanket." The weight came off her shoulders only to be replaced with a gray greatcoat. She saw two dirty boots step over the log, then Royce sat beside her.

"Don't run away, Annie-girl," he said, placing his arm around her. "I'm only trying to get you warm since you haven't got the sense the Lord gave a turkey, sitting out here in the cold instead of inside in front of a fireplace."

He had the most amazing way of making her want to laugh, even now, when she felt herself shattering inside. She seemed to have forgotten how to breathe. Dear heaven, he was beside her, safe and whole, so deliciously warm, so disgustingly calm, while her own heart raced, threatening to leap from her chest. She wouldn't let him do this to her again. She couldn't. She pulled away and scooted down the log.

He held his hands up, spreading his fingers in an exaggerated gesture and then dropped them on his knees. "And all this time, I thought we were friends," he said in a lazy drawl.

"It hardly matters to me what you thought, Major." She stood and dropped the coat in his lap. "If you'll excuse me, I've got work to do."

He moved faster than she remembered, on his feet instantly with her wrist caught in his grip. "I'm taking you home where you belong. Men fight the wars, women stay home."

He stared at her, his eyes flashing silver daggers. Something inside her snapped, and she exploded like a creek in flash flood.

"Wars! I stood on a hill today watching men from both sides falling like lawn pins and heard an intelligent man call it splendid! *Splendid*." She tossed her head and gestured with the arm not held in his punishing clasp.

"Inside those buildings are broken, bloody men, some of them little more than children, many of them dying, and it is *not* splendid. I might be a weak-kneed little woman, not strong enough to fight in your bloody battles, but I'm telling you, sir, I'm strong enough to pick up the pieces you brave men leave behind. Me and thousands of other women like me who get up every morning and deal with the mess you men have made. I don't understand the why of this war, and I'll probably never understand, but I'm telling you that I will not follow your man's orders. I'm staying until I'm good and ready to leave."

She rasped in a chestful of frigid air, suddenly realizing that all around her was stillness. She raised her hand to her face, surprised to find her cheeks wet with tears.

Royce dropped her wrist. A muscle jumped along his jaw as he reached in his pocket, but his eyes showed only the reflection of firelight. Wordlessly, he held out a handkerchief. She ignored his flag of truce, and, after a pause, he shoved it back in his pocket.

She felt foolish and spent and, at the same time, strangely triumphant. The soldier sitting at her feet was the one to break the edgy silence.

"They're here, ma'am," he said in a flat, emotionless drawl.

She turned slowly and looked at the top of his forager's cap. "What?"

"'Cause them Yanks are here, we gotta fight 'em."

And that, she thought, was probably the best answer to *why?* she'd ever hear. One she might even understand.

The same men who had thrown themselves into this morning's battle with savage fury now stood around her, heads bowed, awkwardly fingering filthy caps, shuffling their feet like miscreant little boys. Using both hands, she brushed straggling hair back from her face.

"Please accept my apology, gentlemen," she said. "It's been a long day."

"Heck, Miss Hallston," drawled a rangy soldier. "My wife never put it that kindly."

Somebody laughed, and the tension was broken. Without looking at Royce because she knew she couldn't do so and hold her crumbling composure, she stepped over the log and headed for the barn. She'd taken but three strides when he fell in beside her. She wrapped her arms around her waist and hugged tight.

"I'm taking you home before you collapse," he said in a tone she recognized as an order. She stopped and swung to face him. The air seemed to vibrate between them, like the taut strings of a fiddle.

"There's a boy in there not much older than Bo. He's . . . he's dying, and I promised him . . ." Her words caught in her throat, and she swallowed hard, somehow managing to hold her gaze on his. As usual, his eyes were bathed in shadows. "Peyton sent Clarence. He's helping with the burial details until I'm ready to leave. I don't need you, Major."

The wind caught her skirt, slapping it against his leg. She heard him draw in a breath and let it out slowly. She imagined she could feel his heartbeat, but she knew it was only her own.

"His mother's name?" Annabelle asked Winston.

"Mrs. Alma Reid. Warrenton."

She drew in her bottom lip, holding back a sigh of futile loss. "I have relatives near there. I'll take the Bible to her personally."

"He'd be pleased."

She could sit here forever, holding a lifeless body as it grew cold, but Charlie was gone, and Winston lived. She reached over and touched Winston's good shoulder. "We'll get you into the house now. They've even got a mattress waiting."

Her throat felt raw, and every muscle in her body ached. Wearily, she brushed her hair back and went in search of some stewards. Within a short time, Winston had been carried into the house. She leaned against the wall as Charlie's body was lifted on a stretcher and watched until they reached the door. Then she closed her eyes against a dry, scratchy sorrow, too numb for anything more.

"There's someone outside waiting to take you home," said Dr. Stringer.

Annabelle looked around the barn, torn between an ache to stay and a wish to escape this suffering for a few hours. "You're not leaving."

"No," he said. "I'll be here until I can't stand up anymore, then I'll find a tent and a bottle and drink myself senseless until the next battle. It's almost daybreak, Miss Hallston. You've done enough. Go home, get some rest, and thank God it wasn't any worse this time."

"A splendid victory," she murmured.

"Splendid," he said, and it sounded like a sigh.

She watched him walk down the row, his tired shoulders moving through flickering shadows, and she thought men like him were the real heroes in any war. With a sigh of her own, she picked up her cloak and used it to cover a moaning, jacketless soldier who didn't even know she hovered over him. She picked up Charlie's knapsack, slung it over her shoulder, and pushed open the barn door.

Her gaze landed on the back of a tall man, a caped greatcoat hanging in elegant folds from his broad shoulders. Desperately, she searched for Clarence. Surely, he wouldn't leave her to face—

Royce turned. An icy panic gripped her chest, and her coward's heart gave way. She whirled and began to walk rapidly away from him. Hearing his heavy tread behind her, she quickened her pace.

"Annabelle!"

She broke into a run and ducked into a rose arbor. Her skirt caught on dry, tangled vines, and she yanked, hearing the tear of merino wool. He made a sudden lunge forward, grabbing her wrist. She tried to pull away, but he held on tight.

"Annie, dammit, I'm not here to assault your virtue," he said.

She struggled, careful to keep her face turned away. If she didn't look, she could pretend he wasn't here at all, and then she'd still be safe. He let go of her wrist, roughly grabbing her shoulders instead, and her head jerked back so she couldn't help but see him. His face was sun-bronzed, with harsh lines about his mouth that hadn't been there before. His eyes looked dark and as unfathomable as the sea.

She couldn't bear to look into those eyes and was too tired to struggle. Her head dropped forward against his chest, and his arms came around her, his palms hot against her back. She didn't want this tightening in her chest, this heat wherever he touched. Unconsciously, her hands clenched. She felt the walls crumbling, the walls she'd so meticulously built in a desperate effort to salvage something from the desolation he'd left in his wake.

"Clarence. Where's Clarence?" Her voice sounded hoarse.

"I sent him home hours ago, before some quartermaster spied him and decided to impress him into Confederate service—are you laughing?"

It was true. Her shoulders quaked . . . insanity, absurdity, maybe just exhaustion. "Worry about the horses, the sheep, even the cured hams, but don't worry about Clarence. He's free now," she said, still speaking to his gold buttons. "Peyton gives them a simple test, and if they pass, he signs their papers."

"I'll be damned," muttered Royce.

She stepped back and he let her go without a fight. Flexing her fingers, she stared at her red, raw hands, briefly wondering what had become of her gloves. She dropped her hands, burying them in the folds of her dress, and studied the mud-splatters on his boots. Strands of disheveled hair blew across her face.

She rubbed her dry, burning eyes. She tilted her head and looked at the graying sky. Throughout it all, she felt him watching her as certainly as she felt the harsh cold.

This wasn't how it was supposed to happen. In her imagination, he'd walk into a candlelit ballroom and see her dancing in someone else's arms, smiling into someone else's face. Her hair would be perfectly coifed, her hands white and smooth and her gown not just clean, but elegant. She'd be the haughty lady and cut him to the quick with a few well-chosen words, then, in spite of his height, she'd find a way to look down her nose at *him*.

She forced herself to meet his gaze. The creases at the corner of his mouth deepened into a sudden, dazzling smile.

"At grave risk to my manhood, my pride, and my tattered reputation as invincible among the fair flowers of our Southern cause, I am prepared to escort the lady home. Is the lady, perchance, ready to go?"

The blood drained from her head in a sudden rush. Her vision grayed and the world tilted precariously as the nausea she'd been fighting all day billowed up. She swallowed hard, grabbed her abdomen with one hand and reached out blindly with the other. A big hand grabbed hers, and a strong arm wrapped her waist. She leaned against him, uncertain as to whether she was going to cry or laugh or be sick all over his uniform.

"I think the lady is ready," he said softly.

They rode through the same soup-thick fog as the previous morning, made even more impenetrable by the late sunrise. She was wrapped in fog, wrapped in his greatcoat, therefore, wrapped in his scents, and she didn't think she'd ever be warm or sane again.

Her hands clutched stiff leather in a frozen grip on the reins, her ears ached from the whistle of a northeasterly wind, and her shivering had become uncontrollable. She wanted to be home and didn't think they'd ever get there, traveling by every back trail he'd ever discovered in his errant childhood.

Annabelle decided that alone was reason to hate him.

"C-couldn't we have t-taken a shorter way, maybe the T-telegraph Road?" She'd been trying for sarcasm, but her chattering teeth spoiled the effect.

"Nervous pickets shoot first and ask questions later."

*You had to ask*, she thought. *Men fight the wars, women stay home.* She went back to concentrating on not shivering. She didn't want to think about Royce Kincaid, wounded men, nervous pickets, or her teeth making her sound like a clacking hen.

"You could ride with me—you'd be warmer."

"I'm n-not c-cold." She caught a movement in the side of her vision and slanted him a glance in time to see him tug his hat forward as he tucked his chin down. She'd swear there was a crease at the corner of his mouth, and she wanted to sling Charlie's knapsack against his arrogant, grinning head. She would if the fool thing wasn't already slung over his saddle pommel.

She focused her eyes on a spot between the horse's ears and listened to the creak of saddle leather. Gradually, other sounds burrowed into her consciousness—an unearthly wail floating on the spectral mist; disembodied, smothered moans pierced by shrieks too terrible to hear. Even the horse seemed spooked by the strange ventriloquism, throwing his head and shying fiercely to the side, almost unseating her.

Royce reached out to grab the gelding's headstall. His face beneath the hat looked grim, his lips set in a harsh, cruel line. Her mind flashed vivid pictures of their own soldiers lying in front of a tent-fly, waiting for the surgeon's knife; the gruesome, bloody surgeon with a knife clutched between his teeth—and of blue-clad bodies lying in the carnage of the Sunken Road where there were no surgeons, not even a helping hand bearing water.

"Surely, they're not still there?" She could hardly push the words out.

"They'll lie there with the dead until Burnside asks for a burial truce. As of four this morning, word was he planned another attack."

She couldn't believe the unemotional tone of his voice. Those sounds came from soldiers fighting for the other side, but they were still wounded men lying helplessly on the frozen ground.

"They'll die waiting for help."

"The lucky ones."

It was the ultimate horror in an impossibly long time span fraught with horrors, and she couldn't fight it any longer. She tumbled out of the saddle in her haste to dismount, landing hard and off-balance, so that she scrabbled for purchase on the frozen ground. On some level, she realized she'd spooked the gelding again, maybe by the flash of hoof she saw near her head, but she couldn't think or move. Her insides were trying to get outside, and she doubled over with dry, painful waves of nausea, oblivious to everything else.

Her horse lurched out of his grasp as Royce fought to control his own. For a minute that seemed a terrifying, endless nightmare, he thought Ajaque's rearing hoofs were going to come down square on her bent head.

He got his mount under control and dismounted, hearing the other horse scrambling through brush somewhere ahead in the gloomy fog. He could only hope the valuable animal made it back to Riverbend before some dismounted cavalryman discovered him, but right now, there was a priceless woman bent over the frozen ground, heaving her guts out.

He tethered his horse to a tree branch and managed to coax some water out of his canteen to wet his handkerchief. He tucked the canteen under his arm, trying to thaw more water by body heat, and knelt beside her. His hand hovered over her bent head, needing desperately to touch her, afraid to touch her.

The shock of seeing her inside that barn had cut him like a whiplash. Eighteen months of denial and all it took was one look at her, and he knew he would never want any woman more.

He'd fought the orders to come here and then tried to steel himself for the happenstance of meeting her when the orders held, but never had he expected to find her in that Dante's Inferno—a cold barn filled with the brutally wounded who weren't expected to live and the vermin-laden enlisted men who wouldn't be placed in a decent dwelling until some effort could be made to delouse them. He wondered now why he'd been shocked. She was always exactly where she didn't belong.

His hand settled on her back, feeling each individual knuckle in that ramrod spine of hers, bent almost double now. He stared at her nape, looking so white and vulnerable between the disheveled wisps of hair. He wanted to press his lips against the little protruding knob there, but he didn't.

His concern was growing to fear, she'd be coughing up bloody guts soon; but she gave one massive shudder and settled back on her legs, hugging her waist. He reached around her, holding out the wet handkerchief. She took the cloth from his hand and buried her face in it. He tried to think of something to say, something quick-tongued and amusing, knowing her first reaction would be humiliation and trying to spare her at least that, but he failed.

"Are you all right?" he asked, thinking that was the lamest, most banal statement that had ever passed his lips.

Her hands dropped to her lap as she tilted her head back. "I have just broken the sixth commandment in the Book of Ladies."

"The sixth commandment in the Book of Ladies?" Christ, she was still shaking and he didn't know whether to hold her or not.

"Thou art encouraged to faint in front of any gentleman, but thou must never throw up, especially while wearing a gentleman's good overcoat."

If he could have, he would have smiled. He wanted to take her head in his hands and kiss every pain away, but he wanted more than just that, and therein lay the problem.

"The commandment is only slightly bent, dear heart. My heart is black, my reputation vile, and my soul lost—but on the other hand, it was a pretty decent overcoat." He handed her the canteen. "Just a few sips, or you'll start all over again," he warned.

She used the water first to clean her face and hands, then drank a little, holding the wooden canteen out to her side when she was done. Gray mist eddied around them like a gossamer shroud, and the infernal moaning still sounded in the distance. She was sitting on the frozen ground, shaking like a leaf and evidently still unable to face him. His chest tightened, making it difficult to breathe. He stood and walked over to the horse, stowing the canteen and giving her another minute to compose herself. When he turned, she was back on her feet.

His greatcoat hung from her slender shoulders, puddling around her feet. It gaped open at the front, revealing a rumpled blue dress stained with blood and God-only-knew what else. Wisps of damp, tousled hair fluttered around her face, a face as ashen as the misty fog, her lips white and trembling.

"Annie." He lifted his hands. "Dear Christ, Annabelle . . ."

She started to back up, shaking her head. Her gaze became caught in his, and she stopped. Her eyes grew larger and darker, deep, brown, turbulent rivers, and he fell into them, drowning. He clasped the sides of her face and dipped his head.

She jerked herself back so fast she stumbled. Her hand shook as she pressed it against her lips. She held herself as if she thought she might break if she so much as breathed. His own breath faltered, then came back, raspy and uneven. Dear God, he'd take her now if he listened to his body, sick and vulnerable as she was, take her beneath him on the hard, cold ground and possess her for one heated moment in time.

"Get on the horse."

Her breasts lifted as she drew in a deep breath. "I think I'll walk."

"Get on the bloody horse before I throw you over the saddle."

She regarded him out of solemn, dark eyes. "I cannot bear this again, Kincaid."

He looked in those revealing eyes and saw something too deep for words, something he didn't understand and knew that glimpse into her soul would haunt him for the rest of his days. Love, a word used by the morally self-righteous as an excuse for fornication. Until one party tired of the game. He knew that even if she didn't, and still, he ached for her with a hunger that was a deep, hollow pain in his gut. He swung her up in his arms. She stiffened and pushed against him.

"I'm only going to take you home," he said quietly, and, for an instant, he felt the soft brush of her hair against his neck as she stilled against him.

He lifted her onto the saddle, untethered the horse, and

swung up behind her. He had to reach around her to gather the reins, but she didn't struggle against the contact, and he willed his own body to calm. Eventually, her shivering seemed to ease. They passed beyond range of the wails in the Sunken Road, and, for a long while, the only sounds were the muted plod of the horse's hooves and the dripping of moisture from tree branches.

"How long have you been back?" she asked in a quiet voice.

"Here, two days, before that, Port Royal for three."

"Were you going to visit us?"

He sensed the reluctance in her question, understood the basis for the reluctance, but he wouldn't lie to her. He owed this courageous little woman that much.

"I'm fighting a war, Annie. There's no time or desire in my life for pleasant little family reunions."

He felt her small sigh, then she went so still, he wondered if she'd fallen asleep. He was careful to keep the horse's gait smooth, just in case, but she stirred when Riverbend came into sight, so he knew she'd only been quiet.

Lights beamed through the first-floor windows and the lanterns were lit by the front door. Before he'd had a chance to dismount, the front door opened. He expected Peyton but saw Jules come out on the gallery, followed by a black woman it took him a second to recall. Patsy. He could actually feel Annabelle gathering her strength, the same way he always felt his horse gathering to take a jump. Within moments, he understood why.

"Little missy, what you meanin' staying out all night, soldiers or no soldiers," said Jules, as Royce dismounted.

Royce reached up to assist Annabelle as Patsy interrupted Jules.

"Miz Annie, I done my best, but I'm just the darky as far as all these white folks are concerned, and they aren't about to listen to me. Miz Augusta means well, but she just fit to be tied worrying about Marse Gordon, and you know she gets all flighty when things don't go right. Can't think of much that's gone right since you took off with Marse Peyton yesterday, and Marse Peyton hardly been here a-tall to help."

Annabelle's eyes winced shut, then she looked up into his face. A wan smile took shape at her lips. "I know you have a

war to fight, but could you come in just a minute, get yourself
a cup of coffee and something to take back with you to eat?
Maybe even meet your nephew?"

He had a command waiting on his return, a battle expected
as soon as the fog lifted, and the last thing he wanted to do
was walk inside that house. In the background, he heard
Jules and Patsy arguing and realized Riverbend, like every
other outlying estate, was probably swarming with civilian
refugees.

"When was the last time you slept?" he asked, suddenly
aware that Annabelle was carrying a very heavy load. All he
could see was her small body hunched over in the dirt, sick
from exhaustion. She shrugged and turned to mount the stairs.
Royce followed because he couldn't abandon her to this just
yet.

She took Jules by the arm, wrapping it about her own and
patting the old man's hand as she spoke to Patsy. "We'll
straighten out whatever it is in a few minutes, but right now,
would you get Major Kincaid some coffee and ham biscuits to
take back with him?"

Patsy preceded her through the door, huffing. Annabelle ignored the sounds of disgust and turned her attention to Jules.

"I'm fine, and I stayed so long because there was one soldier
that reminded me of Bo—" She turned so fast, Royce almost
plowed into her. "Charlie's knapsack," she said. "I promised
him I'd send his mother the Bible."

He caught her arm. "Jules will get it."

He steered her through the door as Jules went for the knapsack. Gordon's wife met them inside with another problem,
something about some family named Sutter who had evidently
pitched camp in the dining room. His attention was diverted by
Patsy, who shoved a cup of something hot in his hand, then
joined in with Augusta. Annabelle still stood with her back to
him, but he saw her brush her palm along the side of her head
in a gesture of total weariness.

"*Enough.*" He used his command voice and gained instant
silence.

Annabelle shrugged out of his greatcoat, handing it to
Patsy, then turned. Augusta's hand flew to her mouth as she
gasped, "Annie."

Jules's footsteps came to a sudden halt. His own heart missed a beat.

Annabelle self-consciously brushed her hands down the front of her dress. "I guess I'm a mess," she said in a small, raspy voice. She squeezed Patsy's hand then glanced at Augusta, as if in apology. "Let me get into some clean clothes first, Gussie."

Her clothing was stained, torn, and probably ruined, but he hardly noticed. Inside, with good light, he saw the bruises on her wrist and knew he'd put them there. Her eyes were huge and so filled with exhaustion they were flat and black with heavy circles beneath them that looked like more bruises on her pale skin. She was still shaking and he had a sudden fear she was going to collapse any minute.

Tough and indomitable as she was, after watching her heave her insides out, he wasn't at all sure she'd recover from illness brought on by the cold or her exhaustion.

"Go change," he said into a room so quiet he thought he could hear her heart racing. "Patsy will be up in a minute."

He'd order her to bed, but she'd only defy him. He could hope she'd listen to Patsy, and he'd stay long enough to make certain Patsy and Augusta both understood. Annabelle made it as far as the steps. She swayed and reached for the newel post, missing it.

He caught her before she hit the floor. He was careful to reach the darkness at the top of the stairs before he kissed her. And equally careful to kiss only her brow.

# Chapter 16

❧⟶◦⟵❧

Royce pushed aside the tent flap and stepped inside. He tossed his hat on the cot and stretched the saddle kinks out of his back. The stretch did nothing to relieve the deep sense of futility.

He hated moving with the ponderous army, or not moving as in this case. His men were a different type of soldier, lightning-quick raiders, in fast and out faster, usually under cover of night, usually highly successful, due in no small part to the element of surprise. The only surprising thing about this Battle of Fredericksburg was Burnside's incredible stupidity.

No battle today. All day long the two armies faced one another across the plains, and the only shots fired were from skirmishing pickets. He heard the tent flap open behind him and straightened.

"Sir? I brought your dinner, and Captain DeShields is back," said William.

"Thank you, Sergeant." Royce set the plate on the table without looking at it. He knew what it held, gravy and more biscuits, standard army fare.

"Take care of his horse and send John in here."

Royce ignored the plate of food and picked up the mug of coffee. He took a deep draft, relishing the burning warmth as the liquid snaked down to his belly. The tent flap opened again, letting in a gust of damp cold as John ducked and entered. Royce looked over and smiled involuntarily.

"You been scouting or rolling in a mud holler?" he asked.

"Rolling in the mud holler would have been about as useful," answered John, tossing his plumed hat to land beside Royce's. "Picked up a couple of pickets and more of the same information—are you going to eat that dinner or watch it get cold?"

"That's what I've always liked about you, Captain DeShields. You have such a firm grasp on the truly important issues in life."

He and DeShields had been posted together in Texas. DeShields was VMI while he himself was Point, but they shared the same views on soldiering, a new type of soldiering adapted from the tactics of the Plains Indians, an effective kind of fighting that large armies and War Departments did not understand.

After all these years, they shared more. They'd developed a bond that went beyond language. Royce knew he'd trust DeShields not only with his life, but with even more important things, his command and those other intangibles he couldn't name—those things he saw in Annabelle.

He had a sudden vision of her, actually felt her in his arms. He pushed that thought aside. Later tonight, after the duties were fulfilled. Then, he knew, he would think about her in spite of his effort not to.

Royce gestured toward the makeshift table, an old door, cut in half and set over fence rails, that served as a dining table, map table, and desk. "Eat while you give me your report, then we'll ride over to headquarters."

Royce sat across from John and listened as he gave his report in between bites of gravy and biscuits. John cleaned the plate, wiping up the last of the thick gravy with a hard army biscuit, and leaned back.

"We're being wasted here," said John. "Stuart's men can do this scouting. We should be back up north, hitting the supply lines, keeping Lincoln nervous about an attack on Washington."

Royce leaned forward, his elbows on his knees. He felt like a man with his back to the dike, trying to stem the flood by poking his fingertips in the widening cracks. "Another barren victory," he said in a low voice. "If this goes on long enough,

Lincoln's going to find himself a fighting general, and they'll win by sheer numbers."

"It isn't over yet. If we can hold them back long enough, maybe England or France will come in. Maybe their people will get so tired of meaningless slaughter like yesterday, they'll lose the stomach for fighting and just let us go."

"Maybe the last, not the first. Cotton or no cotton, England's not coming in because of the slavery issue, and King Louis won't move without Britain. He's got his eye on Mexico anyway." Royce thrust his fingers through his hair. From outside the tent, he heard the sounds of men going into bivouac. Another wasted night. "Out West, Sherman and Grant . . ."

"Missed your true calling, Royce. You should've been a politician. All this farsighted vision."

"Hell, I should've been a farmer." Royce leaned back and flashed John a grin. "Let's go see if we can't talk a general into letting us fight."


The rain had stopped, giving way to a light, cold breeze. Royce stood for a minute, absently slapping his gauntlets against the palm of one hand. The Old Man looked tired tonight, too tired. But tiredness hadn't weakened his courtly, ironclad resolve. Royce moved to the fire where John waited with Lee's aide, Taylor. Taylor excused himself and returned to the tent Royce had just left.

"What did he say?" asked John when they were alone.

Royce held out his hands to the fire, breathed in a thick wave of damp smoke, and stepped back. "We split the command. If Burnside doesn't move tomorrow, you go back to the mountains with two companies; I stay here with the rest."

He considered mumbling a few curses, but allowed John the honor. He waited for the wave of profanity to pass, then said, "You're to be ready to come back if something develops here, but we both know it's not going to happen."

"Did he say why?"

"Since when do lowly majors ask generals why?"

"Since when do you follow that law of the army?"

Royce ignored John's bantering and stared at the struggling fire. He'd asked, and the answer even made some sense. Under different circumstances, he might be excited over a new challenge, but there was a danger here that had nothing to do with Federal armies. Every nerve in his body felt the gathering storm, and he had no idea how long his control would last.

Damn Peyton and his matchmaking. Damn the stupid Union general sitting on the Rappahannock and the determined Old Man in the tent behind him. He ran out of targets for damnation, other than the most deserving—himself.

"How long are you stuck here?"

John's question brought him back to this hilltop. "Until he determines what Burnside's plans are. Maybe a week, maybe a month," said Royce, beginning to pull on his gauntlets. "It's not really so bad. I got him to detach us from Jackson, so we can raid on our own. Aquia and Falmouth are pretty decent targets."

John gave him a hefty slap across his shoulders. "You had me feeling sorry for you, and now I'm jealous. A whole new crop of ladies to dance with and a major Union supply depot to harass. You can even spend Christmas at home."

Before he could respond with the denial that sprang up from deep in his gut, he saw Taylor hurrying back toward them.

"General Lee wishes to speak with you before you leave," said the aide.

Surprised, Royce turned, seeing the flash of John's arm as he rendered his own salute. The General of the Army of Northern Virginia returned the salute, then the Virginia gentleman nodded with a small smile at his lips.

"Walk with me, Major Kincaid," said General Lee.

Royce fell in beside him, and they walked toward the crest of the hill.

"I want you here because you know this land as well as any man in the army," said Lee. "I hope you understand that."

"I'm a soldier, I go where I'm ordered," said Royce, unwilling to concede anything more, even to this fine old gentleman. They reached the crest, and Lee stopped. Royce stopped beside him.

The clouds were thinning, and moonlight reflected on the plain before them. It was a commanding view, probably one of the best observation points any army headquarters had ever found for battle. Their own batteries stretched as far as he could see. He heard scattered shots fired from the base of the long hill to the left; the men at the Sunken Road firing at any motion in the thin light, eager to add another bluecoat to the slaughter. Lee rubbed his fingers through his beard.

"We lost two good generals in this fight, Cobb and Gregg," he said. "Good soldiers, good leaders. Where do we replace them?"

Royce suddenly regretted this moonlight stroll with his commanding general. "Sir, we've been through this."

"You must not keep turning down these promotions." Lee's voice was still low, but Royce heard the fire in the tone. "I could use you as a brigadier. Your country needs you, Major Kincaid, and I do not understand your unwillingness."

"I'm cavalry, sir. You already have fine brigadiers under Stuart. You don't need me there."

He felt, rather than heard Lee's sigh. "Your rank precludes me from assigning you a larger command, and your talents are being wasted. You're a leader of men. You should be leading."

"My command is effective because it's small. We hit them in several places at once, hard, and they can't find us to retaliate. I'm not interested in rank, sir, I'm interested in results."

"I'd give you Maxcy Gregg's brigade tonight. I already know the president would approve it."

"Infantry, General. I served under you in Texas, and you know that's not where I can do you, or my country, the best service."

Lee clasped his hands behind his back and seemed to be studying the cloud shadows as they moved across the fields.

Royce studied the plain in front of him, wondering again at the blindness of any general who would throw good soldiers against such a position. Estimates placed the Northern losses at more than ten thousand in a few hours' fighting. He couldn't help but think it was the closest thing to murder he'd ever witnessed in warfare.

Maybe John was right, and they'd win this war when the North grew tired of reading the casualty lists and voted its current crop of politicians out of office. He heard a sound, a dull thud as Lee distractedly struck the fist of one hand against the palm of his other. Three times, then his hands dropped to his side.

"I'm afraid the day will come, Major, when you will be called to higher command."

"If that day comes, I'll do my duty, sir."

Lee turned, and Royce turned with him, walking back to the smoky fire, where several more men had collected. Royce recognized Longstreet and Jackson. He guessed there was a council of war in the offing and wanted to get off this hillside before that event took place. A smart soldier knew when to retreat.

"I saw your father," said Lee in a conversational tone. "He's looking well."

The abrupt change of topic caught Royce off guard. He guessed Lee had been out to Riverbend sometime in the past month.

"I haven't had the opportunity to see him," said Royce.

Lee stopped and gave him a fatherly glare. "I'm speaking as a friend of your family, not as your commanding officer. You're here. Go to Riverbend, Royce. Whatever the past, it's still your future."

*My heaven and my hell*, thought Royce.

A band of crimson flamed across the night sky. Royce stiffened, waiting for the screaming of artillery bombardment, but there was no sound, only a breathless silence, then a broad, iridescent sheet of green streaked across the sky.

Men began cheering, Rebels and Yanks, united by the majesty in the sky above. Fiery lances and blood red banners streaked and billowed into garlands of green and wreaths of gold. Tall columns of pearly white beckoned upward, all of it reflecting off the patches of snow on the field below.

"The Aurora," he said. "I've never seen the Northern lights this far south."

Lee waited a beat, then said, "A humble man might take it as a sign from Our Lord, honoring the dead."

"Whose dead, sir? Theirs or ours?"

"Aren't they all ours, Major Kincaid?"

Most of the snow was gone, washed into the creek by the rain, and the ground was slick and muddy. Cold mud wasn't a deterrent to the poker game. The boys were still trying to teach young Caleb Geary the art of poker. Caleb was one hell of a ranger, but he'd never be a poker player. They'd spread a blanket on the ground near the fire, hung a lantern from a tree, and sat around on the blanket in the growing dark, surrounded by other campfires, the wail of someone's harmonica and an uncommon quiet for soldiers in camp.

Royce sat with his back to a tree, watching. He hadn't the will to join them tonight. It was enough to sit in the darkness near the fire's warmth, passing the time silently, not involved, not needing to talk.

They were camped on Stuart's flank and he'd made it a point to find Gordon today, needing to assure himself his brother had come through another battle unscathed. That had been the only bright spot in the past two bleak days. Yesterday began with another fog-bound, predawn scout only to discover the Yanks had withdrawn across the river, cutting loose the pontoon bridges and escaping again. Wise move on their part. He knew he wasn't the only Reb soldier who felt murderous tonight.

Sacked. In a four-day occupation, historic colonial Fredericksburg had been sacked. He could see it, hear it, smell it, as if he was still there. Buildings cannonaded into rubble. Piles of broken furniture tossed haphazardly out of windows and doors, whole libraries of books thrown in the mud, dishes and fine porcelain smashed to smithereens. Crunching glass with every step taken, winter stores of food tossed in the mud and trampled. Even pianos rolled out into the street and used as horse troughs.

"You're not playing tonight?"

He looked up. DeShields, whose departure had been delayed another day in order to provide what assistance they could to the civilians returning to their ransacked homes.

"No."

John rubbed his mustache with his thumb, then hunkered down on the ground next to Royce. "It's a different war after today," he said in a quiet tone.

"Damn right it is. Ignorant ruffians."

Riverbend had been spared. This time. What would happen next time? What unthinkable depredations would the blue host unleash on defenseless women and children next time they cut a swath down this river byway? What would happen to River-bend, to Annie? Annabelle, already carrying a load too large for her narrow shoulders.

Sweet, skinny, defiant Annie. Why couldn't he put her out of his mind?

John lit a cigar, the match flaring in the darkening night, followed by a cloud of smoke. Royce considered lighting one of his own but it seemed like too much effort. He'd walk over to his tent and get roaring drunk, but he didn't want the sore head in the morning.

"If it was me, and I was this close to home, I sure as hell wouldn't be sitting here in the mud." John took another drag and unleashed another cloud, good Virginia tobacco by the smell.

"I'm not you, and Riverbend isn't my home."

"Touchy tonight."

"Did anyone ever tell you you're a royal pain in the ass?"

"I'm not the burr in your butt." John leaned back against the tree and pulled his hat low over his face. "Go home, Royce. You'll feel better once you see it's still there."

She's *there*, Royce thought, and the thought brought back the vision of Annabelle in that bloody barn, the closest thing to an angel he ever expected to see on this earth. He could feel her in his arms as he'd carried her up the stairs. Christ, maybe she wasn't there anymore, maybe she was dying, already dead, and that was the unspeakable fear gnawing at his guts for two days now.

He stood up and stretched, careful to maintain a casual air. Jarring laughter sounded from the men around the blanket. Caleb had been bluffed again.

"If you're done losing matchsticks, son, you can saddle my horse," he said.

John crossed his arms on his chest and hunkered down a little lower. "Going on a scout?"

"Beats getting drunk."

"Yeah," mumbled John as he crossed his boots at the ankle. "Sure does."

# Chapter 17

A single horseman rode up the lane, the horse's hooves sounding a suck and draw in the muddy ground. The rider passed through the dark barren oaks and pulled to a stop. His hand lifted, tilting a hat back. He sat motionless astride the horse for long minutes, then, with a nudge to the horse's flanks, rode slowly forward.

*No little black boy to meet the Massa this time,* thought Clarence. Rufus was gone like so many others, slipped across the river into the Promised Land. Clarence had heard their talk before they ran, their vision of freedom, and feared for them in the land of milk and honey. White men on that side of the river, too, drinking buttermilk from porcelain cups while the barefooted black man served them honeyed biscuits.

Clarence watched Royce dismount, sensing a vulnerability in the tilt of his head that reminded him of a long-ago boy huddled on the floor inside an old gatehouse with silent tears coursing down his cheeks. *Slavery,* he thought, *could take many forms. Some remained unspeakable.*

Royce pulled off his hat as he approached the gallery. He stopped at the foot of the stairs, placing one booted foot on the second riser, then leaned forward, elbow on his knee, the hat dangling from his hand. His brooding gaze was fixed on the double entrance door, giving Clarence a chance to study that taut, well-bred face in the lantern's dim light.

There was no such thing as a good master, but he could, in

good conscience, call this one a good man. Royce wouldn't want to know it, but there were times when he, the slave, felt pity for him, the master. Royce dragged his own chains wherever he went, whipped himself for things that couldn't be helped.

"You never mentioned Peyton had given you your papers," said Royce, without shifting his gaze.

Clarence smiled inwardly. A good soldier, a good scout; he'd known a man was hidden in the shadows. May he always know and survive this godforsaken war.

"I've always been free where it counted. Didn't see any point."

Royce flashed a lazy smile in his direction, the smile fading as he caught sight of the shotgun. "Expecting trouble?"

"White trash shirkers and two armies full of stragglers. Trouble enough if it comes."

"You might be free, but you're still black. That shotgun could be your death sentence."

Clarence tipped the chair back on two legs, slowly rocking. "No one here but the boy," he said, watching Royce through narrowed eyes. Even through the woolly coarseness of the sack coat, he could see the tension cording Royce's neck and shoulders.

Royce straightened and tugged his hat back on his head. His restless gaze roamed the lawn. He was being real careful not to look at those doors again.

"How is the boy?"

"Good enough, growing. He misses you. Thinks you're the reincarnation of Jesus Christ and drives everyone crazy with the tales he reads about you in the papers. Going to that military institute next fall so's he can learn how to be a soldier."

"Damn."

A cold wind fluttered the brim of Royce's felt hat. Royce turned his head slightly, and his throat jerked as he swallowed.

"Annabelle?" His voice was even lower than usual, as if he was afraid of the answer.

"You're the brave soldier. Go into the parlor and see for yourself."

Royce's head rocked back as if he'd been struck, and only then did Clarence understand the fear that had brought Royce on this lonely pilgrimage to the home he denied.

"Doggone it, Royce," he said, his voice gritty with a mixture of anger and sorrow. "Do you think I'd let you walk in there to find your wife in a coffin without at least warning you first? She was plumb wore out, that's all. Peyton insisted on a few days' rest, and she's back to her plucky little self."

He watched Royce turn without so much as a nod, knowing the famed soldier was running from a battle he didn't want to face. Anger on Annie's behalf overcame sorrow on Royce's.

A sane man would leave these white folks to clean up their own messes, but he wasn't a sane man. Riverbend was the only home he'd ever known, and Royce had walked barefoot through the fires of Hell to protect a helpless slave boy. His own people might call him a white man's nigger, but Clarence knew better; he was his own man, always had been—and as a man, he still felt enormous respect—even love—for this white man who lived on pride alone. This pitiful white man who was still so scarred by that bitch stepmother he couldn't face what he'd come to feel for his wife and call the emotion by its proper name.

"You going?" said Clarence through the tightness in his throat.

Royce swung back around, his hands clenched into fists at his side. "I've got a war to fight, dammit."

"Yeah, just how many wars are you fighting? Go in there, man, what are you afraid of?"

"I've done enough damage." Light from the porch lantern flickered on the bitter set to his mouth. "Don't tell her I was here."

Clarence rose slowly and walked to the edge of the gallery, holding the shotgun loose at his side. The two men stared at one another while the cold wind blew between them.

"At least tell her good-bye this time."

Royce mounted the gray Thoroughbred. He allowed himself one lingering glance at the door. "If I saw her now . . ." His low voice hitched. "If I saw her now, Clarence, I wouldn't be able to leave. Not even for this bloody damn war."

Clarence didn't know how long he'd been sitting in the cold when he heard the door open, then close behind him. He said nothing, listening to the same footsteps he heard moving around their quarters every night, now crossing the wide flag-stone gallery. It was a sound that always made him feel blessed—to have Patsy in his life every night and day, not just the Sunday they would have been allowed if she still belonged to Moulton Johnson at the Willows.

For that gift, Clarence sent a silent thank-you to the lonely man who had ridden away, turning his back on any chance of finding his own blessed state with the courageous little woman he'd married.

Clarence shifted so his shadow would hide the shotgun as Patsy sat on the step beside him. She shivered and drew her woolen shawl closer across her chest.

"It's cold out here, woman. Get yourself back inside where it's warm."

"Not too cold for you to sit out here hiding a shotgun, risk-ing your colored hide to protect the white folks."

*So much for pulling the wool over this one's eyes,* he thought, smiling to himself and ignoring the chiding in her words. He understood the sentiment fueling her reproof.

"Peyton will be back from that meeting soon enough now." Clarence looked down his nose at the top of her head, still wrapped in the dark red turban she wore through her day's chores. "The boys asleep?"

"Sophie's watching them."

"Hmmm." He closed his eyes and breathed deeply, flaring his nostrils wide to make room for all her scents—clove from the kitchen, laundry soap, the milk she'd fed their infant son from her breast, and underneath those scents the hot musk of a woman ready to make love to a man. Or maybe he only wanted to smell that last one. After that scene with Royce he felt a deep, urgent need to bury himself inside Patsy's female body. To forget for however long the loving lasted the sadness that still wearied his bones.

"Was that Major Kincaid I saw through the window," she asked softly, and he held back a sigh.

"Miz Annabelle didn't see him, did she?"

"No, she's already gone upstairs to bed." *Good,* he thought, then Patsy gave a quiet laugh. She said, "I never thought I'd like white folks, let alone feel sorry for them. You're the smart one; tell me why I feel sorry for this family of rich white people."

"Because they're not as lucky as you and me." He felt her milk-engorged breast brush his arm as she moved closer to his body's heat.

"That day Major Kincaid came to the Willows to buy me," she said, "I was scared half out of my black skin when he told me we were going to walk back here. All that way, just me and a white man—I couldn't even think 'cause I knew what he was going to do soon as he found himself a shady spot. And him only talking in that soft way he has, not saying much of anything as I recall, just filling the air with his fancy words until I realized we were here and nothing had happened. Then I meet his wife, who ain't really his wife and don't want to be called Mrs. Kincaid by no one—and it's just as plain as the nose on her face that *she* don't want no truck with owning a slave woman. Lordy, I was so confused I would of thought I'd fallen in a hole and woke up in China if you hadn't been here."

More than two years had passed since the day he'd first met Patsy while delivering a repaired wrought-iron gate to the Willows. For eighteen months she'd lived as his wife, borne him two big, strapping sons. In all that time, with all their conjugal intimacy, this was the first time she had ever spoken so openly. His heart swelled up to fill his throat.

"That horse he traded for you, Jupiter, was worth six thousand dollars."

She straightened and looked at him, her dark eyes studying every feature of his face. He looked back until finally, she said in a disbelieving tone of voice, "That's five, maybe six slave women. Why would he do that?"

"Because I asked him to do that."

"I don't understand, Clarence."

"No, I don't expect you do. Sometimes I don't understand it myself." He circled her waist with his arm and rested his cheek against the softness of her turban. Wispy clouds scudded across a sky gone black and cold.

"Is that why we stay here while just about everyone else is running across the river?" she asked, her voice sounding uncertain now. "Because you owe the massa for me?"

"Aw, no, sweet pea, although I would if that's what it took to have you like this. Royce doesn't expect that. Peyton doesn't even expect that. But we'll stay until the shooting ends because it's safer here for you and the children."

"We could go north like the others. I don't think the white people are shooting each other up there."

He was quiet for a minute, watching the damp leaves swirl at the base of the steps, listening to the sound of his wife's breathing. Taking the time to choose the right words to tell this woman he loved the one thing he knew in his bones about himself.

"My great-gran'pappy was African," he said finally. "Ma knew him when he was an old man, and she said he died still mourning for Africa—for his people there—but mourning for more than his people. Africa was where he was born and where he belonged." Clarence let out a deep breath. "I feel that way about this land. I was born here, in Virginia. I could go north and still be in America, but it wouldn't be to live with my people."

He thought he heard the voices of his ancestors in the wind blowing past his ears. "My people made this land. Every brick on this estate was made by their hands, every shingle, every piece of pottery. They felled the trees, then tilled the fields they'd cleared, and watered those fields with their sweat and the sweat of their children. They threshed the wheat, tended the livestock, and got nothing for their labors. I've got to stay here in this land they made, or die mourning for my great-granpappy. Can you understand that?"

"I can understand it, but I'm still afraid. I thought I wanted freedom more than anything in this world. Now it's here on my doorstep and instead of feeling the Jubilee, I'm scared of both armies of soldiers and scared to death over what's going to happen to us tomorrow, or next week, or next whenever if the shooting ever does stop."

"It will end eventually, and the North's going to win because God can't let it be any other way. When it's all over, we'll take that money I've got buried in the freedom jars and build us a little house down in the colored part of town. We've got enough for that and a smithy, too. I'll make us a good living at the forge, and you can stay home and raise our children."

He turned and gripped her arms, so she was facing him. "I'm not saying it's going to be easy—there's nothing worth doing that comes easy—but if we struggle hard enough, then maybe our children won't have to struggle at all." His hands squeezed her arms with the force of what he was feeling inside. "You've got to want it as much as I do. Tell me you want it, Patsy. For us, for our children."

"Oh, Lordy, Clarence, when you talk like that, I can believe anything."

He laughed a little, feeling pride, chagrin—mostly love. "Come closer, sweet pea," he said, circling her with his arm again. "I didn't hurt you, did I?"

"No." She leaned her head in that spot God had made especially for her head, on his chest near his right shoulder, and she felt so warm, so alive—so right.

"That little boy of yours who got sold, we'll take some of that money and look for him too," he said, talking over her head, carefully not looking at her. She made a funny little hiccupping sound, so he gave her a gentle squeeze and changed the direction of this conversation to back where it had started.

"You hear any gossip in the quarters since you've been here about Celeste, Peyton's second wife?"

She nodded against his chest. "Your mama calls her a bitch in heat."

"No one realized that the first year. Celeste put on such a good show those first months, butter wouldn't have melted in her mouth. I was eight the year Peyton brought her home as his wife; Royce would have been seven. In those days, Peyton wasn't around much—politics kept him away. Royce was this little lost boy, wandering around inside that big house all by his lonesome self. My ma was his nurse, and she'd tuck him into his own bed at night, stay until he fell asleep, then leave him with Jules there in the Big House to look over things.

"Half the time, I'd wake up the next morning to find Royce had sneaked out in the middle of the night and come down to our quarters to climb into the bed between Ma and Pa. He learned to talk colored, he spent so much time in the quarters, and at the same time took it upon his child's shoulders to teach my folks how to read and do sums. I swear, Ma loved that little white boy at least as much as she loved me. But it didn't matter; he desperately needed what she was giving him. I couldn't hate him for taking what she freely offered and then begging for more."

Patsy let out a sigh. "Miz Annie said something like that to me once; that inside that hard soldier was a little boy still crying for his mother."

He looked down at her. "Miz Annabelle said that?"

Patsy lifted her head and smiled softly. "She loves him."

"One day, if he doesn't manage to get himself killed first, he's going to realize that. Then that little woman is going to get more loving than she'll know how to handle."

"Oh, Clarence. I hope so."

"So you've discovered one white woman you can like?"

"I didn't want to," she said in a disgusted-sounding grumble that made him smile over her head.

"It's all right to like her. We're just as bad as the white folks if we can't see beyond the color of their skin to what's inside. I respect that little Miz Annabelle about as much as I respect my own ma, and that's saying something."

"Don't preach to me, Clarence," said his wife. "What are you really trying to say in this roundabout way?"

"I'm trying to explain about Royce and me, but I can't do justice to that if I leave out Celeste." He paused, then said, "This isn't for gossip in the quarters, Patsy. It goes too deep. Ma doesn't know. Peyton, although he eventually came to grief with Celeste, still never suspected how truly awful she was for his son. You can't ever let any of this slip to Annabelle."

"What in tarnation did Celeste do?"

He blew out a breath. What hadn't the bitch done? Hate, yes, he knew hatred for that woman, a feeling so intensely cold he hoped to be spared ever feeling it again for any other human being.

In a low voice that wouldn't carry over the sound of the wind, he told his wife how Celeste had had Clem's father sold down the river, not because Peter, the slave, had surprised her in the act of illicit intercourse, but because, as the slaves knew and Peyton didn't, Celeste had satisfied both her curiosity and her urges by seducing a helpless black man to have sex with her, then wanted to be rid of the danger he posed when she grew tired of his novelty.

He saved the worst for last, coming up on the true sorrow when he touched on that first instance inside the old gatehouse; about Royce's fierce boy's attack against the strange man he thought was attacking his stepmother, and how Celeste had laughed, then threatened them both into silence.

"I was nine," Clarence said when his wife looked up, her dark eyes wide and full of moisture. "The same age as the little boy you lost in just that way, being sold separate from you, his own mother. That's what Celeste threatened to do to me. Royce never said a peep, and of course, I wasn't about to, but we had given her a weapon we were too young and innocent to recognize."

Patsy reached for his hand and folded it between her own two warm palms. "The bitch raped you."

"Not me."

"Oh, God, Clarence. Her own son?"

"Stepson, but still, he was a ten-year-old child when it happened the first time. I'll never forget the look on his face when I found him."

"First time?" she said, but he didn't respond, swallowing hard instead. Patsy must have decided to let it go; she trailed a finger back and forth across his chest. After a while, she said, "And he never told his father?"

"No. It was wrong. I should have told Peyton myself when Royce didn't. But we were just boys, and deathly afraid of that white witch, and not thinking clearly because of that fear." He stretched one leg in front of him, then tipped his head back so he could see the pale, clean light of a crescent moon peeking between the clouds

"Do you understand what that means, Patsy? That white child gave up his freedom for me, a black child. We're brothers under the skin, and he's part of the people I can't leave behind by going north."

She cupped his face between her hands. He drew in shallow, panting breaths, desperately afraid he was going to break down from the old sorrows and cry in front of his wife.

"Hush, hush," she crooned. "You big, ugly, softhearted bear

of a man." She lifted her shoulder and wiped away a wash of her own tears on the woolen shawl. "See, you've made me cry. Of course, we'll stay. Of course, I understand."

She leaned forward and kissed him, hot and wet. It was a womanly kiss of tongues, passions, and all the world's sorrows. Then he took over the kiss, deepening the thrust of his tongue, wrapping her in his tight embrace, holding her hard against his chest so he could feel all her soft womanly curves against his hard muscle.

"I love you, sweet pea," he said against her cheek and felt all-over warm when she wriggled in his arms to get closer again.

"You're right, Clarence. We are the lucky ones."

"I knew you'd see it my way eventually."

Johnson, comfortable and complacent inside his white skin, had traded her for a dumb animal. Clarence, both darker and wiser, wouldn't trade her for all the riches in the world. Just Patsy and their sons: that was more wealth than he'd ever dreamed of, surely more than he'd ever deserved.

He looked over his wife's head to the wide double entrance doors to the Big House. Upstairs, another woman was lying in the dark, cold and alone, worrying her way through the long hours of the night while only a few miles away her soldier husband bedded down on a cot inside a canvas tent.

He had often wondered if Royce thought of Annabelle in those minutes before he drifted off to sleep—but now, after tonight, Clarence knew that he did.

# Chapter 18

❦

Annabelle tied the last bit of lace on a branch and stepped back to admire her handiwork. Bo had managed to find a beautiful fir in Riverbend's disappearing timberland. Yesterday, Bo, Peyton, and Clarence had chopped it and hauled it into the parlor, where it stood so tall the papier-mâché angel crowning the tip brushed the ceiling. The wide branches drooped with garlands of popped corn and cut glass, bayberry candles and fat bows of lacy ribbon. Its spicy scent filled the room.

The sight brought her little in the way of Christmas cheer. She turned away, walking over to the latticed window, where she pulled open the heavy crimson drapes. It was a leaden day, still and cold, the sky hanging low with hoary clouds that promised more snow. She thought of the soldiers out in that bitterness, so far from home for another Christmas, sleeping on the ground with only a small campfire for warmth. She couldn't even begrudge them the vanishing fence rails and livestock.

Sighing, she rested her forehead against the cold glass. She heard the rustle of skirts down the hallway and recognized Patsy's tread. She straightened guiltily, as if she'd committed some sin she had to hide. Hers was not the only sad and weary heart this Christmas, North or South, and she had much to be thankful for.

Annabelle moved restlessly to the fireplace, where she

251

poked a log deeper into the flames, then pulled the tapestry fire screen out to allow more heat into the room. A draft belched down the chimney. She waved her hand against the puff of smoke and pushed the screen back.

She glanced at the lyre clock on the mantel, nearly four o'clock. It would be dark soon. The rest of the family had gone to a reception for General Ewell. She had begged off, claiming fatigue, and Peyton had accepted her lie, looking so concerned for her welfare that she'd been forced to add guilt to the bag of emotions she carried around like a stone weight.

She lifted the glass chimney from an ornately tooled sconce and dug in her pocket for a match, intending to light the bay-berry candle. The door to the parlor opened, and she looked over, expecting Patsy.

Royce stood in the doorway, disgustingly handsome in his dress uniform. The glass chimney dropped out of her hand, shattering into slivers at her feet.

"Mrs. Kincaid," he said in a well-modulated parlor voice, as if he was making a dutiful social call, but his expression was reckless and dangerous.

Her body went cold, and she wanted to run from the house and keep running until she reached the end of the earth, where, maybe, there was no war and no dark warrior to break a woman's heart. As if sensing her thoughts, Royce pulled the door shut.

His gaze flicked to her feet, where shards of glass shim-mered like tears, then back to her face. A mocking smile twisted his lips. He tossed his hat onto a chair and walked to the mirrored sideboard. She watched his reflection in the mirror.

The clink of glass against glass sounded like bell chimes as he poured himself a drink. He turned around and leaned against the sideboard, his pose deceptively casual. Tension ra-diated from every sinew of his being. She swallowed, trying to find her voice, but her tongue had turned to rust.

"Interesting reception at Belle View," he said, still in that lazy drawl that was hiding something dangerous. "Isn't the general some relation to you?"

"Third cousin, once removed." Her voice sounded like a squeaky gate. He was here for a reason, something she couldn't fathom except for his taut anger, and she had no idea why the anger was directed at her. Turning away from him, she dug in her pocket and found a match. She struck it, then lit the candle. A small glow chased the gloom into the corners of the room.

"Very interesting reception," he repeated. "You should have gone."

"I was afraid you would be there."

He clicked his tongue, shaking his head. "Come, come, Mrs. Kincaid, you expect me to believe that? You don't have sense enough to be afraid of anything."

The candlelight bounced off the faceted glass in his hand. He lifted it and one brow in a silent question. She shook her head, declining. He drank his down and poured another.

"I met an interesting gentleman there, but maybe you've already made his acquaintance. Lacy type of fellow . . . talks with an odd accent." His eyes narrowed. "Looks like a bird who swallowed something big and square."

His silver gaze speared her, daring her to lie. She took a deep breath to still her racing heart and hide her sudden amusement at his apt description. She now understood his smoldering anger, but in his current mood, he wouldn't want to hear her laughing at his portrayal of Her Majesty's general.

"Maybe," she said. "British accent, funny-looking red coat?"

He nodded once, then swallowed down the second finger of bourbon. "Goes by the absurd name of Freemantle," he said, pouring another drink.

"Maybe I recall meeting him somewhere," she hedged.

He flashed her a cold, merciless glare, then, with a flick of his wrist and tilt of his head, tossed down the third drink in about as many minutes. He set his glass on the sideboard with a solid thunk and took a step toward her. Her lingering amusement vanished.

"This meeting you might recall took place in a drawing room, I presume?"

She backed up a step, pressing her hand to her chest in an unconscious gesture of self-protection. "I—I think it was on a hill . . . to be exact."

"Let's be exact, little wife." His lips curled and fear flared hot in her belly. He was capable of anything, was Royce Kincaid. He acknowledged no rules, answered to no one, and, in a mood like this, he was as volatile as a stick of dynamite.

"What in bloody hell were you doing on Lee's Hill?"

"I seem to recall I was making coffee." She nodded her head, as if she'd suddenly remembered the event. "Yes, that's what I was doing, making coffee."

He made a sudden, explosive move toward her. Reflexively, she jerked herself back. Her hip struck a piecrust table, knocking over a plaster bust of George Washington. She reached out, catching it before it, too, struck the floor and shattered.

"Have you no sense whatsoever?" he snapped.

For a moment, she allowed the hope to grow. He was a man of deep, unseen currents and something more than anger was twisting inside him.

"Nothing happened." Her hands shook as she replaced the bust in the exact center of the lace cloth. "It was all a misunderstanding, the general forgot to send the escort until after . . ." She realized by the narrowing of his eyes she was headed down a more dangerous path. Briefly, she wondered how much bourbon he'd consumed before he came here, and gave him her brightest smile in an effort to defuse his spirit-fueled temper.

"Why, I was so far away from the fighting, I didn't even see any cannonballs—well, one," she added, in case he'd heard the full story, "but that one didn't explode." As soon as the words left her lips, she realized her mistake.

He clamped her wrist, jerking her forward so violently she lost her balance. His arm snaked around her back as he held her in a punishing grip against him.

"You could have been killed." His eyes flared with a molten glow that could be fury and could be something more, something she didn't dare hope for.

"I forbid any more of this nonsense. Do I make myself clear, little wife? If I have to lock you in your room for the duration of this war, I'll do it. Lock the door and throw away the key."

"How dare you issue orders to me. I've never been one of your soldiers, and I'm your wife only when you find it convenient to remember you have one." She struggled, managing to pull herself free.

"You are nothing to me," she said in a calmer tone, holding

his gaze. She liked the sound of that so much, she repeated it. "Nothing at all, so why don't you just leave again and go back to your manly war because I have no intention of listening to you."

"You'll listen."

"I will not. And you'll stop calling me your little wife since I'm your wife in no way that counts—"

The rest of her protest was cut off as he lowered his head, bringing his face so close to hers she could taste the bourbon on his breath and feel the threat blazing in his eyes.

"Perhaps it's time to remedy that, little *wife*," he said, and she thought the devil's voice would sound no less silky and menacing. He grabbed her shoulders. His gaze moved over her face as intimately as a touch. She turned her head aside. Her neck felt brittle and fragile, like skim ice on the river.

"Let go of me, or I'll scream."

"Indulge yourself but don't think anyone's going to help you. In case you don't understand the reality, Peyton bought a broodmare for his prize stud, and they've all been anxiously awaiting the outcome."

She swung at him, hating him for his ugly cynicism, hating herself for loving him anyway.

He caught her wrist. "Not wise, little wife. I might be the kind of vile, despicable cad who would hit you back."

"You bloody bastard."

"That's the other son," he said, his voice dropping even lower and silkier. "I'm the rapacious blackguard who will get it into your head one way or another that for the duration of this marriage, you obey me."

She twisted and lashed out with her foot, catching him hard on his shin.

"Bloody hell, Annabelle."

He let go to rub his leg, and she whirled, determined to make the door and safety. She was reaching for the knob when he seized her from behind, wrapping one powerful arm around her and flinging her around. Like a cornered animal, she attacked, going for his face with her nails. He grabbed her wrists and thrust her arms behind her back as he shoved her against the door. He held her prisoner with one big hand wrapped around her two, his body pressing against hers.

"Scream, Annabelle. All my women scream." He drew the words out slow, like pulling taffy. "Or would you rather moan? I could enjoy making you moan, dear heart."

His face was like a hawk's, sharp and predatory. There was something intense and dangerous in those quicksilver eyes, and she'd never been so aware of his heat, his smell, or his man's size and strength.

She turned her head to the side, a silent refusal, recklessly provoking him further. She drew in a sharp breath as his hand touched her face and shuddered as he spread his fingers over her cheek, his thumb drifting down to her throat, pressing ever so subtly against her windpipe. His mouth hovered over her ear.

"Scream, damn you."

His whispering breath was in her ear and racing down her spine at the same time. She shuddered again as the realization slammed into her that she would never stop loving this man. Even while she hated him, she would love him, this man with the shadowed eyes and tortured soul. This man with his passionate visions of honor and duty, who owned her heart in a way no other man ever could.

Owned it and didn't want it.

His fingers stroked her neck, then dropped to her bodice, where he held her breast, rubbing and squeezing her nipple through the flimsy silk cloth of her dress. Her heart seemed to clamor just beneath his fingertips.

Annabelle held her breath, fighting to keep her body from shaking. She set her teeth and closed her eyes, needing to deny him the satisfaction of knowing she burned with his intimate touch.

And then he was kissing her, his mouth traveling hot up her neck and across her cheek until she was powerless to resist and turned her face to meet him. He kissed her as if he were starving, sucking on her mouth, drawing the life out of her. He let go of her wrists and tangled his fingers in her hair, bending her head back so he could probe deeper with his tongue. His hand slid down to the small of her back.

Hot . . . so burning hot wherever he touched, hot in places no hand had ever touched. He pressed her into him, grinding his hardness against her belly. A moan vibrated deep in his throat and suddenly, she was kissing him back, tasting him, drinking of him.

She kissed him with all the passion of a young girl's dreams and all the hunger of a woman's yearnings. And the pain of it was piercing, too hurtful to be borne. She slanted her mouth away, her breath shuddering on his cheek.

"Not like this. I—" She bit off the confession of love, unwilling to give him anything more. Her fists gripped his jacket. "I deserve better than this, Royce Kincaid, and so do you."

He cupped her head with his palm and pushed her face against his chest, gently now. He was breathing fast, his chest rising and falling. She gathered her courage and looked up at him. She thought he looked like a dark angel, fallen from grace and bewildered by the heavy landing.

"Sweet Annie, too wise for her years." A trace of a smile softened his lips. "You deserve more than I can ever give you."

He drew her back into him, his hand pressing her head hard against the soft wool of his jacket. He stroked her hair, his fingers tightening in it a long moment, then letting go. He backed away from her.

"Get out of here, Annabelle, before I lose control again and do something we'll both regret."

She wanted to go to him, pull his head against her breast and comfort the lost little boy inside the warrior's body. She didn't. She reached behind herself for the knob, pulled the door open, and slipped into the hall.

She'd taken but a few steps when she heard the crash of glass hitting something hard. She stopped, undecided whether to go back or to leave him alone. He made the decision for her, the door sounding a hammerblow to her heart as he slammed it shut and stalked past her without a glance.

# Chapter 19

Honor kept him away, and duty brought him back. The crepe myrtles were in bloom and two armies returning to this war-ravaged land . . . returning from a little Pennsylvania town called Gettysburg.

Annabelle was in the vegetable garden, pulling weeds that had sprouted with the last rain. She looked up and saw him, a dark-haired man riding long-stirruped and easy on a big gray Thoroughbred. Before him stretched a field gone wild with black-eyed susans and butterfly weed; beyond him, the river flowed brown and muddy in its summer somnolence. She raised up and walked to the edge of the garden. Her movement alerted Major, who stirred from his nap and came to sit at her feet. She reached down and rubbed the dog behind the ear, both of them watching the man on the horse.

He slowed as he caught sight of the Big House, with its sagging back steps and peeling paint, its ravaged grounds gullied by tramping feet. It was no longer the grand estate he'd left, but then, nothing was the same anymore. The world had gone mad and by winter, even starvation would stalk this once provident land.

She wondered if he'd been here last spring when the armies had clashed again, setting the woodlands ablaze while blood ran in waves into the ground. As long as she lived, she'd remember the horror of those days in May. But then, he was a man, a soldier, and maybe he remembered differently.

He reined up to the side of the gallery and her gaze locked on to his face. It was the cavalier's face she remembered, all sun-browned planes and sharp angles, silvered eyes shadowed beneath the brim of a slouch hat. Something inside her tore loose and floated away, the pain of missing him, the pain of fearing for him.

She'd learned that love was not a matter of will; she could no more change what she felt for him than she could change herself into a beautiful Indian princess. She loved him with every breath she drew, and if there was such a thing as eternity, then her soul would go on loving him forever.

He was here, at Riverbend.

He dismounted, then he was walking toward her and she was walking toward him, not running, but walking slow and wanting to laugh, really laugh, because he was safe and whole. Her heart yearned to fling herself into his arms, to love him long enough and hard enough that he couldn't help but love her back.

If she hadn't loved him so much . . . If he had loved her only a little . . .

"Annabelle," he said, stopping first.

She said nothing, only smiled at him, and so they stood like that for a long minute, staring at each other across the space that separated them. A space the width of his arm length, a chasm as wide as war. A trace of wind blew up, heavy with the sweet scent of magnolia. She raised one hand to her temple, brushing back a loose strand of sweat-dampened hair.

"I'll get somebody to take care of your horse," she said. "Come inside where it's cool and I'll make some tea . . ." The words trailed off, caught in her throat, as she looked into his face. He tried to smile, but his mouth stayed tight.

"It is *so* good to see you," she said.

He pulled off his hat and she caught the raw pain that flashed in his eyes before he shuttered them. He reached out, his hand cupping her cheek, and she leaned her head into his touch as her eyes drifted closed.

"I've come to see Augusta," he said.

Royce stopped at the top of the trail, looking toward the bluff. He knew he would find her there, for whenever he thought of her, he always came back to that long-ago day. A day of wind-borne laughter and crashing storm, and one shining moment of holding a woman in his arms, wanting to believe.

A hot wind blew off the river. It fluttered her hair and pressed her skirts against her legs, revealing a thinness made worse by the deprivations of war. Slowly, Royce walked down a once-wooded trail, coming to a stop beside her. She didn't acknowledge his presence, only stared ahead at a river flowing in lazy ribbons of color, from green to gray to the rich, sun-kissed brown of her eyes.

The wind carried other voices to them, the strange intercourse between enlisted men camped on opposite sides of the river, meeting on the islet in the middle.

"Hey, Reb. We got coffee over here. You got any tobacco?"

"Just happens I might. Any newspapers?"

He felt her small sigh. "I come down here to listen," she said quietly. "I hear this and think, maybe, one day it will end . . . the hatred, the bloodshed."

"The war is probably lost, but it's far from over."

A cloud moved across the setting sun, casting her sunburnt face with shadows. His gaze traced the perfect arch of her brow, the gentle slope of her nose, the rose-colored line of full, wide lips. The features were the same, but it was no longer the face of the pure, innocent girl he'd left behind two years before. This was a woman who had tasted from the bitter cup of life. Somehow, she still found reason to hope, and the courage beneath that hope awed him.

The river brushed the sand below the bluff with a gentle touch. She turned her gaze to him, searching his face. "Do you have to leave so soon? You just got here."

Her voice was hoarse, as if her throat hurt. He wondered how she knew he was leaving before he ever said the words, but then, her eyes—those deep, gold-flecked pools that were the windows to her soul—had always been able to see into his own dark depths too well.

"I only came back for Gordon's sake, to break the news to his wife personally."

She stared at him a moment longer, then looked away. "You sound as if he's dead. He's a prisoner of war. He'll come back; he'll be exchanged."

"He's a badly wounded prisoner, and his name is Kincaid. He won't be exchanged. If he lives, he's a hostage."

He heard the bitterness in his voice. He'd only wanted to protect his brother and instead, driven him into Stuart's ranks. Flamboyant, glory-seeking Stuart, whose troops left a wounded cavalry officer behind on a bloody field in Pennsylvania. And now, Gordon would pay twice, for he was Royce Kincaid's brother, and Major Royce Kincaid was a man the Union desperately wanted, dead or alive.

"Why weren't you that blunt with Gussie? She deserves to know the truth."

"Augusta's not as strong as you are."

"You're wrong. We're different, and we deal with this war differently, but she's strong." The trace of a strange smile softened the grave curve of her lips. "You men ride off to fight your battles, but you don't understand what it takes to be the one waiting at home, worrying about the men you love."

She turned to him, her dark eyes stark with pain. He could feel her heat through the thin muslin of her mended dress, sensed her effort to keep from trembling. An aching hunger overwhelmed him, a need to gather her in his arms, hold her. But holding her would only increase her pain, and that, he wouldn't do.

"Will you write this time?"

"No," he said, shocked by the way that single word tore at his throat. "Forget me."

Again, that strange, tiny smile. "I'm trying. You're a hard man to forget."

"Then learn to hate, Annie-girl."

He reached out and brushed her face with his fingertips because he needed to touch her one last time. He was leaving, this time forever. Either he would die on the field once or he'd die a thousand deaths in the future, but in either case, he could no longer deny his fierce, throbbing need for her. It wasn't love, only a hunger, and if he gave in to this hunger, he'd destroy her as surely as he'd destroyed Gordon.

She lifted her hand and placed it over his, pressing it against her cheek. Her hand looked so small and white against his own. The smell of her came to him, of sun-drenched river and earthy woman. Something swelled in his chest so he could barely breathe, a yearning so deep and fierce it left him trembling.

"Leave, Kincaid, before I lose control and do something both of us will regret."

She looked at him as if she knew he was running away from her, from all he could never be for her and all he feared she might mean to him.

He wanted to smile, but his face felt too tight. "Don't waste your tears on this blackhearted scoundrel."

He saw his reflection in her glistening eyes, then she turned away so he saw only her proud profile. She stood perfectly still, the breeze blowing her hair behind her. Flowing water gurgled over river stones, and, somewhere, the tiny peepers began their evening chorus. He thought of another evensong, a time when he stood on a flower-carpeted hillside with this woman—a long age ago and only yesterday.

The setting sun moved from behind the cloud, tinting her face and gilding the tears that spilled over. She dashed them away with the back of her hand, and his heart caught. She was his Hurit, standing on the river bluff, but what she wanted was impossible. Water never flowed upstream, not even in fairy tales.

He turned and left her while he still had the strength to leave. He was running to a war he knew how to fight, away from a battle that scared him witless. And he thought she knew that before he did.

"Major Kincaid," she called after him. "You will think of me."

She was right. He would think of her. Come evening when the sun dropped to the horizon and the wind picked up, he'd think of her, wonder if she'd found a man who knew how to give her all she deserved. And he would hate that faceless, nameless man who owned her in a way he never would.

He didn't intend to look back, but at the top of the trail he stopped. She stood at the edge of the bluff, her slender body silhouetted against the red-gold bands of a Virginia sunset. She was the warrior, seeming so fierce with her head held high, her shoulders drawn back erect and proud. Sweet, defiant Annie, so brave, too brave for her own good.

He supposed one day this brutal war would end, and he knew if he lived to see that dawn, he would think of this moment and wonder. Could it have been different for them? If there wasn't a war . . . If he was a different man . . .

# PART FOUR

*He who sows the wind shall reap the whirlwind.*

—General Phil Sheridan, USA

# Chapter 20

It was a small Bible, bound in green leather with gold-embossed lettering on the front and spine. The thin pages whispered a prayer as Mrs. Reid thumbed through them, pausing at some spot in the middle. She gave a small sigh and closed the book, setting it on a table beside her. She lifted one hand to brush away a tear, and Annabelle looked away, feeling as if she was invading this kind woman's private moment of grief.

"Well," said Mrs. Reid. She folded her hands in her lap and managed a smile. "I can't thank you enough, Miss Hallston. Lieutenant Ellis came to see me last summer, and he told me how kind you were to my Charlie while he . . . after . . ."

"You would have done the same for another mother's son, Mrs. Reid. No doubt, you already have," said Annabelle, interrupting, sensing the woman's difficulty in speaking of her son's death. "I'm just sorry it took so long to get the Bible to you."

"As much as I appreciate your kindness, I sincerely hope you didn't come all this way just to bring me a book. A young lady like yourself, traveling alone, crossing the lines . . . all those hateful Yankees . . . and the weather so cold, too."

Mrs. Reid sounded so much like those long-ago ladies in Lexington, clacking their disapproval, that sudden laughter rose in her chest. Annabelle deftly turned the laugh into a quiet

265

cough, then thought of the mixed reasons for making this journey. Her urge to laugh disappeared.

Peyton had sent Augusta and the baby to Richmond, where Gussie's father had moved after the ransacking of Fredericksburg the previous year. Dr. Raleigh had managed to rent rooms in the beleaguered city for his family and work for himself at Chimbarozo Hospital. Food was expensive there, but it could still be bought.

The same couldn't be said for the counties on the Rappahannock, where there was little to nothing left after the long occupation by two armies. What the Federals didn't steal or burn, the Confederate commissary officers impressed. Even so, the Army of Northern Virginia subsisted on half rations while its horses starved or were sent into North Carolina, where forage could be found to keep them alive until the next spring's campaign. What remained of the civilian population suffered along with its soldiers.

Peyton had sent her here, to the Shenandoah Valley, where the farmlands remained productive, to spend the winter with Aunt Hetty. Annabelle was still torn. She would be closer to Bo and had missed Aunt Hetty and Livvy, was thrilled with the thought of seeing them again after almost three years.

But Riverbend had become her home in a way no other place had ever been; Peyton, the father she'd lost, and she felt a terrible sadness in leaving him to face another winter of war alone. As much as she'd begged and pleaded, Peyton had refused to accompany her for fear Riverbend would fall prey to burning or pillaging in his absence.

"As I said, I'm on my way to visit relatives," said Annabelle. "My brother is at VMI, and he's going to meet me at Merry Sherwood so we can spend Christmas together."

Mrs. Reid made a gesture, and a wiry black man seemed to appear from nowhere. He refilled Mrs. Reid's teacup and moved to refill Annabelle's.

Annabelle shook her head. "I really must be going. It'll be dark soon."

"I wish you'd reconsider and spend the night with me." Mrs. Reid narrowed her eyes. "What did you say your guardian's name was?"

"Peyton Kincaid."

"Any relation to our Royce Kincaid?"

"Father and son."

She secretly wondered if Peyton had some ulterior motive in sending her here, where his famous son ran havoc over the Federal forces, but she was determined to keep herself hidden at Merry Sherwood. If she was careful, Royce would never know she'd been anywhere near him.

"Then you really must stay," said Mrs. Reid with an emphatic nod. "Our young ladies have planned a frolic for the Cavalier and his officers tomorrow night. It's over the Federal line, in Salem. You can stay with me until then, go to the party, and still be in Front Royal in time for Christmas."

A strange ache twisted inside her, part anger, mostly that old longing. *Kincaid's Dominion* this area was called now, as if he were some type of king. An outlaw king to the Federals, some type of savior figure to the Southerners who lived here.

She forced a smile. "It's very kind of you, but I'm anxious to reach Front Royal, and there will be other dances."

*Which I won't attend either*, she thought.

Mrs. Reid accompanied her to the door. "If you change your mind and decide to go, the party will be at Mannsfield, the Gearys' house. It's the big white Georgian, the third house after you go into Salem from here. Maybe you can bring your cousin, and you can both return here afterward."

Annabelle realized the only way she was going to escape this conversation without revealing information she didn't want revealed was to hedge the issue.

"If we decide to take you up on that most gracious invitation, I'll get a message to you by tomorrow afternoon. If you don't hear from me, then don't plan on our showing up on your doorstep."

Mrs. Reid took her hand. "I'd do anything for you, child. You took care of my baby when his mother couldn't be there for him."

Annabelle saw only a young soldier, too young to die. *Was it worth it, Charlie?* He had nodded *yes*, and she hoped, for him and for his mother, it was so. For herself, she had her doubts. Impulsively, she gave Mrs. Reid a hug, then Jules was at the door, grumbling.

"Gonna be dark soon, little missy. A lady—"

"I'm coming, Jules."

She exchanged a final good-bye with Mrs. Reid and followed Jules out to the buggy. They had no sooner pulled away when Jules started in.

"Don't see why you didn't stay with that Mrs. Reid," he said over his shoulder. "Young missies have no business staying in hotels, not when they's traveling alone like you are."

"I'm not traveling alone. I'm traveling with you," she pointed out logically.

"Isn't fitting, isn't fitting at all. Wish your mama had lived a mite longer, teach you something proper-like, then you wouldn't be giving this old man such a hard time."

"I wish she'd lived longer, too, but for some strange reason, I don't think it would have made any difference in my ladylike behavior."

Jules huffed a snort, and Annabelle leaned back in the seat, watching the scenery roll past. A choking sensation filled her throat.

This town had suffered, too, not as much as Fredericksburg, but the growing poverty was evident in the run-down houses and unkempt streets of what had once been a charming little hamlet. They had reached the center of town, almost to the Warren-Green Hotel where they were to spend this last night of their journey, when she stiffened.

The man hurrying down the street was Mrs. Reid's servant, and he was turning into a building with a Federal picket standing guard out front. She leaned forward and tapped Jules on the shoulder.

"Stop here," she said. He grumbled but pulled the horse to a stop, then peered over his shoulder. "I have an errand to run before we reach the hotel."

He glanced around, then turned in his seat. "Little missy, you not be having nothing to do with them Yankees, not while Mr. Peyton's expecting me to look out for you."

She was already half out of the buggy. "I'll be right back. If anybody asks, we're from Merry Sherwood and don't mention the name Kincaid."

She didn't wait for his reply, all she could think of was Mrs. Reid's conversation; a party for Kincaid's Raiders and an eavesdropping servant already inside the provost-marshal's office. She suspected he was intent on furnishing the information he'd overheard to the Federals.

She drew in a deep breath to still her clamoring heart and approached the young guard. She drew her cloak tight against her chest and tried to look demure rather than frightened.

"I can't let you pass, miss," he said.

Her mind raced for a valid reason for entry, and all she could come up with was a lame plea. She gave a silent prayer she could be convincing and lied to the best of her ability.

"My aunty Delia is one of the servants who works here now, and I have to see her. My mama's so sick, and Aunty Delia has the recipe for a root potion—if you don't let me pass, well, Mama simply *must* have that potion."

The boy stared at her, then dropped his eyes to the reticule she held in her hand, conveying an obvious message. Disgust rose in her throat. If this war lasted much longer, she'd learn to hate. It wasn't enough that they burned and stole everything in sight, even the youngest of their soldiers could stoop to extorting coin from a woman dressed in something close to rags.

Annabelle opened her reticule, withdrawing one of the few remaining gold pieces Peyton had given her for the journey. She dropped it in his palm. He clutched the coin, shouldered his rifle, and resumed his monotonous pacing. She slid through the door.

Once inside, a desperate calm replaced her fear. The servants would be working from the basement, but where would the colonel's office be located? Probably upstairs. She was walking as stealthily as she could manage down the long corridor when she heard voices from behind a closed door. She pushed open the door nearest her and ducked inside a dark room.

As her eyes adjusted to the dimness, she made out shapes that appeared to be crates. She heard voices and as she pricked her ears to listen, she couldn't believe her incredible luck. In the room above, she heard the Federals badgering the slave. He sounded frightened, then his tone changed so that she could clearly understand his words.

"I done been promised money, and if y'all give me the money you promised, I can tell you where you can get that Kincaid. But I ain't tellin' you Nawthun gen'mums anymore till you give me the money you promised."

She wanted to be gone before they were finished upstairs, knowing the servant would recognize her, so she left while he was still talking. She nodded pleasantly to the picket outside and crossed the street to where Jules waited.

She shivered, feeling the wind bite cold beneath her cloak. She knew what she had to do. She would have to make Jules understand.

Light from the windows spilled into the shadowed alley behind the Warren-Green Hotel.

"Where did you get the saddle horse?" she asked Jules as she retied her bonnet ribbons beneath her chin, pulling the material as tight against her ears as she could manage.

"Borrowed her. Don't you be frettin' none about that. Won't be anybody talking." He checked the cinch and stepped back, turning to study her face. "Wish you wouldn't be doin' this, little missy."

"He's my husband, Jules," she said in a soft voice. "I have to do this." Deep furrows lined his brow, and she thought she saw tears glimmering in his eyes, but in the gloom, it was hard to tell.

"Shame he don't remember that." Jules nodded toward the horse. "Get goin' so's you can get back."

He bent over, cupping his hands to help her mount, and when she was seated, he fussed a little with the stirrups, then looked up at her.

"Remember them Federal pickets is posted all around the town, then some more 'bout four miles outside. Once you get past them, you should be clear." She nodded her understanding. He reached up, handing her his woolen mittens.

"I have gloves."

"Take them. Just gonna get colder."

She tucked the mittens in her pocket and gathered the reins. "Wish me luck, Jules."

"You just make sure you come back to old Jules in one piece. I always been aiming to breathe my last at Riverbend, and that white-haired old man won't let me back if 'n anything happens to you."

She reached out and brushed his leathery cheek with her hand. "Thank you," she said softly. "I don't know how you managed to find out so much in such a short time, but thank you for helping."

He tucked his chin, as if hiding a strong emotion. "I love that boy, too," he said, and his voice sounded like gravel. "Now you get goin', and you be careful."

She'd lived around too many men and knew better than to say anything more, so she only nodded and nudged the borrowed mare into a walk. She looked back as she reached the end of the alley. Jules stood, holding his hat in his hands, his white head bowed. She thought maybe, he prayed.

A cold, blustery wind kicked up and masses of black clouds scudded across the sky. With the information Jules had obtained, and aided by the clouded dusk, she was able to evade the pickets posted around the town perimeter. She breathed a little easier as she left Warrenton behind and turned onto a country lane.

Her plan was to ride until she encountered a Southern camp of soldiers or, failing that, to continue on to Salem, where she could easily find the house Mrs. Reid had described and pass on her information. She knew she could find her way in full daylight, but it had been a long time since she'd traveled these roads. Although she'd said nothing to Jules, she wasn't at all certain her memory would suffice to keep her from getting lost in the dark.

The temperature continued to drop, the wind picking up higher and higher. Her face ached with the cold, and she was rapidly losing all sensation in her fingertips. She stopped and pulled Jules's mittens over her gloves, then tucked her hands inside her cloak, letting the bridle reins fall across the pommel. She spotted the blaze of a fire through the trees and allowed the horse to go toward the bonfire, thinking, surely, she had traveled far enough to be beyond the Federal lines. She saw no one as she approached.

Annabelle dismounted and drew close to the fire, warming her hands. She looked around and suddenly spied a large tree silhouetted against the skyline. Her heart plummeted. It was an old giant she easily recognized, remembering summer picnics with Aunt Hetty and Uncle Richard beneath its boughs. She must have been riding in circles; she was still only about four miles from Warrenton.

She remounted and rode out of the circle of light. It seemed to be darker than before, but, all at once, the clouds parted, and the glow of a full moon bathed the countryside. She stiffened in the saddle as her heart thumped painfully against her chest. Off to the left, moving slowly in formation, was a body of men, their uniforms blue-black in the moonlight. Each carried a carbine.

She maintained a steady pace, drew a deep breath and steeled herself for the challenge she was positive would be shouted at her. No challenge came, no gunfire, and in a few seconds, the clouds mercifully wrapped themselves over the moon, blotting out the landscape and hiding her from the Federal patrol.

She rode on, her rasping breath making white ribbons in the frigid air, wondering why there had been no challenge, wondering what she would have done if the call had come.

Nerved by that success and thinking she must have passed the last Federal picket by now, she urged the horse along faster. But her spirits sank to a new low when she topped a rise and saw the lights of Warrenton twinkling in the distance below. Once more, she'd lost her direction.

It was deep night now. If she continued forward, she would be heading directly into the Yankee lines. If she turned to try again and became hopelessly lost, she could freeze to death on a night this cold and blustery.

Royce was the man who would always own her heart no matter how hard she tried to take it back. He would not die if she could prevent it.

She turned and rode on. Her breath formed small white clouds around her head as the borrowed dun plodded along. Suddenly, she heard the *thwack* of a snapping twig, followed by a voice calling her to halt.

Annabelle pulled up and waited, overcome with a sense of failure. As the Federal picket approached, she drew in a deep breath, the bitter cold slicing like a knife down her throat.

"Where are you going?" he asked, grabbing hold of the mare's bridle.

"I was trying to go into Salem to visit a sick friend," she said, wondering just when she had developed such an ability to lie on command. "My horse has traveled so slowly that night overtook us, and now I'm afraid I'm hopelessly lost."

"I'm sorry, ma'am, I can't let you pass," he said. "I'll have to take you to the reserve. You'll be detained there tonight and taken to headquarters in the morning."

Suddenly, her cold fear blazed into hot fury. These Yankees had invaded *her* home, despoiling everything they touched. They might win this horrid war, but they bloody well weren't going to tell her where she would and would not go.

"Shoot me on the spot then," she said. "I will not spend a night unprotected among your soldiers. I've seen what they're capable of doing."

They stared at one another, then he stepped back one step. "Salem is about four miles ahead." His voice was low. "You'll see a farmhouse a half mile from here where you can stop to get warm. I'm the last picket, if you stay on the path, you won't be bothered again."

She swallowed and blinked back frosty tears of relief. "Thank you."

He tipped his hat and white teeth flashed in a sudden smile. "I have sisters, ma'am, and I wouldn't want them spending a night unprotected among soldiers either." She held out her hand, in truce if not in friendship, and he grasped it in a handshake. "One day this war will end. We can't be enemies forever," he said

"Let's hope."

She turned her horse to the path he directed and rode on, feeling a strange mixture of relief, fear, and gratitude. She said a silent prayer for one unnamed soldier, *May he return safely to his sisters waiting anxiously somewhere up north.*

She arrived back at the Warren-Green Hotel shortly after daybreak, this time climbing out of Mr. Geary's carriage. As her boots hit the hard ground, she saw Jules push himself out of a rocker on the side porch of the hotel.

She wondered how long he'd been sitting out here in the cold, worrying about her. She wanted to run to him, throw her arms around his neck and laugh but he was an old black man and she was a young white woman and this wasn't Riverbend, but a public thoroughfare. She turned, gave her thanks to Mr. Geary's driver, and walked sedately up to the front porch where Jules waited with his hat in his hand.

"Where's that horse, little missy?"

"Already home. Mr. Geary recognized it and we dropped it off on our way into town."

She wanted to clap her hands and spin around on her toes, she felt so alive. She'd arrived at the Gearys' to find General Early visiting there. There would be no raided party tonight, and Royce would never know where the information came from. General Early and the Gearys had promised to keep her identity a secret.

A party of Union soldiers passed by on their way inside the hotel. She waited until the door closed behind them. "It worked," she said quietly. "Shall we have breakfast here, where I can't say a thing, or take off for Merry Sherwood now, and I can tell you all about it on the way?"

"You wait inside the lobby where it's warm. I'll see to the buggy."

It took her a few minutes to check out of the room she'd hardly used and get a porter to bring down her luggage. When she was done, she took a seat on a faded love seat and waited for Jules. A peculiar sense of relaxation flooded through her, an odd combination of sleepiness, warmth, and relief. On some level, she was aware of the party of Union soldiers talking so loudly over their breakfast their voices floated out from the dining room into the lobby, but she wasn't paying attention to their words.

The front door opened, letting in a frigid draft of air, and she looked over to see Jules coming toward her. He stopped as he reached the dining room entrance and cocked his head, as if listening to something interesting. Slowly, he turned his head and peered at her through narrowed eyes. She walked over to join him, pulling on her gloves and beginning to pay attention to the soldier's conversation.

"Yes sirree," said a male voice harsh with a Northern accent. "Kincaid's men tried to trick us last night, sending one man ahead into our sector, thinking we'd all fire on him and not be ready when the rest came up."

Another voice broke in, "Didn't fool us though. We saw him when the clouds parted but we held our fire and they were afraid to attack us this time. They ran right off!"

"Little missy?" Jules tilted his head and leveled her with a dark glare.

Annabelle made her eyes go wide in a look of innocence. "Would a lady trick those Nawthun gen'mum like that?"

Jules huffed. "Since when was you a lady?"

At Merry Sherwood, Annabelle said nothing about her midnight ride. She was sitting down to an early dinner with Aunt Hetty and Livvy when the First New Jersey Cavalry left Warrenton. They rode without stopping, meeting no resistance from Confederate troops as they crossed the line into Southern-held territory. With a loud clanking of spurs and flash of sabers, they burst down the main street of the village of Salem, halting at a Georgian manor house named Mannsfield.

Mr. Geary, clad in his robe and slippers, politely met the commanding officer at the front door of the dark house. Mr. Geary was home alone tonight, even his wife was absent, spending the night with a Mrs. Reid in Warrenton.

Miles away, near Centreville, a Union supply train, fifty wagons long, came to a fork in the road. Contrary to orders, the lead teamster swung his mules to the right fork. Beside him sat a Maryland man, known as Savage to the rangers watching from hiding places within the trees.

The subdued teamster driving the mules seemed unamused by the recently promoted captain's off-key humming. Maybe the two revolvers in Savage's hands put the damper on the mule skinner's sense of humor. William Savage didn't bother to ask; he just kept humming.

As wagon fifty made the bend, a dark man wearing a slouch hat adorned with a strange feather rang a cow bell. The teamster rubbing his elbow looked up to see a band of soldiers fall in behind the wagon train. The teamster spat a stream of tobacco juice over the side of the wagon and hunkered down for an unscheduled trip into the Blue Ridge Mountains.

"Damned if ain't almost funny," he said to the Rebel officer riding beside him. "In between me and old Jake are forty-eight fools who don't even know they've been captured."

Moonlight glinted off the metal of a Colt revolver as the officer shifted it from one hand to the other. He tugged his hat lower, shading eyes the color of quicksilver.

"Highly amusing," agreed Colonel Royce Kincaid.

# Chapter 21

Annabelle refolded a freshly ironed shirt, then stroked the worn cotton cloth. With a small sigh, she handed the shirt to Bo and smiled involuntarily as he jammed it in his haversack. *So much for wrinkles,* she thought.

He was almost a man, thought himself a man, yet this morning she saw so much of the little boy. Mama's baby, but her boy. He straightened, standing so tall now, and favored her with a wide smile. It was all she could do to keep from lifting her hand and pushing the shock of yellow hair off his forehead.

"Jules is waiting," he said, and his smile faded.

She nodded, accepting that the time had come to part again, hating it. "Make sure he keeps covered with the carriage blanket," she said, "but you have to be careful; he gets all upset if he thinks you're fussing over him."

"I'll take good care of him. You take care of yourself."

"Oh, Bo." Her voice cracked.

He wrapped her in a long-armed hug. "Don't you go all teary-eyed on me. I'm just going back to school."

He patted her back awkwardly while she held on, unwilling to let him go just yet. He was returning to school, one where Clausewitz was revered above God.

"If you're still here in May, I'll ride up and we'll celebrate my birthday together," he said.

She stepped back. "Sixteen. I can't believe you'll be sixteen."

"Makes you positively ancient, doesn't it?"

He grabbed his haversack, and together they walked out to the front porch. Annabelle left Bo on the porch to say his good-byes to Aunt Hetty and Livvy and walked down to where Jules stood by the buggy.

"Don't you go frettin' none," said Jules. "I'll see your boy gets back to school all right."

"I know you will." She folded her cold hands inside her cloak. "Who's going to see that you get back all right?"

He wiped a red mitten under his nose. "All this white hair on my head means something, little missy. I got sense enough to get back to Riverbend in one piece."

"Have Peyton write, so I'll quit worrying," she said.

"Maybe I'll just write you myself. Can't much happen now if a black man's letter gets found out."

*One bright outcome of this bleak war*, she thought. She was at Merry Sherwood, so she gave in to the urge to hug this dignified old black man who found it in his heart to love a white family that had held him in bondage for close to seventy years.

She wondered if the world had always been so topsy-turvy with questions and answers no one could sort out and she had just been too young to realize it. She heard Bo's footfalls on the frozen ground and forgot the big questions as she turned to watch him come toward her.

She saw a flashing vision of another boy-man. Handsome, elegant Carlyle, born with that aristocratic grace inherent in Mama's family, dressed in the distinctive green uniform of the cadet corps as he set off for his first college term. This wasn't Carlyle coming toward her. This man-child was too tall, too lanky and loose-limbed to be considered handsome. But that face, oh, dear heaven, his endearing, freckled, wide-grinning face.

The bright winter sun glinted off a silver belt buckle as Bo came down the walkway in his long-legged, ground-eating stride. The belt buckle had once belonged to Carlyle, and it was the only familiar part of the uniform. Now, these boys wore simple fatigue uniforms of coarse woolen cloth.

He stopped in front of her, the morning sun catching his hair so that it shimmered with a thousand golden lights. She wouldn't cry. Mustn't cry. He straightened his shoulders and drew a deep breath. His long arms hung awkwardly at his sides, a gray kepi hat clutched in one hand.

"I won't break if you give me one more hug," she said, groping for the courage to smile as she sent him back.

"Just one."

He leaned down, and she wrapped her arms around him as he hugged her. "I love you," she whispered.

"I know, sis. I love you, too."

She turned her head enough that her lips brushed the base of his throat where his pulse beat slowly above a stiff collar. Then she stepped back and gave him up to dangerous manhood.

Smiling, smiling. Smiling.

Olivia Sherwood walked down a path strewn with a year's collection of dull brown leaves. She passed through a grove of hemlock and stopped, seeing Annabelle, knowing she'd find her there at the creek. It was snowing again. The accumulating flakes looked like a mantle of lace on the royal blue hooded pelisse Annie was wearing.

Olivia continued down the path and came to a stop beside her cousin. Annabelle turned her head and smiled a wan smile, then lifted her gaze to the mountains rolling upward in shadowy waves ahead of them.

"With a little imagination, you could almost believe God painted that smear on the horizon," said Annabelle in a soft voice. "Even the color seems like a message."

Olivia narrowed her eyes and peered through the snowflakes. "I see gray."

"No you don't," said Annabelle with a small laugh as she nudged her cousin with an elbow. "You see exactly what I see. Blue *and* gray, marching together into the clouds."

"You always had more imagination than I did."

Annabelle scraped through the snow with the toe of her boot, then leaned over and picked up a clutch of pebbles. She tossed one just beyond the skim ice on the creek, and both women watched it sink through the clear water.

Something was bothering Annabelle, had been bothering her since her arrival at Merry Sherwood ten days earlier, and it was more than blue and gray clashing against one another instead of marching together. They'd always shared everything, and it hurt that she was keeping something back now.

"I've missed you, Annie," she said, staring at the spot where the pebble had disappeared. "We've never been apart this long."

"I thought I'd probably be coming back for a wedding long before now." Annabelle tossed the handful of pebbles, then turned so they faced one another. Her brown eyes were still and deep. "All those beaux of yours—didn't you ever fall in love with any of them?"

"Maybe. Oh, heaven's gate, Annie, I don't know." She forced out a little laugh that sounded empty to her own ears, hiding an ache she didn't allow herself to think about often. "There was one, he came back to the Valley just after your father died. He had this way of smiling that made you want to throw yourself into his arms. Here I'd known him most of my life, but it was different all of a sudden . . . like he was the one, only I had to grow up before I recognized it."

"What happened?"

"The war."

"You never said anything in your letters to me."

"It seemed so small when you had gone through losing your father and moving to Riverbend, then Carlyle dying on top of that. Even then, I didn't really understand. How could I? Back in those days, I still had everything."

She reached out and took Annabelle's hand. It was hard, but it felt so good to be talking, sharing this with someone who would understand because she knew you almost as well as you knew yourself.

"When John, that's his name, when he was seriously wounded in one of the first battles, I told myself I'd just wait until this war was over. I didn't want to risk loving some man only to have a bullet take him away from me. Now, with Papa dead . . ." She shook her head, unable to go on without the tears coming.

Annabelle squeezed her fingers and Olivia looked down at their clasped hands, their fingers intertwined like ropes, linked together like in the old days. Olivia felt a surge of resentment toward the Kincaids, stealing Annie away from where she belonged, here, at Merry Sherwood with her real family.

"How about you? In your letters, you sound like you're happy at Riverbend. Are you?"

"As happy as anyone can be these days." Annabelle's voice was as soft as the lacy white flakes filtering from the sky. She slipped her hand free and stepped away, turning slightly as if she wanted to hide her expression.

Olivia brushed a fine dusting of snow from her cousin's shoulder. "You fell in love with him, didn't you?"

Annabelle's body shuddered beneath the concealing folds of her cloak. Olivia thought of the last summer Annie had spent here. They didn't know it then, but it was the last summer of innocent childhood. Together they'd packed Annabelle's trunk for the journey to Riverbend with a new yellow riding habit and a soft lilac ball gown while they shared their girlhood dreams. Royce Kincaid hadn't been there when young Annie Hallston arrived, had never seen the almost grown girl dressed in the new finery, but she supposed, for Annie, the seeds of love had been sown even then.

"How did you guess?" asked Annabelle in a small voice.

"The look on your face yesterday when you heard me tell Mrs. Beal I was waiting for the Last Cavalier to ask me to marry him. If it helps any, I've never even met Royce Kincaid. I just tell the nosy old biddies that to keep them from prying."

The eyes Annabelle turned to her were deep, dark pools, spilling over with anguish. "You wouldn't believe the things I haven't told you." She pressed her fisted hands hard against the bones of her face. "Oh, Livvy, I am so tired of living this lie, so soul-weary, I can't even cry anymore. There's a river of tears all dammed up inside me, but they can't get past the lump in my throat."

Olivia hesitated, then wrapped her arms around the smaller woman and hugged her close. She breathed in a sigh that was soft with the scents of lavender and fresh snow. "Do you want to tell me about it now?"

"It's worse than just loving him." Annabelle's voice was muffled in Olivia's shoulder. "I'm his wife."

Olivia stroked her cousin's back while she tried to sort through the shocked questions piling up in her throat, finally settling on the simplest. "How long?"

"That's why Bo and I moved to Riverbend and why Carlyle never spoke to me again."

Annabelle stepped back, squaring her shoulders and lifting her head high. Olivia almost smiled, the pose was so typical—Annie, ready to do battle.

Olivia listened as Annabelle paced through the thin coating of snow and talked. Annabelle's voice faltered occasionally as she told the story; the bankruptcy of her papa and the coercion employed by Thomas Hallston and Peyton Kincaid to force their children into a marriage neither of them wanted; the marital contract that was so generous and hurtful at the same time and her own shame that caused her to want the marriage kept secret. She seemed to leave out nothing, telling Olivia how she'd come to love her husband and how her husband couldn't, or wouldn't, love her back, even how she'd grown to hate him.

Annabelle finished, turning away and gazing again at the mountains. Olivia picked at a loose thread on her cloak, uncertain what to say. Annabelle gave a weak little gulp of a laugh, and Olivia looked up to see her cousin watching her.

"We're a fine pair, aren't we?" said Annabelle. "You're afraid to love any man, and I'm in love with a man who's afraid to love me."

She smiled—a warm, slow smile—and the warmth of it chased the bite from the cold and spread deep into Olivia's chest. It was good to have her back, this little woman who'd been more like a sister than a cousin. Sharing again.

"Maybe I ought to introduce the two of you," said Annabelle. "You'd be a beautiful couple in more ways than one."

"Don't do me any favors, Annabelle Hallston. I can make my own mistakes just fine, thank you."

Annabelle leaned over and scooped up a pile of snow, rounding it into a ball. "So what are we going to do, coz?" she asked, and heaved the snowball at Olivia's head.

Olivia ducked just in time. Laughing, she scooped up her own handful of snow. "We could tell Mama the story."

Olivia's aim was better. Annabelle brushed snow off her chest with her reddened hands. "Much as I love your mother, we will not tell her anything of the kind. Even Queen Victoria would be twittering by Monday morning." She heaved another snowball, catching Olivia on the chin.

Olivia shuddered as cold snow drifted inside the collar of her cloak. She pretended to think, then gave Annabelle a wide grin. "We'll introduce him to cousin Mae. She drives us crazy, just think what effect she'd have on him."

It was good to hear Annie laughing, and Olivia stopped for a moment to listen to the sound. *Annie was home.*

Annabelle's hood fell back. Snowflakes began to frost her hair, and a faint pink blush washed across her cheekbones. Olivia was struck with the realization her cousin had grown into a beauty, a beauty so delicate it almost couldn't be real, and a deceptive covering for an iron will.

*Let the men fight their wars*, she thought. When they were done, they'd return home to find women they no longer recognized. Strong women. Women who had learned by the necessity of having to run the farms and manage the businesses that the pedestal they had once cherished was really nothing more than a prison. Olivia walked over, linking arms with Annabelle, and the two of them started back up the path.

"Seriously, Annie. What are you going to do?"

"I'll get that divorce as soon as there's a civil authority to grant one." Annabelle gave a small sigh, then nudged her chin up. "I never want to see Royce Kincaid again as long as I live."

# Chapter 22

Six men mounted on horseback rode into the frost-crinkled yard. For a moment, Annabelle's heart ceased thumping, dying another of the thousand deaths she'd died since this war began. One man dismounted and stepped into the circle of light spilling from the windows.

He wore gray. Her heart resumed an erratic beat as the circle of light grew warmer and larger. A cold gust of wind carried Aunt Hetty's voice, followed by the low murmur of masculine voices. She let the curtains drop closed, then pulled the blue velvet drapes to meet in the center. By the time Aunt Hetty appeared in the doorway, Annabelle had tugged on her boots.

"Annie, dear," said Hetty. "Are you decent? You have a gentleman caller."

Annabelle fought to keep her voice unrevealing. "Kincaid's men?"

"Major DeShields, dear. He asked for you specifically."

Olivia looked up from her mending, her green eyes narrowed. Annabelle shrugged. Royce wasn't one of the soldiers, but she didn't know what that meant any more than she understood why this soldier was asking for her now. Her heart seized with the sudden fear they had come to tell her Royce was dead. It was all she could do to keep her knees from knocking together.

"Did he ask for Miss Hallston?"

Aunt Hetty gave her a wide smile, as if she believed this soldier had actually come courting. "That *is* your name, dear."

* * *

He had a strong face, angled cheekbones bronzed by the sun, a prominent nose, bent slightly askew, and a wide mouth framed by the brush of a thick mustache that was long and yellow-brown like fresh honey.

"Major John DeShields, ma'am." He swept his slouch hat from his head with a flourish and held it against his chest. The black ostrich plume floated gently in the breeze. She smiled involuntarily.

He blinked, swallowed. "Strange things happen to a man when a pretty girl smiles, but when you smile, my, but when you smile, Miss Hallston, it's something wonderful to see."

"Silly man. For some strange reason, I don't think that's what you rode all the way out here to say." She glanced toward Aunt Hetty, who hovered just inside the parlor doorway, her plump face beaming. The soldier flashed her a knowing look, and Annabelle followed him out onto the wide veranda.

"Aunt Hetty can be a trifle too chatty."

He laughed. "I've known Mrs. Sherwood for years." His face turned serious. He looked out over the lawn and brushed his mustache with an index finger. "That was a bold ride the other night. I think you might have saved my life and a few more, just as worthless."

"You didn't have to put yourself at risk again to thank me, Major DeShields. And I must beg you to say nothing more to anyone. The general promised to keep my secret."

His gaze drifted down to the plumed hat he held in his hands. "The truth is, ma'am, I wheedled your name out of him because we'd like to ask another favor."

"I see," said Annabelle, although she didn't. For an instant, her thoughts were consumed with a bigger puzzle. Could Royce wheedle her name from General Early as well? She realized Major DeShields was watching her, his face looking grave in the wash of moonlight. "What favor, Major?"

"Would you be so foolish as to direct us to the exact position of the Yankee pickets?"

"Aunt Hetty . . . well, everyone in Washington would know by sunrise."

"Of course, Miss Hallston. I understand." He lifted his hat

to his head and flashed that crooked smile again. "I apologize for being so forward. Good night, ma'am."

Annabelle hesitated. If he found out who she was, would he keep her whereabouts a secret from Royce? If he, or any other in the command, died because of her own selfish fears, she would never be able to forgive herself. She reached for his arm. "Wait, Major. Perhaps I can make up some story she'd believe."

He stared down at her, stroking his mustache with the pad of his thumb. He glanced up. "The moon has risen. Mrs. Sherwood has always had a romantic heart."

"I suspect you've broken more than your fair share of hearts, Major," she said. "Wait here, I'll be right back."

In the space of a few minutes, she returned, wrapped warmly in her hooded cloak. "There's a hill near here where I think I can point out their position." He made a motion as if to help her into the saddle. "We can walk there in a very short time," she said. "I do think we'd be quieter that way."

John DeShields looped the bridle over his forearm and fell into stride beside her. The other rangers followed, their voices sounding a low murmur, like creek water flowing over rocks. The rangers stopped as they reached the barn, and she heard one solitary voice wish them success.

The moon shone brightly, covered only by a veil of fleecy clouds that added strange, racing shadows to the dreamlike landscape. They started across the cow pasture, stepping over gray rocks still buried in the soil.

Annabelle drew in a deep breath. "Major DeShields? You won't say anything about this to Colonel Kincaid, will you?"

He laughed softly. "Not if I can help it. Our colonel is of the opinion all women and children should be locked behind heavy doors until this beastly war is ended. Chances are, he'll shoot me if he finds out I asked for your help tonight."

His big hand grasped her elbow as she stumbled over a root.

"Then we'll just have to make sure he doesn't find out." Feeling a little safer with his assurances, she shifted the conversation. She sensed his spirits lighten, heard the laughter in his low-pitched voice and, for a moment, the moonlight did work magic. The war, with its horror, was left behind; left in the pasture while they traveled on through a small copse of pines and up the rise toward a larger stand of heavy forest.

"Up there," she whispered. "If they haven't moved since yesterday, I can show you from there."

He put his index finger to his lips, and she nodded her understanding. The clouds raced past the moon so that the silver light glowed brighter, catching the sudden movement as a man stepped from behind a tree.

Annabelle stood paralyzed. The night air seemed a solid mass surrounding her skin. Suddenly, it pulsed in a wave of motion as Major DeShields leaped to his saddle, grabbed her arm, and pulled her up behind him.

She clutched his waist as the horse lunged and darted off to the right. A bullet whizzed past her head, a whining sound, gone so fast she thought she must be mistaken. Behind them, men shouted as the entire picket line took up the alarm, shots and shouts ringing out in the mad, silvery night.

Swiftly, with a surefooted gait, the big Thoroughbred carried them into a copse of pines. She gasped in a chestful of frigid air as something—a tree branch—slapped her side with a sharp sting. Still, the shots sounded, bullets scattering to the four winds as they raced through the underbrush.

Then, just as suddenly, there was silence except for the soft plod of shod hooves on a snow-patched trail. She leaned her head against his broad back, gulping air into her laboring lungs, willing her heart to still. She'd lost all sense of direction and closed her eyes, holding on tight, trusting him to get her safely home. He reined up in a clump of trees on the far side of Merry Sherwood. She heard a low chuckle as he half turned in the saddle.

"A little moonlight and romance, raider style," he whispered.

Annabelle closed her eyes against his words. She hurt, dear merciful heaven, she hurt with a physical pain.

His command consisted of ten companies, nominally a thousand men, although no company in either army actually filled its ranks any longer. On a good day, he could muster probably six hundred healthy soldiers. A difficult command to lead since they seldom formed as a single unit, it was still a body of seasoned, hard-fighting men, independent to a fault.

Royce knew he should feel a sense of accomplishment. His rangers had been so successful, the Federals had been forced to post heavy guards on every supply train, rail and communication line, supply depot, and staff headquarters in Union-occupied territory.

With Lincoln's fear for the safety of Washington, Kincaid's Raiders kept more than six thousand Union soldiers bottled up in northern Virginia unable to join with Meade's larger army along the Rapidan. Their raids furnished everything from horses to medicines to boots and blankets for the Confederate Army, strangling in the Union naval blockade.

Royce knew he should feel a sense of accomplishment on this first night of 1864. All he felt was a bone-weary tiredness.

A fire crackled pleasantly in the large fireplace in Mannsfield's parlor. Royce stood in front of the hearth, thawing his hands, listening to the voices of the handful of his men who were here tonight and wishing he'd gone on to his own mountain camp instead of joining them for dinner with Caleb Geary's family.

He'd come along after sending the Union prisoners on their way, hoping to find DeShields and get a report on his raid against the First Pennsylvania Cavalry. DeShields had been here earlier in the evening, but had moved on to Front Royal on another scout. The report would have to wait, and now he found himself in a manor house he hated visiting in spite of the Gearys' hospitality to his soldiers.

Mannsfield reminded him of Riverbend, and what he felt toward Riverbend was so twisted and convoluted with memories of Annabelle he could no longer separate the two.

*You will think of me, Major Kincaid.*

Annabelle's curse on his black soul. He watched the flames in front of him, blazing yellow hot, wrapping and licking at hardwood logs and turning them to cinders. He thought how the hells on this earth were usually of one's own creation.

He moved over, making room for Savage in front of the heat. William Savage handed him a glass of port.

"Ever get the feeling this war's making you old before your

time?" asked William, lifting his own stemmed wineglass to his lips. Firelight bounced off the faceted glass as he bent his wrist, taking a good swallow of the ruby liquid.

"We are the old men of the command," said Royce wryly, thinking how odd it was and yet how true. He was in his early thirties, Savage slightly older at thirty-seven. Hardly old, yet considered ancient by the standards of the younger, mostly single men who made up the majority of the raiders.

William snorted. "DeShields is getting up there, too, but he doesn't seem to feel it. Mrs. Geary was just telling me about another party he was planning while we were off in the cold catching us a wagon train."

Royce thought back as he took a swallow of port. He almost shuddered as the mellow liquid snaked down his throat, settling in his belly with a pleasant warmth. "That would have been just before Christmas," he said, shrugging. "A little holiday cheer . . ."

William snorted again. "Wouldn't have been so cheerful if they'd been caught."

Royce lifted one brow.

Savage stroked his red side whiskers. "Seems the Federals found out about the party from some slave. If it hadn't been for a young lady in Warrenton who made it through the lines in the middle of the night, those Federals would have found more than Mr. Geary here when they came blazing into town."

His mouth tightened. "Who was the girl?" he asked, making a sudden decision to steal into Federal-occupied Warrenton tonight and impress on her family the importance of keeping her under lock and key. Whoever she was, she had about as much sense as Annabelle. Damned if he wanted any dead Pauline Revere on his conscience; it was already black enough.

"Mrs. Geary didn't say, only that she wasn't from around here. Seems she was on her way to visit family. Some place called Merry Sherwood—"

The fragile wineglass shattered in Royce's hand. Dark crimson liquid dripped off his fingertips, looking like blood.

"Good Lord, Colonel," said Savage, pulling out a clean handkerchief from somewhere in his mud-encrusted uniform.

Royce took the linen and wiped his fingers. "Do you happen to know where this Merry Sherwood is located?" he asked in a voice so devoid of emotion they might just as well have been discussing the bloody damn weather.

Savage gave him a strange look. "You think you know this girl?"

"If it's who I think it is, the Yanks won't get another chance to kill her. I'll damn well beat them to it."

He got some part of the story out of Mrs. Geary. She refused to name the young woman, citing some half-baked, bloody damn promise, but she did add the alarming information that Merry Sherwood was John's destination tonight.

Royce knew Annabelle and her flea-brain disregard for her own safety. Christ, all John had to ask was if she knew the position of the Union pickets, and she'd personally lead him into the line.

His fury mounted with every word from Mrs. Geary's lips, and he made no effort to control it. No one ate dinner at Mannsfield, all of his rangers electing to ride along for the fireworks.

Once the small band passed through Manassas Gap, they traveled rapidly down night-blackened back roads and snow-encrusted cow pastures, skirting the Union patrols. Royce fumed in silence, his conviction that Miss Pauline Revere was none other than Mrs. Royce Kincaid growing with every damn hoofbeat.

The manor house was set a good half mile back from the nearest road. As they drew closer, he saw a handful of horses tethered out front and thought he recognized John's favorite mount. Royce whistled the call as each man riding with him faded amongst the trees. Slowing, they proceeded through the sheltering darkness, circling the house as they moved cautiously ahead. He heard this week's answering call—a whippoorwill's trill—and knew it was John's company already here. Royce spurred ahead and was met by a ranger as he drew in at the steps.

"Where's DeShields?" he asked as he swung out of the saddle.

The young ranger saluted and took the dangling reins. "Inside, sir."

"Is there a Miss Hallston here?"

"I believe there is, Colonel."

Not waiting for the rest of his men, he took the front steps two at a time and let himself into the house. He clumped angrily through the door pointed out by a sergeant, handed his hat and riding gloves to a private, and looked up.

John saw him first, flashing a look of surprise over her head as he reached to help her remove her cloak. "Royce?"

Annabelle swung around like a spinning top. She was thin, even thinner than the last time he'd seen her. Still defiant, with her chin nudged up and her shoulders set back, ready to battle him for all she was worth. The streaks in her hair gleamed like a golden halo in the soft candlelight. *Dear Christ.*

Annabelle, with crimson blood spreading in an ominous path across the waistline of her dress.

He thought how strange it was that one person could make such a difference in another's life. Once, his world had been clouded in shades of gray. Then one jonquil-bright day, he'd sat atop a hill watching a wood nymph romp with a mutt in a cold-flowing river. A little woman with bluebells tucked in her hair, joy-light in her eyes, and a sunburst smile on her lips— and for a few bright, shining moments, his world had been colored with her rainbow.

He pictured himself returning to that hilltop and starting all over. Only this time, he would allow himself to dream, a golden dream he would lay at her feet. A dream that would keep the joy-light in her eyes as he took her into his bed.

And perhaps . . . perhaps a miracle would have happened and the joy-light would never have died.

"What happened to her, John?" he asked in a low voice.

Annabelle looked at him strangely, as if unaware she was bleeding, which only served to increase the panic invading his gut. The worst wounds were the ones you didn't feel.

John followed the direction of his gaze, then winced his eyes shut. "Looks like we didn't dodge every bullet tonight."

"Christ."

She looked John over from the top of his head to the tip of his mud-splattered boots, then jerked her gaze back. Her eyes were huge and black in an oval face drained of all its color.

"It's going to be all right, Annie-girl." Royce stepped forward, saying a silent prayer he was speaking truth. He fought the powerful urge to slam his fist into John DeShield's tormented face.

She shook her head as she backed out of reach. "Major," she whispered.

A violent shudder shook her body as the knowledge—and the pain—seemed to hit her simultaneously. She was going to faint, but before he could reach her, John had gathered her into his arms.

Royce yanked her thin, trembling body from John's shielding arms, breathing in the soft scent of lavender as her hair brushed his jaw. She buried her face in his neck as he turned for the stairwell.

No more secrets, dammit.

"Get my wife a doctor," he called over his shoulder.

# Chapter 23

Olivia lifted her hand to knock on the closed door. She paused with her fist in the air. Straightening her shoulders, she lowered her hand to the crystal knob and shoved the door open.

Colonel Kincaid sat on the edge of the canopied bed, holding his wife's hand in his lap. She knew he heard her, but he didn't acknowledge her presence, just sat there, stroking Annie's wrist while he watched her sleep.

Olivia leaned against the doorjamb, crossed her arms over her chest, and took the opportunity to study him. He looked dangerous and blatantly virile, dressed in thigh-hugging buckskins and mud-splattered knee boots—not to mention the deadly-looking revolver holstered at his hip. An innocent young girl's heart would flutter just looking at him. Olivia, herself, felt as if a wild, fierce mountain cat had been let loose to prowl her house.

She wanted to hate him.

"Colonel Kincaid."

He turned his head, still lost in thought. His eyes were filled with a pain so raw and wrenching, she couldn't hate him. He noticed her watching him and lowered his lids, hiding his thoughts as Annie had said he did so well. She felt a sharp and unexpected ache in her chest. Heaven's gate, to be loved with such passion.

"I'll stay with Annie," she said. "My mother wishes to speak with you."

"I told Annabelle I'd stay with her."

She ignored his statement, and said in a low tone, "Annie was born here, in this very room."

Olivia slowly and deliberately looked around the candlelit bedroom; pausing at a bell jar on the bureau holding a nosegay of flowers taken from AnnaLee Hallston's wedding cake, passing on to an old, white-painted rocker with a worn tapestry pillow thrown in the seat, moving to the lusters on the candle sconce twinkling rainbow prisms of light, two of the lusters missing because she and Annie had used them as earbobs in their long-ago dress-up play.

Her gaze finally came to rest on his face. His reputation didn't do him justice. He was sinfully handsome, with his dark hair curling over the collar of a fitted cavalry jacket and his strong lines of bones beneath taut, sun-bronzed skin. Those compelling eyes showed nothing now, only a gray mist, but she'd caught the flash of pain earlier and only wanted to inflict more.

"Her mother died in this room," she said.

His lips turned up in a cynical smile. "What are you trying to say, Miss Sherwood?"

"That Harriet Sherwood is the closest thing to a mother Annabelle has. That you are in Harriet Sherwood's house, and you will go down those stairs and explain to her *exactly* how Annabelle came to be your wife. That you will leave out none of the details, including Richard Sherwood's foolish request that poor Annie pay back fifty measly dollars her father borrowed from him—which request, by the way, is the only reason she and Bo didn't come here when they needed a home. Here, Merry Sherwood, with their *real* family. That while you are telling Harriet Sherwood this lovely story, you will also include just how close you and Annie have been in the marital sense. That's what I'm saying, Colonel, and that's exactly what you'll do."

His gaze drifted back to Annie's pale face. "She told you everything," he said, and it was a quiet statement, not a question.

Olivia shrugged, unconcerned with whether or not Annie had told her everything. She'd shared enough for Olivia to know her pain.

He gently disengaged his hand from Annabelle's and stood. "Not that it matters, but she never said anything to me about Richard Sherwood and a fifty-dollar loan," he said in a carefully modulated voice.

"I imagine there's a great deal she's never said to you."

His gray eyes studied her, then he shrugged, as if he didn't care. But even from across the room, she could feel the tension vibrating in his whipcord-tight body. He leaned over and pulled the coverlet up over Annie's chest, then gently brushed a wisp of hair from her cheek. For an instant, his hand trembled before he controlled it with a fist. Olivia stepped aside to let him pass. She waited until he was into the hall.

"Colonel Kincaid, I think, maybe, Annie was wrong about one thing. Maybe you really do love her."

He stopped and turned around. His face was shut up tight, emotionless, but she saw a strain pulling at his mouth and tense, shadowed lines around his eyes. Suddenly, Olivia ached for him, too, but she ached more for Annabelle.

"If you do, she told me one more thing you might be interested in knowing."

"What's that, Miss Sherwood?"

"She told me she never wanted to see you again."

As he stepped from Harriet Sherwood's back parlor, the front door opened, and DeShields entered, bringing the chill in with him—but no doctor. Bloody hell, he'd treated his soldiers for worse wounds when Farlow was unavailable, but this was different. This was his wife.

There was an odd tightness around John's eyes, and Royce's gut twisted with the certain knowledge their problems tonight had just begun.

John removed his gauntlets and briskly rubbed his palms together. "Brrr, it's infernally cold out there."

"For some reason, I don't think that's what you came back to tell me."

"We found a break in the chain and managed to get in after their picket change. Caught us a couple live ones who didn't mind talking." Candlelight flickered off brass buttons as John's chest heaved in a sigh. "You've got to get her out of here. They're planning a sweep in the morning, civilian homes."

"Christ, I can't move her this soon. Not in this weather."

"They find her with a hole in her side, she's off to Washington." John slapped the gauntlets against the palm of his hand. The sound echoed from the paneled walls.

"Damn, I'm sorry, Royce. It would be bad enough if she was just any young lady, but if she's really your wife . . ."

Royce didn't need an explanation. He knew what would happen; worse than what had happened to Gordon. They'd consider Annie a spy and if they discovered her married name, he had no doubt they'd give grave consideration to the gallows. Her married name was readily available, plain as daylight on the filed deed to Riverbend.

There was no choice. He had to get her away from the Federals even if it meant exposing her to the blasted cold in an already weakened condition. He sucked in a deep breath and let it out slowly.

"Hope Mountain then. Get a call out—a couple hundred men. About fifty at Rectortown and another fifty around Middleburg. I want them seen, no skirmishes unless they're forced into responding to something. What I want is a menacing presence to keep those bluecoats bottled up in camp."

"I see where you're headed," said John. "The others on the ridges between here and the gap."

Royce nodded. "Give Geary the Middleburg command and Chauncey the Rectortown. You and Hank Parker handle the line between Front Royal and Thornton's Gap. If Savage gets back with Doc Farlow in time, they'll go with me."

He couldn't stay with her tonight, not if he was to get her out of here by dawn. Royce swallowed against a terrible dryness in his throat. He felt a weight on his forearm, then a small, plump hand patting him, as if in encouragement.

He laid his own hand over hers and looked down into bottle green eyes that were filled with a warmth he never expected to see after the punishing, hour-long lecture this plump little peahen had just given him. A scathing denunciation far worse than anything Peyton had ever managed to inflict during his rebellious youth: a rebuke both amply deserved and meekly taken.

*It was a scene my troopers would have loved to have witnessed*, he thought wryly.

"Annabelle will just have to understand, Colonel," said Harriet Sherwood.

"She won't," he said, as a small smile creased his lips. It was odd, but he felt almost as if he had a mother of his own.

# Chapter 24

Aunt Hetty gave a funny little sigh, then tossed the blood-stained clothing into the fireplace. Their gazes caught as Aunt Hetty reached for the soot-blackened poker. Annabelle looked away, into the fire, watching the flames consume her last decent dress.

"He *is* your husband, Annabelle."

"That small detail never seemed to matter to him before."

Aunt Hetty's large bosoms lifted in a sigh as she moved to the canopied bed. "I wouldn't be making you do this, dear, if there was any other way," she said as she pulled the coverlet up and under the pillows. Her little hands smoothed the wrinkles from the rose-flowered chintz. "Just last year, the Federals arrested a young lady suspected of giving information to Mc-Neill's partisans. She spent months in Washington, and they couldn't even prove her guilty of any such thing. If it hadn't been for her father having contacts up North, she'd probably still be in the Capital Street Prison."

The idea of spending several months in Washington's Capital Street Prison was vastly more appealing than the idea of spending several weeks in some mountain hideout with Royce Kincaid.

"Aunt Hetty, I'm so sorry." Sorry for what, she wasn't certain, there were so many things: Aunt Hetty's distress, her own marriage, this awful war.

"You've done nothing you need apologize for," said Aunt

Hetty firmly. She straightened and walked over to the window, where she pulled the drapes back. Dawn was just beginning to ease over the mountains. "They've come for you, dear."

Within a minute, Annabelle heard the heavy tramp of booted feet coming up the stairs. She turned her gaze back to the fire as the bedroom door opened, but it didn't help. She smelled him, felt him, as if he were wrapped around her, consuming her in his own dangerous flames.

Annabelle listened to her husband and Aunt Hetty discussing her as if she were some parcel for delivery. She pretended not to hear them and sat like she were part of a granite mountain, stiff and immovable, wishing it were so. Then he was kneeling in front of her with his big hand on her knee. She stared at those long, brown fingers, feeling so hot against her own cold bones. Tiny tremors shook her legs. Her eyes were almost blinded with tears.

"Are you ready?" he asked in a quiet voice that rippled through her with an ache more intense than the ache in her side.

"No," she said.

"That's my Annie."

She wanted to tell him she wasn't *his* Annie, but before she could draw a breath for words, he had her in his arms, and she could hardly breathe at all.

Within an hour of setting out, she was shivering uncontrollably. Royce stopped long enough to cut a hole in his blanket and pull it over her head for additional warmth.

"I don't understand this kindness from you," she said, as he tucked the material around her hips.

He stroked her wind-chapped cheek and tried to smile. "You *are* my wife, Annie-girl."

Her face was as gray as the storm-laden clouds and her lips bloodless with cold. She said nothing more, merely gazing at him through enormous brown eyes with a look that pierced his chest with torment. She was pulling away from him, into that place she felt safe. He could understand why, and with this godforsaken war, he was guaranteed to hurt her again. But for this woman, he'd get down on his knees and beg her forgiveness as many times as it took.

They covered the miles in silence, cordoned within a protective ring of a dozen mounted rangers, with only the clink of horse's hooves on the hard ground and an occasional muttered oath from a cold man.

He couldn't get his fill of looking at her, so achingly beautiful with the hood of her cloak framing her face and tiny wisps of curls fluttering against her temple. There were so many things he wanted to say, things she needed to hear, explanations for what he had done to her, to them. But he couldn't find the words and doubted he would ever find them. He couldn't even begin to explain it to himself. He knew only that he could no longer bear his life without her. He feared the bitter joke would be on him.

Why was it so bloody damn cold?

She fell asleep shortly past dark, almost tumbling off the horse, and he stopped at the next friendly farmhouse for a few hours rest. Savage caught up with them there, bringing Doc Farlow. The farmwoman took Annabelle into one of the bedrooms and helped her undress down to her shift.

Royce leaned against the plank wall as Doc examined his wife. Annabelle said nothing, just lay there, white-faced and still, as the doctor removed the blood-encrusted bandage, probed the injury, then reapplied a fresh linen wrapping. He could feel her haunted brown eyes watching him as he followed Doc Farlow out of the room. Neither man spoke until they reached the kitchen.

"If you survive this war, Colonel, maybe you should consider doctoring," said Farlow as he accepted a bowl of something that smelled like venison stew from the farmwoman.

"What aren't you saying, Major?"

The doctor leveled him with a blue stare. "It's mortally cold out there, and pneumonia's a concern after any wounding. You know that already."

"I've got to get her to the safety of that mountain."

"She's just as dead from pneumonia as from a Yankee bullet."

Royce didn't like the expression on Farlow's face so he studied the insignia on his collar and tried to remember the farmwoman's name. He drew a blank although he'd slept in her barn and eaten at her table many times over the past years.

Mrs. Whomever turned from the large fireplace, holding out

another steaming bowl. "Been weeks since we've seen a Yank in this little valley," she said. "That poor girl's plumb wore out. Let her rest some."

For the first time in the war, Royce ignored his gut instinct, which told him to keep moving before the weather worsened. Annabelle wasn't a hardened ranger; her wounded body was growing weaker with every minute of this forced exertion. But she was a Spartan. She'd die on her shield before she complained, and he wouldn't know how bad off she was until she'd drawn her last breath.

He sent a rider to pull some men off the ridges, enough to post two shifts of guards. Leaving the details to Savage, he returned to the room where Annie rested. He couldn't get her to eat, but Doc Farlow coaxed her into taking some peach brandy laced with laudanum.

Royce sat in a chair near the meager fire while she slept a drugged sleep in the truckle bed. He listened to the sounds of boots clumping in the main room, low male voices and occasional laughter. As night deepened, and those noises ceased, the air became filled with the light sound of her breathing and his heart seemed to hang, waiting for each intake of breath. At some point, he must have dozed because the next thing he knew, Savage was shaking his shoulder and telling him it was near dawn.

They were mounted and on their way before the weak sun crested the mountains. Once again, the miles clicked by in silence as they climbed the ridges on trails so deep in the wooded canopy they were known to few outside the mountaineers who called this hardscrabble land home. It was after they broke through into a mountain hollow that he felt Annabelle shudder.

"They look like scavengers waiting for a carrion feast," she said.

At first, he was so concerned over the raspy hoarseness of her voice, he didn't know what she meant, then he looked to the horizon. From this vantage point, he could see a small coterie of raiders in sharp, cold relief against the wintry skies. Figures on horseback, mysterious, so strangely still and sinister-looking in their black rubber coats it almost gave him a creepy sensation.

"Yankee carrion," he said with a warm sense of pride. Those

were his soldiers, and they'd see his wife got to safety.

The snow started then. Heavy, wet flakes for the first hour, then changing to a wind-driven powder that augured a full-scale storm. Savage rode up beside them.

"I'll take a couple men and ride on ahead," he said as he pulled off his own blanket covering. He held it out and Royce gratefully accepted his sacrifice. "We'll have the fire going and something in the kettle by the time you get there."

As Savage and two other rangers disappeared over the next ridge, Royce wrapped Annabelle's cold body in the folds of Savage's blanket. He hunched over her, trying to protect her from the icy blast of wind-borne pellets, and she seemed to soften against him. He wanted to tighten his arm around her waist and hold her closer to his heat but couldn't for fear of hurting her.

Finally, they crested the last rise. A thin streamer of smoke curled from the chimney of a weathered frame farmhouse and the smaller log cabin just beyond.

The camp looked like nothing more than a mountain dirt farm with a ramshackle barn and dilapidated outbuildings nestled at the bottom of the ridge. Early in the war, they'd come across this abandoned homestead of some hard-luck farmer and adapted it for their own use.

The raiders had several other hideouts strung from Rockfish Gap all the way to Harpers Ferry, but Royce had always considered this one on Hope Mountain the most secure. They'd never been pursued within five miles of this high, narrow valley, and the few human inhabitants of the area were all staunchly Confederate. Annabelle would be safe here even when duty called him away.

Savage came out to meet them as they reined in at the front of the farm house. The horses snorted, blowing great clouds of white smoke. All around him, freezing men were jumping out of hard saddles, stamping cold feet and swinging stiff arms.

Savage reached up, giving Annabelle a gap-toothed grin through his red beard. "Welcome to the Land of Hope, Mrs. Kincaid," he said.

"Well, it ain't the Spotswood, but it's warm," said William Savage.

"I've never been to the Spotswood," said Annabelle in that same hoarse voice. She was standing in front of the fireplace, shivering, obviously not at all warm.

"Then as far as you and me is concerned, this is pure luxury," said Savage, producing another gap-toothed grin. "Even got us some good stew already simmering and real biscuits instead of those bullets the army calls food."

She shook her head.

"You've got to eat, Annabelle," said Royce. He took advantage of her turning away from him, lifting the first layer of wet blanket from her shoulders. She wrapped her arms over her chest, as if seeking protection.

"I'll eat later," she said in a voice so low he had to bend his head down to hear her amidst the masculine voices beginning to fill the room.

Royce exchanged glances with Savage, seeing a concern in William's pale blue eyes that mirrored his own. "When John gets here, let me know," he said, taking Annabelle's elbow in his grasp. "Did you check the cabin?"

"All set. The boys even got her things in there."

Royce steered her toward the rear door, around the wooden tables and benches and the smelly, wet cavalry boots already removed by men too cold, hungry, and war-battered to consider a woman's sensibilities.

The air was grainy with wind-swirled snow and cold as brass. She lost her footing in the deepening powder and lurched sideways, a sharp, pain-filled gasp breaking out of her as she landed against him. Immediately, she stiffened. He wrapped his arm around her and she tried to pull away, but he only firmed his grip. Just now, she was too unsteady for him to consider her pride.

He shoved open the cabin door, thinking of the comforts of Riverbend that could have been theirs for a bridal chamber if he'd had any sense years ago. The single room was spacious enough, furnished with a rope bed with a calico quilt, a small bureau and commode, and a watermarked desk with a cane seat chair. A faded rag rug covered the middle of the plank floor.

Annabelle paused just inside the threshold, her gaze taking in the furnishings. He saw her eyes linger on his rubber coat thrown haphazardly over the back of the chair, a pair of muddy cavalry boots by the side of the bureau, then the valises Olivia had packed for her sitting on the floor at the foot of the bed. Her brown eyes darkened, but she said nothing. Her steps were slow as she went to the window.

She pulled open the bleached sacks that served as curtains and peered out. On any other day, the view from that window was a breathtaking blue mountain vista with a grove of hemlock and mountain laurel in the near distance and a corduroy bridge over the creek. He doubted she saw much in the strange snow-lit dusk that was settling over the land.

He added another log to the smoking fire and managed to coax it into a blaze, then used a taper to light the oil lantern. He stared at the tiny flame, as if it were Aladdin's lamp and would reveal to him how he was going to get his sick wife into the sole bed in the room if she didn't want to be there.

He joined her at the window, standing close enough to touch her, although he didn't. He wondered where she pulled the strength to stay on her feet. He wanted to sweep her in his arms and press his lips to her brow before dumping her in the bed, but he didn't do that either. Instead, he sorted through several conversational gambits in his mind, finally settling on the most direct. But when he went to speak, he found his tongue must have forgotten how to work.

"Annabelle . . ."

She fingered the frayed edge of the tow sack curtain. "Is this your cabin?"

"Yes."

"There's only one bed."

"Yes."

He held his breath, waiting for her to say something, although he didn't know what she could say that would ease the ache in his chest. She nodded curtly, as if he'd confirmed all her worst suspicions of him.

"I suppose you have thoughts of ravishing this skinny body."

"Of course I do." He let his hands rest on her shoulders. "But not until that skinny body's in better shape than it is right now." He lifted the second wet blanket over her head and tossed it on the floor. She turned around to face him.

Her hair, darkened with snowmelt, was the color of fallen leaves and spilled over the royal blue cloak covering her shoulders. Her oval face was as white as the new snow, with bright bands of color across her cheekbones. Her beauty made him ache, but the high color on her cheeks struck terror in his soul.

"Annabelle—bloody damn, Annie. You've got a fever."

She started to shake her head, then her gaze became caught in his. He saw himself reflected in the shimmering pools of her eyes. He smelled the snow in her hair, then he was tasting the snow on her lips.

Gently, very gently, he held her against him while he kissed her and for a long moment, she softened and leaned into him. Her hands gripped his waist as if she needed to hold on to something while her mouth moved beneath his, both seeking and giving while she kissed him back.

She owned him, did this thin little woman with the sinful lips and sunburst smile, owned him body and soul. And he would take care of her this time. He pulled his mouth away and she backed up, bringing a fisted hand to her lips.

"For once, you are going to follow orders, Annabelle." His voice sounded hoarse, not at all commanding. "I am a degenerate Kincaid with nothing to offer you at the moment except a life following the drum. But you are everything I've ever wanted, the only thing I will ever need. I will not lose you now when I've just found you."

She stared at him, her eyes filled with that deep emotion he could never fathom. "You frighten me so. Dear, merciful heaven, I am so afraid."

"So am I, Annie-girl. So am I."

She was shaking so hard, she had to hug herself. He ached to touch her but knew it would only frighten her more. "Annie, I don't know the right words for this sort of thing, but you're going into that bed if I have to knock you out to get you there and you're going to get well, and, by then, maybe I'll find the right words for what I want to do with you."

She wouldn't look at him, but her fingers tugged at the frogs on her cloak, cold, stiff fingers that didn't work. He pushed her hands aside and unfastened the cloak, tossing it atop the blanket. He turned her, and she cooperated by lifting her hair so he could unfasten the tiny hooks on her bodice. The dress pooled at her feet in a whisper of blue cloth.

Her shift was all tucks and frills and lace, and he wanted to rip it, freeing her breasts. He allowed himself to lower his head and kiss the small protruding bone at her nape. Her too-warm skin rippled like silk beneath his lips.

All of a sudden, she shuddered violently and leaned against him. He gathered her in his arms and carried her to the bed. Her hair spilled across the pillow like a pool of fine sherry. Her eyes were enormous and glazed with something he hoped was emotion and not fever.

"You are mine, Annabelle," he said. "My wife."

"Two more years," she said in a raspy whisper.

"Oh no, dear heart." He took her small hand in his own. "Much longer than two years. Forever and a day."

The wind became violent during the night, with the storm rapidly reaching blizzard proportions. For nearly twenty-four hours the winds howled, and when the tempest finally blew itself out, two feet of snow covered the ground with drifts as deep as a horse's flanks. The cold deepened on a world turned white and held for days. Annabelle didn't remember the blizzard. She didn't remember much of anything about those first days of 1864.

She seemed to sleep a lot, and when she opened her eyes it was to a strange room, sometimes folded in shadows, sometimes bathed in sunlight. There was a chair by her bed and different men sat in the chair. Sometimes a big man with a yellow mustache and kind eyes and sometimes a red-bearded man with a gap-toothed smile, both men urging her to drink something. Annabelle thought she should know them, but she couldn't remember who they were or why she should know them.

Mostly, she opened her eyes to her dark angel, a tired-looking man who invariably managed a lazy smile when he caught her gazing at him. She would always remember him, for she had known him since forever, loved him since the beginning of time. Even though it hurt to swallow, she always forced herself to drink something for him because it eased the sad shadows in his eyes.

But a night came, she thought it was night but she might be wrong, when she tried to sip from the cup he held, but she couldn't. She couldn't drink for him, even when she wanted to make his sadness go away.

She had no strength to sip. She needed it all to breathe, and it hurt to breathe, each breath a lung-searing torture. She thought drowning must feel something like this painful gasping for air that wouldn't come and had no place to go.

The world grew dark around the edges, and the edges were growing closer to the center, and she knew the world would soon be black all around.

A strange humming vibrated in her head and she heard Mama and it sounded so wonderful . . . Mama's molasses-sweet voice. The world went black and cold for a timeless minute, then lightened in the middle.

She saw Mama in the light. Mama as she had been before the miscarriages and the sickness, the beautiful young woman who had laughed and played with her plain little daughter, and Annabelle felt no more tortured pain, no more heart-stopping fear, only a sweet peace because Mama would take care of her now. She wanted to talk to Mama and tried to speak, but the words wouldn't come.

Mama held out her arms. Annabelle went into those arms, and a soft warmth seeped into her soul. Annabelle thought she spoke to Mama. "I tried to take care of our men," her heart said.

And Mama's heart answered, "I know you did, sweetling."

The light grew brighter, shimmering, and she could feel Mama all around her; Mama's warmth filling her, and there was no more gasping pain, only a joyous peace. Annabelle wanted to stay there forever with the light and the warmth, in a bright world filled with peace instead of war. But Mama's heart spoke again and the light dimmed, faded . . .

Annabelle knew she couldn't stay in the peace.

Strong hands were clutching her shoulders, hurting her, shaking her, and she heard a man's low, desperate voice saying something she didn't understand.

"Dear Christ, no." A cry broke deep in his throat. "No, Annabelle, *no*."

She pulled hard, sucking in a tortured breath. After a pause, she was able to drag another. She found the strength to open her eyes to the darkly edged world where breathing hurt.

Royce sat on the edge of the bed beside her. His shadowed face looked sharp and wild. She wanted to tell him not to worry, but when she tried to form the words, she couldn't. She wanted to reach up and touch his face, touch him, but when she tried, she couldn't. Her body was weak but inside, she was strong. She drew another breath, and this one didn't hurt so much.

"Royce," she said. It came out as a faint, hoarse whisper, and she didn't know if he heard her or not. But he must have heard something because he buried his face in her neck. She thought she felt tears on his cheeks.

"Hold me." She knew he heard her this time.

His body stretched out long beside her as he gathered her in his arms. The darkness came back to claim her, but she wasn't afraid. Mama said to be strong, and she thought she knew how to be strong. But Mama's heart had said more:

*There are times when we women must take care of our men. And sometimes, we must let our men take care of us.*

It was sounds that wakened her, horses whinnying somewhere, the voices of men carried on the wind. Confused, Annabelle pried her eyes open. Her gaze followed a golden shaft of light from the foot of the bed to a small, frosted window.

She tried to remember where she was and why she was here, but the where and the why eluded her. Wisps of strange dreams clung to her memory: a dream of Mama in a white light, a dream of Royce holding her in his arms.

She heard another low sound and managed to turn her head on the pillow, surprised by the amount of effort that simple movement entailed. She saw Royce then, sprawled in a wooden rocker drawn up near the bed, his head nodding as he succumbed to a restless slumber.

Maybe he felt her gaze because he stirred, then his head jerked up. He saw her looking at him, and his lids drifted closed. He seemed to sigh, then moved slowly, using both hands to push himself out of the rocker. He moved to the edge of the bed and leaned over her.

His face was etched with new lines around his mouth and eyes. A coarse stubble of beard darkened his jaw, and, briefly, her fuzzy mind registered the thought she'd never seen him unshaven. His curled hand stroked her cheek, the haunted look in his eyes fading as his lips turned up in a smile so tender and fragile it hurt to look at him. But she returned his gaze, then, slowly, she returned his smile.

She smiled because she could breathe and it didn't hurt so much to breathe. She smiled because he was here, wherever *here* was. She smiled because she loved him and, maybe, he loved her back.

# Chapter 25

❧❧❧

S he was beautiful, dressed in a simple dress of claret-colored wool, her hair left unbound and falling in lustrous waves over her shoulders. She sat in a high-backed chair at the head of the table with that sunshine smile on her lips while DeShields sat on the other side of her telling some cocka-mamie story for her entertainment. But then, she was always beautiful, his Annie.

Royce frowned. Although she still tired more rapidly than was her wont, his mind told him she was well, almost back to her normal strength. He wanted her—ached with the wanting—but his heart still remembered that terrifying, endless minute when her chest had stopped moving, the long minute death held her in its cold grasp, the blackest minute of his black life.

The simple truth was the avowed rake was sitting at this trestle table with his male member so swollen he'd be embarrassed to stand up, living visions of what he wanted to do to his wife and afraid to do anything except tuck her into that bloody damn bed, alone, one more time.

"I think you're telling me a tall one, Major," she said in a voice filled with laughter. "Did he really do that, Royce?"

Dimly, Royce realized she was speaking to him. "Do what?" he asked, catching the twitch of DeShields's mustache in the corner of his vision.

"Raid the sutler's wagon for hoop skirts." She was looking at him, and he saw the soft candlelight reflecting in her dark eyes. Bloody hell, he wanted this woman. He forced his thoughts to her question before he made a complete ass of himself in front of several dozen rangers.

"The fearless and feared Major sitting beside you had no less than four hoops tied to his horse, one for each of the ladies he was courting at the time." Royce was tired of the knowing smirk on John's face and decided to wipe it away. "Didn't he mention the needles?"

A great shout of laughter sounded from a dozen male throats. She turned a questioning, laughter-filled glance to John DeShields whose mustache was really twitching now. But it was Savage who answered.

"Sewing needles being so scarce in this Confederacy, and especially coveted by the fair ladies, our Big John stuffed packets of needles in every pocket he had, not being able to put them anyplace else because of those hoops he had tied all over his not-too-happy horse. Then we were forced to make a run, those Yanks coming across us before we were ready to end the party. So old DeShields here races away with the rest of us, hoops flapping every which way so that there horse and rider both looked like they had wire wings. Meantime, those sewing needles are shifting in the pockets I mentioned earlier—"

"What they're trying to say, Sarge," said DeShields, his blue eyes sparkling, "is that in the call of duty and honor, my big heart thinking of nothing more than those deserving, Southern ladies in need, I was grievously injured."

Annabelle's eyes clouded in sympathy, probably thinking John had been wounded by a Yankee bullet. Royce snorted. "Bloody damn, DeShields, tell the truth."

Another wave of ribald laughter was followed by Hank Parker's voice from the other end of the table. "Truth was, the dumb ox had holes in places that can't be mentioned in polite society. Took weeks for some of them needles to work their way out."

Annabelle patted John's hand. "I think that was very noble of you, John DeShields," she said, managing to hold back the laughter sounding in her voice.

DeShields winked. "Just happens I've got a few of those no-ble needles left if you happen to know any particularly needy young ladies."

She made some answer Royce didn't hear. Her hand was in front of him on the table now. He wanted to lay his big hand over her small one, pressing hard, until they fused into one flesh. He stared into the muddy brown of his coffee, squeezing the cup hard between his palms. The heat seeped through the tin, adding to the burn inside him. He thought he heard her sigh and looked over sharply.

She was resting her head on the back of the chair. Her dark eyes were fixed on him with the look that always made him feel he *was* the cavalier of her dreams, her knight in shining armor, instead of a tarnished man so frightened by what he felt for her he was sometimes paralyzed with the fear of losing her.

A stillness seemed to come over the room, a sense of breathless waiting. It was like that sometimes between them, as if the rest of the world ceased to exist, and it was only the two of them.

His gaze focused on her face, and she held his stare as the pressure in his chest built and built until it became unbearable. A flush rose on her cheeks. He couldn't read her expression, but the color on her cheeks struck deep into his fear. He shoved his coffee mug aside and stood.

"Say good night to the boys, Sarge," he said, gently pulling her out of the chair. "It's way past your bedtime."

She gazed at him somberly, then a slow smile creased her face as she turned to John. "Major, do you think he's ever going to let me lead a normal life again?"

DeShields gave her another wink. "Not likely, little one. I wouldn't."

"Here, give me your foot."

Annabelle leaned back in the chair and lifted her foot, which he grasped and propped on his thigh. The silver boot hook flashed in the lantern glow as Royce worked the buttons on her half boots.

He pulled off the first boot, and she lifted her other foot. His long fingers wrapped around her ankle, once again propping her muddy boot on his thigh. She saw a prominent bulge where his pant legs joined and looked away as her heart fluttered like butterfly wings in her chest.

She watched his hands work the little instrument, the way the small bones and tendons stood in relief beneath the sun-bronzed skin. His hands fascinated her. Those strong hands she knew could be so gentle, so tender; the same hands that were capable of terrible, violent things she didn't even want to imagine.

He pulled the second boot off, and she looked away from him, toward the oil lamp that cast a spluttering yellow light across the top of the desk where he had maps spread in apparent abandon.

Idly, she fingered one of the leather gloves he'd tossed atop the maps. There were so many things she wanted to say to him. Things he knew how to say but she didn't, so she waited for him to say them. Waited and waited.

"Can you get the hooks on your dress?" he asked.

She nodded. She knew the routine he expected. Go behind the screen he'd put up for her privacy, change into her night-clothes while he built a fire, then climb into the bed, alone. He'd tuck the quilt around her, lean over and kiss her brow, then flop on the cot he'd brought in while she was sick. She'd come to hate the sound of his hard body hitting that hard cot.

She stood. He stared at her. The only heat in the world seemed to come from those silver eyes. And then her heart slowed and slowed, and stopped.

His hand came up. His gentle, callused fingers brushed her neck as they followed the length of her unbound hair, down over her shoulder and along the swell of her breast to where the feathery ends curled at her waist. She felt a strange seizing deep in her chest, as if she'd forgotten how to breathe.

"Annie," he said, although it was more an easing of the breaths they'd both been holding. He traced the line of her jaw with his thumb, so lightly it was almost as if she imagined it.

But she saw in his eyes the echo of the same yearning that cried deep inside her. She wanted to touch the creases at the edge of his eyes with her fingers, wipe away the careworn lines. She ached to touch the hard edges of his mouth with her own and feel the hardness soften. She tried to think of the right thing to say to him, to tell him what she wanted, to give him what he wanted, but she couldn't.

"You'd better get some rest," he said, dropping his hand to his side.

Whatever she'd seen in his expression was gone the way he could do so easily, erasing all trace of his thoughts, his feelings, so that his face might just as well be carved of stone.

"Go on, get ready for bed," he said when she didn't move.

She started to reach for him, then lost her courage. Instead, she walked behind the privacy screen on legs as unsteady as they'd been when she'd first been allowed out of bed weeks ago.

She unhooked her dress and let it fall to her feet, then leaned over, picked it up, and hung the dress on a peg. She peeled off petticoats, stockings, and camisole. On the other side of the screen, she heard the thud of a boot hitting the floor. Then another.

She poured water into the tin basin and washed herself quickly, drying with a rough towel that chafed her too-sensitive skin. She heard her husband's bare feet pad across the floor and knew he was building the fire in the fireplace.

The air was cold on her damp skin. Moving fast, she pulled the nightgown over her head. The thin batiste settled over her like a gentle caress.

She'd never been so conscious of her own body, of the nakedness of her legs and hips, the tightness in her nipples beneath the thin cloth. She felt defenseless without the normal several layers of clothing. Her pulse was beating hard and fast as she buttoned the high lace collar.

Finally, she drew a deep breath and walked out from behind the screen, carrying a hairbrush in her hand and willing her hand not to shake.

Royce was crouched on one knee in front of the fire doing whatever it was men do to make fires burn to their satisfaction. He'd removed his jacket and his shirt was stretched taut over the powerful muscles of his back. He straightened when he heard her and turned. The smile at his lips faded.

"Where's your robe?" His voice was harsh, like he was angry with her.

"I thought—maybe, you'd brush my hair for me."

It was an absurd excuse. Even more ridiculous was the need to tighten every muscle in her body to keep herself from running away from the man she was trying her inept best to seduce.

He came to her, the firelight at his back casting huge shadows in front of him. He stopped so close, she could smell his shaving soap and light sweat. She didn't know what she saw in his face, something intense, maybe anger, maybe longing. Tiny tremors shook her legs, but she wouldn't give up now.

"Annabelle." His hands encircled her arms, gripping so hard it hurt. "You don't understand, Annie, please put that damned robe on."

She looked up, allowing everything she felt for him to show on her face and, just in case that wasn't enough, she said the words with all the ache in her heart and yearning in her soul.

"*I love you.*"

He leaned his head and kissed her, filling her with his breath, his tongue, his taste. The hairbrush dropped to the floor as she clung to his waist. She felt a trembling deep inside as she returned his kiss. His hands roamed up and down her back, pulling her against his hard body. She could feel the heat of him through the worn cotton of his shirt. And a trembling within him as well.

He shuddered and tore his mouth away. "I've wanted you so long." His hand twisted in her hair. "Annie, I'm just a man. I can't see you looking like you do now . . ." He swallowed. "Bloody hell, I want you so bad."

She leaned her head against his chest, hearing his rough breathing as she rubbed her cheek on the soft cloth. "I'm not your kind of woman, but I would very much like to be your wife."

He stepped away from her, and she thought she saw a sadness in his eyes. "I've hurt you so many times, dear heart. For once, dammit . . ." He lifted his hand and ran his thumb over her lips. "Are you cold?"

"I think I'm rather warm," she said, not knowing why he asked, but feeling that strange heat his touch always created deep in her belly.

He gave her another of those fragile smiles she'd come to love. She tilted her face up, asking without words or thought for another kiss. His mouth covered hers in a long, deep kiss that stole her breath. He tangled his fingers in her hair, pulling her head back and moving his mouth to the throbbing pulse in her neck.

"Annie, sweet Annie. You taste like sin." His gaze searched

her face and then, he sighed. "There's nothing in this world I want more than you, Annabelle, but I can't live with myself if I make you sick again."

"Silly man." She smiled, finally understanding him, the worry that had held him back. "I've been fine."

He studied her a moment longer, as if trying to convince himself she wasn't lying. She gazed into those compelling eyes, and the air between them seemed to arc and bristle, like heat lightning.

He grasped her shoulders. "I'm going to hurt you, once, and it can't be helped. But I'm begging you to trust me. Let me be selfish, then I can make it good for you too."

"I'm afraid I'm woefully ignorant on these matters, Colonel Kincaid."

She reached up and traced the line of his lips with her fingers. His mouth moved beneath her touch, the creases at the corner deepening into a sudden smile. He bent, catching her behind her knees and back, sweeping her off her feet.

The rope springs groaned beneath them as he eased them both onto the bed. Her body felt heavy, her skin too hot and tight. He loomed above her, the firelight casting his face in dark shadows.

He lowered his head, claiming her mouth in a fierce, hot, tongue-sucking kiss. A fire began to smolder inside her, twisting her belly up tight. His mouth devoured hers while his hands kneaded her breasts, then tugged and pulled at her nipples through the thin batiste of her gown.

He was becoming too rough, hurting her, but it didn't matter. She was afraid to move, afraid to make a sound for fear he would stop. He raised his head, and she breathed deeply, filling herself with his scent.

"Trust me, Annie." His hands shifted, pulling her gown up over her hips.

His hand cupped her where her legs joined, and she gasped with the shock of him touching her there, then gasped again, bucking against him as his finger slid deep inside her. His hand stilled, only his finger thrust deep inside her woman's place, and she seemed to hang suspended in some eternal world where nothing existed except this exquisite burn, this intimate touch deep inside her.

Slowly, the tenseness eased from her thighs, and he began a thrust and draw, his long finger sliding in and out of her most private place. Something began to build, a twisting, coiling heat. She whimpered, raising her hips, clutching at his shoulders, not knowing what she wanted, only that she wanted something more.

He shuddered, and a harsh, desperate sound erupted from deep in his chest. "Annie, dear heart . . . God, I'm sorry, but I can't—I have to . . ."

She had no idea what he meant, but she was afraid he meant to stop, to pull away from her. "Please," she whispered, and her heart thundered as he did pull away from her.

He wrenched at the buttons on his pants. Her glazed, unfocused eyes caught a brief flash of him as he pushed his pants down over his hips and then he was lowering himself over her. She reached up, wrapping her arms around his neck.

"Just this once, dear heart, I have to hurt you."

He slid two fingers into her, stretching her wider, and it did hurt. Her breath hitched, but he didn't stop. His fingers touched some new place, rubbing her there, building a fiery sensation so frightening, she gasped back a scream. Her hips bucked up against his hand, against the torment, and he pulled away. Something hard and smooth and hot probed her woman's flesh. He wrapped one arm around her shoulders, the other around her hips, holding her tight, immobile.

She knew a moment's fear, then he drove into her. A sharp pain wrenched her and she smothered a cry in his shoulder as her nails dug into his back. He went utterly still. His muscles beneath her palms were taut, tense.

"I'm sorry, dear heart," he murmured, his breath hot and moist on her skin. "Don't move, or I'll hurt you more."

She clung to him, wanting to follow him in this new act, then strained up against him anyway as the pain turned into a warm pleasure. It was so right, to be filled with him. Watching her carefully, he moved his hips, almost pulling out of her, then shoved himself deep, again and again.

She was hot and cold, trembling, mindless to all but the pounding thrust and draw that made her his. She tried to stay still, but she couldn't. Her hips lifted to meet his thrusts, arching against him while the pressure inside her grew.

His head flung back as a groan tore out of his throat. He gave one more powerful thrust, then his body convulsed in violent shudders as something surged hot and wet inside her. He collapsed on top of her with his heavy man's weight and buried his face in her hair.

She stroked his sweating back, feeling the tremors still shaking him, the thud of his heart against her own. Slowly, his breathing eased. She held him tight, not wanting him to move, reveling in his weight crushing her.

She turned her head, brushing her lips against his neck, tasting his man's sweat. His mouth sought hers, and she gave it to him as she had given him her body. He traced the curves with his tongue, parting her lips, drawing her tongue deep into his own moist heat. He pulled away, only to come back again, mouths and tongues mating. And again, as if he needed her breath to live.

He pulled out of her and rolled to his side, gathering her up against him. His hand stroked her hair, a gentle, tender touch, and she thought he probably knew she was crying into his sweat-dampened shirt.

"I hurt you."

He had, but she didn't care. She was really his wife now, and he'd told her it only hurt the first time. She tilted her head back. "I love you," she said softly, her gaze searching his face.

The veil lifted in his shadowed eyes, and, for a moment, she saw his soul, saw his own fearsome need that mirrored her own. He couldn't say the words, maybe he'd never feel safe enough to say them. But for a fleeting moment, he had allowed her to see it in his eyes. Love for him swelled up so fierce, she thought she could die from the pressure in her chest.

He gave her another beautiful smile. "Sweet Annie, you're going to learn now just what you mean to me."

Royce tossed his shirt over the back of the chair and went behind the screen, where he cleaned her virgin's blood off himself. His chest constricted with the certain knowledge he'd hurt her, and hurt her a lot. She'd been so small, so tight, and he'd never been so big, so needful. A damn rutting beast.

He'd make it better this time, his hunger less urgent now, and he'd pleasure her the way a man should pleasure his woman. He wet a fresh rag and returned to the bed, stopping in front of the fire to warm the cloth. He stood for a moment, just looking at her. Her skin was so fair now, stretched smooth over the high, classic lines of her face. Her lips, moist and slightly parted, were a siren song against the whiteness of her skin. Her hair tangled over the pillows in wild abandon, the firelight catching the sun streaks, painting them gold against the brown.

He pulled the quilt back, and she opened her eyes, her lush, sinful lips turning up in a smile. He smiled himself, seeing how she'd drawn her night rail down over her hips, covering herself all the way to her ankles.

"Pull your nightgown up for me," he said as he sat beside her.

"What are you—" She gave a funny little sucked-in breath as he yanked the material up.

"I thought you were going to trust me."

She said nothing but lifted her hips and eased the flimsy cloth up, exposing the dark curls at her woman's mound, exposing the blood on her slender thighs. Gently, he wiped the blood away, then leaned over and kissed her just above the edge of curls.

Hurt, he was always hurting her. He drew a deep breath and discarded the cloth, shoving it beneath the bed where she wouldn't see the traces of her own pain. Pleasure now; he'd give her a pleasure she couldn't imagine, give himself a pleasure he'd been imagining for too long.

"I'd like you to take that nightgown off," he said quietly. Her eyes were huge, and she shook her head as she clutched her hand over the high collar. "A husband likes to look at his wife when he makes love to her." He placed his hand over hers, gently, not wanting to frighten her.

"There's not much to look at." Her voice was low and shaky. Her pulse beat rapidly just above the white lace on her throat, and it was the most erotic movement he'd ever seen.

"It's a beautiful body."

"You've never seen it. It's skinny and—"

"Beautiful." She shook her head again, and he argued by pulling her hand away from her neck then opening the tiny button. "Who do you think took care of you when you were so fevered the sweat ran off that beautiful body in rivers?"

Her dark eyes grew impossibly larger. His sweet Annie, so innocent, she'd never given that detail a thought. He pulled her to a sitting position and gathered the folds of cloth in his hands, ready to lift the gown over her head. She stopped him by placing her hand on his bare chest. He wondered if she felt his muscles reflexively jerk at her touch. He wondered if he was going to have to get down on his knees and beg. Damn, he was hard already, big and hard and aching for her.

"Please, Annie." His voice sounded hoarse. "I want to feel your soft skin, I want to taste you, touch you everywhere."

"Would you take all your clothes off, too?"

He went still, startled by her question, then felt laughter building in his chest, her joy-light, inside him. With a quick, sweeping motion, he peeled her gown away and pushed her back against the pillows, nuzzling his face between her breasts.

"Dear heart, I have every intention of doing just that," he said. "But not yet, I want to make this last a long time."

He took her hands, holding them beneath his own on either side of her head, their fingers interlaced together. He tasted her lips, and she opened for him, offering her tongue. She moaned softly, and he reluctantly gave up her mouth so he could lavish his attention on her neck, the little hollow at the base of her throat, the ridge of her collarbone.

He wanted four hands so he could both hold hers and touch her everywhere while he kissed her and licked her, but he only had two, so he let go. Her nipples were drawn up tight and pointed from the abrasion of his hairy chest against her flesh. He began there, then took his time exploring the contours of her body; feeling the soft skin and firm muscle, the flatness of her belly and swell of hip and thigh, the ridges of bone along her legs, the dimples behind her knees.

When she was purring like a kitten, he came back to her breasts, gently teasing the nipples with his thumbs, watching them draw tight. He lowered his head and for several long minutes, he licked and tasted each one; the white skin where it mounded, the puckered, rosy flesh in the middle, listening to her soft sounds of pleasure. He lifted his head and blew his breath on a wet nipple, watching it tighten and pucker even more.

"I've dreamed of this, Annie, holding these breasts, tasting them."

Her hands had become laced in his hair and he felt her fingers tighten. He raised up so he could see her face and smiled again. As impossible as it seemed, she looked both dazed and disgusted, as if she thought he was lying to her.

"Someday, I'm going to stand you in front of a mirror, buck naked, and point out just how beautiful you are."

She tucked her chin and peered down her little nose, going almost cross-eyed while she tried to look at herself, and he felt an urge to gather her so close she couldn't breathe, an urge to laugh with the joy of her, a terrible, wonderful need to love this beautiful, charming, unaffected little woman forever.

"These for example," he said, cupping her breasts in his hands. "As a decided rake, I am a connoisseur of women's breasts, and yours are wonderful."

She peered down again. "Poached eggs," she said disgustedly.

"What?"

"I wanted lush melons, and God gave me poached eggs."

He couldn't laugh, she was too damned serious, so to keep from laughing he took her breast in his mouth, suckling and teasing with his tongue at the one, teasing with his fingers at the other. Soon, he had her writhing and making more little whimpering sounds. He raised his head and grinned at her.

"I was always partial to poached eggs." He stared into her face, and her eyes were so dark, so filled with that old childhood hurt, his grin faded. "Dear heart, if we're going to compare them to food, I'd say peaches. Golden, ripe Virginia peaches, both soft and firm when you touch them and tasting so sweet."

She gave him a shaky smile, but her eyes seemed to fill with tears. He wanted to pound his fist into her brother, his brother; two young boys who had teased a skinny little girl until she couldn't see the beautiful woman she'd grown into.

He leaned over and brushed her lips with his own, then stood. He hadn't bothered to refasten his pants, and they gaped open at the front. He pushed them down off his hips, and his sex burst free, as big and hard as he'd ever been in his life. She made a little gasping sound, and her eyes went wide before she looked away.

He felt very male and absurdly pleased with himself for an endowment he'd been blessed with at birth. He grinned anyway and lowered himself over her. Supporting his weight on his arms, he rubbed the tip of his sex over her belly.

"This is what you do to me, my beautiful Annabelle. I get like this just thinking about you. Looking at you, the way you are now, deliciously naked and soft and ready for me—Christ, I almost can't stand it."

It started in her eyes, the golden light in the deep brown pools, then the sunburst spread to her lips, and the elusive crease in her cheek appeared. As always when he saw that smile, his heart stopped for a breathless moment.

"I love it when you smile like that." He lowered himself to his side and gathered her in his arms. "Sometimes I get hard just seeing that smile and when you laugh . . . dammit Annie, I hope you're pleased with yourself because you've done something to me I don't understand, and it scares me to death."

She nuzzled her face in his chest, her breath hot and moist on his skin. "I know," she said. "I feel the same about you."

Her hand rubbed down his side, and he almost groaned with the pleasure. His leg was thrown over hers and when she reached his thigh, the jagged scar there, she stopped. Her thumb gently stroked the old wound, and he felt her sigh. It wasn't hard to follow her thoughts. He prayed she didn't discover the second scar tonight.

He tightened his arms around her. "For now, there is no war. Just you and me, together in this room, and nothing else exists. No time, no world. Just us."

She swallowed audibly, then her head nodded against him. He wondered if it was her tears he felt on his chest but didn't have the courage to look. He couldn't stand to see her crying now, not when he hadn't yet found the guts to tell her he was leaving tomorrow. And then, he guessed she was feeling wonderfully brave.

Her hand slipped between their bodies, down his abdomen, to where he throbbed in delicious agony. Her fingers wrapped around him, and he tried not to shudder.

"What do I do?" Her voice was almost a whisper.

"What would you like to do?"

It was impossible; he couldn't get any harder, but he did. He heard her low purr as her hand squeezed and instinctively stroked his length. He shuddered.

She yanked her hand away. "Did I hurt you? I didn't mean to hurt you."

He laughed and drew her against him, nuzzling his face in her sweet-scented hair. "No, you didn't hurt me. It feels good, too good."

He pushed her back on the pillow and leaned over her, staring into her face, trying to memorize every beautiful feature. "Let me love you first this time. Touch me anywhere but there for now, because you make me feel too good when you touch me there."

"Will you tell me when?"

"You'll know."

Her hands came up to his chest, her nails lightly raking through the mat of hair to his skin. He eased himself over her, kissing her, licking her, loving her. He lavished her breasts with wet, hot kisses, more on her belly, the curve of her hips. He palmed her mound, tangling his fingers in her curls, then traced the grooves where her legs joined her body. She trembled, her skin growing slick with her sweat and his kisses.

He didn't have to spread her legs, she opened naturally. He slid his finger deep inside her, then pulled it out; slow, rhythmic thrusts that seemed to match the tempo of his own heartbeat. She was whimpering, almost mindless now.

"This is how you make me feel." He could see the rushing of blood in her throat. He added more pleasure by using his other hand to play with her nipple.

"Dear heaven," she gasped, as her back arched, and her hips pumped hard against his hand.

"You like that?"

"Yeeesss . . ." It was a sigh, then another gasping breath as he increased the pressure on the sensitive nub.

"I'm glad, dear heart, because you're going to get a lot of it."

He kept it up, stroking her hard and deep until he sensed an explosion, then circling her flesh, soft and teasing, slowing her, keeping her just this side of climax. Her sweating skin glistened in the light of the fire. Her chest heaved and her body began to writhe and arch as she reached hard for something she didn't understand.

His mouth was on hers, kissing her. "I'm going to give it to you, but not yet, Annie, not yet."

He held her close in his arms and rubbed her back, calming her so he could take her higher before she plunged. When her trembling eased, he moved down on the bed and raised her hips with his palms.

He took her in his mouth, his tongue delving deep between the soft folds of flesh, tasting her, tasting himself in her. Her hands clutched at his head as she gasped in shock, then moaned from deep in her throat. For long minutes, he pleasured her with his tongue, taking her back to the shuddering heights.

Her thighs instinctively opened wider, begging, needing, and he gave her more. He lightly scraped her tiny nub with his teeth, then sucked it hard between his lips. She went wild. Her head thrashed on the pillow, her hands clutching frantically at the sheets while every muscle in her body quivered.

He felt powerfully male, that he could do this to her. Her guttural moans and cries were sweet music, and he knew he was blessed that after all the hurts he'd caused her, she trusted him enough to allow him to control her this way.

She was climbing higher and higher, so shivering, quivering, heart-thuddering high. He wanted to keep her there forever but he felt the swelling of her folds, the clenching of her muscles, and knew she was too close for him to slow her again. He pulled his mouth away and rose over her.

"Now, Annie."

He slammed his mouth over hers as he drove into her. She cried out, and he swallowed her cries as she bucked her hips, clenching him in her wet heat so tightly he almost cried out. He raised back to watch her, withdrawing until only the rounded tip of him remained inside her, then drove into her again. She exploded, her body throbbing around him, gripping him with her spasms.

He drove her, holding himself back, wanting to give it to her again. She was wild beneath him, her body slick with sweat, her hips thrusting and bucking, meeting his pounding thrusts while her hands grasped him everywhere. He held himself back, driving her. Her thighs were spread so wide, her knees were touching the bed. His rushing blood thundered in his ears.

He slipped his hand where their bodies joined, finding her in the tangle of dark curls, rubbing her in rhythm with his pounding thrusts. Everywhere, he felt her—her hands, her heat, her woman's hot folds around him.

She came, screaming his name, bucking her hips and desperately clutching him as she flew apart, falling from a peak so high, she was an eternity from landing.

Her spasms drew him so deep he knew he was slamming her heart. He didn't feel so powerful now. She was drawing him inside out, absorbing him, reducing him to a pathetic, quivering male who was nothing without her. His head fell back, his back arching as he went mind-numbingly blind, shuddering, shattering. Helplessly lost inside her. He heard a sound and realized it was his own pitiful cries as he emptied himself into her.

He lay on top of her until his heart stopped pounding against his ribs and his lungs remembered how to work. Until he was certain he wasn't scattered in tiny fragments all around the cabin. She stirred beneath him, and he rolled to his side, taking her with him so their bodies remained intimately joined.

"I thought it was impossible to love you more," she murmured in a voice both breathless and raw. "I never knew. Dear heaven, hold me, Royce, please."

"Annie, sweet Annie." He gently wiped the tears from her cheeks, then drew his tearful, quivering, exhausted wife as close as he could. "My dear, sweet, beautiful Annie."

She was his. He was hers. And he wouldn't have it any other way.

For long hours, he watched her sleep, listened to her steady breathing. When he was certain she slept the deep sleep of exhaustion, not illness, he allowed himself to close his own eyes, still holding her in his arms.

Annabelle awoke to the cold of being alone in a bed where she had fallen asleep with her man's warm body surrounding her. She pressed her face in the pillow, afraid to open her eyes, afraid to find him already gone.

She heard a low sound and rolled to her side, opening her eyes to a room still folded in night. The fire, so long ignored, had faded to glowing embers. Royce crouched in front of the fire, silhouetted in the dim light with his back to her.

She watched him shake down the ashes and add more wood. The fire blazed back to life, the light glinting off the revolvers already holstered at his hips. For one blessed night, he had been hers, his fierce and loving touch, his hot and hungry kisses, his man's body buried deep inside her.

*For now, there is no war.*

He raised up and stared into the fire, then turned, as if her gaze was pulling him. His face was strongly beautiful in the flickering light and as emotionless as stone. He took one step toward her and stopped.

He wore his warrior's garb, his cavalry jacket and buckskins, black knee boots polished to a shine. She sat up against the pillows, drawing the quilt to her shoulders to hide her own nakedness, to hide her sudden sense of vulnerability. Her woman's heart could love him beyond pride or sense or reason, but her measureless love wasn't enough to beat the war that claimed him first.

"Were you going to leave without telling me?" Her voice sounded too shaky but she couldn't control it.

"I considered it but even my black heart couldn't do that to you again." He came forward, sitting on the bed beside her. She could see a soft light in his eyes now and that beautiful, tender curve of his mouth. "I was going to tell you last night, but something very special happened. I couldn't spoil it, Annie."

She nodded, swallowing. She would not send him away with a memory of her weakness. She watched him gather her gown from the foot of the bed. He slipped it over her head, and, like a child, she raised her arms and shoved them through the sleeves. He leaned forward and buttoned the single button at the collar.

"You're going to be sore, Annie-girl. This is an order—you're not to move from this bed today. Until I get back, I don't want you doing anything that might make you ill." His expression went hard. "This raid is too important for me to stay behind, and I can't be worrying about you while I'm gone."

She drew her knees up to her chest, holding the ache inside. Not the soreness he mentioned, which was there, but a pain much worse, the belly-slamming pain of fear. He couldn't be worrying about her, and she knew he was right. But this man's war was so unfair. She would live with her fear for him until he rode back over the crest, then live with the knowledge he would leave her again, over and over, until this terrible war either ended or killed him. She blinked and sucked in her lower lip. She would not cry.

"Will you tell me anything?"

"No. I'll never leave you here alone. Savage and some of the boys will stay with you this time. Even here, there's always the chance of a Union raid. The less you know, the safer you'll be."

He studied her face as if memorizing her features. His eyes narrowed, and she knew her traitorous face was giving her away.

"Annie, I don't want to hurt you any more than I already have, but this damn war makes it impossible to keep from hurting you," he said. "Until it's over, I'm a soldier first and a man second; it can't be any other way."

His gaze was tactile, she could feel it against her face as certain as she'd felt his hands on her skin last night. Dear heaven, she loved him, and she was losing him to war, maybe death, and there was nothing she could do to change anything. Not her love, she'd never outlive this love; and not this war, controlled by no one, controlling everyone.

She swallowed against the rawness in her throat. Even so, her voice sounded hoarse when she spoke. "You'll be careful."

"Is that an order, Sarge?"

He held her gaze, his eyes seeming to penetrate through her effort not to cry, then his lips turned up into something almost a smile. She tried to smile for him, but it was so hard, and her face felt stiff, like it might crack with the effort.

"I'll be careful," he said. "There's someone very important for me to come back to now."

He leaned over and brushed a kiss on her lips, so swift and tender, it was only a whisper of a kiss. Her eyes drifted closed, and she placed her fingers where his lips had brushed, holding the memory of his kiss.

"I love you." She opened her eyes for one last look at his warrior's face. He was already gone.

# Chapter 26

Annabelle kneaded her back with her hands as she blew a sigh up into the brim of one of Royce's old hats. The wind had come up since breakfast, chasing away the mist. With the natural beauty surrounding her and the quiet of early afternoon, she could almost forget why this mountain camp existed. Almost.

Royce had been gone for six days.

She coped by keeping busy, driving herself beyond exhaustion so when she fell into the bed at night, her body's aching tiredness overcame the fear in her heart, and she would sleep without dreams of screaming horses and flowing blood.

She picked up the empty washtub in hands that were skinned raw from caustic soap and boiling water. The hem of her skirts trailed through the mud as she slogged toward the farmhouse where another copper was boiling under the watchful eye of William Savage.

When this task was completed, she intended to spend hours on herself, bathing and washing her hair with the scented soap Livvy had packed, then tending her hands with ointment. She would be neat and clean when her husband returned, wearing sweet-smelling clothes, with her hair shining from a hundred brushstrokes. She would never be beautiful like Mama and Livvy, but she could make herself into a woman he could feel pride in, an honest-to-goodness lady.

If he came home. She pushed that thought back. Her feet

squelched through a depression in the ground filled with standing water. The mire of sticky, clinging mud sucked her shoes from her feet. The empty washtub dropped from her hands, and she turned to extricate her shoes. The wet clay felt wonderfully cool and soothing to her burning hands. She raised up, muddy shoes clasped in her hand, feet clasped to the ankles by red mud, and caught sight of Captain Savage headed her way. He juggled another heavy washtub in his arms.

He flashed his gap-toothed grin when he saw her. "Don't know how I let you talk me into this. The colonel gave me strict orders to look out for you. If he was to see you now, barefoot in the cold mud, he'd string me up by my toes and leave me hanging till doomsday."

"What he doesn't know can't hurt him." Annabelle wiped her hands down the front of her apron, spreading a red-brown streak of clay. She gave him a tired smile. "How much more?"

"One more copper of sheets in the rinse tub, but I'll be getting those. You done stirred enough with that broomstick for one day."

She fell in beside him as he carried the full tub over to the strung line. "I've never met a man like you, Captain," she said. "You'd make some lady a wonderful husband, knowing what you do about cooking and washing and not being afraid to help out. Why haven't you married?"

"I had a wife once," he said, and she saw sadness in the deepening creases around his eyes. He set the container on the ground and gazed off into the blue ridges rimming the horizon.

She pulled her handkerchief from her pocket, wet it in the bottom of the tub, and concentrated on wiping the traces of muck from her hands. "I'm sorry," she said. "I have this horrid ability always to ask the wrong questions."

He looked at her, and his face softened. "It was a long time ago, Sarge, and no harm done. We'd only been married a year. She was in the family way when she died of the cholera, and I just never had the heart to go through that kind of sadness again. Kept myself busy being a man for my widowed sister and her kids, and that was enough. I love those four boys of hers as if they was my own, especially the last one."

"I know what you mean. I feel that way about my youngest brother."

"He fighting in this war?"

"Not yet. He's at VMI, so it's just a matter of time. Your nephews?"

"One with Lee, one killed at Gettysburg, and two fighting on the other side."

She knew other families torn asunder by this fratricidal war, brother against brother and father against son. She never knew what to say when confronted by the raw anguish involved in that kind of tearing of families. Sometimes she wondered what possible future the Unionists hoped to gain by winning. Could breaches like those ever be healed?

Captain Savage's gaze had gone distant, and she wondered if he was thinking the same thoughts, wondered if men ever thought those kinds of thoughts. Or did they just pick up their guns and go into battle, fighting for honor or duty or whatever it was that made them fight to the death.

Did they have any notion of tomorrow, of winning or losing or the consequences of either? She wished she had the courage to ask him. His low voice brought her out of her reverie, and she realized he wasn't following her woman's line of thought.

"Did you ever hear how the colonel got that name the Last Cavalier?"

"Wasn't it something to do with the child picket he sent home early in the war?" she said.

Savage nodded. "The boy was just short of his fifteenth birthday, and our colonel saw he was too young to be a soldier. He could have sent the boy to Richmond as a prisoner but sent him home instead, asked me to escort him there since I was from that part of Maryland, too."

He absently slapped his hat against his thigh, gazing somewhere into the distance. "The youngster asked me who the officer was who let him go and back then, we was a secret company, so I just told the boy the last of the cavaliers, making a joke from the question. It was the boy's mother who talked to the fellow from *Harper's Magazine*, and that's how our Kincaid got the name. Back then, it was still a gentleman's war."

The wind gusted, snapping the clothes already hung on the line, making a noise like the rattle of musket fire. Annabelle's chest tightened, as if she was actually hearing the sounds of war, a war that was no longer a gentleman's war, but a killing war already three years old with no end in sight.

"Colonel Kincaid didn't know it when he made the decision," he said. "But the boy he let go was my youngest nephew. Abner had run away to enlist then. He's seventeen now and back in the war, fighting on the other side."

William Savage was a kind man, a friend, and he was hurting for a boy he loved. She placed her hand on his arm. "I'll add Abner to my prayers, Captain."

He snorted a laugh, hiding his ache for the schism splitting his family. "Best add me to your prayer list if your husband gets back before this job is finished. Need help out here, Sarge, or should I go stir the sheets?"

"Stir the sheets and save me some hot water for a bath when I'm done. When he gets back, he's going to find a clean wife waiting for him."

"A smart officer knows it's the sergeants who run this man's army."

She watched him trudge back to the farmhouse and broke into laughter when he hit the same patch of oozing mud and lost a boot. A string of oaths rolled off his tongue with the ease of a man who'd lived among men for too long, and he caught himself, sending her an apologetic glance over his shoulder before he disappeared inside.

She turned and gazed ahead, toward the gap. She breathed deeply. The ache in her back eased as the earth and sky seemed to seep into her.

She loved these mountains—the timelessness and the pure, sweet lonesomeness of the highlands, the blue ridges rolling as far as the eye could see across a bluer sky. The way the sun dusted the valley pastures with gold light and fleecy clouds shed round shadows in the hollows, the way creeks tripped over rocks and ledges on their way to the meandering Shenandoah.

The day was unseasonably warm for March and she could smell the sweet-scented ripening of spring. It was part of the cycle of seasons that melded days into years and brought her a sense of belonging to something larger than herself.

For so long these rocky mountains and fertile valleys had been the place of her heart. It frightened her, this love for the land of the Shenandoah. She didn't like caring so deeply for something the war could destroy.

She watched a red-tail hawk ride a kettle draft, circling in tight spirals, up and up into the blue until he was nearly out of sight. When he was little more than a shadow, he broke off and flew to the south. The air grew still, the day silent, and she could hear her heart pumping in her chest.

She felt so alone of a sudden, separate from everything around her. Fragile and terribly alone.

"Damn, if we'd known Grant was on that train, we could have ended this war in a day," said John DeShields.

Royce glanced at DeShields from beneath the concealing brim of his hat. He'd fought with those same thoughts for the past two days. The success of their raid paled in comparison to the opportunity missed. While they chased a small troop of Union cavalry through Warrenton Junction, a special, unguarded train carrying Grant from Washington escaped their notice. If they'd been a few minutes later arriving at the junction . . . if their intelligence had been better . . .

Grant was now with Meade's army along the Rapidan, while Sherman headed toward Georgia with an entire army. The whole fabric of the war was changing. Lincoln had found his fighting generals, and the South had to hunker down for the finish. Their only remaining hope of winning against the odds was for Lincoln to lose the next election. Lincoln would fight to the bitter end; McClellan would broker a peace.

They were almost back to Hope Mountain, and Royce allowed his mind to focus on something more pleasant. Annabelle. Never had the ground felt so cold and hard as it had on this foray when he bedded down alone and remembered the awesome sensation of holding his wife, soft and warm and trusting as she slept in his arms. Remembered the joy-fire preceding her exhausted slumber.

His body hardened with those thoughts, and he smiled in anticipation. They crested the last ridge and his smile disappeared.

"Bloody hell," he muttered, catching sight of a rope line near his cabin, wet wash flapping in the wind. "I ordered that woman to behave herself. If she's made herself sick again, I'll bloody damn kill her."

"Never thought I'd see the day when Royce Kincaid was bested by a pint-sized female," said John, amusement tingeing his deep voice.

Royce considered landing a fist in John's gut and letting all that amusement escape in a hiss of breath but decided to save his fury for his defiant little wife. He'd hammered Savage's ears with orders to keep her out of mischief. How had she talked him into stringing her a rope so she could kill herself doing laundry? Kincaid wives didn't do laundry.

His wife did as she damned well pleased.

He almost smiled. As they rode closer, Savage emerged from the farmhouse, carrying a tin washtub. A moment later, Annabelle appeared from amidst the flapping folds of a sheet. The line was strung so high she had to stand on two cracker boxes to reach it. He watched her jump down, move the boxes over to an open space on the line, and climb back up. Savage handed her a sheet. John was openly laughing.

"Old Jeff ought to promote our little petticoat sergeant," said John. "She's even got Savage doing the wash. Just think what she could do with an entire army under her command."

"By the time I'm done smacking her backside, she won't be able to walk, let alone command," muttered Royce. He gave the signal for silence, and his men ceased tittering. They approached the little scene as silently as if they were stealing into a Union camp at night.

Savage caught sight of them anyway. Royce shook his head, and Savage followed the unspoken command, saying nothing to Annabelle. She was fighting the wind in an effort to fling a wet sheet over the rope. She wrestled the sheet into place and anchored it with wooden pins.

The wind caught the ends of cloth, slapping the sheet against her. She swayed and grabbed at the rope line. The boxes slid out from under her feet and she landed on her pretty little behind-her with a great splattering of mud and a bone-crushing jar. His heart stopped, and he spurred ahead, certain she'd managed to kill herself before he got the opportunity.

She looked up, and he knew she wasn't dead yet. She ignored Savage's outstretched hand and alarmed curses while she sat perfectly still in the cold, oozing mud, breathing heavily as she watched him ride toward her. He dismounted before the horse had come to a stop.

"Bloody hell, Annabelle. Are you hurt?"

She stared at him with that deep, dark-eyed gaze, then squelched to her feet. His heart resumed an erratic beat. She was covered with red mud from crown to boot. Bloody hell, not boot—the blasted woman was in her stocking feet. He was going to kill her.

She smiled. He blinked.

She wiped at the mud on her face with her sleeve, smearing a wide trail across her cheek. "You're home," she said, her smile glowing through the war paint on her face.

He wanted to grab her in his arms, mud and all, hug her so tight, she'd beg for relief. He reminded himself he was angry. She had no right to put her health at risk again, no right to scare him witless.

"What does it take to convince you to listen to me?" he said, trying desperately to sound angry. He wasn't succeeding, her smile hardly faded.

"You're home," she repeated in a soft voice filled with the love he'd hungered for his entire life.

A chunk of mud fell from the brim of her hat, landing with a *splat* on her bodice. She looked down at herself then back up at him. Any other woman would burst into tears. Not his Annie. She threw back her head and laughed, making that joyous sound, the sound that thrummed through his blood and left him hungry for more . . . more smiles, more laughter, more Annie.

"Dear merciful heaven, you're home."

The sun seemed to blaze brighter, the wind to blow gentler, soft and sweet against his face. But it wasn't the sun and it wasn't the breeze. It was his wife, flinging her wet, muddy self into his arms.

"I love you," she said. Or maybe he only thought he heard it. His mouth was already covering hers, and his arms wrapped her so tight, she probably couldn't breathe.

When this cruel war was over, nothing would keep them apart.

# Chapter 27

Thunder rolled, and Ajaque shied. Reflexively, Royce squeezed his thighs, controlling the horse without use of his hands. It was only after he'd jammed the last cartridge in the last revolver that he gave any thought to his battle-tested mount's odd behavior.

He normally gave no credence to those who claimed precognition before a battle, but something was gnawing at his gut this morning, and he didn't like the sensation. All around him, he heard the click of cylinders as his men readied their weapons. It was a sound so familiar, he seldom heard it anymore. Today, it seemed ominous and filled with foreboding.

He turned Ajaque and rode forward to meet his captains. He would trust each of these men to make their own decisions as the opportunity arose. For the past two weeks, he'd done just that, splitting up and harassing Sigel's forces everywhere from Winchester to deep inside West Virginia and Maryland.

They had higher orders today. Breckinridge was at New Market, a little town halfway up the valley. Their Confederate forces of five-thousand-odd men faced a Union force at least double their number. The prospect was not heartening.

It took Royce only a few minutes to go over their orders. DeShields and Savage would take half the raiders and join with Breckinridge. Royce would take the rest down the Valley Pike, setting up a skirmish line deep in the Federal rear with the goal of preventing reinforcements from reaching Sigel's army.

It wasn't a battle on the scale of the bloodshed taking place at Spotsylvania, but it was critical. If the Union won today, the breadbasket of the Confederacy was theirs, and Lee's army would be starved into defeat.

The Yanks wouldn't win. He and every other Rebel soldier on this wet, muddy field would die first.

As Geary and Savage turned to go back to their commands, Royce stopped John by reaching for his bridle. Rainwater sluiced off the brim of John's hat, the black ostrich plume hanging in a dejected position along the brim.

"They joined him at Staunton," said John.

"Damn." Royce stared ahead into a peach orchard where pink blossoms shivered on the tree limbs. A gray mist hung close to the ground; a mist that would soon thicken with battle smoke, become heavy with the screams of dying men and horses. And maybe, dying children.

"He won't put them in, Royce. He didn't even want to bring them."

His gut twisted again. God willing, today's battle would progress with enough certitude Breckinridge wouldn't feel the need to throw in the boys, VMI's cadets, including Bohannon Hallston, sixteen years old tomorrow. Annabelle could lose her husband and brother in one day's fighting.

"John?" Royce fingered the well-worn leather of Ajaque's bridle. "Annabelle . . . if something should happen . . ." He swallowed against a strange lump in his throat. "There's no one I trust more than you. She'll need someone to look out for her, get her back to Riverbend. I'm asking you to be that man."

It was John's turn to stare into the peach orchard. Finally, he turned his gaze back, his blue eyes penetrating. "I'll look out for her if I'm able. You know that."

Royce lifted his arm, and hand met hand in friendship and oath, then the two soldiers parted, riding silently in opposite directions.

Some men claimed to think their way through a battle. Royce never believed that claim. Some men only reacted. They usually ended up dead. Royce considered himself a fighting man. He fought to live.

The day had been alternating sunshine and rain, but as they

charged into the Union line, the sky hung black and low. Within moments, the heavens unleashed a torrent of pelting rain. Great bursts of thunder mixed with the boom of artillery. Lightning flashed, striking the ground with a sonorous crash and sending quakes rolling across the wheatfield.

Beside him, a ranger went long-legged stiff in his saddle, then catapulted to the ground. Another flash of gunfire, and Ajaque screamed. Royce jumped clear as his great horse fell to his knees.

A Federal swooped out of the fog. Royce waited until he could see the man's eyes. He squeezed the trigger of his Navy Colt, and the Yank fell, dead.

"Colonel." Parker drew up beside him, clutching the wet reins of DeWitt's sorrel in his fist. Royce grabbed the saddle holsters from his own dead horse and swung onto the new mount.

"DeWitt?" he asked, before Parker rode away.

"Dead, sir."

Smoke rolled in waves held close to the ground by the pelting rain. Tree boughs swayed and leaned overhead while the ground shook beneath. Another Yank with a gleam in his eye. Another bullet killing the gleam. Screaming shells. Screaming men. Lashing rain and snapping wind. Noise. Confusion.

A fighting man's high. Sometimes, a fighting man's death.

Annabelle folded the letter from Peyton and slipped it into her pocket. She settled her hands in her lap and tried to compose her features. When she looked up, Chauncey was studying her.

"Bad news?" he asked in a quiet voice.

She took a deep breath and let it out slowly. "Augusta's dead," she said, her own voice calm with the shock of what she'd just read. "Typhoid, it took her mother, too. Peyton's gone to Richmond to get little Gordy."

She thought of Gordon, still languishing at Fort Delaware, a prisoner the Federals refused to exchange. They didn't even know if he was allowed the letters they wrote. Right now, she hoped he never saw them. This news could kill him.

Chauncey fingered the sling holding his left arm. That sling was the only reason he was here with her instead of battling the Federals somewhere on the other side of the valley.

She was surrounded by the walking wounded, those too battered to return to the fight, not wounded enough to be sent to Richmond's hospitals. Normally, her heart ached for their pains, and she devoted much of her time to caring for their needs. Today, they were driving her crazy.

The guns pounded in the distance, and she saw each man look up, saw the soldier's gleam in their eyes—and the frustration. She wanted to hate them. She pushed her chair back and stood.

"It's raining," said Chauncey. They could fight their manly battles in a downpour and think nothing of it. She wasn't supposed to walk in the rain.

She lifted her rubber coat from the peg beside the door and shrugged into it. All she heard was the shuffling of feet as she pulled the door closed.

It wasn't really rain now, more like a steady drip. Heaven's tears, she thought. She trudged up the trail to the ridge. Chestnuts and white oaks raised thick trunks to the sky, their green branches forming a canopy over the path. The understory blazed in color: rose pink azalea, thickets of blushing mountain laurel, the white bracts of blooming dogwoods. It was a spring show she normally relished. Today, the beauty only increased her sadness.

She broke out of the canopy at the top of the ridge. She stopped at the edge of the crest, dangerously close to loose, slippery rocks. Before her spread a peaceful panorama of the Great Valley: the South Fork of the Shenandoah with its lazy bends, the patchwork quilt of green pastures and tilled croplands, the abrupt blue rise of the Massanuttens. To her right, blue lights flashed from Signal Knob—Confederates relaying reports to Richmond.

The deep roll of cannon fire sounded from the other side of Massanutten Mountain. The sky over New Market Gap appeared darker and more ominous. It could be a storm. It could be the dark smoke of battle.

She slipped her hand in her pocket and fingered the letter Chauncey had brought in this morning, news too sad to be borne. One more death, a woman's death; beyond the blue mountain, men were dying.

The sky darkened. Another wave of resonant sound rolled across the valley. Annabelle lifted her face to the dripping sky.

*Please, God. Let Royce live.*

Heaven's tears streaked down her cheeks. Her own were dammed up deep inside her.

General Breckinridge sat mounted on his horse near the Valley Pike, monitoring the battle. Sigel's cannons pounded his infantry, inflicting heavy losses. He watched the gap open in the center of the line, knowing he had no more infantry to throw into the hole.

John C. Breckinridge, former vice president of the United States, turned to his ordnance officer. Tears blurred his vision. "Put the boys in," he said. "And may God forgive me for the order."

# Chapter 28

For miles, the ground was strewn with supplies dropped by fleeing Union soldiers: blankets and haversacks, saddles and boots, oilcloths and cartridge boxes. The fields nearer the Bushong farm were spotted with the dead and the dying, some dressed in blue, some in butternut gray.

Royce walked among the surgeons and litter bearers, exchanging occasional nods with the women of New Market who had come out on this bleak night to nurse the wounded, both blue and gray.

He searched for Bohannon Hallston.

The unrelenting rain washed blood and gore into the shallow gullies formed by tramping boots, easing the stench of death while doing nothing to mitigate the suffering of those still breathing and bleeding.

He watched John plow his way through the thick mud with a cadet in tow. A child-soldier still enamored of the trappings of war, the formalities taught in the classroom and on the parade grounds, where death was a hollow word, honor a hallowed one.

Their initiation had come today. He wondered how many had died in the rite-by-fire. Not Bo, please, not Bo.

When they reached him, the boy saluted sharply. Royce returned the salute, surprised to find that moving his arm was like lifting lead. "Corporal Hotchkiss, sir," said the youngster. "I understand you're looking for Private Hallston."

Royce nodded. He concentrated on the boy's face, still

339

plump with youth, ruddy cheeks and innocent blue eyes. Eyes so like Bo's, he almost choked.

"Bohannon was beside me when he went down," said the cadet. "The first charge. He's already been taken into town."

"With the dead or the wounded, Corporal?"

A startled look passed over the boy's face. Tears glinted in his eyes. "Wounded, sir. I'm sorry . . . I wasn't thinking."

For the moment, Bo lived, and Royce let the relief wash over him. He supposed something must be showing on his face as the youngster relaxed his body. A small boon, he thought, as it saved him the necessity of articulating his thanks and probably embarrassing them both in the process.

Royce reached out and clasped the cadet's shoulder, then fought the urge to squeeze as he felt the youngster's well-hidden trembles. "How old are you, Corporal Hotchkiss?"

"Sixteen, sir, seventeen come November."

"You did a man's job today," he said quietly. "I'd be honored to shake your hand."

Corporal Hotchkiss straightened his shoulders in a stiff parade stance, then held out his hand. Royce clasped it within his own, then impulsively drew the young cadet against his body, encircling him with his arm. The youth didn't resist, almost collapsing against him instead.

Royce fought an emotion he couldn't name building in his chest, squeezing up into his throat. He swallowed hard, clearing the lump so he could speak. "Be proud, son. And don't ever forget the cost." He let the cadet go. "You're dismissed to find a warm meal and a dry bed. That's an order, Corporal."

Corporal Hotchkiss stared at his hand. Suddenly, a wide grin creased his face. "What a day! I fought in the war with General Breckinridge and shook hands with Colonel Kincaid—real, honest-to-gosh famous men."

"Skedaddle, Corporal, before I put you on guard duty," said Royce. The cadet lifted another smart salute and skedaddled. Royce watched the youngster's retreating back as that unwanted emotion tightened his chest.

"Think he'll wash that hand before he eats his dinner?" asked John, in a deceptively light tone. Royce ignored the question, unwilling or unable to hide the tumultuous aftershocks of battle this time.

"What kind of a war is it when we expect our children to fight," he said.

"A helluva war."

Together, they began a return trek across the muddy field. Neither man spoke, Royce's mind beginning to drift from relief back to concern. How badly was Bo wounded? He noticed the cadet had stopped beside another fallen body and angled his steps in that direction.

"I thought he was one of ours," said the corporal. "But he's a Yank."

Royce looked down. Something inside him tore loose and broke away, leaving a hole that bled and hurt. He knelt in the mud and pushed a shock of dark, wet hair off the soldier's forehead. Another boy, a cold, dead child.

"Where's Savage?" he asked. John didn't answer, and he spoke again, his voice revealing the harshness of impotent anger. "Christ, John, where's Savage? This is his nephew, the Union picket you captured on that first raid."

Still no reply. Slowly, Royce pushed himself up. He stared into John's face and saw his answer in the grim lines of John's mouth.

Royce threw his hat down. "Bloody hell, why didn't you say anything?"

"Figured you had enough on your mind for the moment."

Royce fixed his glare on John's face. Savage was dead. Savage's nephew was dead. DeWitt and two other rangers had died in his skirmish lines today; God only knew how many more were dead on this field. Bohannon Hallston lay in someone's house, wounded, and he had to carry that news to Annie. Christ, even his best horse was dead.

And the Confederacy was dying. A slow, painful death exemplified by nothing less than the need to send boy soldiers against the cannon fire. Royce swung around and marched across the field, not knowing where he was going, not giving a soldier's damn.

John DeShields leaned over and retrieved the hat from the ground. He watched Colonel Kincaid as he moved through the thick mud, his lean body silhouetted in torchlight, surrounded by the cries and moans of the dying.

Abruptly, Kincaid stopped. Firelight struck the harsh lines of his face as he turned in a slow circle, as if the hardened warrior was seeing a field of battle for the first time. With the exaggerated motions of a tired man, he sank down on a stump. His head dropped into his hands, and his broad shoulders began to shake.

"What is it?" asked the cadet.

"War, son. Even a brave man cries. All of us have cried." John swallowed, and when he spoke, his throat hurt. "In all this time, he has not."

Troops began gathering, Kincaid's cavalry, infantrymen, and artillerymen, a scattering of VMI cadets. DeShields nodded, and the raiders began to move, cordoning the stump where their commander sat. Hard, silent men, who one by one pulled battered hats from bowed heads. Surrounded by his soldiers, Colonel Kincaid poured out his grief, let go of the pain.

The sounds of death seemed to fade as dark night and heaven's raindrops took over the field. A field of honor for the boys, a field of loss for the Yanks . . . tomorrow, a simple field of grass.

# Chapter 29

Annabelle saw them through the kitchen window, a troop of tired men riding through a thick carpet of dandelions. As always, her eyes searched first for a lean warrior wearing a battered slouch hat with a scraggly gull feather stuck in the band. As always, she forgot to breathe until she found him, then, what remained of life began again, and she counted heads as they rode past her viewpoint.

Today, Caleb Geary was missing. They were her family now, these men. She turned back to her task of drying the dishes, hoping Caleb had only gone to a different camp, fearing he was dead. She tried not to remember a time last May when they had returned without William Savage, but no matter how hard she tried, that time always pushed itself into her memories.

The sun had hung bright in a deep blue sky, the air so clear the mountains were sharp creases against the horizon. She saw them from this same window, tired and dusty men cresting the ridge. Somewhere beyond the window, a warbler sang, and she'd thought the sound echoed her own heart, welcoming the battle-weary warriors home.

And then she was running, skirts clasped in her hands while her bootheels thrummed the ground. She saw her man jump from his horse and open his arms. She ran faster because he was home and he was safe, but she couldn't trust herself to believe it until she felt him. She hit the solid wall of his chest, her laughter ringing out as his arms closed tight around her.

And when he spoke, something inside her died.

Bohannon Hallston recovered. He was in Richmond now with the rest of the cadets, VMI and much of Lexington having been burned by the Federals. Papa's house was gone, but that was a small loss. It was the near loss of Bo that tore her heart into tatters and increased her fear of an even greater loss. Life was so fragile, and war had no mercy, no compassion.

Annabelle hung the dish towel on a peg and made her way to the cabin. She walked past Royce, but didn't stop. She'd seen him, knew he was safe for today, and for today, that was enough.

The summer sun was hot, but inside the cabin the air was shadowed and cool. The rocker creaked as she lowered herself into it, then creaked some more as she rocked. She stared out the window at the grove of hemlock and the corduroy bridge over the creek.

Outside, horses whinnied and men talked loudly. She heard the clink of bits and harnesses. There was fresh coffee and warm blueberry cobbler waiting for them in the main house, so she allowed herself to rock and tried not to think.

She needed to cry, but couldn't let herself cry. Once she began, she'd never stop; all the tears she hadn't shed since this war began, all the tears for all the losses.

It hurt to feel, so she tried to close her heart. It was a coward's answer to fear, and she knew it, but told herself she felt nothing. She told herself so many times, she'd almost come to believe it.

Life was different when you didn't allow yourself to feel.

Royce rode in for a few days and rode back out. When he was with her, they were unfailingly polite to one another. They ate together and did the chores that filled a day. When night came, they slept in the same bed and didn't speak or touch. She would turn her back to him and stare at the pine knots in the wall until she heard him sleeping, then she would roll over and watch him sleep.

Sometimes, she had to touch him, stroking the scars he never talked about, as if by touching him in the night, she could erase the old wounds and protect him in the next battle. But she was afraid he would waken and catch her, so she tried to resist the need to touch him, to protect him.

She rocked and watched the men lead horses toward the barn and heard the rasp of spurs on the floor behind her. She always knew when Royce entered a room, even before she saw him. He was still her man. She didn't want to love him and tried to stop, but it was impossible. She had loved him since forever and would love him for always, and she hated him for making her love him still.

He wasn't really her man. He belonged to the Confederacy. In his own words, a soldier first and a man second.

He came up beside her, so close, she could see his dusty black boots but she wouldn't look at him. She wanted to ask him about Caleb but feared the answer, so she didn't.

"I thought maybe you'd like to ride with me to the falls before I unsaddle the horse," he said.

She peered through the wavy glass, focusing her gaze on a twittering jay as it hopped from tree branch to tree branch. She said nothing. The rocker creaked.

"You're tired, Annie, all these men you think you have to care for. It seems every time I see you you're cooking or mending or nursing. You need to get away from here, feel the sun on your face, the wind in your hair."

"Is that what you feel when you ride into the cannon? Or maybe that's what you're thinking about when you lean over another dead soldier."

He drew in a breath and let it out in a sigh. She clenched her hands in her lap. She hadn't meant to say anything, especially not that. It was too close to feeling, and she couldn't feel because one day, this man would die on a bloody field, and when that bleak day came, she might as well die too because there would be nothing left of her to pick up and go on.

"Annabelle." His hand gripped her shoulder, his long fingers pressing into her flesh. "Talk to me, Annie. I don't know what's wrong, and I can't make it right if you won't talk to me."

Anger surged, hot and burning, driving her out of the chair with such force the rockers skidded across the floor. But anger was a feeling, so she clasped her waist and tilted her head while she pushed the anger back behind the cold. And when she felt nothing but cold again, she spoke in a voice filled with icy scorn.

"I've nothing to say to you."

He clutched her arms and gave her a rough shake. "Dammit, woman, say what you're thinking." She tried to twist free of him, but he pulled her closer so she was filled with his scents. "You're killing me with this. For God's sake, let it out. Talk or scream or curse at me, but say something."

"Don't touch me." She stared into his eyes and saw a pain there as terrible as her own. She wanted to erase his pain, but another part of her wanted him to suffer as much as she suffered each time he rode into his war. "I can't bear it when you touch me."

He dropped his hands to his side and shook his head. "You don't mean that."

She closed her eyes against the torment she saw on his face. She heard a sound and realized it was coming from her, a weak, helpless sound. She turned away from him and stiffened her spine. She felt his touch on her hair.

"Tell me what you want. Christ, Annabelle, I'd tear out my heart and give it to you on a silver platter if I thought it would make you smile again."

She swung around so fast, her skirts billowed around her ankles. "What do I want!" She laughed, a brittle sound, like ice breaking. "I want this war to end. I want all the godforsaken soldiers to go back where they came from. I want my home back and the people I loved back—" Her words caught as a terrible choking grief welled up in her. "I want to wake up in the morning without wondering if this is the day I lose someone else."

"I can't end this war for you. Right now, nobody can."

She tried to laugh again but it got caught up in a hard ball in her throat and came out as a puny, whimpering sound. "Oh no, certainly not you men. You can start it, you can fire your guns and die with your boots on. But you can't finish it. Why, Royce? Tell me why."

He half turned away from her, his face a grim profile. He

was gripping the back of the chair so hard, his knuckles whitened. "I'm fighting for our home, Annie, for you. I'd die for you."

"Don't do me those kinds of favors you stupid, stupid man." Her fisted hand slammed against her breastbone. "I'll take care of myself. I'll bloody well take care of myself."

She turned her back and waited for him to leave. For the longest time, he stood there, and she listened to his heavy breathing. She clenched her fists inside the folds of her skirts and stiffened her spine in an effort not to weaken, then, when he was gone, she had to clamp her jaws to keep from calling after him.

She stared out the window at the wooden bridge and the hemlock whispering in the breeze. The ball clogging her throat grew larger, and larger still, until even her chest was too full to breathe. Her dry eyes burned as if she'd been crying for weeks.

And then she was outside, her shoes crushing the milkweed as she crossed the yard. Royce called out to her, but she only increased her pace, walking so quickly her feet kicked up her skirts. She didn't know where she was going, but she wouldn't stop until she got there. Someplace so far away, she would never know when the bullet found him, would never know he had died for her. When she hit the little bridge, she was running.

Royce heard the door shut and looked back to see her crossing the yard. He called after her, but she only quickened her stride.

Damn her, he was the one who didn't believe in love, wouldn't even think the word until she entered his life. She made him love her, made him believe, and now he was losing her.

Pain twisted his gut while a terrible, cold rage built in his chest. He wanted to hate her. He wanted to thrust himself deep inside her, force her with his maleness to admit she was his. Most of all, he wanted a miracle. He wanted the joy-light back in her eyes.

He untethered his horse and began to lead him toward the barn. He'd taken but three steps when he stopped, staring at the ground, wondering if he should go after her and try again. A large shadow fell in front of him.

"I'll take care of your horse," said John. "She needs you."

"Whatever it is, I just seem to make it worse."

"Lord knows, I'll never understand them, but in her case, I'm one up on you," said John as he reached for the bridle. "Caleb didn't come back with us today."

"What the hell difference does that make?" bit out Royce. It was in her nature to mother the boys, but she was his, not Caleb's, and John was an idiot to think otherwise.

"She worries. She hides it from you, but the rest of us have seen it because we've stayed behind with her. When you leave, something inside her dies, and every time, she's worse off than the time before," said John. He nodded toward the trail they usually followed back over the ridge.

"She watches that hill like a hawk, waiting for us to come back, and I've been here and shameless enough to study her when it happens. She's so caught up in looking for you, she doesn't realize anyone's watching her, so she's not hiding anything."

John pushed the brim of his hat back, clearing the shadows from his face. Royce waited for the rest of his revelation as the light began to filter into his own bloody damn stupid brain.

"Until she finds you in the crowd, there's a look on her face I'd describe as terror, and you can tell exactly when she sees you—something of the old Sarge comes back in her eyes. Then she looks for the others and if someone's missing . . ." He shrugged, as if apologizing. "It's like she's been pummeled anyway."

Christ, how stupid could one man be. He thought of his gut-wrenching fear when she lay sick, dying, a fear so intense it almost killed him, a fear so profound, he was long weeks gaining the courage to bed her. He thought of his flashing anger whenever she did the smallest thing that caused him concern over her health or safety.

What a bloody fool, so damned selfish, he'd never stopped to think she was fighting that killing fear constantly. He forced her to live with it every minute of every day by keeping her here because he wanted to ride back from the war and find a few moments peace in her arms.

Here, in a male world, surrounded by a war she was impotent to control. Where she knew every time a skirmish was fought, knew every man who died, constantly aware the next man to die might be her husband.

Annie, the warrior, fierce and proud. Annie, a woman, with a woman's heart. The only heart in the world that had ever touched his own.

John had opened his eyes, and maybe John could answer another question, a question Annabelle would never answer.

"Does she ever cry?" he asked.

John's face remained somber. "Not where any of us have ever seen her."

Royce thought back over the years. He'd might have seen a stray teardrop or two, but never anything approaching real crying, only that deep withdrawal when her pain became too much to bear.

He watched a hawk circle, fiercely beautiful outlined by shimmering sunlight against a deep blue sky. A predator, a warrior. Even warriors needed to let it out; he'd learned that lesson the painful way. Maybe warriors needed it more than most. He swung up on his horse and gathered the reins.

"Keep the boys away, no matter what you hear. I'll be with her, and we're not coming back tonight."

John's mustache twitched. "Maybe you've got some sense. Thought for a while, I was going to have to go after her."

"Over my dead body." Royce turned the sorrel and rode after his wife.


He heard the falls first, then heard her over the rushing water, great sobs torn from her chest, sounding as if they were ripping her apart.

He should be grateful she'd broken on her own, but damn, he'd rather face the cannons than face this. He forced himself to dismount and tethered the sorrel to a stunted spruce. She'd left the trail and cut through the underbrush. He followed the sounds and saw her soon afterward, hunched on the ground by the creek bank, hugging her waist while she rocked over her knees.

His stomach knotted into a tight ball. He could hardly bear to look at her, his beautiful Annabelle, always fighting her battles alone.

The ground was rocky and unforgiving as he knelt beside her. "Annie, sweet Annie," he said softly as he tried to draw her against him.

She fought, flailing at him with her fists while incoherent cries wrenched her chest. He was stronger and managed to wrap his arms around her. He held her tight while she struggled, and eventually her strength gave out. She buried her tear-streaked face in his shirt as another wave of sobs overwhelmed her.

"That's good, dear heart," he murmured against her hair. "Let it out."

Her sounds became thin and reedy, his shirt wet with her tears. He felt as if her cries were being torn from his own heart, and maybe that was love, when another's pain became your pain, their joys, your joy.

She had a lifetime of tears stored up inside her, but he had all the time in the world, for nothing else mattered right now. So he rocked her and held her, and, finally, she gave one quiet little gulp and collapsed against him. He stroked her back, wishing he could do more, hoping he was doing enough.

"Ladies never cry," she said in a voice still husky with tears.

"Another commandment from the Book of Ladies?" His own voice sounded strange, half choking emotion, half laughter.

"Number three," she said, sounding a bit stronger.

His arms tightened around her in case she decided to pull away. "Dear heart, one day I want you to explain to me why you ignore almost every rule in the book of conduct and decided to follow that stupid one."

"It's a sign of weakness. You never cry."

"I never had any desire to be considered a lady." She gave a faint little giggle, and he stroked the back of her head, wishing he could look into her eyes but unwilling to force her to look at him. "You're wrong on both counts anyway. Crying isn't always a sign of weakness. I *have* cried, and I think maybe, it was one of the bravest things I've ever done."

Her head jerked up. He pushed the damp hair off her face, revealing her red-rimmed eyes. She didn't believe him. He nodded while he brushed the last traces of moisture from beneath those beautiful, soul-revealing eyes.

"After the New Market battle. I was afraid for Bo, afraid of having to tell you he'd been seriously wounded. Then I found young Abner dead on the battlefield, and John told me Savage had been killed. It was too much, and I sat on a stump, in the rain, in the middle of a battlefield with people milling everywhere . . . I cried until I couldn't cry anymore."

"You never said anything."

"Because we're a matched pair, dear heart, both of us too damn proud to have any sense. But that's going to change. When you're afraid or angry or sad, I want to know it so I can fix it or help you deal with it, whatever it is. And I'll try to learn to do the same for you. You're my wife, let me be your husband again."

She didn't say anything, but she snuggled in his lap like a rabbit in a burrow, allowing him to hold her, and for the moment, that was enough. A warbler flew by with a flash of yellow belly. Green leaves waved over their heads with the gentle breeze, a breeze carrying the sweet scent of lilies and columbines. She felt so warm and soft in his arms. So right.

He watched a brightly speckled trout dart in the clear creek water, gold and blue spots glittering in the sun. The only sound was the rushing of the falls, a timeless, eternal sound. There was peace in this quiet world, his wife was back in his arms, and he told himself to remember this moment so it would last forever in his mind.

She was so still, he wondered if she slept, but when he looked down, he saw her dark eyes fixed on his face. He smiled because she was so beautiful, and she was in his arms again. She reached up and touched his lips.

"I'm so afraid of loving you." Her voice was low and shaky.

"Wrong again. You were brave enough to love me when there was nothing about me to love. The only person in the world who ever knew all my faults and still insisted on loving me, in spite of my best efforts to drive you away." He took her hand and kissed the fingertips that had brushed his mouth.

"You're afraid of losing me, Annie, and I can't promise you I won't be killed in this war. I can't even promise you I won't die the day after peace comes. No one can predict the future."

Tears filled her eyes again. He leaned his head and kissed her, then eased her off his lap. He stood and reached out his hand. She grasped it and he pulled her up.

"I want to show you something, Annie-girl. Something very special."

"Wake up, sleeping beauty."

Annabelle reflexively shuddered and came awake, feeling his arm tighten around her. She hadn't meant to fall asleep, but there was something about him that always made her feel safe when he was with her, and so helplessly alone when he wasn't.

She realized her hand was curled over his forearm, and she left it there. She even allowed her thumb to stroke his skin, brushing the soft, dark hairs. She wanted to be brave and independent, but she needed him so desperately.

She wouldn't think about that now. He had come after her when she didn't want him to come after her, and held her when she fought him and allowed her to cry all over his shirt. Maybe he loved her still, in spite of her hatefulness, her efforts to drive him away. Maybe that was enough.

"Where are we?" Her voice sounded strange, thick and hoarse, and her body ached from the wracking tears she'd shed. But inside, there was a lightness, like the lifting of a black curtain.

"A few miles farther along the creek," he answered as he dismounted. He reached up for her, and she leaned into him, her hands on his shoulders, his hands spanning her waist.

Her feet hit the ground, but the world tilted and strange silver dots danced before her eyes. She clung to his arm and after a moment, her vision cleared to reveal his face peering anxiously down at her.

"Just a little dizzy," she said. "But I'm fine now."

His lips thinned and curled at one side. "You're so busy taking care of everyone else, you forget to take care of yourself," he said, as his finger traced the line of her nose. "I'll wager a month's pay you haven't eaten all day."

Her eyes went wide as she thought back, then she shrugged. He was already rummaging in his saddlebag. He gave her one of those dazzling smiles as he handed her a piece of hardtack and an old feed bag.

"Serves you right, dear heart. Don't try to chew it, you'll only ruin your teeth. Just kind of let it dissolve in your mouth."

He was laughing, and a warm rush of love overwhelmed her so that she almost felt dizzy again. She eyed the hardtack doubtfully. "What's the bag for?"

"Blackberries. You pick us some while I get this surprise ready."

Blackberries hung thick and heavy on the bushes. She filled the bag and nibbled on some berries while he watered the horse. She was feeling stronger with food in her belly, the wind in her hair, and her man by her side. She found the courage to ask a question when she still feared the answer.

"Caleb," she said softly. "Is he—did he . . ."

Royce narrowed his eyes and stared at her for so long she knew Caleb must be dead. Then his face softened and a gentle smile formed on his lips.

"John was right," he muttered, and she didn't know what he was talking about but wished he would answer so her heart could start beating again.

"Caleb's fine. Said he had to go in to see his mother, but the truth is, he went to see a girl."

He grabbed a handful of berries from the bag and tossed them in his mouth. He chewed slowly while his eyes studied her face. She wished she could read his expression but, as usual, he was hiding his thoughts from her.

"I'll be back in a few minutes. Can I trust you to be here when I get back?"

"I expect so," she said, a slow smile forming. "Since I don't know where we are or how we got here."

He snorted and led the horse away, disappearing behind a dense outcropping of shrubs and rocks. She sat on the ground and ate more berries, waiting for him to return.

Great clumps of butterfly weed were massed along the stream bank. A buckeye flitted amongst the orange petals, feeding on the nectar. She watched the butterfly, so beautiful with the dark eye-like spots on its fragile wings, watched it seem to disappear against the petals, colors blending so that she saw it again only when it moved. There was a lesson there, she thought, but she wasn't sure what the lesson was. She knew only that she felt as light and free as that beautiful butterfly. And equally fragile.

Whatever he was doing, it was taking him a long time. She

stretched out on her back, her head cradled in her hands, and stared at the deep blue sky. The sun was warm on her face, and she closed her eyes, dreaming this kind of peace was real and war was the dream. She heard his footsteps and reluctantly stood up.

"What are you doing?" she asked, as he tied a rope around her waist. The other end was around his own waist.

"You have this disconcerting habit of going your own direction, and I'll be damned if I'm crawling through miles of cave searching for my lost wife."

She couldn't help but laugh. He took her hand in his own and squeezed hard. Then led her into total blackness.

# Chapter 30

⁓〰〰⁓

They seemed to be traveling downhill, deep into the center
of the earth. The air was colder than outside, and smelled
of dampness and her fear. Only his warm hand gripping her
own kept her from screaming. She stumbled over a loose
stone. His grip tightened.

"You all right?" he asked. His voice sounded so near and at
the same time, so far away. He stopped, and she felt the air
move as he turned, then the pressure of his hands on her shoulders. "What is it, Annabelle?"

"I'm . . . I . . ." She struggled to form a coherent thought.
There was a strange humming in her head, like sound moving
through water. The vibration echoed down her spine and she
trembled. Even her teeth were chattering.

His fingers squeezed into her shoulders. "Annie! What is it,
Annie?"

"I don't know."

He pulled her hard against his chest. His heart thumped beneath her ear, and she tried to concentrate on that sound. "This
sounds so stupid." She dragged in a deep, ragged breath, and it
seared her lungs. The panic grew. "It's like I'm dying— Dear
heaven, *Royce*."

His arms tightened around her. "We're almost there, dear
heart. Just hold on to me for a little bit longer. I won't let anything happen to you."

He took her hand and pulled her forward down the passage.

He turned, and the light became stronger, silhouetting him in front of her, his large man's body blocking her view. Her footsteps slowed, then stopped as he turned to face her. His features took shape in the light, and she saw his eyes searching her face.

"Annie," he said in that low baritone.

She suddenly knew what he was going to say and didn't want to listen. She *had* been here before, if only in a fevered dream. A dream of blackness, then Mama in a bright light. A dream of dying.

"No." She twisted her wrist, trying to pull away. "Please, Royce," she said, hating the cowardice in her voice and unable to hide it this time.

"I cried one other time," he said in a quiet, somber tone. "Annabelle, you did die from that wound—the infection and pneumonia that set in. You stopped breathing for I don't know how long, and I sat beside you, unable to do anything, knowing you died because you'd tried to save my worthless hide. I wanted it to be me in that bed because I didn't know how I was going to live without you."

He was describing the fear that gnawed at her every time he rode into the war. If she had ever felt so small, so selfish, she couldn't remember the occasion.

"I know," she whispered at long last. She finally understood what he hadn't said. That life had no guarantees, even in peacetime. That she could go as well, leaving him behind to suffer alone.

"When I said I would die for you, it was truth but not courage, dear heart. Courage would be living without you." He shook his head, smiling faintly. "This says it better than my poor excuse for words. Come on," he said, tugging her hand.

She followed him through the low archway. Every thought deserted her in that instant. "Oh my," she sighed, awestruck.

He had lit pine torches, fixed in crevices in the walls. The light flickered off rock formations that seemed to drip from the cavernous ceiling and rise up in peaks from the floor. They glistened in every color of the spectrum, bright jewel tones of ruby and emerald and topaz, gleaming golds and silvers shimmering in the soft light.

His arms came over her shoulders, his hands clasped at her

waist as he pulled her back into him. "Beautiful, isn't it?" he said. She rested her hands over his as his chin settled on the top of her head. "Just think, everything you see here was built one tiny drop of water at a time, a time so long we can't even imagine it."

He grew silent and she gazed ahead at the lustrous beauty and listened to the sound of his heart beating. His heat and his strength surrounded her; awesome, God-formed magnificence surrounded her. She was so small, so fragilely human, but it didn't seem to matter. A warm sense of peace eased into her soul.

"In my house are many mansions . . ."

His voice was so low she almost didn't hear him. She turned in his arms, bringing her hands to rest on his chest as she studied his dark, handsome face. The torchlight sent flickering shadows across the strong angles of bone. His hair gleamed, almost black except for the rich auburn glow where the light struck.

Such a complex man, with deep, unseen currents always moving inside him. Sometimes a man so strong and hard as to be frightening, other times, so gentle and tender. Fragile in his own way. A man who was born to love and be loved, so deeply injured as a child he taught himself not to show anything, not to expect anything.

She reached up and stroked her fingers through his hair, then rested her palm on his cheek. "Can you ever forgive me, Royce?"

"There's nothing to forgive." The shadows in his eyes moved as he studied her face. His own face was grave, unsmiling. "You're my wife, and I love you."

Her heart skipped a beat, then skipped another. "What did you say?"

"I said I love you, sweet Annie. For now, forever."

She didn't mean to cry again, there was too much joy in her heart for tears, but the tears streaked down her cheeks anyway. And then, it didn't matter because he was kissing her, and she was kissing him back.

"There's more, dear heart. Are you brave enough to go a little farther?"

"You'll hold my hand?"

He grinned. "I'll carry you to get you there."

She was tempted, not from fear but because it always felt so good to be in his arms. He might think her an even bigger coward than she actually was.

"That won't be necessary," she said in her prim lady's voice. He laughed, as if he'd seen through her, then took her hand in his.

The passageway this time was short, with light filtering from both ends. They emerged into another chamber, this one even more breathtaking than the last. Not even an imaginative child could dream anything like this. Camelot itself, or the inside of a rainbow. Or maybe, a tiny piece of God's heaven.

A lake filled the middle of the chamber, so still and clear, jeweled castles seemed to rise from the depths. But it wasn't from the depths, it was the reflection of dripping stones from the vaulted ceiling.

He led her around the lake. Torchlight glistened on damp stone as he led her up a natural stairway to a wide ledge. This time she laughed.

"No wonder you were gone so long," she said. "You've been a busy man."

At the back of the ledge, against the cavern wall, was a bed that smelled of fresh pine. In front of her, he'd spread a feast of blackberries, a loaf of bread, salt pork, and several of the little cakes she'd baked for the troops before they set out the last time. A canteen and two tin mugs sat in the middle of his improvised table.

"Before you were with me," he said, "I used to come here and think about you, dream about bringing you here, making love to you here."

Her breath caught. He'd never spoken of those years they were apart, and she'd never guessed that he'd spent one moment of that time thinking of her. She watched him pour something into the tin mugs.

"I never knew," she said, as he handed her one of the mugs.

"Because I didn't want you to know." A crease formed at the corner of his mouth. "I was afraid of loving you, afraid I wasn't the man you deserved, and you'd find me out and stop loving me."

"What happened to change your mind?"

His smile broke through, an endearing, lopsided grin. "Not a damn thing. I'm still scared witless you'll figure out what a reprehensible fraud I am. You dragged me into your heart, kicking and screaming all the way."

"Silly man."

"Silly me," he said agreeably. "And if you ever decide to pull away from silly me again, I'll drag you out from wherever it is you go, drag you kicking and screaming back into *my* heart."

"I don't do that!"

He narrowed his eyes and gave her a Kincaid glare. She studied the golden liquid in the mug and, after a long study, admitted he was right. She did do that whenever she felt especially alone or afraid. With a start, she realized she'd been doing that since Mama died.

He understood her better than she understood herself, and he was telling her she wasn't alone anymore. He was telling her in his man's way that he would help her find what she needed, share his strength when she couldn't find her own.

"Colonel Kincaid, you are a very special man," she said softly.

"Ummm."

He took a sip of his drink, then set the mug on the table. He straightened and looked around the cavernous chamber, as if seeing it for the first time. As beautiful as the cavern was, she thought he was even more beautiful, rock-strong and tender-hearted and masculinely beautiful.

"Why didn't you bring me here sooner?"

He grinned again, his smiles seeming to come so much easier for him today. "Didn't need to dream, dear heart. Didn't have anything I wanted to escape from."

She carried her mug to her lips and peered at him over the rim. He was peeling back layer after layer, revealing himself to her in a manner she'd never dared hope for.

She took a deep swallow of the liquid and choked, sputtered, coughed, and choked some more. Vaguely, she heard him laughing and felt him take the mug from her hand.

"That's real Kentucky bourbon, liquid gold these days. You're supposed to savor it, not gulp it." He pounded her back, and eventually, her eyes ceased watering, and she could breathe naturally.

"You could have warned me."

"I suppose I could have."

She looked at him, loving his laughter, wanting to see the creases at the corners of his lips. Their gazes caught. His eyes grew dark and heavy-lidded, his smile fading into a tight line.

"I don't deserve you, Annie, but I'm too much a reprobate not to live this dream with you now."

She started to reach for him, but he was already lowering himself to the camp stool. He tugged off his boots and set them aside. When he reached for his shirt buttons, she impulsively stepped forward to help him.

She saw a smile in his eyes before she looked away. She could feel his breath on her hands as she worked the buttons free, and it seemed so intimate she could hardly lift her eyes when she was done. She slipped the shirt off, luxuriating in the solid shape of shoulders and muscles beneath the cloth.

Without a word, he stepped out of his pants and kicked them aside. His courage fed her courage, and she allowed herself to look at him in all his male beauty: the strong symmetry of bone and muscle, the superb splendor of his body, marred only by the scars of war.

He drew his hand down the curve of her cheek and took her chin, raising it a little. Their eyes were inches apart, and he was hiding nothing from her. She saw heat and desire, and something deeper and timeless.

"I'd like to undress you now," he said.

She swallowed and nodded permission, already feeling the liquid heat spreading inside her. He undressed her slowly and silently, using his big, strong hands to sensuously stroke her skin as he bared each part of her body. He took forever, tormenting her, and when she finally stood naked in front of him, they were both shaking with the need for more.

For a long minute, he gazed at her, and her heart sped to a triple beat. He took her hand and led her to the edge of the pool.

He stood behind her, his hands coming around and holding the sides of her face. "Look into the water and see what I see when I look at you," he said, his deep voice sounding hoarse. "My beautiful Annabelle."

He fondled her breasts, and she wanted to close her eyes with the pleasure, but watched him touching her instead. And the pleasure grew because she saw his reflection, saw the love in his eyes, and it didn't matter that her body was too short, too thin, too bony. He saw something she didn't see and for the first time in her life, she actually felt beautiful, because he believed she was . . .

"Beautiful here. And here." His hand drifted lower, tangling in her woman's curls. "Beautiful everywhere."

She was surrounded by his heat and his love and watched the loving in the mirrored pool and saw him watching the loving in the mirrored pool while his hands burned her skin and his fingers stroked her depths. It was so intense, so special—to see what she had only felt—so that the love itself became real and tangible, touchable.

He played with her, creating ribbons of flame that grew and spread, filling her soft woman's places and her woman's heart until she was weak-kneed with loving him and melting where he touched her. A burn so exquisite, she moaned and leaned against him. He lifted her in his arms and carried her into the lake.

The water was warm and soft against her skin. He carried her to the center so they seemed to float in the middle of a shimmering, liquid castle while jeweled stars glimmered and dazzled overhead.

He lifted her hips and entered her. She gripped her legs tight around his hips and wrapped her arms tight around his neck, trembling and clinging to him for long minutes as her body spasms shook her in immediate release. Then he gently peeled her arms away and took her hands in his.

"I love you," she murmured into the shining, wet hair at his neck.

She saw his smile as he eased her backward—and then she was floating on her back, weightless in a wet, womblike warmth, connected only to him, by him. The jeweled stars shimmered above her and her man was inside her and wet warmth surrounded her. The heat inside her swelled larger, expanding and spreading until she feared she would shatter and float away in a million ragged pieces, never to be whole again.

"Know by this that I love you, Annabelle. In this life and forever."

He pulled her up, his mouth seeking hers as she desperately wrapped her arms around his neck, twisting her fingers in his hair. She gave herself to him, trusting him to protect her when she helplessly flew apart, soaring into the endless, jeweled heavens where he was sending her with his thrusts.

Sending her . . . blind and quivering, heart-stoppingly helpless.

"You're mine." He held her hips, driving into her. "Mine."

"Yeesss."

"I'm yours." His hands moved her to meet him.

Helpless . . . shuddering.

"Say it, Annabelle."

Her thighs gripped him tight, her nails scored his back.

"Mine."

A cry echoed somewhere but the stars were exploding and she knew only her man, holding her tightly . . . tightly . . . tightly as she burned and shattered with flaming stars drifting all around her.

His knees were weak but he stayed in her for a long time for she was warm and wet and welcoming around him and the water was warm and wet and welcoming around him and he wanted to stay inside her forever and drift in this earthly paradise forever.

He held her too tightly, she probably couldn't breathe, but he was unable to loosen his grip. Her silent tears burned his neck. He let her shed the tears for both of them, tears born of an ache and a joy, and both so fierce they almost couldn't be borne. He knew she shared the ache and the joy, for they were one in the spirit and joined in the flesh.

The vaulted castles shivered and dissolved and re-formed as he carried her out of the water. He wrapped her in a blanket for warmth and fed her to keep up her strength, then took her to the pine-scented bed, where he loved her again.

Then he let her sleep and watched her sleep, drawing in the scents of pine and Annabelle and hot, musky love. When he could no longer stand just watching her beauty, he wakened her with his touch and worshiped her with his body again.

Afterward, he let her turn in his arms and nestle against him, her back to his belly, his leg thrown over hers while his hand cupped her breast. He thought she slept, worn-out by the loving, but then felt her sigh.

"What is it, dear heart?" he asked.

"You taught me so many things today, wonderful things I would never have understood without you, but you were wrong about one thing."

He pushed up on his elbow, and she rolled onto her back, staring up at him with that wide, still gaze that always made him feel like he was drowning in her soul.

"What was I wrong about?"

"There's someone else who has always loved you—faults and all."

He brushed the gold-streaked tangle of hair from her brow. "Who's that?"

"Someone so like you, you can't see it."

"Peyton?"

She nodded, and her hand came up to touch his face. "He loves you, Royce. He just doesn't know how to say it any more than you did."

He was going to argue, but then took a minute to look back and see something he'd never wanted to see: the well-hidden pain in his father's gray eyes, a pain he understood too well. And he forgave his father for all the actual mistakes and forgave himself for his own imagined hatred and knew his wife had given him another gift.

"Annie, sweet Annie, too wise for her years," he murmured. He studied her serious, delicate face, then surrendered to the invitation of her lips, kissing her long and deep. After an eternity of floating again in her warmth, he pulled back and looked into her eyes.

"Would you like to know the bravest thing I've ever done?"

Her dark eyes widened as she nodded. He smiled down at her because she was wise and generous and beautiful. And she was his.

"Admitting to myself I loved you. Did I ever tell you how much I love you?" He watched the miracle happen. It began with flecks of gold in the brown depths of her eyes. Annie's sunburst smile.

That golden light. And the joy glowed inside him, too, for he hadn't destroyed her by loving her; he'd brought her joy-light back.

He tangled his fingers in her tangled hair. Christ, how he loved the silken feel of her hair. He considered kissing her again; those lush, sinful lips were moist and parted in invitation, but kissing her always left him aching for more.

"How tired are you, Annie-girl?"

"If you're thinking what I think you're thinking, I don't think I can move."

"Maybe you, maybe me. But I know a way we can find out."

One of them was grinning like a fool, and he didn't think it was her. The smile on her face was . . . Annie's.

Damn, he didn't deserve her, but he loved her. So he loved her again with his hands and his mouth and his body.

"You're moving, dear heart."

"Royce." Her back arched. "Dear merciful heaven."

"Ummm."

And then she touched him.

His body jerked, and he decided to take control of the situation.

"You're moving, Kincaid."

More smiles, more laughter, more Annie. His heart hammered the beat of his body—loving her, loving her, loving her.

# Chapter 31

"I won't go."

"This is not a matter that's open for discussion. You'll go because I said you'll go."

Annabelle bit back a sharp retort, returned his glare, then bit back an absurd urge to laugh at the picture in front of her.

Colonel Royce Kincaid, as bare-bottomed as the day he was born, hunched in a too-small tin bathtub with his soapy arms dangling over the sides while his knobby knees poked at his jutting chin.

Issuing orders.

Then she looked into his glowering face, seeing the deep lines etched by war and an immense responsibility he never allowed himself to shed. She wanted to cry for him. She picked up the pitcher from the commode, crossed the floor, and knelt beside the tub. He actually jerked as she began to massage his neck.

"If you think this is going to make me change my bloody damn mind, you're bloody damn wrong."

"Hush, silly man." She worked the tight muscles along his neck and shoulders, and, gradually, the tenseness eased from his body. With every breath, she inhaled the sharp scent of smoke still caught in his hair. "Lean your head back," she said.

"Why, so you can slit my throat?"

Some of his normal good humor was returning, so she smiled. "I'm still considering it, but I've decided to wash your hair first."

"I can wash my own damn hair."

Slitting his throat sounded very appealing. She poured a pitcher of water on his head instead. He spluttered as he almost jerked out of the tub.

"Take several deep breaths, Kincaid. It works wonders against the urge to kill your loving spouse."

She worked the soap through his hair, then massaged his scalp. She spent long minutes rubbing his temples with her soapy fingers. His head drifted back, and she saw the creases at the corner of his mouth.

"I married a witch," he said.

"You married a woman who's just as stubborn as you are." She leaned forward and kissed his brow, then rinsed the soap from his hair. She pushed up, retrieved the towel, and set it beside the tub. "When you're ready to talk to me like I'm your wife and not one of your privates, I'll be waiting on the ridge."

Her hand was on the doorknob before he spoke. "Annabelle," he said in a long-suffering tone. She turned around. "Put your damn coat on."

She grabbed her cloak from the peg beside the door. "Yes, sir, Colonel, sir."

She pulled the door closed, smiling because she heard him chuckle.

The war creaked on, too stubborn to die. Throughout the spring and into the summer, Lee and Grant played bloody hopscotch from the banks of the Rappahannock to the outskirts of Petersburg where both armies dug trenches and settled in for a long siege. In July, Early marched into Washington, causing panic in the North even though he was turned back. Atlanta fell to Sherman in September; Lincoln's reelection was assured. The war would be fought to its last dying breath.

Summer faded into fall. Autumn began at the mountain crests and crept down from the ridges in fiery shades of russet and red and gold, spreading out into the fertile valleys of the Shenandoah River, where haycocks dried in the sun.

Sheridan took command of the Union troops in Virginia's Great Valley, destroying General Early's army in October. Only the bands of Confederate raiders remained to battle the superior Union forces. Only the raiders, with their continued harassment of supply trains, communications, and rail lines, kept Sheridan from joining forces with Grant, a move that would overwhelm Lee's embattled troops and assure a quick victory to the Union.

Grant issued an order. Sheridan carried out the order.

The Shenandoah Valley burst into flames.

Royce found her sitting cross-legged at the very edge of the ridge. She looked so small and so damn stubborn, silhouetted against an orange sky, with her shoulders set stiff and her head nudged up in that defiant angle. He took a deep breath to still his clamoring heart, then spoke softly so as not to startle her.

"Move back, dear heart. Please."

"You could always hold on to me, keep me from falling."

"Or I could push you over and end my misery," he said, smiling because she was trying to make him smile.

"That, too."

He settled on the ground behind her, wrapping his arms around her waist and pulling her away from the edge. She wriggled a bit, getting comfortable, then rested her hands over his. He nuzzled his chin on the top of her head. They sat for long minutes in silence, both of them watching the billowing smoke from the fires still raging in the valley before them.

He wondered what she was thinking. She loved this land, and now she was watching it burn. Her entire childhood, burned by Federal torches. He fought against the rage billowing up like hot smoke inside him. Soldiers fought soldiers, men against men, fighting for a vision, for a man's honor.

Those People had no concept of honor. War at any cost, especially since the cost was borne by the South's civilian population. This was war waged against the mind: ugly, obscene warfare.

Her hand was squeezing his, as if she read his thoughts. He hugged her a little more tightly. He didn't know how he was going to manage without her; she was the sole beacon light remaining in all this bleak world of war, but she had to return to Riverbend.

"Were you able to save anything?" she asked softly.

"Some. Not enough."

For weeks, his troopers had holstered their guns and turned

themselves into stockmen trying to salvage something before the Federals swooped in with their torches. So far, the Union troops hadn't caught on. They were so busy burning every barn, mill, and chicken coop, killing every cow, sheep, and pig, they hadn't yet figured out the rangers were hiding food staples and driving stock back onto the farms they'd already burned.

It was something, but it wasn't enough. Come winter, women and children, the old and the weak, would die from starvation and cold. This war would end one day, and he feared it would end with a hatred that might never die.

"Royce, I won't leave you to face this alone."

"You'll go, Annie-girl."

"I'll stay with you."

He felt an overwhelming tiredness, one that touched his mind as much as his body. He was going to have to tell her at least part of the story, and the telling only brought back the pain. And the rage.

"Geary and his boys . . . they didn't die in a skirmish." A tremor raced down her spine, as if she already knew. "They were taken alive, six of them, and hanged like common horse thieves. No prisoner of war status, no trial. We found them still dangling from tree limbs, with a placard pinned to Caleb's shirt."

"What did it say?" she whispered hoarsely.

"Thus to Kincaid and all of his outlaws."

The breath came out of her in an almost inaudible sigh. The evening wind blew cold, so he pulled his coat around her, wrapping them closer together. He needed her warmth as much as she needed his, for his heart was cold with the chill of this war and her love was the only warmth left to him.

"You'll go, Annie. Our numbers are too small against theirs, and you're not safe here any longer. If you're captured with us, then you're one of us, and I won't see you hang."

She rose, turning until she faced him. Tears shimmered on her lashes. "I suppose there's no point in asking you to give up this fight?"

He stood and went to her, reaching out and stroking the ridge of bone above her cheek, not answering because she already knew the answer.

Her chin nudged up. "Then I'll stay and fight with you. One more raider. I'm a good shot, and I know how to ride—"

"The hell you will!"

"The hell I will. I'll fight beside you, and if it comes to that, I'll die beside you. Royce, I . . ." Her chin began to quiver, and his chest began to ache. "I can't go. I won't." She lifted her hand and impatiently swiped at her cheek where a tear streaked out of her control. "I'm not going to live without you, and you may as well get that through your stubborn head."

The light over the mountains was fading, the orange glow deepening to ruby and painting her face with a soft wash of color. Annie, so fierce and proud.

He pulled her close against him. "Dear God, Annabelle. "I understand the hell I'm asking you to endure. But you must do it, no matter how hard it is."

"Why?" she mumbled into his chest. "You said once you'd die for me. Why can't I die for you?"

"Because you're carrying our child. Our future."

She pulled back so fast, he impulsively reached for her hands, afraid she'd plunge over the cliff. "Dammit, Annabelle."

He drew a deep breath as she stiffened her spine and glared at him. She opened her mouth as if to speak but her chin quivered instead and she clamped it shut.

"Annie . . ." It wasn't the commander standing on the ridge now. He was only a man, husband to this special woman, the father of their child. And because he had no choice but to love them, to live through them, he pleaded. "Please, Annie, don't make this harder than it already is."

She withdrew her hands and turned slightly. She stood with her arms at her sides, staring ahead, starkly silhouetted against the glowing sky. The wind whistled through the pines, billowed her cloak and lifted her hair behind her. She was so heartbreakingly beautiful, and she carried their child within her. He knew it as well as he knew his own heartbeat.

"It's too soon to tell," she said at long last.

"It's not too soon. You've missed your courses. Your breasts are full and tender, and the nipples dark. You're fighting nausea every morning—"

He pulled her back and brought his arms over her shoulders,

cradling her against his body, his palms gentle on her belly. "I don't want to send you away any more than you want to go, but it has to be. Even without the dangers of war here, there are the risks you'll face in childbirth. I want you someplace safe, where someone is always there for you, where there's medical attention when you need it. You must live so our child can live."

The light was fading fast, the wind blowing colder. She turned in his arms, looking up at him with her soul in her brimming eyes. He knew she understood what he hadn't said. This war was lost, and he was a dead man, a traitor to the Union. If he didn't die from a bullet first, he'd hang by his neck later.

"I'll go," she said. Another tear streaked down her cheek. "Yes, I'll go, for you . . . for our child." He stroked her hair as she cried silently into his shirt.

"Annabelle, my love for you will never die. Remember this vow and hold on to it for however long the years. I will always be near you. Always."

He tightened his arms around her. Holding her, his life, his love.


They forded the Rapidan after dusk of their third day out. An hour later, they arrived at Chestnut Hill. Peyton was to meet them here and take her the rest of the way to Riverbend.

The moon had come up, big and white and hard. Annabelle watched dry, brittle leaves drift in front of the horses. She wanted to be like the leaves, drifting in a westerly wind, lifted back to the mountains where her husband would return on the morrow.

Someone must have heard them approach. The front door opened, spilling a wash of yellow light, then men came out onto the gallery. She recognized Peyton by the silver glow of his hair, his proud Kincaid stance. Royce reached across and took her hand in his own, giving her hand a firm squeeze. Silently, they rode the rest of the distance, hands clasped together between the horses.

Peyton came down the steps to meet them. "Annie-girl," he said, reaching up to help her dismount.

He looked so careworn, so much older since she'd last seen

him. His hair was more white than silver, and the lines were deep grooves at the corners of his eyes now. Sad, gray eyes.

"Hello, Father," she said, trying to keep the choking sound out of her voice.

Suddenly, her feet were on the ground and Peyton's arms were around her and she heard male voices everywhere. She didn't even try to listen, resting her head on Peyton's chest while he patted her back. Then she heard the only voice that mattered and lifted her head.

"Thank you, but my wife's tired," Royce was saying to a gentleman she assumed was Mr. DeWitt. "If it wouldn't be too much trouble, I'd like to get her inside to her room and have a tray sent for her dinner."

"We thought this being your last night together . . ." Mr. De-Witt cleared his throat. "We've got the office dependency fixed up and waiting. I'll have someone take care of your horses and send a tray out for both of you."

Royce tipped his head, his face solemn, then turned to her and Peyton. A slow, fragile smile formed at his lips. Dear heaven, how she loved that smile. She tried to memorize the curve, each crease that deepened around his eyes and mouth.

"I'll bring her to you at first dawn," said Royce to his father. "Tonight, she's mine."

"As it should be, son."

Royce took her hand and led her across the lawn. The wind blew cold beneath her skirts, but Royce pushed open the door to the small brick building and a fire already crackled in the hearth. She stood in front of the fire's warmth while Royce saw to the guard details. A black woman brought in a dinner tray. She thanked the woman and went back to studying the fire, trying not to think of each minute that passed, never to be recovered. She heard the footsteps she'd been listening for and turned.

Royce closed the door and leaned against it. Her dark warrior, so fierce, so handsome. So weary.

"Are you hungry?" he asked. She shook her head, unable to speak around the lump in her throat. He smiled faintly. "Come to me, sweet Annie."

She walked into his arms. He held her tightly, so tightly. She lifted her head, asking without words for his kiss. He lowered his head and kissed her, then lifted her and carried her to the bed.

The night was both sweet and sad, filled with the loving and filled with the parting. And then, too soon, night became dawn.

Peyton stood at the foot of the front porch, surrounded by DeWitt and the band of rangers who had escorted his son and daughter-in-law from the mountains. Beside him stood DeShields, arrived just this morning and bearing news his son didn't want to hear.

The door to the office dependency opened. First Royce exited, followed by Annabelle. Royce took her hand in his own, gripping it tightly between their bodies. Slowly, they began to walk across the white-frosted grass.

The fading moon glow caught her face in silver light, and Peyton thought she looked like an angel must look, a haunting, delicate beauty. She seemed to be watching where she placed her feet, her husband looked only at her. His own vision was blurring as he watched the couple come toward them.

They stopped in the circle of light spilling from the opened doorway, and the glow seemed to radiate around them. Royce wore the caped greatcoat Annabelle had made for him in those days before he wanted a wife. He wanted her now; the anguish was stark on his face.

A horse whinnied and shied. Someone cleared his throat, then someone else. Royce gripped her hands and held them tight against his chest. The breeze caught her cloak, billowing it in a blue cloud behind her. Her head tilted back as she looked up into her husband's eyes. Royce wiped tears from her cheeks, then gently pulled her hood up.

"Are you ready, Father?" he asked, without taking his eyes from his wife.

"I'm ready, son," answered Peyton. His own voice sounded hoarse in the cold. Someone let out a sigh.

Mrs. DeWitt started forward with the basket of food she'd prepared for the journey. Peyton stopped her. Neither of those children needed to face near strangers at this time. He took the basket from her hand, giving her a smile of thanks since his voice didn't want to work properly, and carried the basket to the buggy. He set the basket in the well and stood beside the seat as Royce led Annabelle to him.

Royce lifted his gaze, meeting Peyton's. "Sometimes she forgets to cry. When that happens, you need to pinch her," said Royce.

"I'll pinch when necessary."

She reached up and brushed her husband's hair from his temple, then placed her palm against his cheek. "I love you, Royce. The words aren't enough, but I don't know any others." Her voice trembled as her hand was trembling.

"As I love you, sweet Annie." Royce placed his hand over her smaller one. "Don't look back. I'll watch for both of us."

Her head jerked in a nod as she bit on her lower lip. Peyton walked slowly around the buggy to the driver's side, giving them a last moment alone, trying to regain some semblance of dignity for himself. He feared he would be shedding his own tears any minute now. By the time he climbed into the buggy, Royce had Annabelle seated and was wrapping a carriage robe around her hips.

"If our child is a son, Annie, I would like you to name him Peyton Thomas, after our fathers."

"I'll do that, Colonel Kincaid. It's a fine name honoring two fine men."

Peyton closed his eyes as his heart skipped all over his chest. Annabelle was patting his leg gently, as if she knew the enormity of the gift Royce had just given him. Slowly, he turned his head and met his son's gaze, seeing forgiveness in the silvered eyes peering steadily back at him.

He held his son's gaze, fully aware his tears were obvious as they streaked down his cheeks. He didn't care anymore; maybe Royce needed to see them.

Royce stood alone, watching the buggy carry his wife and unborn child away from him. She shifted, as if she intended to look back, then Peyton's arm circled around her. She rested her head on Peyton's shoulder, and Royce sent his father a silent thanks. She'd suffered enough in loving him and would suffer more in the future. He wanted to bear this awful pain for both of them.

The buggy disappeared from view, then even the sounds of

clopping hooves faded into nothing. He drew in a deep breath, filling his aching chest with cold morning air. He knew this was the only feeling left to him, cold on the inside, so bloody damn cold.

Heavy footsteps sounded behind him, then DeShields drew abreast. John fished a paper from his coat pocket and handed it to him. Royce opened the dispatch, read it, and jammed it in his own pocket.

What price honor? What price duty? He knew the answer: a lonely death. He drew another deep, aching breath.

"Well, Colonel DeShields, we have a nasty war to finish."

"As you say, General Kincaid."

# PART FIVE

*Let us cross over the river, and rest under the shade of the trees . . .*

—Last words of General Thomas "Stonewall" Jackson, CSA

# Chapter 32

*April 12, 1865*

The heat of the sun was warm on his back, but the chill remained deep inside, colder with each passing day. Royce reined in at the top of the rise and studied the grove of hardwoods. A slanting afternoon sun glanced white light off tiny buds that would be broad, green leaves in another month.

One of those old oaks had hidden a Federal picket on a bitter winter night, and Annie had nearly died as a result. He tried not to think of the perils she faced now as she neared her term.

Christ, he wanted to be with her.

Sometimes he wondered why he'd survived so long into this war when so many good men had fallen. Sometimes, he allowed himself a faint glimmer of hope he'd survive to the end, and the conquerors would abide by Lincoln's words: *With malice toward none and charity for all.*

It was false hope. There was already a reward offered for the capture of General Kincaid, traitor and outlaw—the price of a skilled blacksmith in the days before the war. He'd love to share the irony of that thought with Clarence.

He'd never see Clarence again any more than he would see Annie. But he'd come this far. Now he only hoped to live long enough to know whether he'd fathered a son or a daughter, whether child and mother survived the birthing.

He prayed for them. He went to the cavern on Hope Mountain and remembered the loving and thought of Annie and their child. He always talked to God while he was there because it was the only place he felt God's presence anymore. Sometimes while he was there, he even allowed himself to dream.

A daughter. A tiny, little girl with big, brown eyes and golden brown hair, and if he could be her father, she'd grow up feeling beautiful because he'd tell her how beautiful she was every morning when he kissed the tip of her nose and again every night as he patted her to sleep . . .

The sorrel shied, shaking Royce back to the real world. He nudged the horse into a trot and rode through the pasture to Merry Sherwood.

Olivia was crossing the yard as he approached, and she stopped to wait for him to rein in. She was a striking young woman, tall and full-figured, with eyes that were moss green and dark-lashed. She wore her hair coiled at the back of her neck, and it seemed to shimmer like spun gold in the bright spring sunshine.

Her looks paled in comparison to his Annie's delicate beauty.

Olivia smiled as he dismounted. He tried to return her smile, but his face was unused to the effort and felt as if it might crack.

"DeShields here yet?" he asked.

"No, but last time he was here, he brought us some coffee and sugar that we've been saving for a special occasion. Come on inside, and we'll treat ourselves while you wait for him."

"I can't stay, Livvy. You know I don't like putting you and your mother at risk like this."

She gave a ladylike snort. "The Yankees haven't been around here since the night of the burning."

His gaze drifted to the charred remains of what had once been a barn. The stables were gone; everything was gone except for the manor house. The cold gripped his chest again, that clawing, frigid cold. But Livvy was smiling, and the smile spread wider on her face. He wondered where these women found their strength. He wished he could borrow some, enough to get him through these last days of war.

"Someone else is here," she said. "Come on inside."

He draped the reins over his arm and fell in beside her. "Have you heard from Annie?"

"No. Only the one letter has made it through." She took his hand and gave it a tiny squeeze. "You know her anyway. If there was anything wrong, she wouldn't tell us."

That might be true, but it sure as hell wasn't comforting. He tethered his horse to the hitching rail and followed her through the back door into the kitchen.

"Bloody hell." He yanked off his hat. "Bloody damn hell—what are *you* doing here?"

Bohannon raked his fingers through his corn-shuck hair and grinned so wide his lips almost touched his ears. "Do you think he's glad to see me?" he said, shifting his gaze to Olivia.

"Sounds like it to me," she said, smiling.

Coffee beans clattered as Olivia dropped them into the hopper of the coffee mill, then a rich aroma filled the kitchen as she cranked the iron handle.

"Richmond has fallen," said Bo, and Royce wondered if the boy thought that was an answer. He sure didn't think it was.

"I know that, Mr. Hallston, so if you're not in Richmond any longer, why haven't you taken your parole and gone to Riverbend. Your sister needs you."

Bo shrugged. "She's got Peyton and Patsy looking out for her."

"She needs you."

"No, she needs you."

His anger faded into the overwhelming tiredness that seemed to plague him always, tired in every sinew, every bone. He pulled out one of the kitchen chairs and sat, tossing his hat onto the table where it landed with a tiny *plop*.

Annie needed him, he needed her, and he didn't know which of them was the neediest. But it was impossible, and the boy should realize that.

Behind him, he heard the rattle of crockery as Olivia rummaged for something. Bo pulled out the chair on the other side of the table and sat, his gangly legs stretched in front of him. Royce studied the yellow checks on the oilcloth covering the table while he tried to come up with the proper words to get this boy moving on to where he belonged—out of the war, out of the danger.

"Bo—"

"Bo will stay with us until he can take our Annabelle some news of you."

Hetty's voice. Royce looked up, and, this time, a smile came naturally. They should have stayed home and let their women take charge of this war. Maybe the results would have been different.

He started to rise, but Harriet Sherwood stopped him by placing her hands on his shoulders and leaning forward to plant a motherly kiss on the top of his head.

"I wish you would come here more often. We haven't seen a Yankee out this far since the fires."

Royce was going to remind her the Yankees had come close to burning her house down around her ears because of her relationship to him, but before he could speak, she'd already started.

"Livvy, the gentlemen are arriving. I think our Colonel DeShields would rather be greeted by you than by me."

Royce watched Olivia leave the kitchen, her back almost as stiff as Annie's. He heard the door open, then John's deep voice followed by Livvy's hesitant one. Hetty set a steaming mug in front of him, then patted his shoulder. He cradled the mug in his hands, wanting the warmth more than he wanted the taste of real coffee.

"Royce?"

He looked up at John, then pushed himself from the chair. Tired, so war-weary tired, and the war followed him everywhere, even to this house of refuge he seldom took advantage of for fear of bringing destruction upon innocent heads.

"Chauncey and I bumped into each other near Culpeper, so I brought him along," said John. A frown creased his brow, and Royce knew the news from Lee's headquarters was grim.

He nodded once. "Chauncey?"

Chauncey came all the way into the room and handed him a dispatch. Royce stared at the paper in his hand, then broke the seal. The rattle of the paper sounded overloud in the silence around him. He read the dispatch and let out his breath in an inaudible sigh.

He met Chauncey's gaze. "Are you aware of what these orders say?"

"The president made himself very clear, General."

"The president is a damn fool." He turned his attention to John. The light from the window shone off the rough planes of

John's face, deepening the lines of fatigue around his eyes. Even his mustache seemed to droop. "What did Lee say?"

John fingered his slouch hat, then tossed it onto the table beside Royce's. Royce looked at the two battered hats, worn by two battered men, and waited for an answer.

John's voice was low. "Lee surrendered at Appomattox."

He heard Olivia's startled gasp and a choking sound from Bo, but he fixed his gaze on John's haggard face. Several armies might still be in the field, but if Lee had surrendered, the last hope was gone.

He felt a biting sorrow for these two good officers, sorrow for all the men who had fought and sacrificed and lived to see the defeat of their dream. For himself, he felt nothing, as if he were already dead. But then, the light had died in his life that November morning, died the exact moment Annabelle disappeared from his sight.

*Annie, sweet Annie, if I could make it different for you.*

He looked at the dispatch in his hand, a new order from President Davis. Royce made a decision, then made a fist, crumpling the paper into a tight ball.

"Captain Pettigrew, you delivered these orders, now forget you ever heard them. The responsibility is solely mine."

He walked to the hearth and tossed the dispatch into the fire. The paper slowly unfolded as the heat struck, turned brown at the edges, then burst into flame. He watched it burn, hearing nothing but the sound of the fire and Hetty's rapid breathing.

He closed his eyes and concentrated until he saw Annie's face; the curve of cheek and gentle arch of her brow, the pert little nose that always moved him to lean his head and kiss it just so he could hear her breathless laugh.

He'd give up these last days of his life to see her in the flesh one more time, just long enough to tangle his hands in her hair while he kissed her, one more tiny moment of knowing the taste and the feel and the sweet, aching joy of her.

He turned around, catching Chauncey's gaze. Chauncey gave him a small, sad smile. He turned his attention to John, whose expression was as impassive as his own.

"What did those orders say?" John's blue eyes were cloudy and Royce recognized the sign. John's anger was simmering, ready to explode.

"To meet up with Johnston in North Carolina," he said.

"You mean to surrender, don't you?"

"Davis might not realize it, but the war is over. Go to Hancock's headquarters tomorrow and ask for a truce. I'll meet them whenever and wherever they say to discuss the terms of surrender."

"They'll arrest you. Dammit, they'll arrest you and hang you."

"I'll not be responsible for the death of one more soldier."

John gripped the back of a kitchen chair so tight his knuckles turned white. "I'll not be responsible for killing you." He lifted the chair several inches from the floor, then set it down hard. "Hell, bloody damn hell. Think of Annabelle."

"I'm thinking of Annabelle. It might be the last thing I do for her, but it's the only thing she ever asked of me."

The cold was still inside him, but there was a light now, too. He would never hold her in his arms again, never see his child. But he could give them this as his final gift.

"I'm ending this war for her. When our child is born, Virginia will be at peace."

# Chapter 33

Patsy sat in the gathering twilight on a three-legged stool just outside the quarters she shared with Clarence and their sons. She rubbed her thumb over the papers she held in her hand and watched as Peyton Kincaid raised himself from the wicker rocker on the gallery of the Big House. He moved with the slow, exaggerated motions of an old man.

Bottom fence rail on the top now, she thought, and while there was satisfaction in that, there wasn't the jubilation she'd once expected to feel when freedom came for her people. Part of that was the murder of Mr. Lincoln.

So much death—too much death. It was wearying.

In the past four years she'd come to know these white folks, and in knowing them, she couldn't find it in herself to hate them. And maybe that was the true meaning of freedom—to live without hatred eating away all that made you one of God's own children.

She absently swatted a mosquito on her forearm and watched as Peyton brushed a kiss against the top of Annabelle's head. Annabelle picked up her knitting. Peyton disappeared inside the Big House. Behind her, she heard the heavy tread of Clarence's feet and looked over as his dark bulk filled the cabin doorway. Clarence let out a long breath.

"She's alone now," Patsy said. "Sure you don't want to come with me?"

"I wouldn't know what to say."

"And you think I do?"

"Yes, sweet pea, I do. You've known sorrow that deep. At least you won't say the wrong thing."

He was lying, of course. She did it, too, like telling herself she'd find her lost boy one day. Sometimes you needed a certain amount of dishonesty, even with yourself, to . . . to carry on with the burdens each new day presented. Like Annabelle was probably telling herself that if she kept praying, kept writing her letters, someone would listen to her pleas, and her husband would not hang for treason.

Well, maybe he wouldn't.

Patsy took a deep breath and started across the lawn, following the same beaten path she'd followed for four long years. As she reached the gallery, Annabelle looked up from her knitting.

"Nothing wrong with the children?"

"No. They're both sleeping." Patsy settled on the top step, holding the two papers folded in her lap. Fireflies flittered across the lawn. "Word is you got another letter from that nun about Marse Gordon."

*Marse.* She didn't need to say that anymore, but it rolled off the tongue out of habit, and there was a certain comfort in habit. Still, she could learn a different way, one that was the earned respect of one person to another; to one deserving of respect instead of to one demanding it. *Mister* was the white folks' term. She rolled the word under her breath, practicing.

The needles in Annabelle's quick white hands clicked as she worked the yarn. It was a small garment she was making, a baby's sweater. Patsy wondered what she thought each time that baby moved inside her. Babies should bring joy, but it didn't always happen that way.

"Sister Bernadette," Annabelle said in a tired voice. "She's taken Gordon to her family's home in Philadelphia until . . . until we can find some way to get him home."

"He's crippled?"

"He's . . ." Annabelle's hands stilled. She took a shaky breath. "According to Sister Bernadette both legs are useless."

"I'm sorry about that."

"Thank you, Patsy. That means a lot, coming from you."

Patsy leaned her shoulder against the white column with its

peeling paint. She drew in a breath filled with the sweet scent of blooming magnolia and stared across the weed-choked lawn to empty pastures and unplanted fields.

"Clarence and me, we'll be leaving soon."

"Clarence will do well as a smithy. I'll miss you though."

As easy as that. And she suddenly realized she'd miss this kindhearted younger woman who had never understood a white woman and a black slave could never be friends. But maybe now . . .

"We'd like to stay a while longer, long enough to buy a piece of land and put up a house and smithy. Would Mr. Peyton mind? I'll keep working like I've been doing, and Clarence, too, as much as he has time."

"Peyton will work with you, Patsy. I'll tell him tomorrow." Patsy looked over, and Annabelle gave her a small, sad kind of smile. "For whatever it's worth, and maybe what it's worth can never be enough, but Mr. Peyton has always felt responsible for you. For all of you. He wishes you well."

No, not ever enough. The heart could cry for all the sorrow over all the years. Even this poor white woman's heavy sorrow.

"The black folks, we've got to register in town so's our marriages and our families can be legal now."

"You need a name." It was a statement, not a question.

"Yes, a last name. A family name."

There was a smile in Annabelle's voice. "I'd be proud to call you Mrs. Kincaid."

Her own heart felt suddenly—and unexpectedly—lighter. Patsy smiled back at this white woman who *could* become a friend. Equal in their freedom, and in their women's burdens.

"Well see, Clarence was thinking something else. He told me your name before you married was Hallston, and he'd be right honored if he could register our family with that name."

There was silence, then Annabelle said, "I'm honored." After another moment she smiled. "Very honored."

Patsy nodded, smiling in turn. This wasn't as difficult as she'd feared it would be.

"That ain't all Clarence was thinking." Annabelle arched a brow, and Patsy held out the papers. "Read these first."

Annabelle lowered the knitting to her lap. Their fingers

brushed as she took the papers. "What's this? Oh, a bill of sale," she said, glancing at the first one. She looked up. "From when Royce bought you?"

"Yes. But it's the date that's important. Now look at the next one."

Annabelle's forehead furrowed as she tried to make out the words in the gathering darkness. "A writ of manumission," she said finally. She gave a quiet laugh. "The same day. He bought you and freed you on the same day."

"I almost left Clarence when I found out what that paper was," Patsy admitted. "Then he explained the laws to me, about freed slaves having to go to the North."

"I'm glad. I never wanted to own another woman."

"I think I always knew that, Annie. Just like you knew you couldn't own me unless I let you own me."

Their gazes held and Annabelle nodded, a hint of a smile hovering at the corners of her mouth. She gathered the bundle of yarn and set it on the small table beside the rocker. Her skirts and petticoats rustled as she stood. She moved to the edge of the gallery and gazed out over the lawn.

There was picture in Clarence's Bible, of the Virgin Mary, and Patsy was reminded of that picture when she looked at Annabelle's profile. There was a long history of suffering in this world, and it seemed women of every color and every age ended up carrying more than their share of that suffering.

"You're right to leave," Annabelle said softly. "Make a home, raise your children to have pride in who they are and what they come from."

There was a sudden difficulty in her throat, something like a lump of tears too thick to swallow back down. Patsy stood and took back the papers when Annabelle held them out. She walked down the steps, as if she intended to leave on that astonishing note, but at the bottom, she turned and looked back.

She swallowed and found her voice. "There's one more thing. This one was my idea, but Clarence thinks it's a good one. We've got enough money in those freedom jars—real money, not greenbacks—to buy that land and some train tickets, too. You talk to Mister Peyton about that. You folks could go up to Philadelphia and bring Mister Gordon home yourselves, and on the way up, you might could stop in Washington and see someone, maybe General Grant, about your husband."

Annabelle leaned heavily against the column, as if she needed the support.

Patsy lifted the hand holding her papers of bondage and freedom—worthless now, but something to show her children and grandchildren, who could show their children and grandchildren—as proof that there was both goodness and evil in the hearts of men.

"I can think of a few white men that deserve hanging," she said. "General Kincaid isn't one of them."

"I . . . I don't know what to say."

"Thank you will do just fine."

Annabelle came slowly down the steps until the two women stood facing each other. Annabelle gathered her in an embrace, and Patsy was breathing in the soft scent of lavender and feeling the trembling in the smaller woman's body as she fought to hold back tears.

General Kincaid's wife, as brave as her husband in her own way.

"Let it out, child. Sometimes the sorrow's just too much to hold inside."

She felt pity and something more budding inside her heart. It took her a moment to put a name to that new, warmer sensation born of holding a weeping white woman in her own strong black arms.

That something was hope for a better tomorrow.

# Chapter 34

"Mrs. Kincaid, the general will see you now."

Peyton cupped his hand under her elbow and helped her rise from the hard wooden chair. She felt as big and ungainly as a steamboat and always slightly off-balance. She pulled the edges of her redingote together, hoping to hide her enormous belly, and looked into Peyton's worried gray eyes.

"Just pray I don't make it worse."

"If anyone can do this, you can, Annie-girl."

She wasn't so certain but knew she had to try. She followed a lieutenant down a narrow hallway. He stopped in front of a paneled door and pushed it open, then stood aside. She drew in a deep breath and stepped through the doorway.

General Grant was seated behind a wooden desk, scribbling something on a large sheet of paper. She tried to remember the last time she'd seen white writing paper. Sometime before Chancellorsville, she decided. She stood quietly, waiting for him to finish and used the time to study him.

He wore the plain uniform of a private soldier, the only sign of his rank the officer's insignia stitched to the shoulders of a worn frock coat. He wasn't a big man; she guessed when he stood, he'd be several inches shorter than Royce, and his shoulders were stooped and rounded.

She didn't know what she'd expected, but it wasn't this man who carried the air of dusty roads and little farms and small-town shops. He set down his pen and looked up. His red-brown beard was bristly and cropped short. He didn't smile, nor did she.

He rose and gestured toward a velvet armchair. "Mrs. Kincaid, please . . ."

"I'm afraid if I sit in that chair I might never get out of it."

"In that case . . ."

He carried the wooden chair he'd been using around the desk and gestured again. *A man of few words*, she thought as she seated herself. He lowered himself into the comfortable chair she'd declined.

"I suppose you've come today to beg for your husband's release."

"I shouldn't think begging would be necessary. He's the only general officer imprisoned at Fortress Monroe, and you and I both know he's not guilty of anything more than any other Southern officer in the late war."

"Your husband was a bushwacker, an outlaw."

"My husband was regular army, detached service. A guerrilla fighter, General, not a criminal."

"He knew what he was doing when he chose to fight his style of warfare."

"Exactly. My husband waged an honorable war—against soldiers, supply wagons, communication lines—only targets of military significance. He never once harmed a civilian or destroyed civilian property, nor did he allow his men to behave in that reprehensible manner. Your General Burnside allowed Fredericksburg to be pillaged. General Sherman ravaged two entire states. You, yourself, gave the order to Sheridan that resulted in the devastation of almost every farm in the Shenandoah Valley—my God, even the Quaker farms were burned. Do you consider yourself a criminal for issuing that order?"

"I consider that order one of the most difficult I ever issued and one of the most necessary. It led to the end of the war."

"It led to starvation."

One corner of his mouth lifted. "Maybe you should try begging, Mrs. Kincaid."

She realized her hands were twisting together in her lap. Inside her gloves, her palms were sweating. Inside her chest, her heart was tripping. If she failed today, Royce would hang. If she continued to put her foot in her mouth, Grant would probably play hangman.

Annabelle took another deep breath and met the general's steel gaze, unable to read anything in his expression. She had a hard time getting her throat to work. "All right, I'll beg. I'll get down on my knees if it will help."

"That won't be necessary."

She thought she heard amusement in his tone, and for the first time since she'd entered this unpretentious office of this unpretentious man, she felt a faint glimmer of hope.

The lines at the corner of his eyes deepened as he favored her with a real smile. "I happen to agree. General Kincaid surrendered his troops when he could have easily disbanded them, in which case, I've no doubt we'd still be fighting in the Virginia mountains. He knew he faced arrest as soon as he stepped into Hancock's headquarters, and only a courageous, honorable man behaves in that manner. His misfortune was to surrender the day after Lincoln died."

"So you'll speak for him again?"

"I'll try, Mrs. Kincaid. I won't promise you anything will come of it."

"I suppose I can't ask for anything more."

The interview was clearly at an end; he was gazing somewhere over her shoulder with a distant look in his eyes. She pushed herself up, and her belly contracted with one of those sharp, tight twinges that had plagued her the past few days. Suddenly, she wanted desperately to be back at Riverbend.

"Thank you, General. I'll go home now and pray my child will have a father."

The man of few words remained seated and only nodded. She was almost to the door when he spoke.

"Is there anything you would like me to say on his behalf?"

She turned back slowly, groping to come up with the right words. She knew in her heart why Royce had joined the Confederacy, why he had continued the fight to the bitter end. "Tell them Royce Kincaid hated the whole idea of the war. He fought for his home, General, for Virginia. There was no other reason."

"I'll tell them."

He sounded sad, as war-weary as the soldiers who were floundering to adapt to life in a conquered land. Suddenly and unexpectedly, she ached for him, too. "I'll add you to my prayers, General Grant," she said. "Thank you for taking the time to speak with me."

"Good day, Mrs. Kincaid."

He was already staring out the window, his gaze unseeing. She looked and saw the newly completed Capitol dome. From the top of the dome, a large flag snapped in the wind—the Stars and Stripes. Her heart seized at the sight of that familiar symbol. The United States of America, the country of her birth, was once again her country, and she wasn't certain how she felt about that.

She wondered what he was seeing as he stared into the wan light of a cloud-shrouded morning. She thought it might be the bloody past, but it might just as well be the problems of putting a country back together again. She thought he understood hanging an honorable man wasn't going to make those problems any easier to solve. She could only hope he'd be able to convince President Johnson.

Annabelle heard the hiss of steam as Patsy touched the hot iron to another shirt. She heard the tiny *plink* of shelled peas hitting the wooden bowl in her lap. She suddenly realized those were the only sounds she heard in the cookhouse.

She looked up sharply. "Gordy?"

Patsy's eyes went round. "He was right here."

"Well, he's not now." Annabelle set the bowl on the table in front of her. "Gordy, where are you," she called as she pushed her ungainly body out of the chair.

"I mistif," answered a little voice from somewhere nearby.

Patsy chuckled and went back to ironing. Annabelle followed the sound of the voice.

"You're not in mischief, you're in trouble."

Gordy sat in the dirt just outside the cookhouse door, a molasses crock between his dimpled knees and Major between his feet. The dog licked the traces of sorghum molasses from Gordy's fist while his bushy tail fanned the dirt into a gritty cloud around the two of them.

She didn't know what she'd do without little Gordy to brighten the days. She still tried to hope for Royce's release, but the hope grew dimmer with each passing hour. It had been two weeks since her visit to Washington, and they'd heard nothing: no amnesty, no trial date.

She wouldn't allow herself to think about the gallows. She tried not to think about his suffering, in a solitary prison cell, but she failed. She dreamed the terrible vision every night, and it haunted her throughout each long day.

If only they'd let her see him, just once. Just long enough to hold him close to her heart and run her fingers through his hair while she kissed him. Long enough for him to rest his hand on her belly and feel his child move. It might be all he would ever know of his child.

She shook her head hard, clearing the terrible vision, and saw instead a chubby, towheaded toddler sitting in the dirt.

Gordy held up his fist. "Taste, Aunty-Ann."

"Sharing won't help, you little cutie. Come here, Aunty-Annie's too fat to lean over."

"Aunty-Ann pitty."

"That won't help either."

The child seemed to decide if bribery and flattery weren't going to work, cooperation might. He struggled to his feet and came to her with a wide smile on his face and an excessive amount of dirt stuck everywhere. Major tagged along, tongue still licking and tail still wagging. Annabelle gingerly wrapped her hand around Gordy's wrist and led him into the cookhouse. She went to lift him onto the chair and grimaced as a sharp pain gripped her back, and her belly clenched tight. Patsy was beside her instantly.

"You got no business lifting that child in your condition," said Patsy. "I'll get him cleaned up."

"It's nothing, Patsy."

Annabelle kneaded her back and let Patsy take over cleaning little Gordon anyway. She moved restlessly to the ironing board Patsy had vacated and picked up the sadiron.

"Put it down, Annabelle. You got no business ironing in your condition either."

Annabelle forced a little laugh. "Who did your ironing when you were in this condition?"

"Clarence."

Annabelle set the sadiron back on the trivet. "Clarence?"

"Don't tell him I told you that."

A bout of real laughter shook her. Good gracious, she was going crazy today, hurtling from near tears to silly laughter to ungodly fear. Another spasm gripped her monstrous belly, and she bit her lower lip hard.

Her body was betraying her, deciding to bring her baby into the world early. Early babies were fragile babies; Mama had buried several. She rubbed her stomach, as if the gentle massage would calm the infant into staying inside her womb for another month.

Royce's child. She wouldn't lose it, she *wouldn't*.

She moved to the cookhouse door and leaned against the post, staring across the yard to where the stables had once stood. Behind her, she heard Patsy and Gordy in silly conversation. Major came and sat at her feet.

She was rubbing the dog behind the ears and trying not to think of early babies or imprisoned husbands or mamas who had died giving birth when she saw him silhouetted against the horizon. A man on a sorrel horse, a dark-haired man sitting tall and easy and graceful in the saddle. She straightened slowly.

"Patsy, come here."

Patsy came and stood beside her. She shifted Gordy to her other hip and let out a long breath. "Might be. But don't get hoping yet. He's still too far away to tell for sure."

Annabelle gripped Patsy's hand and watched the rider. She wanted it to be Royce. She wanted it too much, and things you wanted too much never happened. But sometimes they did; she had wanted him to love her and he loved her . . .

"Keep an eye on Gordy," she whispered hoarsely, and walked into the yard.

The rider disappeared in the deep shadows cast by the oaks, then emerged into the bright sunlight of a cloudless May afternoon. He might have seen her then because he pulled up sharply. The horse reared, and she knew by the way he handled the sorrel.

She didn't want to believe yet. To believe, then not have it be true would be more than she could bear. She closed her eyes, testing the vision. When she opened them, Royce was riding hard toward her.

His shaggy hair hung long over the collar of a worn cavalry

jacket with all traces of the Confederacy removed. The gull feather was gone from the slouch hat, but it was the same frayed hat he'd worn through four years of war. He pulled the horse to a hard stop and swung down from the saddle. They both stood for a moment, simply looking at one another. A tremor raced down his throat as he swallowed, but he didn't speak.

He thumbed his hat back, and she looked into his eyes— those intense, silver eyes—and saw all the words he wasn't saying and she couldn't say. Her heart seemed to stop beating, so she fisted her hand against her breast, just above her swollen belly. His eyes followed the motion.

"Annabelle," he said, and his voice broke over her name.

She could say nothing at all, only look at him, and the joy and the ache of loving him pushed her heart into her throat. Tears welled up in her eyes, and he wavered in her vision until she feared he might be only a dream after all. Then he spoke the words he'd spoken the last night they were together, and her heart resumed beating because she knew he was real and had remembered as she had remembered.

"Come to me, sweet Annie."

"I can't seem to move," she whispered.

His lips turned up in that fragile, tender smile and he came to her of a sudden, all powerful man. His arms wrapped her tight, so tight, as he kissed her. He kissed her long, and he kissed her deep, and then he jerked back so fast, his hat tumbled from his head.

"*Christ*, Annie." His hand trembled as he placed it against her hard belly.

Time had carved new lines at his eyes and mouth, and silvered threads showed in the dark hair at his temples, but, as always, it was his eyes that drew her. She saw an anxious, almost frightened look in those eyes. An overwhelming tenderness swelled up in her chest. She brushed his hair where the silvered threads showed, then placed her palm gently on his cheek.

"General Kincaid, I think you are about to become a father."

"That's Mr. Kincaid, dear heart." He lifted her into his arms as carefully as if she were a crate of eggs. "Annie. Oh God, Annie, couldn't you have done this closer to the right time?"

"Everything will be fine, Royce. Women do this every day."

His throat clenched as he swallowed, but he did manage to shoot her a lopsided grin. "Of course everything will be fine. We're together again."

Bo sprawled on the brocaded love seat, his mouth gaping open while he slept. The sounds coming from his throat were as rusty and squeaky as an old pump handle. And equally annoying.

Jules lounged in the tufted wing chair with little Gordon curled in his lap. The toddler had been asleep for hours. Jules's eyes were closed, but Royce knew he wasn't sleeping because nobody hummed in his sleep. And if Jules didn't stop humming about chariots coming to take people home, he knew he was going to stuff something big and hard and round in the old man's mouth.

Royce clenched the fists jammed in his pockets and paced another length of the library.

*Tap, tap, tap.*

"Dammit, Father, if you don't put that bloody letter opener down, I'm going to use it to commit patricide."

Peyton leaned back in his desk chair, fingering the sharp edge of the bronze instrument while he fixed his gaze somewhere over his son's shoulder. Peyton was trying to hide his concern, but Royce was wiser these days and saw the reflection of his own growing fear in the distant, unseeing look of his father's eyes.

"These things take time, Royce."

"Sixteen damn hours!"

"Fix yourself a brandy."

"I don't want to be drunk, I want to be with my wife."

The humming stopped. For a moment, Royce felt relief—the angels were being called into someone else's house.

"Isn't fitting," mumbled Jules. "Gennulmens aren't supposed to be in the room when their lady-wife's birthing."

Royce drew on his last remaining shred of patience and said nothing. He paced another length of the library. He stopped and stared at the brandy decanter. He considered jamming the big, hard, round object into Bo's rattling throat. He paced another length of the library.

*Tap, tap, tap.*

"Bloody hell."

No one spoke as he stalked from the library, which was just as well since he probably would have punched them a good one. He took the stairs two at a time, fully prepared to toss the doctor from his wife's room before he'd allow the doctor to toss him.

He heard Annie as he neared her bedroom and broke out in a cold sweat. His little warrior was in that room, gasping and panting and maybe fighting for her life. His hand shook as he reached for the knob, then he didn't have the strength to turn it.

It turned in his hand. Dear Christ, she *was* dying. They were coming to tell him she was dying. He jerked his hand back and panted himself. The door opened, revealing Patsy outlined in the lamplight.

"Thought I heard you," she said.

He wished she would smile so this terrible terror would leave his heart. "She needs me, I'm coming in," he said in his best general's voice.

Patsy quirked one brow. "Always made it easier for me when Clarence was there."

"She's not—I mean—how is she?"

Patsy stepped into the hallway and pulled the door closed. "She's having a hard time. I wanted to come get you hours ago, but she wouldn't let me. Said you'd suffered enough, and she didn't want you to have to watch."

"Sweet Annie," he murmured.

Patsy snorted. "Stupid Annie. Every husband should be forced to watch his wife give birth."

"I'm going in now, and no one's forcing me." He pushed the door open, then stopped as her words belatedly reached his brain. "Did Clarence really stay with you?" he asked.

Patsy smiled, and he suddenly understood what Clarence had seen in this woman, not just her striking good looks, but the warmth in her smile and the quiet strength in her eyes.

"First time, it took him about ten hours before he came barreling in. Big as he is, wasn't anybody going to stop him. Went through the whole time with the second baby."

"He was always a little quicker to catch on than I was."

Royce placed his hand on her shoulder. "I'll be out to see him in a few days. In the meantime, tell him thanks for lending Annie the money to get to Washington. I wouldn't be here now if she hadn't made that trip."

She touched his hand and smiled softly. "Go to your wife, General."

Dr. Chatham stopped him just inside the room. The doctor's forehead was creased with the worry that showed clearly in his eyes. He spoke in such a low voice, Royce had to lean his head to hear him.

"She didn't want us to send for you." He shook his head. "Another hour or two like this . . ."

"She's strong, Doctor."

"Let's hope she's strong enough."

She'd be strong enough because he'd give her every ounce of his own strength. Surely, they'd come through too much to be parted now. *Please, God.*

Annie was clinging to the brass rails of the headboard so hard her knuckles were white. She panted and huffed and didn't seem to know he was here. He sat on the edge of the bed and peeled her hands off the bedstead.

"Hold on to me, dear heart."

She raised her head and peered at him through bloodshot eyes. "I don't want you here, Kincaid," she said, yet she gripped his hands so hard it hurt.

"I can tell. Getting ready to leap up and throw me out on my behind—him any second now."

"This is no time for your blasted—"

Another pain gripped her, cutting off her temper as she panted and gasped and gritted her teeth against the pain. He willed his hand not to shake as he pushed a sticky strand of hair off her cheek. Her chest heaved violently, her heart visibly straining as she fought her way through the endless contraction. Sixteen hours she'd been battling like this. His throat tightened. *Please, God.*

"That's good, dear heart, don't fight it. Easy now . . . you're doing real good."

She panted in a breath and shot him a murderous glare. "Fight it! Shows what you know, you arrogant man."

He tried to flash her a cocky, arrogant grin, and maybe he succeeded because her murderous glare faded into a soft, tender smile.

"You don't have to go through this, Royce."

"Try to keep me away." He laid his hand gently on her belly. Her muscles quivered, then hardened beneath his palm.

"Oh, dear heaven—" She grabbed for him again as her eyes winced shut. She huffed and heaved and clenched her teeth, her lips curling back in a grimace of pain. He couldn't stand it.

"Annie, scream, holler. Let it out, woman."

"Can't—scare—Gordy."

This time, he squeezed her hands hard because he suddenly knew a brown-eyed little girl had cowered somewhere alone, listening to her mother's pain.

He pushed away the thought her mother had died this way, a woman who hadn't been suffering the debilitating weakness of malnutrition. He circled Annie's wrist with his fingers, then before she might guess his purpose, brushed his palm down her thigh. How could she be so thin while carrying a child? She looked at him through pain-filled eyes, and he forced a smile.

He lost track of time. Maybe three hours passed, maybe more, all of it in brutal, unrelenting labor. The contractions were coming so close together she could barely catch her breath between them. He followed the doctor's instructions and rucked her shift up to her waist. She gave a little puff of a sigh and bent her knees. Her legs opened wide, and they were trembling from exhaustion. He could see the rapid slamming of her heart against the walls of her chest.

He wiped her face and neck with a cool, damp cloth and pushed her wet, tangled hair off her face. She was fighting to bring this baby into the world and she was fighting to live. He knew because he saw the fierce, warrior gleam in the dark eyes staring back at him. She was steadfast and brave and beautiful, and he loved her with a depth of feeling he would never understand.

And if she didn't give birth soon, her heart would give out from this awful strain.

He leaned forward and kissed her sweat-salty forehead. "Hold on there. I need you."

She tried to smile, she was way beyond talking, but then her back arched and her stomach contracted violently. Her hands flew up to the bed rails, and her teeth clenched so tightly the corded muscles of her neck stood out like ropes. The doctor moved suddenly as a great, wrenching sound ripped from her chest.

Royce couldn't move. He couldn't breathe. He couldn't tear his eyes from his wife's pain-contorted face.

"It's coming," said Dr. Chatham, the relief in his voice coming out in a shout. "It's coming. I can see the head."

From there, everything happened so fast, Royce knew he would never remember exactly what happened. Annie was crying and laughing and grunting and heaving. He was raising her up so she could see and reminding himself to breathe and trying hard not to cry because he knew this was going to be the daughter of his dreams and the father of a beautiful, tiny, brown-eyed girl had to be strong and manly.

Then he was kissing his wife's dry, cracked lips and his cheeks were wet with somebody's tears and his heart was in his throat while a wonderful, awful, magnificent love filled his chest . . .

And their daughter was squalling.

Their daughter. Arm-flailing indignant and red-faced angry— and the most beautiful baby ever to enter this beautiful world.

# Chapter 35

⌒⌒

A nnabelle wondered how long she could hold her breath. If she moved, Royce would know she was awake and the scene would end. She wanted to fix this in her memories first so it would last forever.

He cuddled their sleeping baby close to his heart as he talked and cooed and gently rocked back and forth in the old rocker. She wanted to hear all the silly promises he was whispering. She wanted to watch forever the joy in his eyes and the peace on his war-ravaged face as he rocked their tiny daughter and patted her little behind-her and made up fairy tales with happy endings.

She would never know what horrors he'd endured to bring the silver streaks into his hair—he'd spend the rest of his life protecting her from that knowledge—but he was home now and peace was restored and he was finding his own restoration in their child. She was afraid if she so much as breathed, he and their daughter and the peace would all disappear.

But she could close her eyes for a moment, and she did. *Dear God, thank you.* When she opened her eyes, Royce was looking at her as if he knew she'd been awake for a long time. Awake and watching him love their child and loving the watching of him loving their child.

"She was stirring, and I didn't want her to disturb you. You need your rest," he said. The look on his face put her in mind of Gordy whenever he was caught in *mistif.* "Now that you're awake, I suppose I could share," he said, sounding doubtful.

"You don't have to share until she's hungry."

"Actually, I think she is, not that I know anything about babies, mind you." He looked down at the baby in his arms and spoke in his teasing drawl, "Innocent babes and defiant virgins have always terrified me. Set my knees to quaking and my heart all a-quivering—"

"If that black heart is quivering, it's not from terror, Kincaid."

"Think you have me all figured out, do you?"

His face creased in a broader smile, bringing out the dimple at the corner of his mouth. He rose slowly, cupping their daughter in his large, strong-boned hands. To Annabelle's surprise, the baby's arms started flailing, and she heard tiny whimpers.

"She really was awake?"

"Dear heart, when have I ever lied to you?"

He put the squirming bundle into her arms, then sat on the bed beside her. They both looked down at their daughter, at her round, pink face with its tiny mouth preparing to wail. Her brown eyes were opened wide, seeming to take in this conversation, and Annabelle inwardly laughed at herself. No day-old infant, not even her own exceptional one, was that aware of the world.

She looked at Royce, saw the awe and the love plain on his face as he gazed at his daughter. She looked back at the baby. The baby was watching her father and Annabelle choked back a laugh. Their daughter *was* aware of the world. She already had her father's number, all bluff and bluster and tenderhearted pushover.

"She's beautiful, Annie, so beautiful," he said. His curled finger stroked the baby's cheek, then he looked up and touched Annabelle with his eyes. "As beautiful as her mother."

There was a lump of joy all knotted up in her throat, a joy so sweet and scary and precious because this perfection couldn't last forever. But it was here for now, and the knowing of it was like the rainbow's promise. No matter how cold the winter, how bad the storm, sunshine and spring always returned. Even Royce had returned when she'd lost all hope of ever seeing him again.

"She has your hair," she said around the joy-lump in her throat.

"And your mouth, which is all puckered, getting ready to squall any second now."

"Yes, sir, Father, sir."

She returned his smile as she unbuttoned her gown and put the baby to her breast. The sun pouring through the window struck the baby's hair, turning the color from near black to deep chestnut. Her tiny fists were thrown to the side of her head as her little rosebud mouth sucked greedily. They both watched their child, both of them caught up in the miracle.

"You're not too disappointed it wasn't a boy?" she asked after a minute.

"Annie . . ." He leaned forward over the baby in her arms and gave her a sweet-gentle kiss. When he raised back, another dazzling smile creased his face. "Whatever made you think I wanted a son? I wanted you to suffer through raising you, not me to suffer through raising me."

She laughed because he was alive and home and because he sounded so happy. She laughed because together, they had created the skinniest, boniest, most beautiful baby girl ever born to this world and together, they would be her parents.

"Did you think of a name for this beautiful daughter of yours?"

He leaned forward and adjusted the pillows behind her head, then brushed the hair off her brow. His smile was gone but his eyes were warm, like a misty gray summer morning. He took her hand in his own, his thumb stroking the inside of her wrist as he studied her face.

"I did," he said at long last. "I went to our cavern a lot after you were gone. Went there and thought of you and dreamed of living so I could be a father to my daughter."

She didn't try to hide her sudden tears, and he allowed his face to be naked before her.

"I would like to give our daughter a special name. A name from our past but more for our future," he said, and Annabelle saw the light of love in his eyes. And she saw something more. She saw . . .

"*Hope*. I would like to name her Hope Ann Kincaid."

"It's a beautiful name, Royce," she said softly. She lifted her hand to his dark angel's face. Slowly, he turned his head and kissed her palm. "A beautiful name."

Royce took her hand in his own as an unexpected tightness gripped his chest. He swallowed, blinked against a sudden, stinging heat in his eyes. Their fingers were interlaced together, and he tightened his grip, insensibly afraid it was all an illusion—peace, Hope, this special woman with the golden brown hair and golden brown eyes who, for some reason he couldn't fathom, loved him.

"Sweet Annie," he whispered. "Did I ever tell you how much I love you?"

It began with flecks of gold in the depths of her eyes. Annie's sunburst smile.

That golden light, the joy-light. And he knew it wasn't an illusion, for the joy-light glowed within him, too.